Praise for Jonathan Wylie's earlier titles

SHADOW-MAZE
'Exceptionally good at constructing sound plots, rounded characters and pacey narratives . . . the telling is often adroit and ultimately very entertaining . . . an intriguing and colourful fantasy setting a bit different from most'
Stan Nichols, *The Dark Side*

DREAM-WEAVER
'All accolades should go to **Dream-Weaver** which starts with a world-making bang and continues without unnecessary diversion along a path of high originality . . . It is engrossing, marvellously written and most surely one of the best of its type. Applause all round'
John Gilbert, *Fear*

'A strong new fantasy . . . makes the most innovative use of salt since Lot's wife'
Carolyn Cushman, *Locus*

'The whole book may be classed as a good read . . . it leaves a satisfying aftertaste'
Pauline Morgan, *Critical Wave*

'This is a marvellously realized tale of intrigue and growth into adulthood. The plot is easy to follow yet excitingly woven. Nothing is predictable; everything is riveting. The best book I've read this year'
Graham Ing, *Auguries*

The **SERVANTS OF ARK** trilogy
'Unlike most trilogies, these books can be read separately; each focuses on a different character and a separate crisis . . . Kings, queens, princes and wizards all live like regular folks, loving and quarrelling and raising their children as best they can in the face of a magical war . . . **Servants of Ark** is enjoyable fantasy reading, with plentiful light touches that bring a gentle humour to the books'
Carolyn Cushman, *Locus*

Also by Jonathan Wylie

SERVANTS OF ARK

Book One: THE FIRST NAMED
Book Two: THE CENTRE OF THE CIRCLE
Book Three: THE MAGE-BORN CHILD

THE UNBALANCED EARTH

Book One: DREAMS OF STONE
Book Two: THE LIGHTLESS KINGDOM
Book Three: THE AGE OF CHAOS

DREAM-WEAVER
SHADOW-MAZE

and published by Corgi Books

Island and Empire
Book One

DARK FIRE

Jonathan Wylie

CORGI BOOKS

ISLAND AND EMPIRE: Book One: DARK FIRE
A CORGI BOOK 0 552 13978 5

First publication in Great Britain

PRINTING HISTORY
Corgi edition published 1993

Set in 10/11pt Linotype Times by
County Typesetters, Margate, Kent.

Corgi Books are published by Transworld Publishers Ltd,
61–63 Uxbridge Road, Ealing, London W5 5SA, in Australia
by Transworld Publishers (Australia) Pty Ltd, 15–25 Helles
Avenue, Moorebank, NSW 2170, and in New Zealand by
Transworld Publishers (NZ) Ltd, 3 William Pickering Drive,
Albany, Auckland.

Made and printed in Great Britain by
Cox & Wyman Ltd, Reading, Berks.

AUTHOR'S NOTE

Thanks are due to Alfred
for toads, bats – and Grongar!

PROLOGUE

Kerrell Adjeman watched her closely as she saw the city for the first time. On the surface, Ifryn was the calmest woman he had ever known, and yet he could not help wondering whether her serenity was just a façade. What was really going on behind those gentle brown eyes? Surely her heart was racing beneath that small, slim frame?

'Xantium,' she breathed, unaware of his scrutiny. 'The city that never sleeps?'

'It has been called that, my lady. Among other things.'

They had brought their mounts to a halt at the top of a dusty ridge. Behind them, the long line of horses and carriages had also stopped. Ifryn had delighted Kerrell that morning by insisting that she wished to ride in the open, now that they were crossing the Deadlands. She wanted to be able to study her surroundings more closely. Forsaking the relative comfort of the covered carriages, and the company of her parents, she had proved to be a capable horsewoman, endearing herself still further to her escort.

Now she turned to look directly at Kerrell, her long brown hair framing her charming face.

'I have a name, *Captain*,' she said, amusement sparkling in her eyes as she deliberately emphasized her use of his title. 'I wish you would use it.'

'I fear that would not be appropriate, my lady,' he replied, his expression neutral. 'In a few days' time, you will be the Empress. I am a mere soldier.'

'You are no *mere* anything,' she told him pertly. 'You forget, I know who you are.'

Kerrell bowed his head slightly in acknowledgement.

7

'My ancestry guarantees my loyalty, my lady,' he said seriously. 'Not my ability.'

'And you believe I cannot judge that for myself?' she retorted, her eyebrows raised.

Kerrell was the latest in the long line of the Family Adjeman and he, like his father, his grandfather and many earlier generations, was a sworn servant of the Emperor. Kerrell's father had died tragically soon after Southan III had ascended to the imperial throne, depriving the young Emperor of his best general and wisest adviser. Even though Kerrell was as yet only twenty-two years old, it was expected that he would take his father's place in due course, and that he would become Commander of the Imperial Army before too long.

Even in the few days that they had been together, Ifryn had seen enough to know that he suited his supposed destiny perfectly. The very fact that he had been chosen to lead the escort for the Emperor's bride-to-be spoke of a trust that disregarded his tender years. Many of the men under his command were much older than him, yet it was clear that he was universally respected, his authority accepted with no hint of resentment.

Even Ifryn's own father, King Fyles, had been won over. Kerrell's first appearance at their modest court had caused some surprise, but the captain's manner and bearing had soon made it clear that no offence had been intended by the choice of one so young and of comparatively low rank. Indeed, once they learnt of his traditional link with the Emperor, it was obvious that any other choice would have been inappropriate.

'Besides,' Ifryn went on now, before he had a chance to reply, 'I am not asking for familiarity, merely your friendship.'

'Within the bounds of propriety, my lady,' he replied gravely, with a slight stress on her title, 'my friendship is something you can count on for as long as I draw breath.'

8

He smiled then, and the sudden warmth in his dark brown eyes was worth far more to Ifryn than the use of her name would have been.

'I'll hold you to that, Kerrell,' she said, returning his smile. *It will be good to have at least one friend at court.*

She studied him for a moment longer, liking what she saw. His broad, deeply tanned face and wide-set eyes promised honesty and good sense. His long, mid-brown hair was tied back, a style which she had found faintly ridiculous at first – none of the men in her own country affected such – but which she now admitted suited him well. Several of his junior officers, she had noted, wore their hair in the same way. Kerrell's sturdily built body, which was so lithe when in motion, now rested at ease astride his mount, his strong hands resting lightly on the pommel of his saddle.

'I'll hold you to that,' she whispered, and looked away, her smile no more than a memory now.

Acutely sensitive to her change of mood, Kerrell turned to look back at his men, pretending to check that all was in order. The escort detail consisted of more than a hundred mounted soldiers, picked for their fighting expertise rather than ceremonial grandeur. These were unsettled times in the Xantic Empire and each journey, whether long or short, carried its perils. The cavalry were accompanied by several carriages and baggage carts, and it was these which dictated the pace at which the convoy travelled.

Several days on the road had given Kerrell time to study the girl chosen to be his master's wife – and to form a high opinion of her. Yet the sudden uncertainty in her quiet voice reminded him how strange this must be for her. Her homeland was a remote but strategically important region of the Empire, far from the intrigues of Xantium. His heart yearned to help her. After all, she was only eighteen.

Politics made demands on all those in positions of power, but Ifryn was being asked to make an enormous sacrifice, to marry a man she had never met for the sake of strengthening various alliances – and to send subtle messages throughout the world. Her marriage – and, in due course, her children – would be counters in a vast game which she could not hope to understand. Whatever the honour, the riches and the opportunities that awaited her, Ifryn's life would never again be her own.

How did she react when she was first told? Kerrell wondered, not for the first time, as he glanced again at her now solemn face.

Ifryn's thoughts were running on similar lines, remembering her initial reaction to the Emperor's choice. First had come disbelief – this could not be possible! – but then, as the reality had sunk in, her customary calm had deserted her. In the privacy of her own chambers, witnessed only by her maid, Doneta, Ifryn succumbed in turn to horror, fear and then anger. 'Why me?' she had cried as unaccustomed tears had filled her eyes. 'How can they do this to me?'

Later, she realized that her parents had had no choice. With their country in the forefront of the Empire's struggle against the rising tide of barbarianism, they were in no position to displease Southan – even if they had wished to. The advantages that they would accrue from their new status were also too numerous to reckon.

Eventually, Ifryn had regained her equilibrium, even managing to laugh with Doneta about the insanity of the Emperor's choice. Princess she might be in her own small realm – but *Empress*? The very thought was ridiculous!

Kerrell had arrived some months later; in the intervening period, Ifryn had become reconciled to the fact that she must do her duty, and had accepted the responsibilities of her new role in a manner which made her father's heart swell with pride. She learned all she could about what she would be facing in the future, and had even half-persuaded herself that this was all a great adventure, something that was truly beyond her wildest dreams. Even so, it was still a journey into the unknown – and one with which she felt ill-equipped to cope.

The days spent travelling in Kerrell's company had done much to help her relax. His calm manner, consideration and dignified courtesy, as well as the unexpected pleasure of finding a companion so close to her own age, had restored a measure of her own self-assurance, and made the prospect of what lay ahead a little less daunting. She would count herself truly fortunate to have him as a friend in Xantium.

Ifryn's gaze returned to the city, which towered above the barren plain like an immense fortress. The sun was beginning to set beyond it, distant clouds painting the sky shades of pink, gold, blue and grey. From this distance, the city itself resembled a strange, glittering cloud formation, but unlike the others, its shape did not change. It simply became more mysterious as the shadows deepened.

The sight of her new home evoked a curious mixture of emotions in Ifryn. It brought back many fears and un-certainties – and a sense of being out of her depth. But at the same time, she felt as though she had never seen any-thing so beautiful. In the midst of the desolation of the Deadlands, Xantium was like a magical creation, full of wonders and enchantments. She knew, without under-standing how, that fate had brought her to the right place.

'Shall we continue, my lady?' Kerrell asked softly, startling her out of her reverie. 'We can be at the gates by nightfall.' He noticed that the princess was fingering one of her earrings – a gift from her mother – as if it were a touchstone. But she continued to stare at the city, and did not speak.

Into the silence came the distant sound of a bell ringing.

'Your arrival is expected, my lady.'

'Can they really see us from so far away?' she asked quietly.

11

'There are many keen pairs of eyes in the uppermost towers of Xantium,' he replied.

His comment broke the city's mesmeric hold on Ifryn, and she glanced at him questioningly. But Kerrell offered no further explanation.

'Then we'd better not keep them waiting,' she said determinedly.

Ifryn spurred her horse forward, and led the way towards the heart of the Empire.

CHAPTER ONE

*I hear them – shouting, when there is no need. Blighted
words full of fire. I could stop them if I wanted to – that
made him angry before. But there are so many of them
now, and I am so tired. So tired. Even flying with the bats
does not refresh me. Perhaps I should sleep? No. Dreams
are more tiring still.*

*Why can't they be quiet? The whole world must know
of the little one by now. The bells have rung, have they
not?*

It was the wedding that the whole population of the
island of Zalys had been waiting for – all except one, it
seemed.

'I don't see why there has to be all this fuss,' Dsordas
complained.

'That's because you're an unromantic pig with the soul
of a rock!' Fen retorted. 'Gaye and Bowen have loved
each other since they were children.'

'I know that.' Dsordas looked hurt, his brown eyes
hooded beneath thick, dark brows. 'But why all the
ceremony? We've been together almost as long. We're
all right.' There was a faint note of challenge in his voice.

'You're just lucky,' she replied. 'I put up with you. My
sister has different ideas about how things should be
done. And Bowen would not deny her.'

Dsordas gave her a strange look, trying to work out if
he was being criticized.

'They deserve their day,' Fen stated firmly.

'It's just . . .' His expression had turned sullen, and he

13

would not meet her gaze. 'It's just that it seems so inappropriate . . . with things the way they are.'

Fen exploded in quick-tongued fury, her words flying as fast and sharp as knives.

'All the more reason then to take this chance to celebrate,' she exclaimed. 'To spread a little joy! Can't you ever think of anything else?'

'When Zalys is free,' he answered softly. 'There will be time then to celebrate.'

'And in the meantime we should all stop living?' she snapped back. 'No one is to laugh, to dance, to enjoy any of life's small pleasures? Just because injustice exists, it doesn't mean that nothing else is important.'

Dsordas looked at her then, shocked by the vehemence which coloured her pale skin and brought fire to the gold flecks in her startling green eyes. He stared, his thoughts distracted by her beauty, wondering how such a slender frame could contain such spirit.

'Well?' Fen demanded.

'I love you,' he said quietly.

'Oh!' She tossed her head in exasperation, her blond hair flying. 'You are impossible!' She did not stamp her foot, but it seemed as though she did.

Dsordas smiled sheepishly, and her expression gradually softened. He held out his arms and, shaking her head in disbelief, she went to him. Enfolded in his embrace, Fen ran her fingers through his dark curls. His colouring was so unlike her own that the couple were known as Light and Dark. She resisted the temptation to take him by the ears and shake some sense into him.

'For you,' he whispered, 'I will get trussed up like a chicken on Old Year's Night, and come to this wedding. For you, I will even try to enjoy it.'

'You'd better,' she threatened, but there was laughter and love in her voice.

The ceremony was set to take place in Fournoi Square, the only large area of open space on dry land in the town

14

of Nkosa, the island's capital and main trading port. The imperial garrison would not ordinarily allow large gatherings in the town but, perhaps because Bowen was a son of the influential Folegandros family, the authorities had relented on this occasion. Permission had been officially granted by Commander Niering, the Xantic Emperor's representative on Zalys, but everyone knew that he would not have done so unless Marshal Farrag also approved – and some people muttered that Farrag must have devious reasons of his own for granting the request.

Nominally Niering's second-in-command, Farrag's position as Marshal of Information actually made him the most powerful and most feared man on the island. His network of spies and informers reached into every section of island society; it was he who controlled the all-important Far-speakers, and his personal abilities bordered on sorcery. In addition, the way Farrag used his power was moulded by his sadistic and cunning nature, made all the more terrifying by his own bizarre and repulsive appearance.

The Marshal had been short and fat even before the accident some years earlier which had robbed him of the use of his legs. What could be seen of him now was immense, folds of limp flesh in rolls around his face, neck and arms. But the lower half of his body was permanently encased in a kind of flexible box which moved as if it were on wheels. Such a man should not have been able to move fast, yet his pudgy hands were incredibly nimble, and his 'carriage' glided across even quite rough surfaces with a speed and grace quite out of keeping with the bulk and shape of its occupant. He had even been seen to complete the apparently impossible task of climbing stairs without assistance or visible effort.

His head and body were entirely hairless, and a series of four tattoos of ever-staring eyes – one in the centre of his forehead, one on each side of his head above his ears, and one on the back of his skull – gave him an even more sinister air. His own small eyes, hidden deep within gross

15

flesh, were very pale blue and always alert. Those eyes and his surprisingly delicate ears missed nothing, and he was fond of remarking that he saw and heard everything that mattered on the island. And when he spoke, one final revolting aspect of his appearance was revealed. His tongue was stained purple, so dark that it was almost black, testament to his depraved habits.

In the two years since Farrag had been on Zalys, several attempts had been made on his life. It was even rumoured that some of his own soldiers had tried to kill him; they evidently hated and feared him almost as much as the islanders did. All attempts had failed, however, and the rumours concerning his methods of survival – and the appalling punishments meted out to the would-be assassins – were enough to ensure that only the insane or the truly desperate would try again.

The spectre of Farrag's evil presence hung over the island like a poisonous cloud, but nothing had been seen or heard of him in the two days prior to Midsummer's Day, the date appointed for Gaye and Bowen's marriage. Most people had managed to dismiss him from their thoughts.

The longest day of the year was considered by the islanders to bring especially good luck, but the ceremony would not be held until the early evening, thus avoiding the stifling heat of the summer sun which made the canals steam and stone too hot to touch. However, there had been plenty to do during the earlier hours of the day, and many of the preparations had already been under way at dawn.

While Zalys was remote, many leagues from any land mass, its position near the centre of the warm Larenian Sea had made it the crossroads of many important trade routes. The island's history was one of constant occupation by various remote powers – the Xantic Empire being only the latest – and this, together with the constant flow of commerce, meant that its population was cosmopolitan. Even so, most of its inhabitants had the swarthy complexions of life controlled by the sun and sea, and so some of the Amari children – those who had inherited the far northern traits of pale skin and blond hair from their mother, Etha – were always noticeable. That the eldest two, Fen and Gaye, were also beautiful, made them doubly so. This, combined with the fact that Gaye and Bowen had been sweethearts from childhood, and the local importance of the Folegandros family, ensured that the wedding was a major event in the island's calendar.

Fournoi Square was bordered on three sides by high buildings of three or more storeys; the spacious homes of the more well-to-do merchants, some of the town's more luxurious taverns, jewellers and other shops, as well as quarters for the most senior imperial officers. Yet even here there were genteel signs of decay caused by the town's proximity to the sea. Paint was peeling and plaster crumbling – and each year the deterioration grew worse as – in the belief of most of its inhabitants – Nkosa and the island were slowly sinking. However, all such signs were forgotten now, hidden by the banners, flowers, lanterns and flags which decorated nearly all the surrounding walls.

The floor of the square, which was paved with sun-bleached stone of pink and yellow, was crowded with people, and there was a carnival atmosphere as evening approached. There were eager faces at most of the windows overlooking the scene and every balcony, save one, was filled with spectators who would watch events from above. The last balcony was left empty; for it was here that the spirits of some long-forgotten party gathered to witness all such entertainments. The ghosts were assembling now, pale shadows in the evening sunlight, but few people paid them any attention. Their presence did no harm, their conversations were silent to living ears – and they took no offence when children laughed at their old-fashioned clothes. On a night such as this, the revenants were merely part of the scenery –

and their absence would have been more disturbing than
their appearance.

The fourth side of the square, to the north, was
defined by the Nkosa Canal, the port's main thorough-
fare, and one of hundreds of waterways which criss-
crossed the town. The canal was thronged with boats of
all shapes and sizes, waiting for the arrival of the bride.
Excited chatter and laughter echoed from the square and
over the water.

The only discordant note, which the islanders did their
best to ignore, was provided by the presence of dozens of
imperial soldiers. There were pairs of sentries at inter-
vals around the edge of the square, archers lined the
rooftops and sat in several windows, and there were
many guards stationed at each entrance to the square,
including the waterfront. These men searched each and
every arrival, confiscating anything that might conceiv-
ably be used as a weapon. Having granted permission for
such a large gathering, Niering was evidently taking no
chances.

At last, the shadow on the ancient sundial at the
southern end of the square touched the line of the seventh
hour after noon. By unspoken agreement, the crowds
drew back, leaving an empty aisle down the middle of
the square. At the very centre stood Nias Santarsieri, the
island's Patriarch, who would perform the age-old rite of
joining. At his signal, the members of the two families
gathered near him on either side of the aisle; Etha, Fen
and Dsordas, and all the younger Amari children on the
western side; Bowen's parents and younger brother,
with their relatives, forming a much bigger group to the
east. As was only natural, the families were to be
granted the closest view of the proceedings.

A hush fell over the entire square as the old man in
black robes waited silently for the arrival of the
principals.

Bowen came first, riding into the arena from the
south-west corner. His mount was a beautiful white

stallion, one of the few horses on the island. Its mane and tail were interlaced with colourful ribbons, and the saddle and tack had been decorated with flowers. Bowen himself wore loose-fitting trousers and a shirt of white, belted with a purple sash. He was a solidly built young man, tall and handsome in an undemonstrative way. The onlookers were impressed by the way he held himself in the saddle, and by the gleam of expectation in his dark brown eyes. It seemed that the many lanterns ready for use later in the evening would not be required; Bowen's smile would have lit up the whole square.

It was obvious to all that he was intent on enjoying every moment of the most important day of his young life – a day he had waited for for so long – and there were tears in the eyes of many of the onlookers after he had passed by.

He walked his horse slowly to the central point, dismounted, handed the reins to a servant, then knelt before Nias for the Patriarch's blessing. When he rose to his feet again, his eyes and those of every other person in and around the square turned towards the canal.

They did not have long to wait. Within moments, Gaye's barge came in sight, threading its way through the flotilla in the canal. The slim boat was newly painted white, with yellow flowers attached to its high prow, the single oarsman at the stern proudly dressed in scarlet. In the centre of the boat sat Antorkas Amari, his solid, dark figure contrasting with that of his daughter beside him. His face was solemn, acutely aware of so many eyes upon him, but Gaye was smiling joyously, her flowing dress a pale but vibrant yellow, the colour of spring flowers. It complemented her own light skin and hair perfectly.

The barge pulled smoothly alongside the quay, and as willing hands steadied the boat, Antorkas stepped out, then turned to help his daughter ashore. Gaye alighted from the barge so gracefully that she seemed almost to be floating. Taking her father's arm, she went to meet her love. Even the dignified Patriarch could not help but smile as she approached and knelt to receive his blessing.

Antorkas withdrew to his wife's side, running a finger round the tight collar of his formal shirt. He and Dsordas, who was also fidgetting in the unaccustomed attire, exchanged self-pitying glances, and Fen leant closer to her lover's ear and whispered, 'You promised!' Then all eyes were on Gaye and Bowen.

Fen, like many of those present, paid little attention to Nias's opening words of welcome. When she saw the two of them together, she began to see Dsordas's point about the ceremony being unnecessary. They seemed to be radiating happiness. That they belonged together was so patently obvious that no one with a grain of sense could imagine them any other way. The only wonder was that they had waited for so long – until they had both reached the age of twenty – before formalizing their relationship. Fen suspected that Bowen's family had had something to do with this. She had often heard various elders speak approvingly of the example the couple were setting. But that was all history now. The Patriarch's voice brought her back to the present.

'Now we may begin!' Nias called, raising his voice to the sky.

At that moment, though, there was a rush of whispers, and sudden movement in the crowd at the northern end of the square. Then a breathless silence fell as the dread figure of Farrag came into view at the end of the aisle. He glided towards the centre in an obscene parody of Gaye's graceful approach, a self-satisfied smile upon his ugly features. Tattooed eyes stared at all those about him. In his wake came a detachment of six soldiers, big, hard-faced men in armour and helmets, spears and shields ready at their sides. The regular crunch of their booted footsteps was the only sound as the whole of Zalys held its breath.

After what seemed like an age, Farrag and his guards stopped before Nias and the white-faced couple.

'I bring greetings and good news from Emperor Southan the Third, Lord of Many Lands!' Farrag cried. His voice rang out cheerfully, but his smile did not reach his deepset eyes.

'You choose a strange time to bring them, Marshal,' Nias replied. The old man's brave words were loud enough but there was fear in his eyes and his thin hands were trembling.

'Forgive me, Patriarch. I could not wait.' There was no hint of apology in Farrag's tone. 'And this gathering provides an ideal setting for the release of such joyous tidings.' He paused, smiling at the people around him as if remembering them for future reference. The onlookers waited, exchanging fearful glances. Fen felt Dsordas's grip on her hand tighten until it hurt, but outwardly he remained perfectly still, his face a mask.

'You all know,' the Marshal went on, 'that the tenth anniversary of our beloved Emperor's marriage to Empress Ifryn will be celebrated in five days' time. That in itself is good reason for all his subjects to rejoice, but this morning I received news of an even happier event.'

Again he paused, relishing the obvious anguish he was causing. No one needed to ask how he had received this news. Fen wriggled her fingers to prevent them from being crushed, and Dsordas released her hand without looking at her.

What is he playing at? Fen wondered apprehensively. *Get to the point!*

'In the early hours of this morning,' Farrag announced, 'the Empress Ifryn gave birth to a son, Southan Azari. The Imperial heir is born!'

Please let that be all he has to say, Fen begged silently. *Please.*

Others evidently shared her thoughts, as faint signs of hope and relief showed on the faces in the crowd. Even Gaye regained a little colour.

'Hail, Southan Azari!' Farrag cried unexpectedly.

The guards behind him repeated the shout, and it was

21

echoed by other soldiers around the square – but that only seemed to make the ensuing silence all the more pointed. Farrag again looked about him, his expression one of mock surprise. His gaze rested on no one for more than a moment, but each of them – Nias, Bowen, Gaye, Fen, Dsordas and all the others – felt their hearts shrivel in that instant. They knew, with terrifying certainty, what was coming next.

'What is this?' Farrag asked in feigned disbelief. 'Such quiet! Can it be that the citizens of Zalys are disloyal to the Emperor?'

Fen swore silently, feeling the tension around her grow unbearably. *Don't let him do this. Don't give him a reason.*

'Again!' the Marshal snapped, clicking his fingers at the guards, who cried out once again:

'Hail, Southan Azari!'

This time a few islanders, sharing Fen's apprehension, joined in, albeit half-heartedly.

'Again!' There was anger in Farrag's voice now. His false smile was gone.

The performance was repeated, and this time the shouts were much louder. Fen's voice was among the strongest, even though it made her feel sick.

If this is the price we have to pay . . .

Once more the imposed ritual was signalled and obeyed – and now enough people realized what was needed. The response this time was very loud.

Farrag looked around again, smiling smugly once more, as the echoes died away.

'That's better,' he commented mildly.

'May we proceed now?' Nias enquired with timid indignation.

'I think not,' Farrag barked.

A sudden ominous stillness fell over the square.

Oh, no. Please. What now? Beside Fen, Dsordas was like a wine-skin stoppered before the fermentation was complete, ready to explode.

'I have one more duty to perform,' their tormentor explained quietly. 'Less pleasant than the first. Xantium has sent word that another hostage is required from Zalys.'

Time stood still as the horror implicit in his words sank in.

'And I have chosen Bowen Folegandros,' Farrag said, raising his voice again.

'No!' Gaye screamed. She staggered as though she were about to faint, and Bowen went quickly to her aid.

Several people began to move, amid a sudden clamour, but they stopped as the soldiers tensed, spears at the ready. Dsordas had taken a step forward, but Fen held him back. It was her turn now to grip him tightly. For his part, Farrag seemed unconcerned by the massed hostility around him, as if he were impervious to any threat.

Then Bowen's father stepped deliberately into the open, and the noise died away.

'Why must this be?' he pleaded. 'You already have my eldest son. What can this cruelty gain you?'

'Sagar is no longer in Xantium,' the Marshal replied, unmoved. 'He is dead.' Further gasps of horror and pain greeted this news. 'He was killed attempting to escape,' Farrag went on evenly. 'It is only fitting after such treachery that his brother should take his place.'

At this, Bowen's younger brother, sixteen-year-old Nason, pushed forward, heedless of the adult hands trying to hold him back and of his mother's cries of anguish.

'Then take me instead,' he implored. 'I am Sagar's brother too.'

'Get back, boy!' Farrag snapped. 'I have evidence that Bowen is involved in treason. He too plots against the Empire.'

'That's a lie!' Bowen cried desperately.

Gaye struggled out of his embrace and rushed towards Farrag as though she would beat him to death with her bare hands. The Marshal gave a disdainful wave of his hand, there was a flicker of light, and Gaye's legs crumpled under her. She fell to the floor, sprawling like a discarded rag doll.

'Arrest him,' Farrag ordered, pointing at the shocked Bowen. 'Now!'

As the soldiers began to move, Antorkas surged forward, intent on murder. This time, Farrag did not even attempt to conceal his contemptuous response. His hand flashed out and a crackle of blue fire, like miniature lightning, sped from his fingertips. The blast hit Antorkas squarely in his broad chest, throwing him backwards. He landed heavily on the stone floor.

In the failing light there was a faint aura about the Marshal, a shield of power made tangible by his malice. Without that, perhaps the enraged islanders might have overwhelmed him, although the unarmed men and women would have been slaughtered by his guards – but this last sign of Farrag's invincibility made them hold back.

No one else tried to attack him or the soldiers as they marched Bowen away. He struggled in their iron grip, his distraught face turning back to see the limp form of Gaye for as long as possible, hopelessly calling her name over and over again.

Torn between the need to scream, to stop Dsordas from doing anything reckless, and to go to the aid of both her sister and her stricken father, Fen's mind gave up the unequal struggle. She buried her face in her hands and wept.

CHAPTER TWO

From far above, I roll the dice of augury. Yet the hands are not mine. They are blighted and burn, but the flames are cold, like ice.

Seven dice; four red, three white. The whites settle first. All skulls – for death and danger. Of the reds, one is the lantern of knowledge, one is water, for travel, and two show the moon for other realms. But the moons wane, darken, and disappear. And the dream ends.

Awake, the dice are too heavy for me to lift. My hands are like clouds.

The crowds left Fournoi Square quietly, in an atmosphere of numbed outrage. The decorations looked forlorn and abandoned, and the shutters were closed quietly, the windows blind to the dismal scene. As the islanders melted into the night, hurrying along the few narrow alleys and sculling through the latticework of canals, the soldiers watched them go. Some of the guards were grim-faced and tense; others smiled maliciously, enjoying Farrag's cruel joke.

The square was soon empty and silent. The imperial forces returned to their own quarters, to celebrate the birth of Southan's heir.

The Amari family got no sleep that night. There had been many volunteers to help them back to their home, willing hands to row the boats and lift Gaye and Antorkas to their beds, but then the family had been left to their own devices, at Etha's request. Their grief and fears were private now.

The only outsiders who stayed for a while were Habella Merini, whose knowledge of the lore of herbs was unrivalled on the island, and Foran Guist, a physician, and an old friend of Antorkas.

To Fen, her father appeared half-dead, a grey pallor beneath his sunburnt skin. His back and arms were badly bruised, and there was a lump on the back of his head the size of a hen's egg. However, Foran confirmed that there were no broken bones, and that the damage to Antorkas' head would heal if he simply rested quietly. Of more concern were the marks on his chest, where the sorcerous blast had struck. The skin there was raw and pink, as if it had been burnt, and the matt of black hair seemed scorched. Habella brought a soothing ointment and tended to Antorkas as best she could, but neither she nor the physician could guess at what internal damage might have been done.

Much to everyone's relief, Antorkas woke up briefly around midnight – only to lose consciousness again from pain and rage as he remembered the evening's events. Even so, the healers had seen enough to be confident that he would recover, albeit slowly. Sleep was the best thing for him now.

In repose, Antorkas' dark face was strikingly handsome, the flecks of white in his dark mane of hair the only sign of his fifty years. Etha sat alone at his bedside after the others had gone, holding one hand in her own and watching his face with mixed emotions. His breathing was deeper and more regular now, but she could not rid her mind of the memory of him being struck down, and the worry bit deep.

The door to their bedchamber opened slowly, and Fen looked in. When she saw that her mother was still awake, she came in quietly and joined her.

'How is Gaye?' Etha asked.

'No change. We've done all we can.'

'I'll go to her.'

'Stay a while and talk to me,' Fen said quickly.

'Habella and Anto are with her. She's in good hands, and you need to rest.'

Etha frowned, but remained where she was. Her gaze returned to her husband. The night silence surrounded them.

'Look at him, the great oaf,' Etha complained fondly, her eyes suddenly brimming with tears. 'Why didn't he have more sense?'

Fen made no answer. None was expected.

'He's handsome still,' her mother went on, talking almost to herself, 'but you should have seen him when we first met. Like fire in the midst of snow. All the girls were fascinated by him, yet he chose me.' She shook her head in disbelief. 'I still don't know why.'

'He's always said that you were the most beautiful girl he'd seen in all his travels,' Fen insisted gently. 'And the one who made him laugh the most.'

Her mother did not appear to hear.

'When he first told me of his home, I didn't believe a word,' Etha whispered, her eyes full of memories. 'To hear him, this island was a place of wonders. The warm sea and the sun so hot it could burn stone; giant fish that could fly underwater; ghosts and *magic*. What did *I* know of such things?' Her voice faltered for the first time. 'Now look where it's brought us.'

'Do you ever regret coming to Zalys?' Fen asked softly.

Etha smiled at her daughter.

'No,' she replied with heartfelt conviction. 'I would have followed him to the ends of the earth.' After a moment, she added, 'Besides, without him, none of you would have existed. I was already carrying you when I stepped ashore here for the first time.'

Fen nodded. She knew the story well. As a young man, Antorkas had travelled widely, making and losing fortunes, surviving perils of all kinds and – if the stories she had not been meant to overhear were to be believed – making the acquaintance of many women. All that had changed when he met Etha. She had captivated him completely and, when he brought her home to the island as his wife, he was content to give up his wanderings, using one of his many skills to earn a living as a jeweller. Over the years, his craftsmanship had grown, and so had their family. Natali, at three years of age the youngest boy, was their sixth child.

Fen expected her mother to continue with her tale by relating how they had at first mistaken her morning sickness for a malady of the sea – the voyage to Zalys had been her first long trip on water – and of Antorkas' unconfined joy when the real reason was confirmed. Instead, Etha's voice took on a note of helpless appeal.

'There's much of the northern lands in you, Fen,' she stated. 'I've only to look at you to see that. Do *you* understand all this?' A tear rolled down her cheek.

Fen was so disconcerted by her mother's outburst that she could not respond immediately. Etha almost never cried. She had always been the true strength of the family, feisty and good-humoured, but businesslike and full of commonsense when it was needed. That innate good sense had saved her more volatile husband from many unwise decisions. Etha's figure was well-rounded now, but her green eyes still sparkled and her face retained the signs of beauty and strength that had first drawn Antorkas to her.

Even so, Fen had often wondered about the price her mother had had to pay for the romantic, bewildering start to her marriage. Fen had been born on Zalys and had lived there all her life, but she sometimes dreamed of her mother's original homeland – a land she had only seen in her imagination. *There's much of the northern lands in you.* For her mother, those memories were real, faraway and lost in innocence, but perhaps all the more painful for that.

At last Fen found her voice, wanting to help, to heal the unexpected doubt in her mother's mind.

'I understand some of it,' she replied. 'One day we'll

all be free, and then dreadful things like this won't happen any more.'

Her daughter's voice seemed to be the catalyst Etha needed. She visibly pulled herself together, impatiently wiping tears away from her eyes, and rose to her feet.

'In the meantime,' she said in a firm tone, 'we women are left to make the best of the mess these men and their politics have made. Be careful of your Dsordas, child. I don't want you to be hurt too.

'Watch him for a while,' she went on. 'I'm going to see Gaye.' She got up, kissed her husband gently on the forehead, and left. The door closed quietly behind her.

How much does she know? Fen wondered anxiously. *Or is she just guessing?*

She looked back at her sleeping father, wondering if he realized just how lucky he had been in his choice of a wife.

Gaye's malady proved to be a greater source of worry than her father's. Outwardly, her injuries were less serious: minor bruises and grazing, and none of the 'burns' which had afflicted Antorkas. However, she remained unconscious, hardly even seeming to breathe, despite all their best efforts to rouse her. None of Habella's potions had the slightest effect and the herbalist eventually left to consult the copious records of her late grandmother, from whom she had inherited her mantle. Foran was also baffled. He could find nothing physically wrong with Gaye, and could only speculate that perhaps the shock had damaged her mind more than her body. That filled her family with dread, and even his hastily added opinion that such effects would surely be temporary did little to reassure them.

They all took turns to watch over Gaye during the night, but there was no change in her condition. The duties were shared between Etha, Fen and the next three Amari children. The younger Antorkas, known to everyone as Anto, was at seventeen the eldest son, and

29

his solemn disposition was evidence of how seriously he took his responsibilities. Unlike his elder sisters, Anto had the dark colouring of his father, and had also inherited his artistic flair and sometimes fiery temperament. Only his startlingly green eyes spoke of his mother's ancestry.

The next was Tarin, a serious minded ten-year-old boy with his father's dark good looks, and below him came Ia, at seven the youngest of the girls. She too was dark, in contrast to her older sisters. Although she understood little of what was going on, she insisted – in spite of growing tiredness – on playing her part in the all-night vigil. She had always doted on Gaye, and bravely sat at her bedside, talking to her sister about everything and anything as if she could hear. The little girl's earnestness brought a lump to the throats of those who heard her.

The only one who played no part in the night's proceedings was Natali, the infant son, whose blond hair and blue eyes meant that he was doted on by many of the island's women. They called him 'the little angel', and would spoil him at every opportunity. That night, however, Natali was red-eyed and tearful, unable to understand what was going on, and no one – not even his mother, who tucked him into bed – could explain it to him. He cried himself to sleep, feeling sad and neglected.

The morning brought no improvement in Gaye's condition, but the early sunlight revealed a strange and disturbing fact. Her hair, which had been slightly darker than Fen's, was no longer blond. All colour had drained from it overnight. Her shining tresses were now pure white.

Dawn also found Farrag with much on his mind. It had been an eventful night, and one which might still have unexpected repercussions. But now he had a duty to perform.

After a little thought, he decided which one of the Far-speakers to use. The young man inside the cell was hardly more than a boy. He wore a tight-fitting head-band with an amberine stone sewn into it over close-cropped hair, and his body was draped with a filthy, loose-fitting robe. He lay slumped on the pallet, his limbs sprawled out and his back resting against the unadorned stone wall. His face was slack when Farrag entered, and his dull eyes registered no interest in his visitor.

'Roll three skulls, Iceman,' the Marshal said.

The hypnotic code words brought the young Far-speaker to life, and he sat up, his eyes alert now. But he was not his own master. The words had given Farrag complete control over the boy.

'I need to talk to Xantium. Will your voice carry that far?'

The Far-speaker known as Iceman touched a tentative finger to the stone on his headband, then to his temple, and shook his head slowly.

'Barely.' His voice was hoarse, little more than a whisper.

The Marshal considered the possibility that he was being deceived, then discarded the notion. Taking a small glass phial from a pocket, he glided over to the rough wooden table below the cell's only window. On this lay a crude clay cup and a jug of water. Carefully, Farrag let a single drop of black liquid fall from the phial into the cup, then filled it with water and swirled the mixture around. Iceman watched his every action avidly, his eyes burning.

Farrag turned and offered the cup to the Far-speaker, who all but snatched it from the thick fingers, draining it instantly. His eyes closed and he shuddered as the Marshal watched, a thin smile upon his face.

'I am ready,' Iceman said after a few moment's silence.

'The message is for Chancellor Verkho,' Farrag stated

promptly. 'No other ears. You will transmit and then forget.'

Iceman nodded, calm now.

'Bowen Folegandros has been arrested as instructed. I have questioned the prisoner, but his answers make no sense. He may have lost his mind, at least temporarily. Do you wish me to use other methods to extract information? When is shipment required?' Farrag paused. 'Add my signature code.'

'The message has been sent and received,' the Far-speaker said evenly a moment later.

'When a reply comes through, summon the guard to notify me,' the Marshal ordered. He turned towards the door.

'The reply is being sent now,' Iceman told him.

Farrag struggled not to let surprise show on his face. He had not expected an instant response and anxiety welled up within him. Was Verkho keeping an especially close watch on him for some reason? A tremor of fear shivered through his obese frame. That man was uncanny! Perhaps he wanted something else. The consequences of failing to provide exactly what the Chancellor wanted were not to be contemplated.

Farrag became aware that the boy was still looking at him.

'Relay,' he ordered impatiently.

When Iceman spoke next his voice sounded quite different; it was stronger, no longer hoarse, and of a different pitch.

'Send the Folegandros boy to the mainland immediately. He is to be unharmed. Remain vigilant. V.'

The message complete, Iceman lapsed into silence, while Farrag fumed. The instruction about Bowen was disappointing but not wholly unexpected. But why had Verkho added *Remain vigilant*? It was unnecessary, an insult.

Is he trying to test me? Farrag wondered. *To tell me something? Is there some subtlety I have missed?*

He waited for a few moments, just in case, but there was nothing else, no explanation.

'Discard the pair of moons, Iceman,' Farrag said in disgust.

As the released Far-speaker flopped back, his eyes blank once more, the Marshal left the cell. He found a guard and gave the necessary orders for Bowen's transportation, then hurried away, his thoughts still in turmoil. It was bad enough to have been posted to this ridiculous little island at the furthermost reaches of the Empire. The petty intrigues on Zalys were hardly worthy of the name, and were certainly not fitting for one of his talents. But to be treated with such contempt was intolerable. And now Verkho had even robbed him of the pleasure of interrogating his prisoner!

Without thinking, Farrag set his course towards his private garden.

CHAPTER THREE

I see a new beacon shining in the distance. Does she know what this waking means? Her head is too full of thoughts about the other one. His light was always there, even if he denied it.

What a pair they could have made. But now they are separated by the cruel darkness of the sea.

They must learn to fly.

As the sun rose with the promise of another searingly hot day, Fen and Dsordas were slumped side by side on a couch, bleary-eyed from lack of sleep but still too disturbed to be able to rest.

The night before, Dsordas' rage had been frightening to behold. His jaw had locked and he had literally been unable to speak for hours, so great were the forces warring within him. Eventually, Fen's distress had released him, and he had spent the hours of darkness like one of the family – as indeed he was in all but name. As well as being Fen's long-time partner, Dsordas worked for Antorkas in his jewellery business, and was trusted with much of their buying and selling. It was a job which enabled him to move freely within all the strata of Zalysian society – something he had found to have considerable advantages.

At first, Dsordas had wanted to call on the men he knew he could trust, to retaliate immediately – many members of the island's secret resistance movement would want and expect just that – but Fen had persuaded him otherwise. These discussions were usually the other way around, with Dsordas remaining infuriatingly calm while she fretted and fumed – but something of Farrag's evil purpose had sunk a barb deeper into his heart than any of the earlier injustices. For a time he had seemed uncharacteristically out of control.

'You mustn't react to Farrag's provocation,' Fen argued. 'That's just what he wants!'

Eventually, Dsordas' fury had abated and he agreed with her, becoming his usual controlled self once more – but even then the hurt still showed in his eyes, and he was suffering from a crushing headache.

'You have responsibilities,' Fen told him. 'So many people depend on you. When you move, it must be because you are prepared, ready, not because you've been forced into it. Much as I hate not being able to act, we *must* remain quiet, or we'll destroy all our plans, all our hopes.'

'But it's your own sister!' he said, wide-eyed.

'She'd say the same if she could,' Fen answered with conviction.

Dsordas stared at her, but she did not falter.

'You know I'm right,' she told him quietly.

Some time later she asked a question which had been at the back of her mind for a while.

'*Is* Bowen one of the Children?' The Children of Zalys was the name of the island's clandestine organization.

'No,' Dsordas replied bitterly. 'I wanted him, but he wouldn't have anything to do with us because of Sagar. That was just another of Farrag's lies.'

'But does he *know* anything?'

'Nothing of use to them,' he reassured her.

Dsordas was about to say more, but then Etha came in, looking exhausted.

'Papa is awake again,' she said, forcing herself to smile. 'Complaining as usual, so he's on the mend.'

'And Gaye?' Fen asked quickly.

Her mother's smile disappeared, and she suddenly looked much older than her years.

'Nothing's changed, except her hair,' Etha reported. 'You know about that.'

They nodded. No one knew what it meant. Long moments passed in awkward silence.

'Dsordas . . .' Etha began tentatively, 'would you . . . ?'

'Not that again, please!' he begged. 'There's no point.'

'You have the hands for it,' Etha responded, undaunted by his scowl of anguish.

'No, I don't.'

'Your mother was a healer, and so are you!' she retorted, angry now. 'Why do you deny it?'

'Much good it did my mother!' Dsordas shot back. 'She died.' It sounded like an accusation.

'But before she died,' Etha answered him fervently, 'she did all the good she was capable of. She helped people. You won't even try.'

'I won't try because I *can't* help!' he shouted back. 'Leave it to those who know what they're doing.'

'We've tried everything else,' Etha said, calm now. 'Gaye needs you.'

As the ensuing silence stretched unbearably, Fen racked her brain for some way to end the painful argument, but she could find none. Both Dsordas and her mother were so entrenched in their own beliefs that nothing she could say would make any difference. As always, it became a contest of wills.

Surprisingly, it was Dsordas who backed down.

'All right,' he whispered, not looking at Etha. 'It won't do any good, but I'll try.'

'Thank you.'

They went to Gaye's room, and the women stood back as Dsordas laid his hands on either side of the invalid's head, just as he had seen his mother do so many times. His own lack of faith was reflected in his expression, but he persevered, and after a while, Gaye's breathing seemed to strengthen a little, and the lines of her face relaxed. But she remained as deeply unconscious as ever, her ghostly appearance accentuated by her white hair.

'It's no good,' Dsordas said weakly, withdrawing his hands. 'I don't know what I'm doing.'

'You're doing all you can,' Etha told him. 'No one can ask more.'

'Come on,' Fen said. 'Let's go and get some food.'

He allowed himself to be led towards the kitchen.

'How's your head?' she asked.

'Much better!' he replied, sounding surprised.

Farrag's 'garden' was in a small courtyard, boxed in by the three-storey high walls of the surrounding buildings. The windows overlooking it were all securely shuttered, and there was only one entrance, through a set of double doors. Inside, the air was humid and rank, even at this early hour, and insects whined and buzzed threateningly. In the centre of the courtyard was a small, stagnant pond with a rotting tree trunk half-submerged in its murky depths. It was surrounded by sickly-looking grass and anonymous shrubs and trailing vines.

As Farrag entered, there was a sudden stillness, as if the garden were holding its breath. Beside the pond were several large and ugly toads, all frozen in position, hoping not to be seen. Their mottled green-brown skin blended with their fetid surroundings, but the Marshal was not fooled. His cruel blue eyes fixed upon the largest of the toads, and he began to hum a single, low note which reverberated in the confined space. His chosen victim became insensible, sinking down on its belly, its eyes closing.

As Farrag moved forward, the other toads all leapt for cover, moving with remarkable speed. The biggest could not resist as the Marshal leaned down and scooped him up in both hands. Holding the creature in front of his face, Farrag stopped humming. The toad's eyes snapped open and it struggled desperately, suddenly aware of its peril and terribly afraid. Farrag's experienced hands held it easily, however, and the animal resorted to its last defence. A thick black substance oozed from nodules on its back and on the top of its head. The Marshal deftly scraped most of the dark slime off with one thumbnail and deposited it in a small glass phial he had ready for the purpose. Then he turned to the final nodule and slowly, deliberately, licked the poison directly from the head of the terrified creature, his stained tongue rasping over the rough skin.

Then he dropped the toad to the ground and it scurried away, unheeding. Farrag's body twitched massively, rolls of fat quivering, and his eyes rolled up towards the sky in ecstasy.

By mid-morning, Fen and Dsordas had forced themselves to eat, but had still been unable to get any sleep. Now at least they were alone together and resting comfortably in each other's company. Their peace was short-lived, however, as they received an unexpected visitor.

'May I come in?' Nason asked.

'Of course,' Fen replied, wondering at the determined expression on the face of Bowen's younger brother. 'How are your parents?'

'They're all right,' Nason answered without thinking. 'They sent me to see how Gaye and your father are – but it's really you I came to see,' he added, looking at Dsordas.

'Why?'

'I want to join the underground,' Nason stated. 'The Children.'

'Then you've come to the wrong place,' Dsordas told him evenly, his face a neutral mask which Fen struggled to match. 'I don't know anything about it.'

Nason stared at him, shock and incomprehension making him temporarily mute.

'But you must,' he whispered eventually.

'It's dangerous even to talk of such things,' Dsordas

said quietly. 'What makes you think I know anything?'

'I . . . I know I'm young,' the boy exclaimed, as his brain began to function again. 'But I'm not stupid! And I'm not going to make the same mistake Bowen did.' There was a touch of anger in his voice now. 'You can trust me.'

'We trust you,' Fen said quietly.

'But we can't help you,' Dsordas added firmly.

'What was Bowen's mistake?' Fen asked, knowing that they needed to learn more but that they must do so very carefully.

Nason was silent for a few moments, youthful pride making his eyes defiant, even though he was obviously still confused.

'He thought if he stayed out of it and didn't choose sides, then he'd be safe,' he said at last. 'He was a fool.'

'Did he talk to you about these Children?' Dsordas wanted to know.

'Not exactly.'

'What do you mean?'

'Awake, he wouldn't even discuss anything,' Nason replied, 'but he used to talk in his sleep. Our rooms are next to each other and I heard him sometimes, arguing with himself. I couldn't help overhearing,' he added defensively.

'And?' Dsordas prompted, trying to sound only mildly interested.

'He talked about someone called the Stone Eye,' Nason told them. 'He shouted sometimes, and said things like "I should help him. I should help him. But I can't. I mustn't."'

Fen looked puzzled.

'But the Stone Eye is a place, not a man,' she said.

'I know that,' Nason put in. 'But Bowen talked as if it was a man.'

'How did that lead you to me?' Dsordas asked.

'He mixed things up sometimes,' the boy answered.

39

'The Stone Eye became the Swordsman or the Sword – and sometimes I swear he yelled out Dsordas.'

No one said anything for a few heartbeats.

'I could have been mistaken about the name,' Nason said uncertainly, 'but it was pretty obvious that he was talking about the underground.' The boy's voice trailed away, his earlier confidence evaporating.

'So you came to me?'

'Yes.'

'I'm sorry, Nason,' Dsordas said. 'I can't help you. And if I could, I wouldn't. Do you understand?'

'No.' Then the boy's indignant look slowly faded. 'Yes,' he amended quietly.

Dsordas beckoned him closer, until their faces were only a handspan apart. When he spoke his voice was quiet but calm, and full of authority.

'I know how you must feel, Nason, but you're not stupid. You know that if any of this family or yours was involved with the Children – whoever they are – now would be the worst possible time for them to make any move. After what happened yesterday, Farrag and his men will be watching us all even more closely than usual.'

'I hate them!' Nason breathed.

'So do we all,' Dsordas went on, 'but there's no sense in risking our freedom and our lives to no purpose. So don't talk to anyone about this for now. All right?'

Nason nodded reluctantly.

'I wish there was something I could *do*!' Frustration made his voice shrill.

'In time, there will be,' Dsordas responded. 'But not now!'

'You *do* know something!' Nason exclaimed.

'No, I don't,' the other replied, smiling. 'But when the underground decide to make their move, don't you think they'll call on all of us – you, me, Fen, everyone who wants Zalys free. You'll get your chance, when the time is right.'

Nason regarded him thoughtfully.

'In the meantime,' Fen said gently, 'be careful. Don't get yourself – or anyone else – into trouble.'

The young man nodded, his expression solemn.

'Do you think Sagar's really dead?' he asked suddenly. Nason had been a young child when his eldest brother had been taken hostage nine years earlier, and retained only the vaguest memories of him.

'I don't know,' Dsordas replied honestly. 'Farrag and his kind lie all the time, but we have no way of knowing for sure.'

'I'll find out one day,' Nason vowed, then moved towards the door. 'I'd better go now. Thank you for talking to me.' He paused on his way out and glanced back anxiously. 'You won't tell my father about this, will you?'

'No,' Dsordas replied seriously.

Fen waited for the door to close before letting out a long sigh of relief. Then she put her arms around Dsordas and hugged him tightly.

'Oh, my love,' she whispered, 'I hate this.'

'Me too,' he replied. 'He deserved better than that.'

'Do you think he believed us?' she asked, drawing back to look at his face, seeing the preoccupation in his deep brown eyes.

'I'm not sure,' he said. 'But he's a sensible lad. Even if he has his suspicions, he'll keep them to himself.'

'Did Bowen know about you?'

'No. All the messages I sent him were anonymous.'

'The Stone Eye?'

'Yes.'

'What about the Swordsman? Is that you too?'

'No. I'm not foolish enough to choose a code-name so like my own. I'll have to do some quiet investigating.'

'Farrag will interrogate Bowen, won't he?' Fen said, shuddering at the thought. 'What if he tells them about the Stone Eye?'

'It won't mean anything. No one will connect the name with me.'

'I still don't like it,' she said, thinking that this was the understatement of the year. Then another idea occurred to her. 'You'll probably be faced with a few eager recruits in the next few days,' she suggested. 'Not all of them will have as a good a reason as Nason, but a lot of people will be very angry at what happened yesterday.'

'I know,' he replied. 'And what better time for one of Farrag's informers to infiltrate the organization – while feelings are running so high.'

'You'd better spread the word to the Children to be on their guard,' she told him, fighting down her fear.

'I already have,' he replied, with a smile that was almost smug.

'And you be careful too!' Fen ordered brusquely.

'I'm always careful,' he answered.

Fen was at her sister's bedside when Gaye finally awoke later that day.

'Bowen!' she cried in anguish, her lovely face suddenly distraught. 'Bowen!'

'I'm here,' Fen said helplessly. 'How are you feeling?'

'I hurt,' Gaye answered gratingly. 'Is it still night?'

'No.' Fen was puzzled. 'It's the middle of the afternoon.'

'Fen? Fen!' Gaye sat up, her eyes wide. 'Where are you?' Her voice had risen to a scream. She stared frantically around the room, but could see nothing. She was completely blind.

CHAPTER FOUR

Walls have never mattered much to me. There is always a way through. Even the bats know that.

Yet the ones who need to see are fed darkness from the fire. They will not listen to the light; their senses are no more than smoke. It is beyond my strength to wield the burning sword.

Sagar Folegandros had no idea where he was or how he had got there. And that made him all the more fearful.

The cell was almost completely dark. It had no windows, and the only light came from the faint reflections of a distant lamp that filtered through the bars in the door slit. The unyielding stone walls were cold but dry. Sagar had never before been in a place like this within the hostage enclave, but he had heard of such . . . and the thought made him shudder.

What have I done to deserve this?

He had spent the last nine years of his life in the small world of the enclave, never once allowed to venture past the walls to the city beyond. He had been only thirteen when he arrived, bewildered, frightened and angry – not only with his captors but also with his parents for letting him be taken away. As one of the first 'guests' to be installed, Sagar had witnessed the arrival of other hostages, some of them much younger than himself.

Since then, his life had been full but not difficult – except for the chafing lack of freedom and his longing for his home. His quarters, while certainly not luxurious, were comfortable enough; most of his needs were catered for, and the food was more than adequate, although it had seemed strange at first. His schooling – in languages, logic and imperial law – was thorough, something he only regarded as an advantage in the later years of his captivity, and he had the companionship of the other hostages. Some of these were girls, the oldest of them now grown to womanhood, but romance was not something that had entered Sagar's life. His friendship was bestowed warily and his trust even more reluctantly, for the hostages were always watched, and who was to know who was really friend or foe? Self-reliance had become his watchword in an enclosed realm where tensions ran high and real knowledge of the outside world was strictly rationed. It had been a strange adolescence.

There were many more hostages now than when Sagar had first arrived – and they had all realized that escape was impossible. The enclave ramparts were strong, and their guards sharp-eyed and efficient. Even if they could have slipped through this formidable net, they would have been alone in an unfamiliar city where the army was reputed to be all-powerful and the inhabitants hostile. And then, of course, there was the ever-present threat of reprisals in their homelands. Some kept their anger and will-power alive, but they suffered for it, and even if they were willing to die themselves in the name of freedom, few were content to risk family or friends at home, just as those in faraway lands would do nothing to endanger their loved ones in Xantium. The Empire benefited from the use of this double-edged weapon.

It was true that some hostages had disappeared without trace, but no convincing explanation was ever given for this. The more optimistic among the prisoners suggested that they had been released to return to their homes, their purpose served, and in spite of the lack of any proof, this was a hope which many clung to. However, there were also terrible rumours – which their captors did nothing to dispel – about the fate of those who were foolhardy enough to attempt to escape. It was said that they were chained alone in the dark for years on end, catching only fleeting glimpses of reality as silent gaolers brought their meagre sustenance. Unable to move or even stand erect, these unfortunates were said to go mad long before they died, festering in their own degrading filth. Such a prospect was enough to strike fear into even the boldest heart.

Instinctively, Sagar moved his limbs, as if to reassure himself that no manacles clamped his wrists or ankles. He found some relief in this small freedom, but greater terrors weighed heavily upon him.

What have I done to deserve this?

His head still felt fuzzy, filled with the darkness that had engulfed him earlier. As soon as he had woken, he had tried calling out. His cries had echoed into silence in the half-seen corridors of the dungeon, and there had been no response. After that he had forced himself to explore every corner of the cell. All he encountered was bare stone, a straw pallet and an empty wooden pail. Nothing else.

He steeled himself to wait, clinging to his dwindling supplies of patience and resolve. Surely someone would come and explain soon. They couldn't just leave him here. Could they?

The last thing Sagar remembered before his incarceration was that he had been sitting reading in his own room and had been visited by an Information Officer – the white-faced one with the thin, pale hands and red-rimmed eyes. He had ordered Sagar to drink a draught of colourless liquid, but would give no explanation. Reluctant, but aware that the consequences of refusal would be far worse, Sagar had obeyed. Experiments upon hostages were not unknown, but if this potion was one of their supposed truth serums, then he had nothing to hide. He had not feared poison. Cooperative hostages were not killed for no reason.

He had tossed back the liquid, tasting only a fleeting

bitterness – and then the blackness had overwhelmed him so suddenly that he had not had time to be afraid.

How long had he been unconscious? He had no way of telling now whether the sun shone or night had fallen. Days could have passed for all he knew. He was not hungry, but that meant little. Even if the potion had not affected his appetite, it was certain that his anxiety did. In the forlorn hope of finding some clue, Sagar went to the door again, peered through the slit and listened. Nothing moved; even the air was silent.

It was then that he remembered the message, and his skin suddenly felt cold and clammy. He had received it three days earlier, a small piece of paper secreted in the folds of his bed.

But I burnt it! he protested silently. *Can they decipher ashes?*

The message was still fresh in his mind, however, no matter how hard he had tried to forget it, to dismiss it from his thoughts.

'Not all the citizens of Xantium wish
to have your imprisonment on their
consciences. If you want to know more,
leave us a sign. Leave a drop of blood
on a shirt collar when you next send
washing to the laundry. Whether you
respond or not, destroy this note.'

The dangerous letter had been written in the common trading tongue in use throughout the Empire. It was not signed, but there was a mark at the bottom which Sagar had at first taken to be a cross. He had later realized that it was a sword.

He had agonized over his decision for most of that night, but had eventually decided not to respond. There had been no blood on any of his clothes when they were next sent out, and he had held the paper in the candle flame, seen it reduced to dark powder. But the possibility remained that he had admitted receiving the message while he was drugged.

Surely they can't blame me for that? he thought helplessly. *I didn't answer!*

He went back to sit on the straw mattress, his back leaning against the wall, and brooded on the possible injustice of his fate. All the time he watched the door, clinging to the hope that he would be released.

However, his first visitor, when he came, arrived through one of the solid walls of the cell. The ghost appeared without warning, slipping from the stone in absolute silence. His pale luminescence made the cell seem unreal.

That's a useful trick, Sagar thought. He was surprised, but not afraid. His childhood on Zalys had accustomed him to such spectres. The living, he knew, had nothing to fear from the dead.

The ghost looked around the chamber, then turned his translucent eyes upon Sagar. His mouth moved but made no sound, and Sagar did not have the skill to read lips. He did not bother to reply, knowing that sound could not pass between their worlds. Instead he studied the visitor's appearance. He was curious – he had seen spirits in Xantium before, but never this close. The man was dressed in military uniform, apparently of high rank, but Sagar did not recognize the style. His face was an ever-shifting blur.

'Next time, bring a key,' Sagar suggested, more to hear the sound of his voice than for the hope of any response.

The ghost's lips moved silently once more.

'Oh, go away!' Sagar was exasperated, wanting some-one real.

The spectral image vanished in an instant.

After the midwives and the court physicians had completed their work and satisfied themselves that all was well, they allowed the Emperor to see his new heir.

While Southan III stared in awe at the tiny boy in his wife's arms, Ifryn lay still, as the pain slowly faded and contentment began to flow through her. It had been a long time since she had given birth to the second of their two daughters, and she had almost forgotten the agony of confinement and the joyful relief when it was over. At least Southan Azari's arrival in the world had been reasonably quick and without complications – and the look on his father's face was worth a great deal.

The Emperor looked fondly at his wife, his eyes still full of wonder. Ifryn smiled weakly.

'You've done well,' he said.

The words were so solemn and so inadequate a reward that Ifryn laughed aloud, regretting it instantly as the movement made her wince with renewed pain. Southan was immediately concerned.

'Are you all right?' he asked anxiously. 'Should I fetch a nurse?'

'No, I'm fine,' she answered softly. 'Just don't make me laugh.'

'I wasn't trying to,' he said seriously.

'Kiss me instead,' Ifryn suggested, smiling.

He leant carefully forward over the baby who was destined to become Southan IV. Unexpectedly gentle for such a big man, he brushed her lips tenderly. The bristles of his moustache tickled, but Ifryn did not mind.

'A boy!' the Emperor breathed, as though he still could not quite believe it.

'He has your eyes,' she told him. Father and son both had deep blue eyes.

'Yes,' he said. 'And my dark hair.' There was a touching note of pride in his voice.

'What there is of it!' Ifryn remarked.

Southan seemed lost for words for a while.

'I'm sorry it took so long,' she told him. 'Ten years is a long time to wait for an heir.'

'I never doubted that it would happen!' he responded, uncharacteristically passionate. 'It has been worth the wait. Why such things take time is known only to the gods, not to men.'

'It wasn't for lack of trying,' she said. 'That's certain.'

In the face of her mischievous smile, Southan blushed. He looked so ridiculous that Ifryn almost laughed again, but she lacked the strength to tease him further.

'Go and fetch the girls,' she instructed him. 'They'll want to see him, and I need to sleep.'

Southan backed away from the bed without taking his eyes off his son, then turned and strode purposefully towards the door. In doing so he regained his habitual military bearing. He had hardly touched the handle when the door burst open and the imperial daughters flew in. Vrila, the eldest at eight and a half, was quickest to the bedside, her long fair hair flowing, blue eyes open wide, but Delmege, who was barely seven years old, was only a pace or two behind. She had dark hair like her father, but her huge eyes were brown and gentle, like her mother's. Both girls stood in silence for a few moments as Southan walked back to join them, then they began to chatter so eagerly that neither could be understood.

'Hush,' Ifryn told them. 'You don't want to make Azari cry.'

'He's so little!' Vrila whispered accusingly.

'And your tummy was so big!' Delmege added.

'He'll grow soon,' Ifryn said, smiling at their incredulity. 'Like you did.'

'I was never that small,' Delmege decided.

'Can I hold him?' her sister asked hopefully.

'Not now, my sweet. Look, see. He's gone to sleep.'

'Can he talk?' Delmege asked.

'Not yet, little one.'

'Of course not,' Southan added, trying to sound stern but failing miserably. 'He's only just been born.' The Emperor smiled at his wife from behind the girls.

A knock on the door put an end to their conversation. Doneta, Ifryn's maid, who had accompanied her from

49

their homeland ten years ago, peered around, then entered and curtseyed.

'I'm sorry to interrupt, your majesty,' she began. 'But the Chancellor requests that you join him for an urgent conference.'

Southan's smile vanished.

'Of course,' he replied, casting an apologetic glance at Ifryn. 'Will you be all right?'

'Doneta and I can manage quite well,' she told him. 'But take these two out with you, or I'll never get any rest.'

Southan began to usher the protesting girls out, and turned to flash a brief, bright smile as the door closed. Doneta came and took the sleeping infant, placed him in his cot, then retreated to her own chair in a corner where she could watch over baby and mother while both slept.

The Empress lay still, thankful for the quiet, but sleep would not come and she fell to reminiscing about the last ten years, the period since her life had been turned upside down.

The first time she had met her husband-to-be, she had been daunted by his physical presence – he looked every bit as imposing as an Emperor should. He had been very formal then, obviously pleased by his bride's unexpected beauty, but still making her fully aware that she was little more than a possession, a single piece in a vast, complex game of politics and power.

The wedding was an appropriately glittering event, but it left Ifryn cold. The ceremony and the words meant little. The real significance of their union lay in the shifting influences and renewed alliances that came in its wake, and the new Empress was aware of this. Nevertheless, she also knew her duty. She performed her part in the charade to perfection, appeared radiant as required, and accepted her role with as much equanimity as she could muster. Within the year she was pregnant.

However, even before Vrila was born, Ifryn had begun to view her husband in a different light. The months at his side taught her that he was, after all, just a man – like all the rest – and she soon realized that his outward appearance – the dominating physique and dark good looks – was misleading. Inside his impressive, gaudy shell, he was weak in both character and intellect, and she had found it easy to bend him to her will when she chose.

At the same time, a curious metamorphosis took place within her heart. What had begun as duty gradually turned to genuine affection and finally to love – even though, or perhaps because, she saw his faults so clearly. Southan was always tender and eager to please her, and was a devoted father.

Unfortunately, others also found the Emperor easy to manipulate – and many had less benign motives than Ifryn. Because of that, she steered as clear as possible of all politics and court intrigue, and contented herself with the responsibilities of her family and her household. Of course, her self-imposed separation could not blind her to all that went on in the outside world. She was unhappily aware – increasingly so in the last few years – that even if Southan was the Empire's figurehead, the real power lay elsewhere. His hurried departure this very hour was proof enough of that.

No man could afford to ignore a summons from Chancellor Verkho. Not even the Emperor.

CHAPTER FIVE

*From here the sky is hollow. I can read the signs. Clouds,
smoke, the patterns made by the wings of birds. They all
tell a story of the future. Is it my responsibility to choose?*

*Long ago I looked at the patterns of silt beside the river
bank. They told me that I would lie here, looking up at the
bright sky. The bright and hollow sky.*

Prophecy is not a gift. It is a curse.

Chancellor Verkho Yulsare was alone in his austere
study when one of his lieutenants opened the door to
announce the arrival of the Emperor. Southan strode in,
already feeling the familiar unease of that place. There
was none of the opulence of Verkho's living quarters
here. It was a working room, starkly functional, with no
adornments, no softness, no humanity. It was a place
dedicated to the Chancellor's greatest weapon of power,
information. A large, wooden desk stood in the centre of
the room, row upon row of books and boxes lay on the
shelves which covered two of the walls, and cabinets
along the other walls housed yet more mysteries.

Verkho rose from his chair, preserving the formalities,
but both men were aware of their real standing, their
relative power. The Chancellor executed a perfunctory
bow. He was an imposing figure, one of the few men
who was as tall and as broad-shouldered as the Emperor.
His long, lustrous hair and unruly beard were as black as
midnight, but his eyes were his most striking feature.
They were grey – but so bright that they appeared almost
silver. It was said that Verkho's eyes shone in the dark,

like a cat's. Even now, in the subdued light of the study, they glittered, making it difficult for Southan to meet his Chancellor's gaze.

'I am sorry that I was forced to request an audience at this time,' Verkho began. He did not sound at all apologetic. 'I trust that all is well with the Empress and your son?'

'All is well.'

'Let us hope that it remains so.'

'What do you mean?' Southan demanded angrily.

'I have just received intelligence that the conspirators led by the traitor who calls himself the Swordsman are becoming active again,' the Chancellor replied gravely. 'I fear that the birth of an heir might spur them into fatal action. They may even plot against your son's life.'

'That's absurd,' the Emperor spluttered. 'What would they gain from the death of a baby?'

'Time,' Verkho answered, 'and uncertainty. If you were once again left without an heir, it is doubtful whether another would be born for some years. Forgive me for broaching such a delicate subject, but it has been seven years since your last child, and if you had to wait as long again, the Empress would perhaps be growing too old for childbearing. And during that wait, the Imperial succession would be uncertain. In such a climate, with the Empire under threat from beyond our borders and possibly from within, anything might happen.'

'But the Empress is in perfect health!' Southan objected. 'There's no reason why we shouldn't have another son.'

'Perhaps not,' Verkho agreed coolly, 'but the very possibility of such difficulty, the inevitable rumours, would be enough to make your realm unstable.'

It sounded horribly plausible to Southan. He did not trust Verkho completely, knowing him to be devious, a consummate politician, but the Empire was indeed in a parlous state. Financially, militarily and politically, there were problems which seemed to grow worse daily. The Xantic borders were pressed on all sides by increasingly ambitious neighbours, and unrest was growing in some of their own provinces. After centuries of expansion and vigorous stability, the last few years had seen only stagnation and decay. The imperial armies had recently fought several minor wars not of their own choosing; wars not of conquest but of defence, and there were more to come. Xantium itself depended heavily on the outside world for supplies and taxes to sustain the city – and that was another perilous situation. In such an atmosphere, alliances shifted daily, and only the army and Verkho's wide network of spies, with the help of the Far-speakers, held the Empire together. No wonder then that various factions within Xantium were exploiting the uncertainty of the times to further their own ends. But to threaten the imperial heir, his own son – that was too much to bear!

'What evidence have you about the Swordsman?' Southan demanded.

'There has been much clandestine activity recently,' Verkho answered promptly. 'And the timing can hardly be a coincidence. My agents have witnessed several meetings between unreliable elements, junior members of the nobility.'

'Who?'

The Chancellor reeled off a list of names.

'That's hardly surprising,' Southan countered. 'Young men prefer the society of their peers.'

'But the frequency of their gatherings is unusual,' Verkho went on, unruffled. 'Some of these hotheads are indeed friends. And yet those who are reputedly enemies also meet regularly, in the gambling halls. A few have even been foolish enough to carry weapons in the forbidden areas. Something is brewing – and what better cover for their activity than the preparations for your tenth anniversary celebrations – and those for the birth of your child.'

The two men stared at each other over the desk, one agitated, the other icy calm.

'Was there anything else?' Southan asked eventually.

'Unfortunately, yes,' the other answered. 'Several foreign merchants have recently visited the city for no apparent reason. They did not even attempt to conceal their real purposes with genuine trade. I do not like spies in Xantium.'

No – unless they're your own! Southan thought, but said nothing.

'Several hostages have been contacted by the organization which uses the sign of the sword,' Verkho continued. 'They have been very clever.' The admission was drawn from him grudgingly. 'We have not managed to catch any of them red-handed yet – but we will.' He paused, bringing his flare of anger under control. 'Why would the agitators promote unrest in the enclave unless something grave is afoot? One of the hostages has even dared to escape.'

'Who?'

Verkho consulted some notes on his desk, but Southan guessed, correctly, that the Chancellor had no need to do so. His memory was phenomenal.

'Sagar Folegandros, from the island of Zalys,' he said. 'There is no doubt that the Swordsman had something to do with it.'

'Zalys?' the Emperor said, puzzled. 'What harm can they do?'

'On their own,' Verkho replied, 'little or nothing.' The rest of his answer went unsaid. 'I've taken steps to reprimand the island for his folly.'

'What does all this have to do with my son?'

'The timing of their activity is suggestive, as I've said. But we also have this.' Verkho picked up a scrap of paper from his desk. 'It's part of a message delivered to one of the hostages. The rest has been burnt, as you can see, but what is left speaks eloquently.'

The Chancellor handed the paper over, and watched

the Emperor carefully. Southan took it gingerly.

'It's one of several such missives,' Verkho added, 'but all the others, including Sagar's, were completely destroyed.'

The Emperor stared at the scrap in his hand. It was the right hand side of a larger piece of paper, with only a word or two remaining at the end of each line. The left hand edge was jagged and black, left by the devouring flame that had obliterated most of the message. Most of what was still readable seemed innocuous enough; the word 'wish' on the top line; '—w more' on the third; '—xt send', 'er you,' and 'note.' on the last three lines, but Southan's eyes were drawn again and again to the other fragments. They were indeed eloquent. On the second line, the single word 'heir' was like a beacon, and the fourth bore the ominous message 'of blood'. In the bottom corner was the unmistakable sign of a sword.

Southan wanted to believe that the message was a fake, one of Verkho's bizarre tricks, but it felt real. And for the life of him, he could not see what Verkho would gain by such elaborate subterfuge. It seemed that his safest course was to treat the note as genuine.

'What steps have you taken?' he asked quietly.

'We have redoubled our vigilance in the enclave and in the city as a whole,' the Chancellor responded. 'I have already asked General Kerrell to reinforce the guard on the imperial quarters – inconspicuously, of course – and my own men are observing the kitchens.'

'You suspect poison?'

'It pays not to neglect any possibility,' Verkho answered patronizingly. 'However remote.'

'But the baby feeds from his mother,' Southan objected.

'There are poisons which can be passed from mother to child in the milk,' the Chancellor said. 'The Empress may be in danger too.'

Some hours later, when Midsummer's Day was more

than half over, Verkho received another visitor. This one had not been summoned – there had been no need. He had known that she would come of her own accord. The only surprise was that she had waited so long. Verkho had looked forward to the meeting.

Clavia Bhazak had once been beautiful, but years of scheming and partially frustrated ambition had taken their toll. Lines of discontent now marked her face permanently and her green eyes, while still sharp, no longer made men turn their heads. Her once willowy figure showed signs of indulgence and excess that no finery could disguise, and even her cloud of red hair had lost the fire of her younger days. She was tall for a woman but still a handspan shorter than Verkho, who was her half-brother. The two, who were so different in looks and temperament, shared the same mother, and it may have been from her that each had inherited their talent at social and political intrigue. Whatever the source of their expertise, they made a formidable pairing. Verkho would never admit to it now, but Clavia's wiles had played a big part in his own rise to fame and influence in Xantium.

'So the bitch has finally whelped,' Clavia spat, without preamble. 'Would that we could drown the pup.'

'How prettily you put it,' Verkho mocked, smiling nastily.

Clavia glared at him malevolently.

'Don't provoke me, *brother*.' She made the word sound like a curse. 'You know what this means. Why couldn't she have had another girl?'

'A boy suits our purpose better,' he said calmly.

'Are you mad?' Clavia screeched. 'Southan now has an heir!'

'Exactly.' Verkho nodded, smirking.

'I swear I'll kill you one day,' his half-sister hissed in frustration.

'That's treason, my dear. Perhaps I should have you imprisoned.' He seemed to delight in goading her, but then relented abruptly. 'Let me explain. I'm surprised that you haven't sufficient wits to work it out for yourself.'

Clavia waited impatiently, scowling, but resigned to his sarcasm.

'Before this boy arrived,' Verkho explained, 'our hands were tied. If Southan had died, half the nobility would have been clamouring for their sons to marry his daughters and claim the throne. Our own claims would have been dismissed. At best we would have been embroiled in chaos. But now . . .' He smiled rapaciously. 'Now the succession is clear. The boy will be the next Emperor. If, for argument's sake, Southan met with an *accident* while his heir was still a child, who else but his Chancellor could reasonably claim the responsibility of regent? From there it would be but a small step to my being recognized as Emperor in my own right. No one would stand in our way. Ifryn is of no account. Kerrell's loyalty is sworn to the Emperor, or his regent, whatever his personal feelings. Who else is there? I . . .' He hesitated, then nodded deferentially to Clavia. '*We* shall have our rightful places at last.'

Clavia's angry expression had gradually turned to a smile as her half-brother spoke, but now she looked doubtful.

'Perhaps you underestimate Ifryn,' she suggested. 'She is worthless on her own account, but I think she would fight for her children. And Kerrell might side with her,' she added in disgust. 'You know those two are as close as twins in the womb.'

'Your disapproval wouldn't have anything to do with the fact that the general has rebuffed your advances, would it?' Verkho asked, feigning innocence.

'Answer me!' Clavia demanded angrily, her cheeks flushed.

The Chancellor nodded smugly. His thoughts were way ahead of hers.

'Our beloved Empress is the perfect mother,' he said

sarcastically, 'and that is how we can break what little
spirit she may show. How would it be if, through some
mischance or even her own negligence, the boy turns out
to be a halfwit, fit only to drool and wallow in his own
filth? Would she have the stomach for the fight then?
Would Kerrell?'

'Could this be done?' Clavia asked admiringly.

'Naturally,' he replied. 'It can be arranged simply
enough. I was warning Southan of the perils of poison
only this morning.'

'You did *what*?' she exclaimed.

'Let him be on his guard,' Verkho said, laughing. 'It
will do them no good. I will be the last to be suspected,
having forewarned the Emperor of such a possibility.
And think how it would affect Southan if such a thing
escaped his vigilance. Even though the so-called
assassin's attempt will fail, his son, his heir, will be
reduced to the status of an animal. What better reason
for an Emperor to lose his reason and hasten his own
death?'

'My apologies, brother. You are even more devious
than I had thought.'

'Thank you, my dear,' he said, bowing his head in
acknowledgement. 'Would you care for some wine?'

'Only if you drink from the same bottle,' she replied.

They laughed together, knowing that even that precaution would do her little good if she forfeited Verkho's
trust. He fetched the wine, poured, and pushed one of
the goblets across the desk. She sipped appreciatively
and watched him over the rim.

'I don't suppose you had anything to do with the
excitement in the hostage enclave?' she asked curiously.

Verkho spread his hands.

'I can't conceal anything from you,' he said.

'One of them escaped?' she said, ignoring his tone.

'So it seems,' he admitted happily. 'A lad named

59

Sagar, from Zalys. He's one of those who had received a message from the Swordsman.'

'Him again!' Clavia grimaced.

'An opponent worthy of my skill,' the Chancellor said, sounding almost eager. 'Most of them are no challenge at all, but he . . .' His eyes gleamed as he sipped his wine.

'He's getting bolder,' she remarked.

'Yes, but everything can be turned to our advantage,' Verkho responded. 'I used a fragment of one of the notes we recovered to set Southan thinking. Dullard that he is, he'll not ignore this. Look. Here's a copy of the whole note.' He waited while Clavia read the message. 'And here's what Southan saw.'

She scanned the charred fragment and burst out laughing.

'That must have taken some careful work with the flame,' she commented admiringly.

Verkho shrugged, accepting her praise nonchalantly.

'Why Sagar?' Clavia asked.

'He's of no importance at the moment. We just need to have him safely out of the way for a while. But his brother Bowen might be another matter,' Verkho added enthusiastically. 'I've heard some interesting reports about him.'

'So you arranged for Sagar's "escape" to provide you with the perfect excuse to summon his brother to Xantium?' she said.

Verkho nodded, a sudden frown creasing his forehead.

'Unless that grotesque bungler Farrag fouls it up,' he said bitterly. 'I wouldn't put it past him.'

'Ah, but you have such a delightful way with people who fail you, brother.'

They smiled at each other.

'Is there any other news from Zalys?' Clavia asked pointedly.

'No. But there must be soon,' the Chancellor replied.

'The ship should be there any day now, but Farrag's not such a fool that he won't notice anything. I can't afford to let him know too much.'

'And in the meantime, we have much to do here,' Clavia concluded.

'I try to keep busy,' he replied, smiling.

CHAPTER SIX

I have been lost in a dream of rolling dice for thirty-seven years. But whose dream is it?

I was here long before he came, for all that he would rewrite history. The fire is everywhere now, but it was not always so. Before that, only the gods saw beyond the waking world. Therefore . . .

I am tired of gambling with gods.

Verkho had been busy ever since his arrival in Xantium, but his story began long before that. Technically, he was a distant cousin of Southan III, but the illegitimate son of an impoverished minor nobleman in the northern part of the Xantic homeland counted for little. He grew up wild and ignorant, skilled only in a variety of cruel sports. His father publicly disowned the illiterate wastrel, though Verkho took his father's name, but privately, as was the way of many petty lords, he admired the young man's violent and stubborn-headed nature and revelled in the tales of his hunting prowess. However, all that changed dramatically in Verkho's sixteenth year.

It was then, according to popular belief, that the young man experienced a 'divine revelation'. No one knew exactly what had happened, but the effect upon Verkho was quite remarkable. Hitherto, he had been relentless in his torments of anyone weaker or less fortunate than himself, but now there was a warmth in his gaze, and healing in his hands. His suddenly bright eyes held others mesmerized, and he preached devotion to love and to the gods. The faithless boy now spoke with a man's voice in praise of the ancient pantheon, with a fluency that defied understanding. Even more extraordinary was the fact that the illiterate young man could now both speak and write several languages to a standard which put many scholars to shame. It was even said that Verkho had been granted the gift of prophecy and that it was this talent which drove him to leave home. Whatever the real truth of the matter, it was obvious that the undistinguished town of his birth had suddenly become too small for the new prodigy.

The next few years of his life were shrouded in mystery. Some said that he had retreated to the remote mountaintop monastery of a peculiar sect, whose barbaric rituals had a profound effect on the young, awakening mind. Others believed that he had lived as a hermit, meditating and dedicating his every breath to the gods and their service. An even more bizarre theory suggested that his time had been spent bargaining with the gods or their servants, and that Verkho had traded his soul for a variety of worldly talents. Yet all such ideas were mere speculation. The only man who might be able to set the record straight remained implacably silent.

Verkho eventually reappeared in the world of men as a wanderer. His time of exile had made his appearance all the more striking. He was still wild looking and unkempt, but his dark hair and beard shone with perfumed oil and his eyes blazed, captivating women and making even strong men falter before his gaze. Yet his reputation as a starets – a self-proclaimed holy man – continued to grow. He used his healing talent to good effect, living on donations – whether gold coin from a rich merchant or a share of the communal stewpot from a grateful peasant – but he also gained much favour by the sale of curses for enemies as well as healing for friends. The effectiveness of both were known to be reliable.

Nevertheless, Verkho's two greatest claims to fame, if popular belief could be trusted, were best illustrated by tales which were now well-known throughout the

Empire and which, no doubt, had grown more fanciful in the telling. The first of these concerned the young man's refusal to gamble. In the Xantic Empire, where wagering was as close to a common religion as existed, this would have been noteworthy enough, but the reason Verkho gave for his refusal was even more incredible. He would not play because – or so he claimed – he would always win! The starets was challenged many times, but always declined. Eventually, one drunken young lord pressed him too far, saying that he would be willing to wager his own wife against one hair of Verkho's head that he could beat the holy man at the dice game known as Emperor's Fortune.

At this Verkho became incensed, and had to be restrained from violence. The young lord's men could not restrain the starets' tongue however, and his insults and venom only convinced his host that he was afraid to play. Verkho gradually calmed down and, after a few moments of almost eerie silence, requested that the wager be amended. The loser of the contest would submit to the barber and have his entire head shaved. His would-be opponent suddenly felt that his insistence had been a mistake, but he could not back down now. And, after all, he was no longer risking his bride but only his hair. Even if he was more than a little vain about his good looks, the risk seemed small.

Emperor's Fortune is played with two sets of seven six-sided dice. There are seven symbols marked upon the flat surfaces, so that a different symbol is missing from each die. Both players begin by throwing all seven dice, but thereafter, depending upon what their opponent has thrown, they can choose how many to throw on each of seven tries to improve their hand. The seven symbols are, in order of rank, a crown – known as 'the emperor', a skull, a moon, wavy lines indicating water, a star, a scythe and a lamp.

After six throws apiece, the young lord held four emperors and three scythes, a very powerful hand.

However, Verkho held four moons, and should he get a fifth on his last throw he would win. After much consideration, the young lord decided to defy the odds and try to improve his hand. He picked up all three scythes, even though one of these could not be converted into an emperor, and threw them. The result sent a wave of gasps, disbelieving laughter and cheers through the crowd of onlookers. He had rolled two emperors and a skull, giving him six emperors and the next highest symbol as the add-on. It was the best he could possibly have thrown. Verkho's moons were now useless. Even if he rolled two more, he would still lose. As seven of one symbol was impossible, only one hand could beat six emperors. That was 'the circle' – one each of all seven symbols – and the odds against that were too enormous to be calculated.

The noble host sat back, smiling triumphantly.

Verkho, who until then had played without seeming to care about the contest's progress, glanced at the table and scooped up all seven of his dice. Several people protested, telling him that the odds would be better if he let some of them lie, but he ignored them.

Opening his fist slowly, he let the dice fall to the table. Six of them settled quickly, each die showing a different symbol. A sudden quiet fell on the room as the last die skittered between the others, then spun on one corner for what seemed like an age. The quicker eyed among the crowd had seen that all that was missing to complete the circle was a skull.

The final die settled at last, leaving everyone except Verkho stunned into speechlessness.

'Appropriate,' the starets muttered. 'Now let us see what *your* skull looks like. Bring me the shears. I will do the barbering myself.'

After that, no one was ever eager to test Verkho's gambling prowess.

The second major accomplishment claimed for the wanderer was demonstrated in spectacular fashion while he was staying in the home of a well-to-do merchant. During the few days of his visit, Verkho had not only cured the man's gout and arranged for ill fortune to befall the businessman's rivals, but he had also taken his reward from the household by seducing both the merchant's daughter and his wife. When he learnt of their downfall, the cuckolded merchant had determined to exact the ultimate revenge. The next time the two men met, he offered Verkho a goblet of fine wine. The starets swallowed a healthy mouthful and then frowned as the merchant waited breathlessly. Wife and daughter entered at that moment to witness the scene.

'A touch sour perhaps,' Verkho commented. 'What do you think?' He offered the cup to his host, who recoiled involuntarily, thinking that the poison should have been effective by now.

'It's not that bad,' Verkho remarked, his glittering eyes fixed on the merchant's perspiring face. 'Drink some.' The last two words stabbed home like blades. The merchant found that he could not look away from those uncanny eyes, and felt his fingers close around the stem of the goblet. He meant to toss the tainted wine aside and make some excuse, but his hands would not obey him. He slowly lifted the goblet to his lips and, after one last imploring glance at those unforgiving eyes, he sipped.

At once, the pain sent him into convulsions and he fell. But as the women rushed to his side, Verkho reached out and plucked the goblet from his grip, saving half its blood-red contents. The merchant died within moments as Verkho watched coldly. Then, with every sign of enjoyment, he gulped down the rest of the fatal drink and left without another word.

From this grew the legend that he was immune to all forms of poison, and even if this was not wholly true, it had been tested enough times to be given credence.

Eventually, after several years of travelling throughout the Empire, Verkho's ambition began to take form and brought him, naturally enough, to the gates of the capital city. His arrival in Xantium was marked by events so sensational that they were still remembered vividly some twelve years later.

Somehow a rumour had begun, growing in force with every hour, that a wild man 'with stars in his eyes' was to reveal wonders at the old temple. No one could account for this tale or determine who had started it but, by mid-afternoon of the appointed day, a sizeable crowd had gathered at the hilltop site. No one was sure what was supposed to happen, but there was a carnival atmos-phere in the mild autumn sunshine, with all the sights, smells and sounds of a merry and expectant throng.

The old temple had not seen such a gathering for centuries. Only a handful of eccentrics still worshipped the old gods, and the temple, which had once been a proud and lavishly decorated hall covered by a gilded dome, was now a ruin, its bare stone walls and columns open to the sky. Only here and there, where the carvings were less worn, were the images of the pantheon still visible, but few could even put names to the gods, let alone pay them any reverence.

Afterwards, nobody could recall how Verkho had arrived in their midst, leading some to believe that he had travelled through stone like a ghost. One moment there was no sign of the promised wild man, and the next he was standing on the stone altar in the centre of the crowd. He towered over them, resplendent in iridescent black robes which mirrored his own hair, and with eyes that might indeed be full of stars.

The crowd instinctively drew back, leaving a wide circle around the altar. Silence fell as the holy man turned slowly to stare at all of them. Even the children, the dogs, the very air itself grew still. When Verkho finally spoke, his voice rang out, seeming to shake the foundations of the city.

'This place still has power!' he cried. 'Magic is in its very being. Why do you neglect it?'

67

No one answered his impassioned plea.

'Are your memories so short?' he demanded. 'These stones have not forgotten.'

The crowd stirred uneasily. This wasn't what they'd expected.

'The gods may forgive you, but I cannot,' Verkho thundered. 'Do none of you have the eyes to see?'

The spectators were now beginning to wonder why they had bothered. This was just another madman. But no one left.

'Show us!' someone called out. 'Show us the magic.'

Others voiced their agreement.

'Some magic – if it's still there!' one sceptic cried.

'Aye, show us!'

Verkho raised his arms until the noise subsided. He was calm now, determined and businesslike.

'This altar,' he said, looking down at the grooved slab upon which he stood, 'this has witnessed much.'

Suddenly, a naked boy appeared at his feet. He was struggling, but could not avoid the shining blade wielded by invisible hands. Again and again it plunged down, until the boy lay still and his life's blood ran in rivulets along the grooves and on to the floor below. The vision drew forth screams and gasps of horror from the audience, but most watched in fascination, wide-eyed and open-mouthed, until the image vanished as abruptly as it had come.

An excited clamour broke out. This was more like it. Perhaps this madman would put on a good show after all. They were already eager for more. And that is exactly what Verkho gave them.

'There!' he shouted over the noise, pointing with an imperious finger. 'Beneath the image of Meyu.'

Those standing in the area he indicated scattered quickly, leaving the floor open below the carving of the sun-god.

'The stones remember their wrath!' Verkho cried, and as he spoke, two armoured men sprang into view out of nowhere. Swords crashed upon dented shields, each blow a signal of fury. Around and around the combatants fought, oblivious to their awestruck audience, until the final blow struck home. The warrior's blade caught the joint in his opponent's armour at the armpit, and drove deep. Blood fountained from the wound and from the visor of the vanquished soldier as he fell.

'And other passions have held sway here!' Verkho shouted, without giving the crowd time to catch their breath.

As the armoured men vanished, the figures of a man and a woman appeared, standing braced against the altar. Their robes of office, marking them as adherents of the gods, were drawn up, bunched around their waists, as their naked lower bodies thrust at each other in a frenzy of lust.

Laughter swelled from the crowd, who roared lewd comments, but the lovers pursued their own course unperturbed. After a few moments, Verkho swept them out of existence. The noise of the throng increased, but he waited patiently for quiet. He had them in the palm of his hand now, anticipating his next display of magic, no longer wondering if the climb to the temple had been worthwhile.

'Do these things amuse you?' he asked eventually, smiling for the first time. 'Then how about *this*?'

Each person there became aware that the size of the crowd had doubled. The whole space was full of kneeling worshippers, their eyes closed in penance or in contemplation. The afternoon suddenly felt chill, and the carnival atmosphere disappeared.

'Their prayers are remembered,' Verkho told the crowd. 'So would yours be if you only knew it.'

Many people fell to their knees then, but only a few knew how to pray or to whom. A small number tried, but fell silent in the growing cold. The images from the past faded away, leaving the crowd alone – for Verkho had gone also, his departure unnoticed.

The gathering dispersed quietly, unnerved and feeling suddenly cheated – but no one would forget the wild man with stars in his eyes. It was only after the hill was empty of life once more that some people looked back – and saw that the temple was now populated with ghosts. What had drawn *them* to the show was beyond anyone's comprehension.

News of the events at the old temple spread through Xantium like flame through dry bracken, and soon everyone wanted to see the wild man and his miracles. However, having made his indelible first impression, Verkho chose to proceed in less dramatic style. He visited several private homes, using his various talents to convert the curious into devotees, but his next public appearance was some days later. He took over a stall in one of the market places in the southern part of the city, and called upon the sick to come forward so that he could heal them.

At first people were reluctant, but eventually some volunteers were cured of minor ailments, and as the crowd grew, so Verkho became more ambitious. Most of his patients were put into a hypnotic trance and simply told that their maladies would be gone when they woke up, but his most memorable success came in quite a different manner. He was attending to a girl who had been suffering from seizures, when a boy staggered across the open space before the stall with his arms outstretched before him. The unlooked-for interruption appeared to anger Verkho and he struck out, catching the child an open-handed blow on the side of his head. The boy, who made no attempt to defend himself, staggered and fell as the audience muttered angrily. They knew that he was blind.

'That's no way to . . .' someone yelled, but was interrupted by the incoherent shouts of the fallen child. He was sitting up now, staring around in wonder.

'I can see!' he screamed. 'I can see!'

The audience, whose mood had been on the verge of

70

turning sour, drew back in awe. Verkho took no notice of the commotion and finished his work with the girl. Then he withdrew, escorted by a number of his growing band of followers, and was not seen again for many days.

No doubt Verkho could have continued in this way and amassed riches and influence of a sort but, by now, his ambitions were far greater. He had tasted power, and it was to his liking. His ultimate aim now was absolute power.

He continued to use his remarkable talents to gain access to ever higher levels of Xantic society, biding his time until the opportunity he was waiting for presented itself. This came when he was approached by the Imperial Minister of Treasuries, the man who controlled the vast bureaucratic network that enforced the taxation laws and held the purse strings for the entire Empire. The minister's name was Padin Uldara, and his only child, Maissa, was afflicted with a mysterious disease which caused her to lose consciousness. The frequency and duration of these attacks were increasing steadily and, while she was insensible, her blood flowed so slowly that her pulse could scarcely be felt. Physicians pronounced themselves baffled, and the fear grew that every attack might mean her death.

When Verkho was first called to her bedside, he did not touch her, but just stared unmoving at her pale face, then knelt as if in prayer.

'She will wake as soon as I leave this house,' he told the girl's disbelieving parents. They attached little hope to his claim; even if this fit lasted no longer than the previous one, Maissa would not wake for nearly half a day. However, when Padin returned to her bedchamber, having escorted the starets to the door, he found his wife and daughter crying in each other's arms. Maissa was fully awake!

Thereafter, as Verkho had prophesied, her attacks grew less frequent, and on each occasion the healer was able to bring them to an end quickly. During many of his later visits, Verkho insisted upon being left alone with Maissa, saying that his healing would take effect more quickly that way. Over the same period, Padin grew to like the holy man, realizing that there was far more to him than his wild appearance would suggest. The starets showed a keen appreciation of the complexities of the minister's work, and even suggested solutions to some of his problems. Little wonder then that Verkho was soon rewarded with a post within the treasuries and, with Padin's help, began to acquaint himself with those in power at the imperial court.

Padin and his wife were so overjoyed at their daughter's recovery that they failed to notice her increasingly odd behaviour. She became forgetful and sometimes listless, and ignored the various suitors who came to pay their respects now that she was well again and of an age to be thinking of marriage.

When the minister finally discovered that Verkho was not as benevolent as he had seemed, it was too late. Maissa was found to be expecting a child, but would not, or could not, reveal who the father was. Eventually, Padin saw through the spell that Verkho had woven about his family, and accused him of rape. Verkho, however, was ready with his reply. He denied the charge, and in turn accused Padin of falsely denouncing him. Verkho claimed that the minister was involved in a massive fraud, and the evidence he presented was impressive, though Padin denied it to the end. As a consequence, Padin and his family were exiled in disgrace, and Verkho, who already had many admirers and supporters in the court hierarchy, was promoted. Four years later he had risen to the position that Padin once held.

It was during his early years at the treasuries that Clavia came to Xantium. She immediately proved to be an invaluable ally in Verkho's war of intrigue, but whether she realized it or not, he always held the upper hand in their relationship. After she had been in

Xantium for a while, Clavia began to form plans of her own. But her half-brother did not yet have the influence that could have introduced her to the upper echelons of court society, and so they were powerless to prevent the Emperor's match with Ifryn.

In spite of this early setback, Verkho's rise was now unstoppable. He proved himself to be a genius in matters of finance, intelligence and manipulation. The next few years saw his network of contacts and spies spread throughout the city and the Empire, and he boasted that he saw everything and heard everything in all of Xantium. In due course he rose to the position of Chancellor.

At the same time, he naturally made many enemies, and no one could deny that he was the most hated and feared man in the Empire. Although many of his opponents were either exiled or met untimely ends, this did not prevent several attempts against Verkho's life. His contemptuous avoidance of such plots only strengthened his now legendary status, and the vile punishments meted out to the traitors only served to increase the awe in which he was held.

On one famous occasion, Verkho had secretly encouraged riots and insurrection in the city by blatantly unfair decisions about taxes. He made sure that he especially enraged certain enemies whose habitual meeting place was the city's Stadium. He even went so far as to allow the rebels some small victories – which they took for a sign of weakness – and then allowed them to claim victory by reversing some of his earlier decisions. The riotous celebrations naturally centred on the Stadium.

During the disturbances, Verkho's spies had been in action, ensuring that the ringleaders were identified, and had kept their master informed of all developments. Secure in this knowledge, the Chancellor bided his time. When the rebels were well and truly drunk, he surrounded the Stadium with his own loyal troops. Most of the troublesome conspirators were killed, some imprisoned or exiled, and a few were set free to bear witness to the fate of those who opposed Verkho.

However he achieved his ends, it was unquestionably true that Verkho brought a new strength and stability to the Empire, and in doing so, he won the gratitude and loyalty of Southan III. Even Kerrell, who disliked the Chancellor intensely, could not deny his influence, and admitted that Verkho's methods of gaining intelligence had proved invaluable in his own military campaigns.

By the time Southan's heir was born, Verkho's influence was in reality second to none. All that was left for him to achieve was the title of Emperor itself.

CHAPTER SEVEN

Love is strange, and calls itself by many names. Tenderness, affection, respect, yearning and protectiveness. It is all of these things, and yet none of them alone. Love is beyond definition.

I will not know it in this lifetime. But I have seen it in others.

Apart from short periods of wakefulness when she catered to the needs of her son, Ifryn slept until early evening. When she was properly awake, Kerrell came to see her.

He had changed in many ways over the years. He was now a general, in overall command of all the field operations of the Imperial Army. He had filled out in the ten years since their first meeting, presenting a sturdy compact figure to the world, but he was still strong and fit – a man in his prime – although he was weighed down now by responsibilities he had not known as a younger man.

And yet, in so many other respects, he was the same as he had always been. His brown eyes still smiled on Ifryn, whatever his troubles; his face was still tanned from his predominantly outdoor life, and he wore his long hair tied back. Also, true to his word, he had always remained her friend – even though his duties meant that he spent much of his time away from the city. They missed each other when he was away, but a strict sense of propriety had always ruled the relationship between the Empress and the general. Many things were left unsaid.

Tactful as ever, Doneta made herself scarce as soon as Kerrell came in.

'I am glad to find you awake, my lady,' he greeted her. In all the years they had known each other, he had never once called her by her own name. 'Are you well?'

'Well enough,' she answered, smiling. 'The better for seeing you.'

Kerrell peered into the cot where Southan Azari was still asleep.

'My next master,' the general commented softly. 'My sword is at your service, my lord,' he added formally.

'He won't need it yet awhile,' Ifryn told him, smiling.

'No.' Kerrell was aware of Verkho's theories, having talked to Southan, but he saw no reason to disobey the Emperor's order not to tell Ifryn. They felt that there was no need to worry her unnecessarily. But she saw through his pretence.

'You don't sound so sure,' she said.

Kerrell hesitated, then realized that the hesitation itself spoke volumes to the woman who had always been able to read his mind.

'Chancellor Verkho senses unrest,' he confessed. 'But he sees shadows everywhere.' His words sounded unconvincing, even to his own ears. 'He's asked me to double the guards on the palace.'

'Because of him?' Ifryn looked towards the baby's cot.

'Yes,' Kerrell admitted. 'You're not supposed to know.'

'I won't say anything,' she promised. 'Is there any reason to be afraid?'

'I don't think so,' he replied, 'but I have no choice but to take it seriously.'

'Because Verkho decrees it?'

'Yes.' The general's distaste was obvious.

Kerrell was unswervingly loyal to Southan, and although this was one of his greatest strengths, it was also one of his biggest problems. He was too diplomatic to say anything to the Empress, but his feelings were clear to Ifryn, even though he hid them well. She knew that he loathed Verkho and fretted about the Chancellor's influence over Southan, and there were times when he felt great regret that the Chancellor's authority exceeded his own. He even wondered if he would have been exiled, like so many others who opposed Verkho's dominance, had he not been such a fine general and military tactician.

'You suspect his motives?' Ifryn asked, her anxiety born out of his distrust.

'That is not for me to say, my lady,' he responded formally.

'He has helped the Empire beyond measure,' she prompted uncertainly. It was only in recent years that she had come to realize just how dependent Southan was on Verkho.

'Unquestionably,' Kerrell conceded.

'Then why can I not find it in my heart to like him?' she wondered aloud.

'Liking for someone is never measured by their professional abilities,' he replied. 'The two of you are so very different.'

'Meaning that I am useless to the Empire?' she teased, trying to lighten the tone of their conversation.

Kerrell caught her slight smile.

'But highly decorative, my lady,' he answered, a glint in his eye.

'So are tapestries, General!' she exclaimed, pretending to be angry. 'Have I no more worth than a few stitches?'

'All men of sense know your true worth,' he replied, suddenly serious.

'In truth, I might as well be made of cloth,' she said, plunged into a sudden gloom. 'I've hidden myself away, concerned myself only with my children, my husband . . .' Her voice trailed away. *Could I really have done more? What do I know of such things? How could I compete with such as Verkho?*

'What else should an Empress concern herself with?' Kerrell asked.

'Affairs of the Empire?' she suggested.

'That's men's work.'

So Ifryn had thought. And had acted accordingly. But now . . .

'Besides,' the general went on, 'cloth cannot produce such as this.' He indicated Southan Azari. 'And *he* is the very future of the Empire.'

'Any pod can shell peas,' she responded with a touch of bitterness. 'I carried the imperial burden for nine months, but my work is done now. It's time to hang me back on the wall.'

'Never speak so!' There was genuine anger in Kerrell's voice now. 'You . . .' He swallowed what he wanted to say. 'You are the Empress, but any man who says that your importance ends there will have to answer to me!'

'And to Southan, I would hope,' she added mischievously, touched by his outburst.

'Naturally,' Kerrell stammered. His face had turned a deeper colour and he turned away, aware that he had gone too far.

Southan Azari awoke then, and started crying. They were both glad of the interruption.

'Hand him to me, please,' Ifryn requested, her tone businesslike.

Kerrell was taken aback, and wanted to refuse, but her encouraging smile convinced him to try. He picked up the baby very carefully, holding him away from his body. His face was full of the fear that he might hurt such a delicate creature, and he smiled with relief when the infant was safely cradled in Ifryn's arms.

'Thank you,' she said, then, as he continued to stare, she hinted, 'I think propriety demands that you leave now.'

'Of course.' Kerrell's blush deepened, and he almost ran from the chamber.

Doneta entered and saw Southan Azari contentedly feeding at his mother's breast. Her quizzical expression faded.

'I wondered why the general came out of here like a startled rabbit,' she remarked, smiling.

'I don't think men like to be reminded that they were once this tiny, this dependent,' Ifryn said thoughtfully.

'It's not the baby he was fleeing from,' the maid told her.

'Hush, Doneta. Our general flees from no one.'

'From no *man* perhaps,' the maid replied, unabashed.

When the message from Farrag came in, Verkho had already been at work in his study for over an hour. Whichever Far-speaker originally received a report, anything meant for the Chancellor was immediately relayed to his personal assistant, who was known as the Focus. She was a plain girl, whose talent was great enough and whose mind was alert enough to be able to cope with the demands of her particular role. She then passed the messages on to Verkho as soon as possible.

On receipt of this latest report, a quick mental calculation told Verkho that it was barely dawn on Zalys. In Xantium, further to the east, the sun had already been up for almost an hour. The Chancellor pondered the message and its timing for a few moments, feeling an abrupt irritation at Farrag's words. The Marshal on Zalys had his orders, yet he still felt it necessary to meddle.

'Reply thus,' Verkho instructed his assistant. 'Send the Folegandros boy to the mainland immediately. He is to be unharmed. Remain vigilant. Add my code and send now.'

The Focus nodded. A moment later, she reported, 'The message has been sent and received.'

'Good. You may go.'

As she withdrew, Verkho smiled to himself at the probable effect his instant response would have. He was especially pleased with the words 'Remain vigilant'. That would give the fool something to think about.

But the Chancellor's smile faded before he returned to his work. He had remembered the other shipment he was expecting from the island.

CHAPTER EIGHT

I swim with the dolphins sometimes. Their whistles and clicks mean more to me than most of what passes for human speech. Yet I have never left this land, never seen the sea.

'As far as I can tell, there's nothing wrong with her eyes,' Foran said. 'The lenses are clear, they react to light, and there's no evidence of any damage to her skull.'

The physician was sitting with Etha and Fen at Antorkas' bedside. Gaye's parents had been dismayed and shocked by the news of her blindness, and even Etha had fallen into a deep depression. Antorkas was recovering his own health rapidly now, but that only made him feel more wretched.

'Why her and not me?' he muttered sadly.

'There must be some cause,' Fen said.

'Whatever power Farrag uses, its effects are beyond my knowledge,' Foran replied, 'but my guess is that it's not Gaye's body that's been hurt, but her mind. She doesn't *want* to see any more.'

'Without Bowen,' Etha agreed, nodding sadly.

'That's ridiculous,' Antorkas rasped. 'Of course she wants to see!' He glared accusingly at his old friend, but Foran did not back down.

'Consciously, yes,' he responded. 'But her grief is affecting her so badly . . . there are levels of the mind we'll never understand.'

'What can we do?' Fen asked, trying to keep their discussion as practical as possible.

'We're already doing all we can,' the physician assured her. 'Habella's given her a soothing draught, but I think the only one who can heal her is Gaye herself.'

Antorkas struggled to hold back his anger, guilt and aggrieved helplessness welling up within him.

'He'll pay for this,' he vowed. 'One day . . .'

'One day, but not yet,' Fen put in quickly, then repeated the arguments for not reacting to Farrag's provocation, for biding their time. Her father listened, though with an ill grace, but her mother's thoughts were elsewhere.

'We'll keep a watch over Gaye,' Etha said. 'There'll always be someone for her to talk to – if she wants to. She'll never be alone.'

'Good,' Foran commented approvingly.

'We can't replace Bowen,' Etha explained, glancing at her husband and Fen in turn. 'But perhaps *our* love can convince her to see again.'

Foran smiled with satisfaction to see the determined look that had returned to Etha's eyes.

'Anto's with her now,' he said.

'And Ia,' Fen added.

'Gaye was asleep when I left . . .' the physician began, but was interrupted by a terrible, piercing scream that brought their conversation to an abrupt halt. After a moment's shocked silence, they realized that it had been Gaye's voice, distorted by some unknown fear, and there was a sudden scramble to go to her. Even Antorkas struggled out of bed, heedless of his own pain.

The scene that greeted them at the door of Gaye's room was heartwrenching. Ia was huddled in one corner, curled up as if she were trying to hide, crying miserably. Anto sat on the bed, his arms around his trembling sister who was sitting up, sightless eyes staring over his shoulder.

'It's all right. It's all right,' he murmured. 'You're safe. It was only a dream.'

Etha hurried to Gaye's side, with Foran close on her

heels, while Fen went to comfort Ia. Antorkas reached the doorway, breathing heavily.

'What happened?' Foran asked.

Gaye did not answer. Her face was ashen, and she gave no sign of having heard the question.

'She was asleep,' Anto answered for her. 'Then all of a sudden she sat up and screamed.' His voice wavered, betraying his own shocked state.

'I saw it,' Gaye breathed, still clinging to her brother.

'What, my sweet?' Etha asked.

'It filled the sky!' Gaye sounded terrified.

Antorkas reached the bedside and knelt down painfully. Etha looked at the two invalids, her eyes full of worry.

'It was just a nightmare, Gaye,' Foran told her gently but firmly. 'You're safe. We're all here.'

Gaye did not react to his words, but her grip on Anto tightened.

'It's coming!' she cried.

Then her body went limp as she fell into a dead faint.

The merchant, whose name was Ravel Alexi, rode slowly towards Nkosa, his thoughts full of his own good fortune. Behind him came a second donkey, stoically pulling a heavily laden cart. It was here, among the jars of olives, oil, spices and herbs, as well as the box of precious amberine crystals, that the reason for Ravel's jubilation lay. His purpose in making this long-planned trip had been to collect a carefully sealed, square casket, which was big enough to contain a human skull.

In front and behind the donkeys walked the ten soldiers he had hired from the imperial garrison. The use of such guards was standard practice for merchants travelling to the remoter parts of Zalys, especially when they were trading in amberine.

The road here, even so close to the town, was little more than a track – narrow, rutted and strewn with rocks. On Zalys, most trade and travel was done by boat and so the roads were neglected, but Ravel had very good reasons for not wanting to risk this cargo on the water.

The soldiers had no interest in the merchant's means of travel or in his goods, and saw this trip as an enjoyable change from barracks routine. They had amused themselves by terrorizing villagers – once the merchant had completed his trading and thus given them licence to do so. Even now, they were laughing about how they had burnt down an isolated hut after the owner had annoyed them by trying to prevent them from stealing his pig. The islander had fled, watching from a distance as his only animal was roasted in the embers of his ruined home.

'We should have roasted him too!' one of the guards commented now.

'Aye,' another agreed. 'These poxy islanders are no better than pigs.'

'There was no meat on him, though,' a third objected. 'Not like that sow.' He smacked his lips in remembered appreciation.

'All string and bones,' the first soldier agreed, nodding.

'And no crackling!' his companion added, provoking a burst of laughter.

By late afternoon, they were passing the rock pools where the shark fights were held, but all was quiet now. Here the trail crossed rocky terrain, becoming even narrower, but once they were across, Nkosa was only a few hundred paces away. Rounding a promontory, they came face to face with an elderly peasant farmer, leading a moth-eaten donkey and a rickety wagon piled high with sticks and straw. There was no room to pass by. There was open space a short distance behind the soldiers, whereas the farmer was almost across the stony tract, but the guards had no intention of giving way.

'Out of the way,' the squad leader ordered, waving an indifferent arm.

'But . . . I'm almost over,' the farmer pleaded, pointing ahead.

'We don't back away before scum.' The soldiers marched on relentlessly. 'Move!'

The farmer tried to reverse his wagon but the donkey baulked at the unfamiliar movement, twisting in the shafts. The cart swung sideways and came to a shuddering halt across the path.

'Get it out of the way,' the leader ordered his men. The soldiers moved forward purposefully, grinning.

'No. Please,' the islander begged.

'Untie the donkey unless you want it to go over too,' one of them told him.

The farmer hesitated in despair.

'Hurry up, or you'll go too!' The commander snapped. 'This man has a ship to catch,' he added, pointing at the merchant.

With fumbling hands, the farmer loosened the ropes. The soldiers heaved the wagon over the side and it ran down the rocky slope, gathering speed until it tumbled in a slow somersault and smashed to firewood on the boulders below. The straw was blown to the four winds as the farmer watched aghast.

'Now stand aside!'

The peasant and his frightened animal flattened themselves against the outcrop of rock as the party moved by. Shortly afterwards, Ravel was ensconced in one of the town's public warehouses, supervising the unloading of his goods, the incident forgotten.

He had already received the news that *The Serpent* had docked earlier that day, and had sent word to Ilest, the ship's second officer. The pinch-faced young man arrived within the hour, the insignia of an Information Officer worn on the shoulder of his tunic.

'You have it?' Ilest asked without preamble.

'Of course,' Ravel answered. 'It is safe within my office. Come. You have the payment?'

Ilest nodded, and Ravel led the way to a room at the

side of the warehouse. It was one of several such chambers rented by merchants who traded regularly on Zalys and who needed somewhere secure and private to store particularly valuable items. Ravel unlocked the door with one of a bunch of keys attached to his belt, went inside and lit a lamp. Then he unlocked a metal-clad trunk and took out the obviously heavy casket. He placed it carefully on a table and selected a third key, then paused and smiled at his companion.

'May I see the scrip?'

Ilest removed a sealed paper from the inside of his tunic and handed it over without a word. Ravel broke the seal and glanced at the contents. It was a promissory note for one thousand gold imperials, signed by Chancellor Verkho himself. Any treasury in the Empire would honour such a document, and Ravel's credit would also be guaranteed. The merchant's mouth began to water.

'And a small bonus,' the seaman added. 'For your promptness.' He tossed a bag on to the table. The clink of heavy coins came from within. 'My master appreciates loyal service,' Ilest explained. 'You will lack for nothing when you next visit Xantium.'

'Thank you.' Ravel was pleasantly surprised by the gesture, but had no intention of travelling to Xantium. He had other plans. He opened the casket.

Inside was a dull sphere, the size of a man's head, securely padded with clean straw. The sphere's rough surface was like glass which had been in the sea for many years, opaque, but with the promise of clarity just beyond sight.

'May I?' Ilest asked.

'Of course.'

The second officer leant over and lifted the sphere, his strong young arms making light of the task.

'See, there,' Ravel said, pointing. 'The ignorant peasant who found it tried to break it open with an axe.'

The surface was indeed chipped, missing a jagged piece the size of a thumbnail. The glass beneath the flaw was as clear as crystal. Ilest moved closer to the lamp, put his eye to the hole, and smiled. There, deeply embedded in the centre of the solid sphere, was a rounded shape the size of a fist, sheathed in silvery metal etched with indecipherable markings.

'The talisman is unharmed,' Ilest pronounced. 'You have done well.'

Ravel bowed in acknowledgement, and the seaman replaced the glass sphere in the straw.

'The man who found it?' Ilest asked.

'Dead,' the merchant reported quickly. 'His wife too.'

'No one else saw it?'

'No one.'

'And the . . . authorities here . . . ?'

'No word has passed to them.'

'Then you have truly earned your reward,' Ilest concluded.

His hand flashed out without warning, and a tiny needle knife pricked Ravel's neck. The merchant's eyes went wide but he had no time to cry out; the lethal poison worked instantly. Ilest caught him as he fell, lowering him gently and silently to the floor, then cut free his keys.

He calmly closed the casket, and locked it. He pocketed the bag of gold and carefully folded the scrip before putting it back in his tunic. Then he picked up the casket, turned and left the room, locking the door behind him, and walked unhurriedly back to his ship.

The Serpent sailed on the evening tide. Its cargo included shipments of amberine, a cage full of toads, a prisoner named Bowen Folegandros, and – unlisted on any manifest – a casket now stowed away in the second officer's cabin.

CHAPTER NINE

*I feel the stones growing cold in the valley of ghosts.
Memories sink deeper, and stories sleep. Who is left now
to coax them back to life, to heal their pain? Even my own
eyes are blind. I see only sky.*

Dawn came to the Larenian Sea, and the helmsman of
The Serpent squinted past the bows towards the rising
sun. Yet, for one passenger at least, time had ceased to
have any meaning. All Bowen could see, over and over
again, was Gaye falling to the ground. He felt himself
being led away, unable to believe what was happening,
as she lay still.

The four walls of his small, locked cabin had no reality
for him. The sway of the ship as it cut through the waves
meant nothing. All he could think of was Gaye. His
longing for her was something desperate, a physical
yearning and an emotional denial. It simply was not
possible that they would not be together, not after all
this time. He wept, called her name, shouted with futile,
incoherent rage, hammered fists and forehead into
unforgiving wood.

His dreams, always troublesome, now invaded his
waking hours. There was no escape from the torment of
self-recrimination, hatred and bottomless dread which
filled his very being. But the most painful emotion, and
the most helpless, was love. No torturer could have been
more effective than the memory of Gaye's face, her
smile . . .

On that fateful Midsummer's Day, something had

snapped inside Bowen, and his ravings had unnerved even the hardy sailors of the Imperial Navy. Once locked in his cell, his only visits had been from a galley hand, who shoved his tray of food inside quickly and fled, and from a thin-faced young officer who merely stared at him briefly, then left, his expression impassive.

Bowen had had no sleep during his first night on board. His despair fought any weariness he might have felt. And, whenever he closed his eyes, something grey loomed over him, filling his world with a terrible, inescapable presence.

'Gaye came out of her faint by late evening, then slept normally,' Fen said. 'And nothing happened during the night.'

Fen and Dsordas were walking, hand in hand, through the olive groves south of Nkosa. It was a beautiful morning, clear and sunny, but with the summer heat made less oppressive by the cooling westerly breeze that blew down from the mountains. In other circumstances they would both have taken great pleasure in the sweet-scented countryside, but this day was marred by Gaye's misfortune.

Even so, they took comfort, as always, in each other's company, and once persuaded to go, had been glad to escape from the house for a while. Etha had shooed them out, recognizing their needs better than they did, saying that she wanted to get them out from under her feet.

They were both tired from lack of sleep, but had decided to walk. They needed to find space to breathe, to be alone, to talk. Without thinking, they had chosen a course which led them via alleys and bridges to the southern edge of the town. From there they crossed the dunes and took the coast path, heading towards the Arena.

'Hasn't she suffered enough?' Dsordas said fiercely. 'It's as if someone is deliberately torturing her.'

'She didn't remember anything about it this morning,' Fen told him. 'That was a blessing at least.'

'What was it she said?' he asked.

'Something about filling the sky. And then, just before she fainted, she said, "It's coming".'

Dsordas looked thoughtful.

'It must have been about the same time as she was dreaming that I felt ill,' he murmured.

'What's the matter?' Fen asked quickly. 'You didn't tell me.'

'Nothing. I'm fine now,' he replied reassuringly. 'I felt much better when I got home – and there were other people needing your concern then. But I'd felt sick, and my head hurt so much I thought it was going to burst. It was as though a great weight was pushing down on me.'

'You think the two things might be connected?'

'I can't see how. Unless it's more of Farrag's foul sorcery.' He made the suggestion in an off-hand way, but Fen was shocked by the idea.

'Come on!' Dsordas protested quickly. 'No one's that powerful. Especially not that disgusting dungheap.'

They walked on in silence, climbing towards a hilltop which was a favourite vantage point. Near the summit the trees gave way to scrub, bushes and flowers.

'Look!' Fen exclaimed, pointing at a five-petalled, scarlet bloom with a long yellow stamen. 'I've never seen that before.' She went forward and bent to sniff the scent – but Dsordas caught her arm and jerked her away.

'What did you do that for?' she asked, rubbing her arm, surprised and a little hurt by his actions. He was invariably gentle with her.

'It'll hurt you,' he said flatly.

'But it's only a flower!'

'Trust me,' he replied defensively. 'I'm sorry if I scared you.'

'You *know* something!' she accused him. 'Like your mother used to. How could it hurt me?'

Dsordas became sullen in the face of her conviction.

'The pollen is bad for you,' he told her gruffly. 'If you'd breathed it in, it would have made you sick.'

'But *how* do you know?' Fen persisted, not allowing herself to be put off.

'I'll prove it to you.' He touched the stamen, and the tip of his finger came away stained yellow.

'Won't it hurt you too?' she asked.

'No. These things are different for different people,' Dsordas replied. 'Give me your hand.'

He carefully dabbed a tiny amount of powder on to the back of her hand and then, almost immediately, blew it away. A tiny red mark showed on Fen's fair skin, while his own hand remained unblemished.

'Different people react to different things,' he went on. 'Like Tarin can't eat fish without coming out in a rash.'

Fen nodded. In an island community, not eating fish was a rarity.

'You're the same with those,' Dsordas explained, pointing at the flower.

'That still doesn't explain how you knew,' she said.

'You're my responsibility,' he told her, smiling. 'I have to look after you.'

'You're not answering my question,' she stated, her green eyes flashing.

For a few moments the only sounds came from the insects and the soft rustling of leaves in the wind.

'I get feelings about things sometimes,' Dsordas admitted eventually. 'I can't explain it,' he added, holding up his hands to forestall her comment. 'I don't want to talk about it any more. All right?'

Fen nodded, having the sense not to push him any further. She contented herself with a flippant remark.

'It's a good job my mother isn't here. You'd never hear the end of it!'

They walked on up to the hilltop, and stood looking around them. To the west were the mountains at the centre of the island, where the bat colonies lay hidden in gigantic caves. To the north, beyond the town and obscured by distant, tree-covered hills, were the beaches where most of the amberine was found. The bright blue sea stretched away to the eastern horizon, studded here and there with fishing boats.

Closer to the hill, the land was a patchwork of green and gold. Olive trees covered the terraced slopes, and in the valleys, where the streams made the soil more fertile, there were many different crops, and pasture for goats and sheep. Only the bare upper ground was left wild. Every other space was utilized to the full.

A little further off on the northern side, the town of Nkosa lay spread out below them, its buildings a mixture of red, ochre and white. The network of canals laced them together, finally leading out into the lagoon which was encircled by massive sandbanks. These natural defences were pierced by two wide portals which allowed the tides and shipping to pass in and out.

'The flood tides are due in four days,' Dsordas said quietly.

They both knew what he was thinking. Much effort had already gone into the attempts to stop the periodic flooding of the town, but each year the situation got worse. The river-formed sandbanks, which gave Nkosa the advantage of a safe harbour, also posed a threat to the town – they were always in need of reinforcement and the channels within silted up and shifted, making navigation hazardous. Worse still, if a high tide co-incided with a strong easterly wind, the water level in the lagoon would rise so high that alleys, basement floors and even Fournoi Square itself could be flooded. The townspeople erected ever more elaborate defences, but they could not fight the forces of nature. Nkosa was slowly sinking into the sea.

'Let's hope the wind doesn't change,' Fen said.

Dsordas nodded absently. His thoughts were far away as he pictured the apparently inevitable catastrophe in his mind. The garrison had taken over almost all the best protected buildings for their own use, leaving the islanders to fend for themselves, but even the soldiers recognized the value of Nkosa's warehouses and other places of trade. If the worst happened, Niering would order his men to help in the operation of the pumps and in shoring up the barricades.

'Perhaps we'd better get rid of our imperial masters quickly,' Fen suggested with a grin. 'You know what the old legend says.'

'That the only way to stop the island sinking is to free ourselves from tyranny?' he said harshly. 'Very convincing. Since when has the sea taken any notice of mankind?'

'It was only a joke,' Fen protested feebly, taken aback by her lover's vehemence.

'There's another myth,' Dsordas continued as if he hadn't heard her, 'which says that one of the old gods was dumped in the sea because he annoyed his fellow immortals. Perhaps we should get *him* to help us by pushing the island back up again!'

His sarcastic words were a measure of his contempt for such notions, and he stared angrily at the harbour as if he sought to reshape it by the force of his thoughts. Fen knew that some people took the old stories more seriously than Dsordas, but she knew better than to say so while he was in his present mood.

'Come on,' she said gently. 'Let's walk.'

She led him away from the town, heading over a series of ridges on a barely perceptible trail which led to a place known as the Arena. This was a rock-strewn, natural amphitheatre, which had once been – and still was on occasion – an important meeting place for the islanders. Over the centuries, it had witnessed religious ceremonies, political rhetoric and arguments of law, as well as hosting innumerable performances by actors, storytellers and musicians. It had seen rejoicing and mourning, merriment and sorrow, drunkenness, insanity and violence. It had nurtured love in all its forms, seen the results of hatred, and felt the chill of indifference. Fires had burned here, ice had formed. The sun had turned it into a baking cauldron, but wind, rain, thunder and hail had all visited the place. Men had been born here; others had died while the impassive stones looked on. To many this was the place where the island's history still lived. If Zalys had a soul, it lay in the Arena.

Dsordas and Fen came to the rim of the small valley at a place marked by the curiously shaped outcrop of grey rock known as the Stone Eye. The name derived from the hole which ran through the rock at an angle, so that it seemed to gaze down on those within the Arena.

From below, all that could be seen through the pupil of the Stone Eye was a tiny patch of northern sky, but on the rim it was possible to climb the outer side of the tor and look down the sloping tunnel which framed the centre of the valley.

Fen clambered up and peered through. The sides of the hole had been smoothed by the passage of generations of small children, who believed that to crawl from one end to the other would bring them good luck. Fen smiled, remembering her own passage, the eager hands reaching up to help her out at the lower end. She was too big to make the journey now, but she felt no regret. The place no longer felt the same.

All was quiet and still inside the Arena. An air of emptiness hung over the place, and a sudden over-whelming sadness swept over Fen.

'It's dying,' Dsordas said quietly, putting her un-formed thoughts into words.

'What does it mean?' she asked, climbing down to join him.

'What it means,' he replied, 'is that looking to the old ways to solve our problems is hopeless. We have to learn to be self-reliant. If there ever was any magic here, it's gone now.'

'But it can't just vanish,' Fen protested. 'This place *knew* too much.'

'It's just rocks and earth now.'

'But it listened,' she persisted. 'You know it did. And it had its own voice. Everyone heard it, in one way or another.'

'Or thought they did,' Dsordas said.

'Isn't that the same thing?' she asked.

Dsordas shrugged.

'It doesn't matter any more,' he said. 'It's been dying for a long time.'

Fen knew that he was right, but could not accept it so easily. Farrag and their foes had forms of sorcery at their disposal, and it seemed only fair – indeed necessary – that the island should have some magic of its own. She could not have explained how they were supposed to use this strange resource, but she felt its loss keenly.

'There were always ghosts here,' she said sadly.

'Not any more,' Dsordas stated. 'It's as if they're avoiding the place.'

'Let's go back,' Fen said, feeling inexplicably chilled.

They turned away from the Arena, realizing that they too had avoided actually entering the amphitheatre, and set off towards the town.

'I wonder why only a few people come back as ghosts,' Fen said. 'Why doesn't everybody?'

'I've often wondered the same thing,' Dsordas replied, smiling. 'My mother would have made a good ghost.'

'Perhaps they can't choose where or when they appear,' Fen suggested, gladdened by his change of mood.

'Mother could probably have talked her way round that if she'd wanted to,' he remarked ruefully. 'What's more interesting is *why* they come back. Their appearances seem so pointless.'

'Does everything have to have a purpose?'

'All forms of life, yes,' he replied with unconscious irony.

'Even me?' Fen asked pointedly.

Dsordas looked at her questioningly.

'What are you getting at?' he said.

'It's easy to see your purpose,' she explained, 'but all *I* do is watch. I'm only a passive spectator, but I need to be self-reliant too. Let me be a part of it.'

'You already are,' he told her.

'Not really. I've *done* nothing. And all I know is the little you tell me.' *Could I really have done more?* Fen wondered. *How could I hope to compete with such as Farrag?*

'It's too dangerous,' he began. 'The less you know . . .'

'Don't you trust me?' she demanded, interrupting the familiar refrain.

'You're being ridiculous,' he said tolerantly. 'This is men's work.'

'I thought so once,' Fen shot back. 'But now . . .'

'I couldn't bear it if you were hurt,' he argued, stubborn to the last. 'I love you too much.'

'So you're the only one who can take risks?' she added incredulously. 'My love for *you* counts for nothing?'

She stared at him as the last of his resistance crumbled into dust.

'All right,' he whispered, then drew her to him and kissed her soundly.

'You promise?' she asked breathlessly as they drew apart.

'As long as you promise to be careful,' he replied.

'I'm always careful,' she told him, grinning.

Farrag swept past the nervous sentry outside the broken door of the merchant's chamber. Ravel lay where the officer in charge of security at the warehouse had found him.

Farrag bent to feel the merchant's cold skin and to study the tiny puncture in his neck. He straightened up, and turned his gaze upon the officer. Outwardly, Farrag appeared calm, but inside he was seething with fury. This had been a professional assassination, and one for which there had been no forewarning. The Marshal did not like mysteries on his island.

'What's missing?' he asked, glancing towards the still open trunk.

'Nothing,' the officer replied promptly. 'I've been through his records, and his stores are complete. Even the amberine is still here. But the door was locked from the outside.' The young man sounded worried. He had been efficient and thorough once he had found the nerve to order his men to break down the door, but now, as well as facing Farrag's possible vengeful displeasure, he had come up against something inexplicable.

'Who was last in here with him?' Farrag asked.

'A seaman from *The Serpent*, out of Xantium,' the officer replied, glad that he had already been able to glean such information. 'But that was last evening,' he added reluctantly. 'He was an officer by all accounts, but no one here knows his name.'

'Well, Ravel obviously knew him,' Farrag said, almost to himself. 'Where is this seaman now?'

'*The Serpent* sailed last night,' the young man reported, and waited anxiously for the explosion. It never came. Instead, Farrag grew very still, his hands clenched at his side.

'Someone is going to pay for this,' he vowed quietly.

CHAPTER TEN

*There is unquiet in the world, and poison in the wind.
The bats are not the only ones to sense it. Why can't I
see?*

*Some things are too big to be seen. How deep is the
sky? Do the gods know their own limitations? Where does
the wind begin or end?*

*The fates ride on wings of pain. I see their shadows but
not their substance.*

Since the discovery of Ravel's body, Farrag's men had
been busy interrogating the soldiers who had formed the
merchant's escort, warehouse officials and dock workers
– and anyone else who might have witnessed the naval
officer's return to *The Serpent*. Yet, despite their
diligence, they learnt little. The only significant addition
to their knowledge was the fact that the merchant had
sometimes travelled alone when collecting goods. A
squad was despatched to retrace his footsteps, and
returned with the news that two peasants, a couple who
lived in a remote cottage on the northern shore, were
dead – apparently poisoned. However, no one knew for
certain that Ravel was responsible and, in any case, it
was inconceivable that such people had owned anything
of sufficient value to cause the subsequent mystery.

Even the weather conspired to thwart Farrag's investigation. The wind continued to blow strongly from the
west, so there was no chance of overtaking a sleek vessel
like *The Serpent*, but Farrag vowed that if she ever
returned to Zalys, her captain and crew would answer

some very pertinent questions. The Marshal even considered contacting Xantium about the ship, but hesitated to commit himself. *Remain vigilant.* Verkho's words still haunted him. Had he failed? Or was this some devious scheme of the Chancellor's, of which he was supposed to remain ignorant? If either was true, he must proceed with caution.

In the end, Farrag handed down a few trivial punishments to those he felt had failed him, then cast the matter from his mind. He had other things to attend to in the aftermath of Bowen's exile. He had, of course, heard of Gaye's blindness, and contemplated this unexpected bonus with undisguised delight. So much the better! If that did not provoke a reaction from these stinking island clods . . .

However, all remained quiet – on the surface at least – so the Marshal decided on further action. This was the sort of game he enjoyed. The time chosen for his next move was the day of celebration which would mark the tenth anniversary of the imperial wedding.

'That's him,' Dsordas said quietly. 'The one in black, to the left of the second pool.'

'He's not in uniform,' Fen whispered.

'He's off duty. And Information Officers aren't supposed to mix with the riff-raff on occasions like this.'

Dsordas and Fen were sitting in the midst of a sizeable crowd of islanders who had gathered on the rocks overlooking the tidal pools. They had come there to watch – from a distance – the shark fights which had been organized by some enterprising soldiers as part of the imperial celebrations. Below the islanders, much closer to the sport but still a discreet distance from the water's edge, were clusters of soldiers and officers together with their civilian guests.

The organizers had paid local fishermen to provide sharks, knowing that their profits from the subsequent gambling would more than justify their initial outlay. A great deal of money had already been wagered on such things as which of the young divers – islanders who were also paid performers – would draw first blood; how long they could stay in the water; who would make the final kill; which of the men would be injured or even killed – and many more variations dreamt up by the devious minds of the gamesters.

One contest was already over. The mangled remains of a small shark were being dragged out on to the rocks by the fishermen, who would reclaim the carcass for its meat. The water of the pool was stained pink, and the breeze carried occasional wafts of the stink of flesh and lacerated skin, but most of the spectators agreed that it had been a disappointing contest. The shark had apparently given up the fight once its small, ferocious brain had somehow recognized its captivity. The divers had had a relatively easy victory, and none of them was so much as scratched.

Many of the islanders shared the soldiers' sense of disappointment, although they took a quiet pride in the skill of the divers. As sea-faring people, they feared and hated sharks, and saw nothing wrong in using them for sport in such a way. Matching man and knife against teeth and fin was a long-held and respected tradition on Zalys, but it was not until the Xantic garrison had become involved that betting had been accepted as an integral part of the spectacle.

'Did Panos win?' Fen asked, trying to follow the bewildering flow of transactions.

'I'm not sure,' Dsordas replied. 'He was certainly wagering heavily.'

'Desperation?' Fen suggested.

'Let's hope so,' her lover answered quietly.

The couple would not normally have attended such an event. Fen already felt saddened and a little queasy, and Dsordas was contemptuous of such cruel and senseless activity, but he had promised to provide Fen with a purpose, some active way of helping the Children.

Observing Panos was the safest task he could think of.

Their gaze returned to the second of the four pools. This shark was larger than the first, swimming in angry circles within its prison, giving every promise of a better fight. Even so, one of the organizers, a burly, bearded soldier, decided to liven the proceedings up a bit. After the pitiful capitulation of the first creature, he was taking no chances. From somewhere he had found a stray dog, which he now picked up by its hind legs. He swung it round and pitched the dog, yelping, into the pool. Cheers, laughter and a flurry of betting on the mongrel's chance of survival followed.

The dog surfaced, spluttering and barking, and thrashed towards the shore. For a moment it seemed as if it might make it, but then the shark's blunt snout reared up, and a single bite cut the terrified animal in half. Soon there was nothing left but a small red patch on the swirling surface. Money changed hands amid more merriment and excited speculation. The shark had tasted blood; now it was ready for more.

Some of the divers appeared apprehensive, while the eyes of others shone in response to the challenge. One young man in particular stood with his gaze fixed upon his opponent, as drops of seawater ran down his bronzed, well-muscled torso, reflecting the morning sunlight. He was Helian, known as 'the Blade', an illiterate peasant from one of the northern villages, revered in some quarters for his shark-fighting prowess. The young man was a favourite with the crowd, and he knew it. He was one of the three men who dived in to begin the combat, and it was he who scored first, raking a long, jagged gash in the shark's back with his hooked knife.

Thereafter, the fight – and the wagering – proceeded in a frenzy. Two divers were hurt; one with a hand bitten clean off and the other's left calf torn to shreds, but both were dragged out alive, and eventually the shark succumbed.

Fen had long since stopped watching the actual battle, feeling sickened by the baying of the crowd and their bloodlust, and was glad of the excuse to concentrate her attention elsewhere. Panos was enraptured, his face flushed, shouting with the others and busily placing bets. Money and scrip passed back and forth, although the transactions were almost unthinking, the gamblers' eyes rarely leaving the churning, polluted water for more than an instant.

When it was over, Panos seemed to come back to his senses, looking down at the coins in his hands, then delving into pockets to study the scrip there. Even from a distance, the look of dismay on his face was unmistakable.

'He's losing,' Fen whispered.

'Good,' Dsordas replied. 'Will you be all right on your own now? I have people I need to see.'

'Yes.'

'You know what to do?' he persisted, obviously reluctant to leave her. 'We already know that he's deep in debt – but not by how much or to whom. See how he fares here, then follow at a distance. Whatever you learn, however insignificant it seems, might just be the lever we need.'

'Yes!' Fen repeated, with a touch of impatience.

'Malo is waiting with his boat at the third jetty from the bridge, in case you need to follow him on water. All right?'

'Go!' she told him. 'I can cope.'

Dsordas could not resist one last instruction.

'Whatever you do, don't get too close,' he said quietly. 'You can walk away at any time. This is not the time for heroics – from anyone.'

For answer, Fen drew him to her and kissed him.

'I'll be as careful as you,' she promised in a whisper.

As Dsordas stood up to leave, a gasp went up from the crowd and he turned back to look at the third pool in time to see a huge splash.

'What was that?'

'A sea-bat,' Fen answered in disbelief. 'They've got a sea-bat in there, not a shark!'

'A big one by the look of it,' he commented.

'But they're gentle,' she protested. 'I used to swim with them. Why kill them?'

'I've seen them overturn small boats,' Dsordas told her. 'If it leaps like that again, the blow could easily stun a man and drown him.'

As if to demonstrate, the manta ray erupted from the surface again, its vast, triangular wing-fins undulating, horns seeming to grasp at the air, while its long, whip-like tail lashed overhead. The thunderous crack as it hit the water echoed like a scream of protest as spray flew in all directions.

Fen was suddenly chilled, but Dsordas merely took the ray's plight as one more piece of evidence for humankind's depravity.

'Perhaps if they goad it enough, it'll give them a show,' he remarked, disgusted but resigned. Kneeling down, he added quietly, 'Keep your eyes on the job. I'm relying on you.' He kissed her cheek quickly and was gone.

Fen struggled to focus her attention on Panos, but kept turning back to look at the imprisoned ray. There was a buzz of conversation all around her; it was clear that she was not the only one who had sensed the cold, unnatural malevolence of the creature. *It's only trying to escape*, she told herself, but was not convinced. She remembered swimming with a beautiful pair of sea-bats as a girl. They had been intensely curious, and not at all dangerous. True, there were tales of how a blow from one of their fins could shatter boats, but Fen believed that such things were caused by overexuberant playfulness, not malice. There was little doubt that large rays possessed prodigious strength – one had reportedly towed a fishing boat for a full two leagues after being harpooned, and others had apparently lifted heavy anchors – but Fen had never felt even remotely threatened by them. In fact she had been charmed by her inquisitive friends. But now she was not so sure. *Perhaps if they goad it enough . . .*

The attention of the whole crowd, including Panos, was now centred on the manta ray's pool, and the wagering was fiercer than ever. Once again, Helian stepped to the forefront, confident and smiling, but this time he dived in alone. Instantly the surface of the water roiled, making it impossible to see beneath, then exploded as the ray leapt into the air. With it came the diver, apparently clinging to the creature's underside before arching away, his arms outstretched.

To the mesmerized onlookers, man and ray appeared to fall back in slow motion, and in those few moments, everyone saw that Helian's face and chest had been flayed, his torso ripped asunder and his stomach ruptured and gaping, as blood glinted amid the spume. The diver was dead before he hit the water again and, an instant later, the ray crashed down on top of his eviscerated body.

For a long, breathless moment the crowd was silent as the echoes of the fall died away. Then screams, shouts of anger and amazement rang out – and one man laughed, unable to contain his glee, as all those about him passed over their money. Panos' losing streak had come to an end.

Fen gaped stupidly, knowing what she had seen but unable to believe her eyes. A sea-bat's teeth were tiny and flat; there were none at all in the upper jaw! How could it have done this?

Soldiers were gathering round the pool now, spears at the ready, as the divers drew back in horror. From her perch, Fen saw several lances thrown, and a cheer went up as one of them evidently struck home. An instant later there was hurried movement among the soldiers as the successful spearsman was attacked. The ray leapt towards the boulder on which he stood, its tail whipped forward, and its tip slammed into the man's face. He fell back screaming as the ray landed heavily and slithered back into the water, leaving a glistening trail of blood.

Everyone drew back to a safer distance then, and the injured soldier was seen writhing and screaming, clutching at his face. After one last convulsion, he lay still. The word 'poison' spread through the crowd on breathless wings.

Only one man remained unconcerned. Panos was too busy pocketing his money and adding up his notes of good fortune. He turned away and began to walk back towards the town.

Fen was too shocked to react immediately, but eventually scrambled to her feet and began to climb, her legs shaky, over the rocks, back towards the track. Thus she never saw how the ray was beaten at last, skewered by a dozen lances and then butchered by the now vengeful divers.

Not too quick, she cautioned herself. *Don't get too close.* She had hoped to leave with the rest of the crowd, hiding herself among the throng, but the unexpected, horrifying turn of events meant that she was glad to get away, even if it made her task a little harder. She waited until Panos was well ahead, then followed, her legs still trembling.

At the river, Panos hailed two soldiers in a boat. They picked him up, then rowed across and into one of the canals. Fen kept out of sight until she was sure where they were going, then ran to find Malo. He was a strong, young boatman and he knew the currents better than the soldiers, so they were not far behind when they too entered the canal. Following them through the maze without being obvious could have been difficult, but it was soon clear where Panos was headed.

'Fournoi Square,' Malo muttered.

'Drop me at the far end,' Fen said, then watched her quarry disembark, dismiss the soldiers and walk jauntily away. Malo leapt out to hold his boat steady.

'Do you want me to wait?' he asked.

'No. Thanks.' Fen's thoughts were following Panos.

'Go carefully,' were Malo's parting words.

Fournoi Square was busy with people and preparations for the celebrations later in the day. Fen experienced a momentary qualm when she remembered what was due to happen that afternoon, but pushed aside her unease and made her way across the sun-warmed stones.

Panos was easy to follow, not least because he was evidently in a jubilant mood, whistling, greeting other members of the garrison and heading for an open-air tavern. Sitting at a vacant table, he called loudly for wine, and the waiter who scurried to obey was rewarded with a handful of coins thrown negligently on to his tray. The Information Officer drank deeply with evident satisfaction, beaming at the world, while Fen pondered the best place from which to observe him. She eventually chose a neighbouring establishment, and ordered tea. She sipped the fragrant brew gently and tried to quiet the frantic beating of her heart.

You can walk away at any time. Dsordas' words calmed her, but made her all the more determined to learn something useful. He obviously hoped that Panos' gambling debts might make him vulnerable – and thus a possible source of information or, if he was really desperate, aid. That seemed a forlorn hope now, but Fen had resolved not to fail at her first attempt to prove her worth to the underground.

Panos was soon joined by several other officers. Their conversation was loud and jovial, much of it revolving around the sensational events at the rock pools and Panos' equally astounding luck. The party consumed several bottles of wine, and became the focus of attention for many of the other tables. Fen noticed especially that two hard-faced men glanced that way frequently, scowling and talking closely. After a while, these two got up and walked away without looking back, and Fen forgot about them. People were coming and going constantly, and she could not possibly remember them all.

At last Panos rose, and took his leave with words to the effect that he had better go and pay off his creditors.

'Wouldn't do to upset *those* sharks,' one of his companions agreed.

Panos laughed and set off, coins clinking loudly in his pockets. Fen made herself wait for a few moments, then got up, waved to the proprietor and followed. Panos led her to one of the square's main exits, making it easy for Fen to remain inconspicuous among the many other people passing to and fro, but then he turned off into a narrow alley in the cramped heart of the town. Here there were fewer pedestrians, and she had to be more circumspect. Pretending to walk past the entrance, she was just in time to see him turn again and hurried after, not wanting him to be out of sight for too long. Before she reached the second corner, however, she heard running footsteps, a shout, and then the sounds of a fight. It lasted only a few moments, and Fen winced at the thud of blows and the groans of pain. She hesitated, shrinking into the deeper shadows of a doorway. Two men emerged, each carrying items she could not identify, and ran off in the opposite direction. No sound came from the second alley.

Eventually, Fen overcame her indecision and crept forward, unable to resist peering round the corner. Panos lay curled up by the far wall, a few paces away. The shutters in the alley were all firmly closed. It was quiet and still.

Panos groaned.

Still alive.

Gingerly, he tested his pockets, then swore softly, coughed and spat. He tried to sit up, to lever himself up against the wall, but fell down again with a sudden gasp of agony. Involuntarily, Fen took a step forward, then stopped as Panos looked up and saw her for the first time. His face was swollen and bloody, with one eye closed and his upper lip split, but nevertheless he could not hide his surprise at seeing her.

'Are you all right?' Fen asked quietly, not moving any closer.

'Do I look all right?' he rasped painfully, levering himself up to sit with his back to the wall. 'You can stop gloating now.'

'I'm not . . .'

'Friends of yours, were they?' he grated, his voice thick with contempt.

'No!'

'You islanders are all the same.' Panos coughed again, dabbed his lips with a grimy sleeve and winced. 'They closed the shutters fast enough. Rather not see. And you . . . you, of all people, no reason to help me.'

He knows who I am. Fen was close to panic. *Don't get too close.* Yet her feet refused to move.

'Help me then!' he growled spitefully. 'Fix this mess.' He indicated his ruined face. 'Mend my ribs. Better still, get me my money back. This's nothing to what my *friends* will do if I don't pay them.'

He sounded so pitiful, looked so helpless and in pain, that for a moment, Fen saw only the suffering of a human being. Panos coughed again, and more blood dribbled down his chin.

'You'd be doing me a favour if you finished me off now,' he muttered, sounding unutterably weary.

'Your commander, can't he . . .' Fen began.

Panos spat.

'He'd never lift a finger. Farrag has decreed that his officers do not gamble, never get into debt. It's not natural!' His bile was suddenly replaced by self-pity, as if the full implications of what had happened were only now sinking in. 'Gods, what am I going to do?' he breathed, sending a fine spray of red over his black shirt.

At that moment, they both heard the sound of approaching soldiers, at the far end of the alley. Panos glanced up at Fen and, afterwards, she could never decide whether his expression held a plea or a warning, but he did not speak again.

Fen turned and ran.

CHAPTER ELEVEN

The dial shows two different times; one for the sun, one for the stones. The shadow of the stones is deep and rich, but limned with dark fire. It fragments, spreading its strength. How clearly they see! How powerful – yet directionless – they are. They have not learned the pitfalls or the pleasures of the world. All will depend upon what they are taught.

I hear echoes of their voices and long to answer their questions, but I cannot control the dial.

Time changes.

'You did *what*?' Dsordas did not shout, but his shock was clear.

'I talked to him,' Fen repeated sullenly.

'You little idiot. What did I tell you?' He was infuriatingly calm, almost resigned, and this filled her with resentment.

'I couldn't help it!' she shouted.

Dsordas let that pass.

'Did he know you were following him?'

'No.'

'You're sure?'

'Yes!' Fen paused, then added reluctantly, 'As sure as I can be.'

'All right. So he might have thought it was a chance encounter,' Dsordas went on relentlessly. 'Tell me exactly what was said.'

Fen related the conversation, as best as she could. Dsordas did not interrupt and, by the time she had finished, Fen had regained her composure.

'He's really in trouble now, more so than ever – and he hates Farrag,' she concluded. 'He'll get no help there. Doesn't that make him ideal for our purposes?'

Dsordas nodded absently, deep in thought.

'And we'd never have known it if I hadn't talked to him,' Fen added triumphantly, daring him to disagree.

He nodded again, his expression serious.

'Say something!' she demanded. 'Admit I'm right.' There was no response. 'Let me win an argument with you, just once,' she pleaded.

'I thought you always did,' he answered distractedly, his thoughts elsewhere.

'What harm can it have done?' Fen persisted, unnerved by her lover's continued preoccupation.

'Did you recognize his attackers?' Dsordas asked, ignoring her question.

'I didn't see them properly.'

'Islanders?'

'By their dress, yes,' Fen replied, then realization dawned. 'Wait a moment. I'm almost certain I saw them earlier – they were at the tavern, watching Panos get drunk. They left before he did, and waited for him to fall into their trap.'

'Which implies that they knew where he was headed,' Dsordas commented.

'I suppose so.'

'But you didn't recognize them?'

'No.'

'Would you know them if you saw them again?'

'Yes. I think so.' Another idea occurred to Fen. 'Could they have been your people?' she asked.

'If they were,' Dsordas answered, 'they were acting on their own initiative. I'll know soon enough.' He paused. 'They could just have been opportunists,' he added thoughtfully. 'Panos was an easy target, after he'd been bragging and drinking like that. Or perhaps someone had their own reasons for wanting to stop him settling his debts. Or maybe . . .'

'What?' Fen prompted.

'It's just possible that the whole thing was set up by Farrag.'

'That's crazy.'

'Think about it,' he argued. 'It's almost too convenient. What if the entire performance was staged for our benefit?'

'But he was beaten half to death!' Fen protested.

'It'd have to look good,' Dsordas went on, nodding. 'You can't fake injuries like that easily.'

'They weren't faked!' Fen exclaimed, unable to believe her ears. 'You're not serious?'

'Just imagine that somehow Farrag got wind of our interest in Panos,' he explained patiently. 'So he sets up a big win, makes his man as conspicuous as possible – just in case we're not paying attention – then gets two of his own men, in disguise, to rob Panos and leave him to sob out his story to whoever was following.'

'No. It's too far-fetched,' Fen responded, but with less conviction in her voice.

'With what Panos told you,' Dsordas continued evenly, 'he was practically begging for us to help him out and give him the chance to become a paid traitor. But, in fact, he'd be the man Farrag's always wanted inside the Children.'

'You don't really believe that, do you?' Fen was horrified by the idea.

'Even if it's only a remote possibility, we have to take it seriously. Farrag is more ruthless and cunning than we can imagine.'

'But if you're wrong, we'd miss a wonderful opportunity,' she objected. 'If Panos is *really* in trouble, then it may not be long before he's killed – and he'll be no good to us then.'

'On the other hand,' Dsordas countered, 'if I'm right, and we approach him, we expose ourselves to a double threat. Revealing our plans to a possible informer would be bad enough, but . . .'

'But what?'

'He recognized you,' he replied, allowing his emotions to show for the first time. 'If this supposedly chance encounter leads to contact with the Children, then Farrag will have another way to attack us . . . through you. That's something I'm not prepared to risk.'

The sun had risen five times since Midsummer's Day, but Gaye's condition had not changed. She was still blind, and still deeply depressed. Her other physical hurts were receding, though, and she was determinedly learning to find her way about her home – a place which was now full of unexpected perils. Her family, including Antorkas, who was now almost fully recovered, spent much of their time with her, helping, coaxing, learning to deal with her anger as well as her sorrow.

The fact that today was the tenth anniversary of the Emperor's wedding would have meant little to the Amari household – except for one thing. An edict had been issued the day before, requiring the parents of all children between the ages of three and five to present them in Fournoi Square in the late afternoon. The purpose of the gathering was ostensibly to give the children gifts from the Empire, as part of the celebrations, but the wording had made it clear that this was an order, not a request. Everyone sensed Farrag's hand behind the anonymous decree, but no one knew what his motives were. This uncertainty added to the general misgivings about the occasion but, even so, everyone knew that to disobey would be to risk severe punishment. Consequently, as the sun travelled its downward path, Natali was dressed in his best clothes. The little boy was the only one who had no qualms about the gathering, and was evidently looking forward to being the centre of attention. His family's preoccupation with Gaye's misery had left him feeling neglected, sad and angry at the same time. Now they would all be watching him for a change!

*   *   *

Fournoi Square was a cauldron of noise, colour and heat. Most of the surrounding buildings were draped with banners in the imperial colours of blue and gold. The edges of the square, especially the shaded areas on the western side, were crowded, and the taverns were doing a roaring trade. Some of the younger children were still with their families, but most had escaped, and the sun-baked open space at the centre of the square was now their province. They alone possessed energy in the still considerable warmth, running, shouting and playing all manner of games, while their anxious parents looked on, wondering what was to come next.

So far, apart from the usual sentries, there was no sign of the imperial presence, except for soldiers busily working on some mysterious apparatus in a roped-off area next to the canal. A long line of trestle tables had also been set up along the southern side, but as yet they were bare and unattended.

Etha and Antorkas sat side by side at a small table outside one of the taverns. This was the first time either had been to the square since the traumatic events of Midsummer's Day – indeed, it was the first time Antorkas had been out of the house – and they were both suffering. Their eyes rarely left Natali, who ran to and fro, playing happily with his friends. Fen was with her parents, but she was still preoccupied by her own experiences earlier in the day, and she glanced around constantly, as if expecting to see Panos' battered face in the crowd. The rest of the Amari children were at home with Gaye, and so it was left to Dsordas to greet the many people who came to give their condolences or good wishes. He alone remained aware of everything about them, his own apprehension hidden beneath an outward serenity. The islanders all knew instinctively that Antorkas and Etha would not want to attract undue attention, but many felt honour bound to say something. Dsordas' discreet wardenship made it easier for all concerned.

114

The official start of the proceedings was marked by Niering, in one of his rare public appearances. He addressed the crowd from a balcony of the imperial garrison's headquarters, at the southern end of the square. Once even the children were quiet, he gave a speech which was both brief and bland, expressing the wish that everyone would partake in the festivities that marked such a joyous event. The commander was clearly uneasy in his unaccustomed role, but his final words caused a stir, for a variety of reasons.

'Some of my men will shortly be bringing food and drink to the tables below. This is a gift from their Imperial Highnesses Emperor Southan and Empress Ifryn.'

An appreciative murmur ran through the crowd. A free meal and wine were always welcome – whatever the source.

'Please feel free to help yourselves to as much as you like,' Niering went on, 'but let the youngsters go first. This is their day after all, and when they have eaten, the children aged between three and five are to gather in the centre of the square. There they will receive their own special gifts.'

Niering waited for a wave of excited chattering to die down, and then continued.

'Later on, our celebrations will end with another special event, which promises to be spectacular. It would be foolish of you to miss it.' Over the renewed speculative whispering, he raised his voice again. 'You are all welcome in the name of the Emperor, but the children of Zalys are especially welcome.' Niering smiled.

Fen felt the sudden tension in Dsordas beside her, and fought against the urge to look at him. Dsordas himself remained still, outwardly impassive, but others were not so controlled. The crowd's murmuring grew louder and glances were exchanged.

Fen wondered how closely they were being observed, and hoped fervently that Niering's choice of phrase had

115

been innocent. Somehow she doubted it. Surely it was another attempt to gain information – however inconclusive – about the underground. She sensed Farrag's influence in the ploy, and wondered where the Marshal was now. Who was he watching?

'Let us begin,' Niering declared with a wave of his hand. His duty done, he disappeared into the dark room behind him.

Men strode into the square carrying trays, platters, bowls, wineskins and rolling barrels. Some of them obviously resented this duty and remained sour-faced, but others grinned as they watched the children's expectant faces. In the sudden rush of noise and movement, Fen felt that it was safe to look at Dsordas at last. At first he would not meet her gaze, then his expression softened and he took her in his arms.

'Laugh,' he whispered in her ear. 'We're supposed to be enjoying ourselves.'

Fen did her best, drawing back to look at his smiling face. Only his eyes betrayed his true feelings.

'I'm going to see that Natali doesn't eat too much and make himself sick,' she told him. 'Look after my parents, will you?'

Dsordas nodded.

'Keep your eyes open,' he said softly. 'There have been too many surprises already today.'

'I'm never stupid twice in one day,' she replied, forcing a smile.

By the time all the children had finished eating, and most of the adults with any appetite had been up to the tables, the sun had left the square. The ghosts on their eastern balcony were now in shade and clearly visible, talking silently as usual, watching over the living like ineffectual guardians.

By now the specified children, perhaps a hundred in all, had congregated in the centre as requested. Most were sitting on the stone, though others ran and played, still full of energy.

At last, Farrag made his long anticipated entrance, gliding in at the head of a line of men carrying boxes. Some of the children looked frightened now, and a few started to cry, but they fell silent when Farrag looked at them. Others, including Natali, had eyes only for the boxes. Without further ado, each child was called up in turn to face the Marshal. After a brief scrutiny, he passed most of them on to his assistants, who gave them a trinket from the boxes and sent them on their way. A few, however, were told to wait to one side, and they all seemed quite excited by this, as though they had been singled out for a special treat.

When Natali's turn came, his family held their breath, but it came as no surprise to Fen when her brother was chosen to wait. Idle speculation was useless however; all they could do was hope for the best.

After what seemed like an age, the children had all been seen, and Natali and the others gathered round Farrag. He looked them over slowly, blue eyes staring at each of the twenty or so faces for a few intense moments. Then he spoke quietly, so that no one but the children could hear, before turning to one of his lieutenants and taking a small box from him. From this he drew forth a handful of pendants, and held them up. Even in the fading light, it was clear what the stones were. Only amberine glinted in such a mysterious and seductive way, winking a rich golden brown.

There were gasps of amazement from the crowd. Surely he did not intend giving amberine away? It was much too valuable!

But that was indeed Farrag's purpose. Each member of the chosen group was called forward and a pendant hung about their small necks.

'What's he up to?' Fen whispered.

'I've no idea,' Dsordas answered tersely.

Then the children were dismissed, and they ran back to their parents to show off their trophies. Natali went

117

straight to his father, the jeweller, his small face flushed with pride.

'Look!' he cried breathlessly.

'It's beautiful.' Antorkas smiled at his son, trying not to let his fear show. To the others, he said, 'It's amberine all right. The chain's cheap and the setting's clumsy but the stone is excellent.'

Etha held out her hand.

'Give it to me, Natali,' she asked. 'Let me see.'

'No!' The little boy clasped his prize protectively.

'Mind your manners!' his father scolded him. 'Do as your mother says.'

'No.' Natali tried to back away, his face angry.

Antorkas caught his son's arm, angry himself now.

'Give it to me at once!' he demanded.

'I'll give it back, I promise,' Etha added, more kindly.

Natali shook his head and looked at the ground, his eyes beginning to fill with tears. Elsewhere, other children were reacting in similar fashion. Some screamed, others wept or tried to fight or run away – but none would be parted from Farrag's gift.

'Leave him be,' Dsordas said unexpectedly.

They all looked at him, recognized his conviction and reluctantly obeyed. Natali glanced up and gave him a watery smile.

While this was happening, Farrag had slipped away unnoticed. The sudden darkness of the island summer had fallen, and this was intensified when, at an officer's command, most of the torches and lamps around the square were doused.

What now? Fen wondered. *There have been too many surprises already today.*

An expectant, fearful silence fell over the square, until a sudden flare of red from the cordoned-off area caught everyone's attention. Moments later, a million sparks of blue and gold shot up into the air, glittering like jewels for a few incredible instants before melting back into the darkness. After that, the spellbinding display presented an almost continuous vision of enchantment. Fireworks had never been seen before on Zalys, and the islanders, especially the now wide-awake children, all felt that it was the most beautiful magic they had ever seen. Each new pattern, each variation of colour and sound, was greeted with cries of amazement and delight.

Then the darkness settled once more, and the audience groaned in disappointment. Was it over so soon? But the fire-masters had saved the best till last, and one last rocket sped upward in a huge blaze of orange sparks. High above, as every eye followed its course, it exploded in a dazzling brilliance of blue and white. Yet that was not the end of the wonders. Instead of spreading randomly, the sparks coalesced, seemed to take form, to become a shape. Everyone fell silent, mesmerized. Even the fire-masters gaped in awe; they had not expected *this*.

For a few heart-stopping moments, a huge glittering eye eclipsed the stars. It was as if one of the old gods was looking down on them, watching them all.

In the wide-eyed silence, there came the sound of a single voice.

Farrag laughed at a joke only he understood.

CHAPTER TWELVE

*There are signs here that have never been seen by any man
– except those who wrought them. Stonemasons left their
marks where even the birds would not see them. Why did
they do it? I understand their longing for immortality, but
when they climbed back down to earth, their hopes went
with them. Only the signs remain, here among the
gargoyles, the lichen and the wind.*

*This is a special place. But I am the last of those who
think so.*

'He's asleep,' Etha reported, joining the others in the
kitchen.

'Good,' Antorkas said. 'We can take that accursed
pendant off him now.'

Etha shook her head.

'He's still clutching the stone,' she told them. 'He'd
wake if we tried now – and I can't face another
argument.'

Her husband swore softly.

'What is that damned man up to?' he demanded angrily.

They had been discussing Farrag's intentions for
hours. Fournoi Square had emptied quickly after the all-
seeing fire-eye had faded from the sky – but, from what
they had seen and heard, the other children had been
similarly obstinate about their pendants.

'What can he hope to gain?' Fen wondered aloud.

'Maybe just this,' Dsordas suggested. 'To make us
nervous, trying to outguess him. That sounds like his
idea of a joke.'

'An expensive joke!' Antorkas exclaimed in disbelief. 'Those stones must be worth a small fortune.'

'He's not playing for money,' Dsordas replied, then turned to Etha. 'Did Natali tell you what Farrag had said to him?'

'No,' she answered. 'He won't say anything. To tell the truth, I'm not even sure he remembers. But he got defensive and tearful when I asked.'

'Farrag's obviously made them react like that on purpose,' Fen commented anxiously. 'What else can he make them do?'

'I won't have this!' Antorkas exploded, slamming his fist on to the table. 'We'll cut the chain off if we have to!'

'It's just a piece of jewellery,' Dsordas said. 'It can't do anything on its own, you know that. If we take it off, we'll just make Natali miserable and resentful, and we might not achieve anything else. And then we'd *never* have a chance of discovering what Farrag's up to.'

'So we do nothing?' the older man growled.

'We'll watch Natali,' Dsordas replied, 'just as all the other parents will be watching their children. If anything unusual happens, we'll know soon enough.'

Antorkas subsided, looking unhappy and very weary. Etha looked at her husband and stood up, holding out her hand.

'Come, my love. You need your bed too,' she told him. 'Nothing more is going to happen tonight.'

Fen and Dsordas also went to bed then, but after a time lying in the darkness listening to each other breathing, they knew that sleep would be a long time coming. There was too much on their minds.

'Are you awake?' Fen whispered.

'No.'

'Me neither.' She moved closer, and Dsordas put his arms around her. 'What are we going to do about Panos?'

'The gods know,' he replied, obviously at a loss.

121

'Can we afford to miss such an opportunity?' Fen asked.

'Can we afford to take such a risk?' he countered. 'It's bad enough trying to ward off all the new recruits just now, but this . . .'

'Did I do so badly?' she asked, hoping for reassurance.

'I can't tell,' Dsordas answered, surprising her. 'That's what scares me. You're too important to me.' In a lighter tone, he added, 'Maybe if you weren't so beautiful . . .'

Fen rose to the bait.

'Jewellery is beautiful,' she told him. 'Is that all I am to you? Just something to display?'

'We both know your true worth to me,' he said, grinning.

'And because of that, I can't help you in your work?' she demanded.

'It's men's work,' he mumbled.

'You said that before.'

'That doesn't make it less true.'

'So I should just sit around being beautiful and doing nothing?' she concluded.

'But you do it so well,' he protested innocently.

There was a long pause, then they both burst out laughing. *More and more of our conversations are like this,* Fen thought. *We only seem able to talk about serious things by joking about them.* She couldn't decide whether that was something to worry about or not, so contented herself by calling him several rude names, snuggling closer at the same time.

'Do you want to . . .' she whispered.

'Not now.'

'Have you got a headache?'

'No,' he answered, laughing. 'I have to be up very early. The first of the flood tides is due the hour before dawn.'

They lay quietly for a while. The events of the day had quite removed the threat of the floods from Fen's mind.

'I can't forget the sight of that sea-bat,' she whispered. 'I'm sure I'll dream about it.'

'Dreams can't hurt you. They're not real,' he told her.

'They're real enough when you're in them!'

'Wake me up if you get scared,' he suggested. 'I'll make the monsters go away.'

They finally fell asleep in each other's arms.

Farrag neither wanted nor needed any sleep that night. He was swimming in a sea of wine and self-congratulation. He had enjoyed the celebrations immensely, not out of any joy for the faraway Emperor who commanded his nominal loyalty, but because the occasion had given him the opportunity to indulge in his passion for games. All his experiments had worked beyond his expectations. Niering's speech, which he had helped to write, had been a splendid joke, and the fire-eye had been very impressive. But best of all was the ceremony with the children! How those stupid islanders had gaped when he handed out the amberine! Of course, the gesture had cost him nothing – the stones had been appropriated from Ravel's stock – and might gain him a great deal. It was a long shot of course, but what was the point of gambling unless the stakes were worthwhile?

Most of the children had been hopeless clods, as expected, but he had seen sparks of talent in some of them, and it had been those children that Farrag had singled out. If his gifts brought out any of their latent abilities, they might become a rich source of intelligence for him. His experiments with his own Far-speakers suggested that starting young was a considerable advantage. If his plan worked and a suitable adept could be trained to monitor them, the children would be working for him without even knowing it.

Ensuring that they kept the pendants on had been simplicity itself. Their little minds were so malleable, so open to the most basic of hypnotic techniques. Perhaps it would all come to nothing, but at the very least it would give his enemies something to think about. And it would be fascinating to see what his embryonic spies did with their new toys!

When the wine and the company of other officers began to bore him, Farrag made his way to his private garden. He needed no sleep that night. His dreams were steeped in poison.

Gaye was flying. It was a crooked, skittering flight, but it was effortless, as though she had been born to it. It was night, with a red moon and bright stars above, and the landscape was seen only dimly, yet the air was full of tiny sounds and echoes that formed pictures of towers and ramparts. Spires jutted into the sky, insane sculptures leered as they swooped by, and all around were the others, mere shapes in the darkness, flying with her. Their presence was welcoming but remote, and their voices were filled with a deep, indefinable sadness.

Gaye awoke crying, her sudden sense of loss made even more acute by her return to the constant darkness of her waking world.

Ia was woken by her sister's sobs.

'I'm here,' she called out softly. 'What's the matter?' She had taken to sleeping in Gaye's room, watching over her even while she was at rest.

'If only I could learn to fly,' Gaye said wistfully.

'Where would you go?' Ia asked, then realized the stupidity of the question and berated herself silently. She tried to think of something else to say, rubbing her sleep-filled eyes.

'I'd follow him wherever they take him,' Gaye answered.

'I know,' her younger sister said, still uncertain.

'One day you'll understand,' Gaye told her gently. *And one day I will learn to fly.*

CHAPTER THIRTEEN

There is beauty in the designs of nature. No gift of prophecy is needed to foretell the shape of the moon, the movement of the stars or the shifting of the tides. Perhaps that is why I like them so much.

But if omens predict that the sun will not rise – what then? It would be a joy to be proved wrong. And yet, what if I am proved right, and the whole world shivers beneath an endless night? Would they burn me on the sacrificial pyre? Or make me a god?

Humankind has its own tides.

When Bowen stepped ashore, he had no idea where he was. He moved as if in a dream, taking each step only because a guard prodded him down the gangway. Once on the dock he staggered, unbalanced by the unexpected rigidity underfoot, then stood aimlessly until he was led away by his captors. He did not know why he was there, or where he was going. Nor did he care.

In fact he had just entered the port of Brighthaven in the western province of Nadal, a country which bordered the Xantic homeland to the south-west. The town's name was singularly inapt, and not even the summer sunlight could make the place look inviting. The streets were drab and dirty, and the inhabitants all had a dour, hangdog look to them, like gamblers perpetually down on their luck.

It was strange to see signs of a recent celebration in such a place. Pavements and cobbles were strewn with debris from the night before, and there were some bright blue and gold banners still draped from balconies, looking absurdly out of place amidst the general grime. None of this meant anything to Bowen. He passed a girl who was clearing up the mess of an outdoor tavern, and she looked up at him and smiled sympathetically. But her hair was the wrong colour so Bowen ignored her and walked on.

Behind him something stirred, something vast and grey. He spun around and stared, and his already nervous escort reached for their weapons. Unaware of his peril, Bowen remained still, watching as an officer carried a box the size of a man's head down the gangway. He exchanged a few words with another man on the dock, then passed the box over.

Bowen felt the whole world begin to tilt and slide. He staggered again, blind now, and covered his face with his hands. A little of his memory returned, cruelly.

'Gaye!' he cried in agony.

He collapsed, matching her endless fall.

Fen woke as the first light of day filtered through the shutters, but Dsordas had already gone. She was seized by a sudden terror for a moment, but then remembered the flood tides. She got up and dressed quickly, and went down to the kitchen where she found her mother, alone, preparing food.

'I'm glad you're up,' Etha said. 'I could do with the company.'

'Has Papa gone too?'

'Yes, and Anto and Torin are with them,' her mother replied. 'It's going to be a bad one. The wind shifted in the night, so they'll need every pair of hands they can get.'

Not for the first time, Fen was grateful for the fact that her own home stood in one of the driest parts of Nkosa. Here at least they would be safe, but she wanted to join Dsordas and the other men, to help in their frustrating battle.

126

'The worst of the morning tide will be just about over now,' Etha went on, 'but I don't think they were planning to come home. There'll be plenty for them to do before evening. Will you go and find them, and take some food? They'll need it.'

'Of course,' Fen answered gladly. 'I may stay to help.'

'It's men's work,' her mother informed her.

Why is everyone always telling me that? Fen wondered irritably. 'I'm as much use as Torin,' she objected.

Etha shrugged.

'He shouldn't be out either,' she remarked, 'but try telling him that.'

'We all do what we can,' Fen said defiantly.

'None of my children listen to me any more,' her mother complained, and sighed theatrically. 'Where have I gone wrong?'

'You let us grow up,' Fen told her, laughing. 'Big mistake, that.'

Etha nodded philosophically and the two women went on with their preparations in companionable silence. Shortly after the sun rose over the distant horizon, the food was ready, and Fen left. Two of the family's three boats were gone, but the smallest had been left behind, and it would be easy enough to handle on her own. The tide was indeed very high, lapping at the uppermost steps of their courtyard. If it was so close to flooding here, Fen knew that other places would have been very badly affected. Although the currents were running strongly, she cast off confidently. Like all the children of Nkosa, she had learnt to row almost before she could walk.

Even so, it took her most of the morning to locate Dsordas. There was evidence everywhere that this had been the most destructive tide yet. In some places, the so-called permanent defences – hastily built walls and solid, tight-fitting wooden gates – had been overwhelmed, as had the temporary measures, dams built of sacks full of sand and run-off channels. The lower levels of some buildings had been inundated. Elsewhere the damage was less severe, but a mopping-up operation was in progress all through the town.

Worst affected were the residential areas in the eastern side, closest to the lagoon. The docks themselves were well protected and of sturdy construction, but beyond them was chaos. Already many people were effectively without homes, and a repeat of the morning's floods would cause such far-reaching damage that some houses would be in danger of collapsing. Fen went there first, thinking that this was where most men would have been needed, but her family were not to be found. After that, depressed by what she had seen, she went to the area around Fournoi Square. The square itself had survived intact, helped by the manpower and resources of the imperial garrison. Indeed, the whole of the centre of the town seemed to have escaped with relatively light damage.

Fen made her way to the northern section of the town, where the river made navigation treacherous at times like these. Carefully avoiding the worst of the tidal currents, which were now ebbing strongly, she searched methodically, asking anyone she met about her family. Most were too busy to respond with more than a weary shrug or a few words, and she noticed that they kept glancing at the sky. Far above, a few thin clouds still moved westward, boding ill for the afternoon highwater.

At last, her arms aching, Fen spotted Torin's dark, slender form, and called out to him. He waved back, and came over to catch her bow rope, pulling her to the shore. The others were all there, taking a brief rest. Dsordas hugged her, and she saw the tiredness in his eyes. They were all glad of the provisions and ate ravenously, sharing the food with the men who had been working alongside them. All too soon, every scrap was gone.

'Do you want me to fetch more?' Fen asked.

'No. We must get back to work,' Dsordas told her.

'There's much to do before the next tide. We can eat this evening at home.'

'I'll stay then,' Fen said firmly. 'And if you tell me this is men's work, I'll throw you in the canal.'

Shortly before noon, the three remaining Amari children were sitting round the kitchen table. Natali still wore the amberine pendant, but seemed perfectly normal and quite happy. Ia had slept little the previous night; she was tired and kept rubbing her eyes. Gaye was quiet and thoughtful, eating carefully. The kitchen was a potentially dangerous place for her – the heat of the stove and the boiling water could have harmed her – but she was getting used to the restrictions of her new life. Etha bustled about, keeping busy to stop herself from thinking. The last few days had seen her life grow much more complicated, and there was little she could do about it – a situation she did not like at all.

The meal was interrupted by a hesitant knock at the front door. Etha went to open it, her heart in her mouth as she half-expected more bad news, but she was unprepared for the sight which greeted her. Nason stood on the step, wild-eyed and dripping wet from head to toe.

'I need to see Gaye,' he declared.

'You need to dry out,' Etha told him, ushering the unexpected visitor inside.

Nason started towards Gaye's room but Etha caught his arm and swung him round towards the kitchen.

'I have to see her,' he gasped.

'Not like that,' she decreed. 'Besides, she's in the kitchen.'

'Who is it?' Gaye called, having heard the use of her name.

'Nason's all wet!' Natali exclaimed admiringly as they returned to the kitchen.

'Ia, go fetch some of Anto's clothes,' Etha ordered. 'Nason, get out of those things.'

'But . . .' Nason began, as Ia departed obediently.

'It can wait,' Etha stated. 'Gaye's not going anywhere.'

'What is it?' the blind girl asked. 'What's going on?'

Nason glanced at Etha, then began to undress self-consciously, feeling awkward in front of Gaye even though she could not see him.

'Go behind the pantry screen, you great lump,' Etha said impatiently. 'We've no interest in looking at you. Talk at the same time, if you can manage that.'

Nason retreated gratefully.

'Last night,' he began, 'I thought I saw someone in Bowen's room.'

'Oh.' Gaye let out a quiet sigh of anguish.

'So I went in,' Nason continued, 'and there was a ghost in there. He looked angry, and was stamping about and talking, though I couldn't hear him of course. At first he took no notice of me, but then he stared at me and said something. It felt as though he was asking me a question, and he kept pointing at the empty bed. I told him . . .' He hesitated, but couldn't find any easy way of putting it. 'I told him that Bowen wasn't here any more . . . but he didn't seem to understand.'

Ia returned with the clothes, anxious to know what she had missed, but her mother quietened her, took the clothes and a towel to Nason and left him to it.

'Thank you,' he said, then resumed his tale. 'The ghost went out then, walked straight through the door, but when I followed he'd vanished.'

'What has this got to do with me?' Gaye asked quietly.

'He came back a short while ago,' Nason replied. 'I'd been helping with the flood defences – that's how I got so wet – and I'd just gone upstairs to change when I saw him. He beckoned to me, and I went in.'

Nason emerged barefoot, dressed in his borrowed garb, rubbing his unruly hair.

'Nason's not wet any more,' Natali commented disappointedly.

'I could see him more clearly this time,' their visitor went on. 'He seemed stronger somehow, and he was certainly in a better mood, but I still couldn't hear him. He was dressed in strange clothes, and there was a sword at his belt, so I thought perhaps he was the Swordsman Bowen used to talk to in his sleep.'

'What swordsman?' Gaye and Etha asked simultaneously.

'Didn't Fen or Dsordas tell you?' he asked breathlessly, then gulped, realizing that he was on perilous ground. *It's dangerous to talk of such things.* But that had been about the underground; this was a different matter altogether.

'Tell us what?' Etha asked pointedly.

Nason explained, leaving out the reason for his earlier visit, while the others listened quietly. The pain on Gaye's face almost made him wish he had never come, but he pressed on.

'Today, the ghost really seemed to be trying to tell me something. He looked *so* frustrated. I felt terrible. It was obviously very important to him, but I just couldn't read the words his lips were forming. Eventually he pointed to the bed, then at the floor in front of him, as if he wanted me to bring Bowen to him. I shook my head, tried to make him see that I couldn't. He made some other signs that I couldn't understand, then pointed to the bed again, and to his own ears.'

'He was saying that he and Bowen could hear each other,' Gaye put in.

'That's what I thought,' Nason said eagerly. 'Then he saw a book on the bedside table and got quite excited, pointing and talking. He even tried to pick it up, but of course he couldn't. He gave that up, and then covered his eyes, shaking his head and walking as if he was blind; after that he pointed to his ears again and nodded, his eyes still shut.'

'Someone who can't see, but can hear,' Gaye interpreted softly.

131

Nason nodded.

'Then I remembered that the book was one you'd given Bowen,' he told Gaye excitedly, 'so I ran straight over here. I'm sure he wants to see you!'

'You think I might be able to hear him too?' Gaye asked. 'I've never . . .' She paused. *I've never been blind before either*.

'Will you come?'

'Now?' Etha asked.

'Yes,' he replied, his enthusiasm bubbling over. 'The ghost was still there when I left. He might still be there.'

'I'll come,' Gaye said.

'Sweetheart, do you think . . . ?' Etha began.

'Mama, I have to. Bowen might be trying to contact me.'

'How do you come to that conclusion, child?' She did not want her daughter hurt by false hopes.

'What harm can it do?' Gaye replied. 'Will you take me, Nason?' Her mind was clearly made up.

'Of course,' he answered, and looked at Etha expectantly.

She glanced back and forth between them.

'All right,' she conceded. 'I'll come with you.' Turning to the two smaller children, who had been fascinated by Nason's tale, she issued her instructions. 'Ia, you look after Natali. See that he doesn't get up to any mischief. We'll be back soon.'

'Yes, Mama.'

'Come on, then,' Etha said determinedly. 'Let's go and see what this Swordsman has to say for himself.'

Both houses were in the western section of the town, and the journey between them was possible by a roundabout route using several bridges. A boat would have been quicker but none was available, so they set out on foot, guiding Gaye as best they could, warning her of steps and obstacles. This was her fist time outside the house, and the process was difficult, time-consuming and a little frightening.

At last they reached their destination, finding the house empty. Everyone else was out helping in the more vulnerable parts of the town. Between them, Etha and Nason led Gaye up the stairs to the landing where the door to Bowen's room stood open. They saw the ghost immediately, standing on the far side of the chamber, apparently looking out of the window. Etha wondered briefly what it was he saw. All three entered the room.

'Are we here?' Gaye asked.

The ghost turned towards her, his expression a mixture of surprise and delight.

Do you hear me?

'Yes. Who are you?' Gaye sounded nervous.

'Can you hear him?' Nason asked, greatly excited, but Etha quietened him swiftly. She, like the boy, had heard only her daughter's words.

My name is of no importance. I have a message for you.

'From Bowen?'

No. I had hoped to speak to Bowen. But your skill is even greater.

'Is he alive?' Gaye asked. Although disappointed, she hoped she might learn something.

Bowen? Yes. He is not among us. That is all I can tell you.

'Oh.' Gaye sighed with relief at this small comfort, but wished she could have more. 'Nothing else?'

No.

'What is the message?' she asked, deciding bravely that the little she had gleaned would have to be enough for now.

The ghost's transparent face grew grave.

Zalys is in great danger. If you are to save it, the Stone Eye must be reawoken.

Gaye waited, but there was no more.

'Is that it?' she exclaimed. 'What do you mean?' She heard Nason gasp beside her. 'How are we supposed to do that?' she cried desperately.

'He's gone, sweetheart,' Etha told her gently. 'He's gone.'

'No!' Gaye protested. 'There must be more than that! Come back!'

'Here,' her mother said, guiding her to the bed. 'Sit down and tell me about it.'

Gaye obeyed, suddenly feeling very tired, and repeated the conversation.

'The Stone Eye?' Nason asked. 'By the Arena. Bowen talked about that too. What does it mean?'

'I don't know,' Gaye said helplessly, on the point of tears.

'Nason, fetch something to drink, please,' Etha said.

'Yes. of course.' He hurried to obey.

'Why am I so tired?' Gaye asked plaintively. 'What's he done to me?' She lay down on Bowen's bed and curled into a ball. By the time Nason returned she was fast asleep, with Etha sitting in a chair, on guard.

'What have you brought?' Etha asked quietly.

'Wine,' he whispered. 'Is that all right?'

'Perfect,' she replied, taking the goblet. 'Just what I need. We'll make her some tea when she wakes up.'

The afternoon tide had come and gone. The flooding had been less severe this time, because the wind had died away to an almost flat calm, but it had still been a long day for the residents of Nkosa. Dsordas, Fen and the others, all of them wet, tired and dirty, arrived home in their boats at the same time as Etha, Gaye and Nason arrived on foot. As they entered the courtyard, the front door flew open and Ia burst out, her cheeks tear-stained. She ran to her mother and threw her arms about her.

'Oh, Mama,' she cried, beginning to weep again. 'I fell asleep and Natali's gone. I can't find him anywhere!'

CHAPTER FOURTEEN

*A white owl flew past my balcony, the harbinger of death.
I do not fear to hear her call. I will fly with her one night,
when my time comes.*

As the convoy rumbled slowly across the Deadlands, the
baggage cart bumped and swayed on the rutted, dusty
track. Baylin shifted position for the hundredth time that
day and tried to tell himself that this was better than
walking. After his most recent, hectic journey, his horse
had been in no fit state to continue over the parched
tract of land that surrounded Xantium, and Baylin could
not afford to buy or hire another. Travelling alone across
the Deadlands was a risky proposition at the best of
times, and so he had eagerly accepted the offer of a ride
from the transport commander.

For a while the slow pace had suited his mood, but
now his back ached, his buttocks were numb and the
endless dust, churned up by the hooves of horses and
oxen, had parched his throat. For all that he was
returning with bad news, Baylin wished that the journey
was over.

Baylin Parr was an inveterate traveller who generally
put his time to good use, but who would willingly em-
bark on a voyage even without a commission. He had
left his home in Xantium more times than he could
remember and he always felt the same way; a keen
anticipation of new places, new experiences. His feelings
on returning, however, varied enormously. Sometimes
he was elated, if a job had been well done and he

was looking forward to his reward; at other times he was relieved – when he was weary or glad to be rid of a burden; occasionally he was already bored and could not wait to be off again. Today he felt an odd mixture of unease and irritation, with a touch of glee that kept him from growing morose. Baylin was an optimist at heart and preferred, whenever possible, to dwell upon the future's more pleasant aspects. The Emperor's anniversary celebrations would be in four days' time, and by then Baylin's unpleasant duties would be over, he would be able to forget his worries, and would have money in his pocket again. In all his travels, he had found no better place than Xantium for the provision of hedonistic delights.

Not that you'd think so looking at this! he thought ruefully. All about him, for many leagues in every direction, there was nothing but dry, red earth. The rolling, barren landscape of the Deadlands was oppressive, especially in the heat and dust of summer. Winter was not much better; the little rain that fell here merely produced sickly mud. Nothing grew here.

It had not always been so. Baylin knew that many years ago this area had been fertile, its produce supporting Xantium and a considerable rural population. But greed, the ever-increasing burdens of taxation and quirks of the weather had combined to ruin the land. In truth it was a man-made desert. The constantly increasing demands on its resources had led to overuse of the acreage. Too many animals grazed upon larger and larger fields as trees were cut down and the hedges that formed necessary boundaries were uprooted. Soon crops began to fail and animals grew sick. Some people left when they were unable to meet the tithes demanded by the city and their farms fell into ruin. Eventually a series of droughts dried out the earth and the once fertile topsoil blew away as dust storms scoured the land, blasting every living thing and coating the few remaining homes in a red-brown shroud.

The whole process had taken many years, but finally nothing remained, just a few tracks in the wasteland and the abandoned ruins of the last houses. These could be seen occasionally, their stones and broken timber bleached white by the sun, like skeletons in a desert. They served as reminders that an ill-prepared traveller could die crossing this land.

That the city should have survived at all in the midst of such desolation was remarkable, and was due to two main factors. The first of these was the prosaically named Brown River. This flowed from the mountains far to the west and meandered across the Deadlands, becoming warmer, dirtier and more sluggish as it went. Even so, it was still a formidable size when it reached Xantium, which was situated inside one large loop. A few tiny enclaves of cultivation still clung to the river banks but the water itself was the main resource for the city. A system of reservoirs, cisterns and filters, fed by pumps powered by animals or slaves, ensured that the population's needs were met.

The second reason for Xantium's survival was that its administrators had become adept at the ruthless exploitation of the empire. The city drew tribute from far and wide; money, food, goods of all kinds flowed into the capital from every region. Their arrival was enforced by military power and political pressure that only the far-reaching influence and trading prowess of a historically mighty empire could achieve. Every day dozens of convoys crossed the Deadlands or sailed slowly up the silt-laden, twisting river, bringing everything from essential provisions to the most bizarre luxuries – which Xantium demanded as of right. Baylin had no doubt that there had been even more traffic in the last month as the city prepared for the imminent festivities.

He sighed with relief as Xantium appeared upon the horizon at last. He had approached the Empire's heart countless times, from every direction and at all times of year, and was never less than impressed by the sight. The city rose like an impossible mountain, layer after layer revealed as Baylin drew closer, starting with the uppermost level – the lunatic maze known as The Spires – and ending with the massive city walls themselves. Once those were in sight, the journey was almost over.

From a distance, Xantium appeared almost unreal, resembling a huge cloud formation or a demented mirage, but it grew in substance with every step. By day, the first impression was of a white mass which later resolved into a bewildering collage of many different hues. At night, the first magical glow separated into a thousand points of light, as if one of the old gods had decorated a giant tree with stars.

Xantium lay on the southern bank of the river inside a long loop, so that for three quarters of its circumference the walls ran parallel to the water's edge, a hundred paces or so away. A traveller could only approach the city directly from the south, using either of the two Great Gates which stood in the wall, facing south and south-west respectively. All the trails over the northern half of the Deadlands led to one or other of two huge bridges which spanned the river, one to the east of the city, the other to the north-west. Each of these in turn led to one of the remaining city gates, massive structures of wood and metal set in stone archways and flanked by defensive towers. Such was the confidence of the city garrison that these gates were rarely closed, even at night.

The walls themselves were fashioned from pale grey stone whose crystalline structures made them glitter in sunlight – although this was often obscured by the ubiquitous red dust. They were truly massive, fully twenty paces high and ten paces thick at their base; the solid, immovable rock was surmounted with battlements and studded with even taller towers, and formed an imperfect circle, flattened from both the north-west and south-east sides. The walls had been built by the unimaginable labour of artisans and slaves centuries before, and had never been breached by any aggressor.

Indeed, no one had ever tried to lay siege to Xantium. The city's one weakness was its constant need for supplies from other parts of the Empire. But the massive reservoir to the north of the city, which lay on the easily defensible strip of land between the walls and the river – and which was itself protected by spur walls running from the city to the river bank – together with the vast cisterns within the walls, meant that water was controllable. In addition the city maintained several vast warehouses of food and other essential goods in case of emergency. While the citizens fed upon these stores, any besieging army would have to haul their own supplies many leagues across the Deadlands.

Within the boundary walls, Xantium was built upon a large conical hill, whose slopes grew increasingly steep as they neared the centre. The vast majority of the area was known as The Levels, where the land rose only gently and was itself marked with a few minor hills, such as the knoll on which the ruined temple of the old gods stood. Here the general populace lived, here were most of the storehouses, the Great Dice Hall, the Stadium and all the buildings of commerce and daily life. Generally speaking, The Levels was the poorest part of Xantium, except for sections around the gates where both army garrisons and merchants' guilds held sway, but the nearer to the centre – and therefore higher up the main hill – the more affluent the neighbourhood became. This culminated in the first of several ring-shaped terraces, each with its own outer wall, which formed the heart of the city. First came the area housing most of the merchants, minor nobility and anyone else of sufficient wealth or wits. It had no official name but was known to the citizens as The Circle – and was the place in which any businessman aspired to own a home. Inside that was The Domain, which housed the bulk of the city garrison and the vast bureaucratic apparatus of imperial administration. Arsenals, treasuries, barracks, endless official archives and storerooms made up a hive of activity which buzzed at all times of day or night. Here at least, Xantium truly never slept. The hostage enclave was wholly contained within The Domain, high on the eastern side of the circle, its uppermost boundary marked by the outer wall of the next ring – the imperial court itself. Here Southan, his family, his advisers and the most high-ranking nobles had their quarters.

As Chancellor, Verkho had extensive quarters, which were unique in that they cut across both the court and The Domain in a wedge-shaped section, which also bordered the hostage enclave at its northern end. This wedge housed the Chancellor's home and facilities for all his private pleasures as well as his work place and most of the Ministry of Information offices. From here it was possible to gain access to all parts of the city via hidden entrances, tunnels and secret rooms, as well as by the more conventional routes. If all the parts of Verkho's realm were counted as one, he had more space than even the Emperor.

At the very centre of the city, on the crown of the hill, lay a small circular area known as The Spires. This was an architectural folly of a long-dead Emperor, and was built on such a scale that it had never been worth the effort of replacing. Instead, it had simply been abandoned, and was now uninhabited except for birds and bats. There seemed no overall design to the place, the various pieces apparently thrown together in a bewildering jumble. Narrow, pointed spires rose like arrows into the sky next to solid square turrets whose ramparts crawled with grotesque carvings of men, goblins, beasts and huge insects. Severe straight lines stood next to sinuous, almost organic curves and arches that made the structure look as if part of it had actually grown, rather than being built. Saw-tooth edging on some of the spires provided roosts for many birds, while the endless buttresses and irregular openings in the masonry were home to colonies of bats.

At ground level, the pathways were like a maze, with

perspectives changing dramatically at every turn. It was even worse higher up; stairs led to dead ends, bridges crossed precipitous canyons only to end in bare rooms too small for more than one man, and unguarded walkways left even the bravest explorer prone to sudden vertigo.

It was the landscape of nightmare, the product of a diseased mind or of an army of insane artists. The children of the imperial court used to dare each other to play there but now even they were absent, banned by parental disapproval, fear – there had been several injuries and even a few deaths caused by falls or broken masonry – and, more importantly, by the barring of all known entrances. The Spires were left to moulder into dust.

Yet one mystery remained, to remind the inhabitants of Xantium of the strangeness of the place. Every so often, especially at times of great joy or sorrow, the bells in one of the deserted towers rang out. Some said they were being rung by the ghosts of the madmen who had built the place, but the sound was heard by all – and ghosts cannot move anything in the real world. Some thought that sorcery was responsible, suspecting Verkho of playing tricks on their hearing. Others claimed that it was merely the wind, or the settling of old stones that set the bells ringing, but they were unable to explain the uncanny timing of the peals. It was also suggested that a hermit still lived hidden within The Spires, but most people dismissed that theory as absurd. Only a very few knew the real truth, and each of them kept it secret for reasons of their own. Baylin had heard the bells on several occasions but was no nearer to understanding them than he had been when he had first stared up in wonder at The Spires as a small boy. He rather liked the mystery.

Just before setting camp the previous night, the convoy had met another heading in the opposite direction. They had reported that the bells had rung that very morning, and presumed that the Empress Ifryn must have given birth to her long-awaited child. The soldiers of the outward bound party were doubly irked at missing the celebrations that such an event would have engendered, because they already knew that they would be absent for the imperial anniversary in four days' time. However, those in Baylin's group, and the merchants who accompanied them, were delighted, anticipating a double celebration when they reached home.

Not long now, Baylin thought, staring ahead. From long experience, he reckoned that they would be at the gates by dusk, which suited him perfectly. A night in a soft bed, after some discreet celebrating of his own, would do something to offset the disagreeable task that faced him the next morning. There would be hell to pay if Kerrell found out that he had not reported immediately, but Baylin lived by his own rules. *I'm probably already too late to be of any use*, he thought glumly. He settled down again, trying to ignore the jolting of his cramped and bruised body.

Ifryn had been asleep when the bells rang the previous day, but Doneta had told her about it, and the Empress smiled, wondering how long it would be before her strange friend came to visit her. The answer came that afternoon.

Ifryn awoke from a comfortable doze to find Alasia standing at her bedside. She had no notion of how the other woman had arrived or how long she had been there – Alasia moved silently when she wished to. Doneta knew and trusted the visitor and had left the two women alone. When the Empress opened her eyes, Alasia curtseyed – an elaborate and formal, yet very graceful, movement. Ifryn had tried to make her friend stop greeting her this way, needing no such recognition of her status, but Alasia persisted. It was one of her many foibles.

'Well, what do you think?' Ifryn asked.

'He is healthy.'

Azari slept peacefully, unaware of the scrutiny of the two women. His tiny hands twitched.

'He is dreaming,' Alasia stated.

'I wonder what he's dreaming about?' the Empress said quietly.

'All dreams are about the past or future.'

'Future then,' Ifryn said, smiling. 'He hasn't got much past yet.'

'Past and future are all the same for him,' Alasia said.

It was one of the pronouncements which would have seemed absurd on anyone else's lips, but seemed quite natural coming from Alasia. Ifryn did not question her judgement or her meaning, but looked sharply at her friend, trying to guess her mood. She seemed very solemn.

As always, Alasia's physical appearance was striking and – to some – unnerving. Her smooth skin was very pale, almost translucent, and her hair was wispy and white-blond. Even her eyes were almost colourless, the irises having just the faintest touch of pale blue. The fact that she was small and painfully thin – almost like an undernourished child – meant that she sometimes seemed to have no real existence at all. She was a creature of air and light – a gossamer sprite whom the wind could blow away.

And yet Ifryn knew that Alasia was a woman, some years older than herself, whose hands were warm and comforting and who brought with her an atmosphere of love and brightness. Very few people shared the Empress' perception, however. All others saw was a pale madwoman with no more substance than a ghost, who appeared out of nowhere at the most unexpected times, and who spoke in riddles. Most of those who knew of her existence avoided her when they could; their loss, as far as Ifryn was concerned.

Alasia's origins were equally obscure. It was said that she was a distant cousin of Southan on his mother's side, but no one even knew her family name. She was just there, one of Xantium's many eccentricities.

'Thank you for ringing the bells,' Ifryn said.

'My duty,' Alasia whispered, still looking at the baby.

'You have no duty to me,' the Empress told her. Or to him.'

'My duty to the bells,' her friend replied gravely, as if this explained everything.

'Oh.' Ifryn eyed her thoughtfully. 'You seem sad today. Are you all right?'

'You will have a visitor,' Alasia replied, as though this answered the question.

'Who?' the Empress asked with a puzzled frown. 'I receive many visitors.'

'I will watch over him,' Alasia remarked.

Ifryn did not know whether her friend was referring to Azari or to the unknown visitor. The memory of an earlier time rose up in her mind, of Alasia watching over one of her daughters. It had been very soon after the birth of Delmege, and in all the activity and pain that had entailed, Ifryn had not noticed that Vrila, who was then only a year and a half old, was poorly. She was soon near to panic, however, as the little girl's condition worsened rapidly. Vrila became cold, lost her natural colour, had difficulty in breathing and coughed incessantly. The physicians were helpless. Ifryn became frantic, torn between the needs of her newborn baby and the sick child. She was on the point of exhaustion when Alasia arrived, unasked and unexpected, and took Vrila from her. The girl grew calm almost immediately, slept peacefully for a while, and then took solid food for the first time in three days. The court physicians were suspicious, but Ifryn saw only her daughter's improvement and insisted that Alasia stayed. The pale woman nursed Vrila throughout the night, allowing the Empress some much needed rest; in the morning the girl was so much better that she was barely recognizable as the same child. Alasia left then, saying that her work was done.

Vrila emerged stronger and healthier from the ordeal, and had rarely been ill since.

Ifryn also remembered, with a shudder, that a young healer then working in the treasury had been brought to see her that day. It was the first time she had met Verkho. He had looked at Vrila with glittering eyes, announced that she would recover, then left. He subsequently claimed some credit for the girl's return to health, but Ifryn knew the truth. Nevertheless, others, including Southan, found it easier to believe in the powers of a proven healer than in those of a madwoman – and it may well have been a turning point in Verkho's career. He had certainly come a long way since that day.

'But he *is* healthy?' Ifryn queried, her natural concern for the baby making her forget the promised visitor.

'Yes,' Alasia confirmed, then paused as the sound of movement came from the outer chamber. 'I will take my leave now.'

As Alasia curtseyed again, Azari woke and began to cry. Ifryn leaned over and picked him up, holding her son tenderly. When she looked up, Alasia was gone.

That night, Ifryn dreamt of her father for the first time in years. He stood over her, smiling, his eyes filled with tears of pride as he watched her and his sleeping grandson. Fyles appeared strong and happy, but something made Ifryn feel afraid. *All dreams are about the past or future.*

In her dream, she sat up in bed and opened her eyes. Her father was still there, still smiling, but there was a painful lump in Ifryn's throat.

You will have a visitor.

Her father spoke, a single word.

'Farewell.'

Ifryn woke, finding herself sitting up in bed. An odd light was fading at the foot of her bed, and Fyles' goodbye still echoed in her ears. Her cheeks were wet with tears.

CHAPTER FIFTEEN

In times past, mourners at a funeral vied with each other to wear the most elaborate clothes. To come enrobed in finery was a sign of wealth and status because, by ancient tradition, the garments would all be burnt that same night. The spirits of the dead would then choose their raiment from the smoke.

At my funeral I will appear wreathed in flame. Can I not be allowed one last joke?

'So the wanderer returns.' Kerrell looked up from his desk as Baylin came in, and smiled.

'I thought to find you at the practice yards,' the traveller said. It had always been Kerrell's habit to spend the early part of each morning training with his soldiers.

'A general's life is all paperwork,' Kerrell answered ruefully. 'Look at these reports.'

'Anything from Idiron?' Baylin asked, naming Ifryn's old homeland.

'Not recently. Why?' The general studied his old friend for a few moments.

'Some things are best not entrusted to the Farspeakers, I suppose,' Baylin said ominously.

'You've come from there?' Kerrell asked. 'Trouble?'

'Yes. When I left, the place was in a mess. Fyles is ill and, with Ifryn here, the succession is in a shambles. If the in-fighting between the nobles gets any worse, the country will disintegrate into factions and leave it wide open from the east.' He had no need to add that the eastern borders of the Empire were already under pressure from barbarian tribes. 'One of the possible claimants to the throne was even suggesting an alliance with the easterners, breaking away from the Empire,' Baylin added.

'Gods!' Kerrell exclaimed. 'That would leave Tilesia and Agrea isolated. The whole eastern front could collapse.'

'Like a house of dust,' the traveller agreed laconically.

'Why haven't we heard this before?' the general demanded angrily. 'What's the matter with our people out there?'

'They're under some pressure,' Baylin remarked mildly.

'That's what they're paid for!' Kerrell controlled his anger and asked, 'When did you leave?'

'Twenty-three days ago.'

'You made good time, then.'

'For the most part, yes,' Baylin replied smugly. 'A lot might have happened since then, though.'

Kerrell nodded, considering.

'The Chancellor will want to hear this,' he decided. 'And the Emperor, given the circumstances. I'd better arrange it.'

'I was afraid you'd say that,' the traveller said resignedly.

A short while later, the four men were seated in Verkho's office.

'You arrived last night,' the Chancellor pointed out without preamble. 'Why have you waited until now?'

Kerrell looked sharply at his friend but Baylin was ready with his response.

'I was drunk,' he answered simply. 'I was in a lot of pain for the last part of the journey. I wouldn't have been able to present a proper report.'

Baylin was the only man Kerrell knew who could lie with a straight face while looking into Verkho's eyes.

Perhaps, in some strange way, the Chancellor admired the traveller's nerve and thus tolerated his aberrant behaviour.

'I trust you can do so now,' Southan said coolly.

'Yes, sire,' Baylin answered, then went on to give the other men a detailed account of the situation in Idiron. Both Southan and Kerrell interrupted him every so often but Verkho remained silent, listening intently. Only he showed no emotion or alarm.

'Why has all this escaped our notice?' Southan demanded, turning to his Chancellor when Baylin had finished.

'The army should have been on the march a month ago,' Kerrell added.

'There is no need for military intervention at present,' Verkho assured them calmly. 'I have been kept in constant touch with the situation in Idiron, and I believe the problems have been resolved.'

'Why did you not keep us informed?' the Emperor asked coldly.

'I had no wish to burden you or the Empress while she was in the last stages of her pregnancy,' Verkho answered. 'Worry about her father might have caused difficulties. And I felt that any significant movement of our army would have been detrimental to the Empire as a whole.'

'Kindly explain that,' Kerrell put in harshly.

'First, let me bring you up to date,' Verkho said evenly. 'I regret to inform you that King Fyles died during the night.'

'Gods,' Southan breathed.

'But the succession is secure,' the Chancellor went on. 'The hot-headed baron who suggested an alliance with the east is also dead. Fyles' cousin, Latif, has taken the throne unopposed and the nobility are now united behind him. They are mindful of the threat from the east and remain vigilant. Our borders are secure.'

'More by luck than judgement,' Kerrell growled.

'I beg to differ, General,' Verkho responded complacently. 'If the Imperial Army had indeed been on its way to Idiron a month ago, it would have made civil war there much more likely. Knowing that the barbarians would be repulsed by your reinforcements, the Idirians would have been free to slaughter each other. As it was, knowing that they would have to face our common enemy alone, they were forced to compromise and choose a new leader. We have thus saved ourselves men, time and expense – and they have learnt a valuable lesson.'

'With a little help from you,' Southan remarked. They all knew who had been responsible for the death of the treacherous baron, and who had made it clear that no reinforcements would be sent from Xantium. Verkho bowed his head in acknowledgement.

'I appreciate your concern for the Empress, Chancellor,' Southan went on, 'but in future you will keep me informed of such events.' It was a weak protest, which Verkho appeared to accept meekly, but both knew it was of no real consequence. Southan rose to his feet. 'I must tell Ifryn,' he said, his reluctance obvious.

Kerrell also stood.

'I hope your strategy works in the long term, Chancellor,' he said gruffly. 'Idiron is the key to the whole eastern border.'

'I am aware of that, General,' Verkho replied. 'But the Empire also includes many more places where your men and your talents can be utilized to greater effect. Our perils are not confined to the east.'

He's right about that, Kerrell thought ruefully.

The meeting was at an end.

Once outside, Kerrell and Baylin took their leave of the preoccupied Emperor and strode away quickly.

'Damn the man!' Kerrell exclaimed, once they were far enough away. 'Nothing ever touches him.'

'I wonder how long he'd have kept it secret if I hadn't come along?' Baylin said.

'*Were* you drunk last night?' the general asked.

'No.' The traveller grinned. 'But I will be tonight.'

'I may join you,' Kerrell said, but his face was sad as he thought of Ifryn.

The Empress was out of bed, seated at her dressing table by the open window, while Doneta brushed her hair. She looked round as Southan came in, and he saw the grief in her eyes. The maid, needing no urging, slipped quietly from the room, and Ifryn stood up slowly as her husband came towards her. He folded her tenderly in his arms.

'I have some bad news, my love,' he whispered, but she did not respond and Southan took a deep breath. 'Your father died last night.'

'I know,' she said in a small voice.

'Who told you?' he asked in surprise.

'He came to see me, to say goodbye.' She had started to cry again.

Southan held her, feeling helpless, not knowing what to say.

Another meeting took place later that morning. Alasia was alone with her thoughts in one of her spire-top eyries when she heard footsteps on the stairs below. She knew it was the stranger. No one else came here.

He greeted her with a smile, taking her pale hand in his own and kissing it. He was always gallant, although Alasia knew that this was through courtesy rather than affection for her. She had not seen him for a long time. His visits were always unannounced, yet she was never surprised. They were part of her life now. It never occurred to her to wonder how he found her or even how he reached the secluded realm of The Spires. The stranger moved silently and in secret, and she had told no one of his existence. Alasia had known his real name once, but he called himself something else now.

'How are you?' she asked politely. It was always important to be polite.

'I am well,' the Swordsman answered. 'And you?'

'It is a fine day to sit in the wind,' she replied, looking down at the city spread out below them. 'You have questions for me?'

'Yes. Is all well with the Emperor's son?'

'The child is healthy,' she said happily, remembering. 'I have seen to it.'

The stranger nodded, frowning.

'The guards on the central quarters have been doubled,' he went on. 'Do you know why?'

'They are of no account.'

'They make my task more difficult,' the Swordsman said thoughtfully. 'Are they being over cautious now that Azari has been born, or do they know something?' He was talking to himself and expected no answer. He got none. 'One of the hostages is missing,' he went on, trying a different tack. 'Sagar Folegandros. Do you know where he is?'

'In the cells under Verkho's quarters in The Domain,' Alasia answered promptly.

Her visitor swore softly. That would make getting him out very difficult; even contacting him would be hard. But neither was impossible. It had been done before, after all.

'Thank you.' He never thought to consider how Alasia knew such things but simply accepted the information. She had never been wrong before. 'I must go now.'

Alasia held out her hand and the Swordsman kissed it once more, brushing it lightly with his lips.

Like a butterfly, Alasia thought. She did not watch him go, but in her mind the stranger flew away.

Ifryn stood looking out of her bedchamber window. Her private apartments were in the upper part of the court circle, on the western side of the hill. The window gave her a wide view over the western part of the city and the wasteland beyond, and it had always seemed symbolic to Ifryn that it should be so. She looked away from her old

151

homeland, a sign of her abandonment of her earlier life. The idea had never seemed more poignant.

Down below, throughout all the levels of Xantium, preparations for the forthcoming revelries were under way. She could see some of the banners from where she stood. But Ifryn had never felt less like celebrating. How could she dance and laugh beside a funeral pyre? She had not seen her father since his last official visit to the city three years ago, and she had never returned to Idiron. Fyles – his ghost? – had come to say farewell, but she had been unable to respond. Two days ago, she had brought a new life into the world, and now one had left it – and she was powerless to bring him back. She felt so tired.

There was a quiet knock at the door and Doneta's head peered round.

'You have a visitor,' she said, making Ifryn's heart thump at the repetition of those fateful words. 'Would you rather be alone?'

'Who is it?'

'General Kerrell.'

The Empress felt a tremor of gladness, despite her grief.

'Send him in, please.'

Ifryn stayed by the window, gazing into space. Kerrell came in and slowly crossed the room behind her, until he stood at her side.

'I'm sorry, my lady,' he said quietly.

He laid one hand over her own as it rested on the sill, and Ifryn stared, feeling a surge of warmth run through her body, her wrist tingling. Kerrell rarely allowed himself even the most fleeting physical contact with the Empress, and only did so now because of the extreme nature of the circumstances. Even so he withdrew quickly and they looked at each other. He saw her red-rimmed eyes and wanted, more than anything in the world, to take her in his arms and comfort her, to make it all right. She too was within an instant of throwing herself into his embrace, but both of them had been schooled by long years of severe self-control and they stayed apart, each fighting a lonely battle.

'Southan asked me to come, my lady,' he began hesitantly. 'He is unavoidably detained by imperial business and regrets that he cannot be with you himself.' In fact, Southan felt helpless, not knowing how to deal with his wife's mourning, and so had sent her friend in his place. It was a measure of the complete trust that Kerrell and his position engendered that he should be invited to visit the Empress' bedchamber alone – and nothing thought of it. However, his formal words broke the suffocating tension between them.

'He thought I . . .' the general began.

'Oh, Kerrell,' she exclaimed. 'I feel so lost.'

'I know,' he said soberly. 'I still miss my own father.'

'But you were with him when he died,' she sighed. 'At least you had a chance to say farewell.'

'Only by chance, my lady. It could easily have been otherwise. Not many are so fortunate.'

Falteringly, fighting tears as she spoke, Ifryn told him of her dream.

'How did he seem?' Kerrell asked.

'Happy. Strong. As I remember him from my childhood.'

'Take comfort from that then,' he told her. 'He's given you a sign that he is well, whichever world he is in now.'

'I hope so.' How was it, Ifryn wondered, that she could talk so easily with Kerrell about such matters, but not with her own husband? How could he understand her better than the father of her children? In her heart she knew that answer, but dared not admit it openly – even to herself.

'Can I get you anything?' he asked, noticing her preoccupation. 'A drink perhaps?'

Ifryn shook her head and waved him to a chair. They sat facing each other in silence for a few moments.

'Do you have any news of my mother?' she asked eventually.

'She is well but grieving, naturally,' Kerrell answered. 'Latif has the throne now and is treating her with all honour.' From the transcribed reports of the Far-speakers, which he had now read, this was as near the truth as it was possible to know. 'I believe she has plans to come here after the funeral,' he added, hoping this news would cheer her a little.

The Empress reacted quite differently, however.

'I won't even be able to go to his funeral,' she said, her tears welling up again. 'To burn my robes in his honour.'

Kerrell went down on one knee before her, his face showing the agony he felt on her behalf.

'You cannot do what is not possible,' he told her. 'Don't cry, my lady.'

'I need to,' she sobbed defiantly.

Still kneeling, Kerrell bowed his head, no longer able to contain the hurt her distress caused him.

For a few moments, all was still. Then he glanced up again to see her staring at him in astonishment. Ifryn had never seen him display his emotions so openly, and she ached for them both. There was danger even in looking into his overflowing eyes now.

'It's a wonder we haven't set Azari off,' she said, smiling bravely.

As if on cue, there was a rustling from the baby's cot and the indrawn breath that preceded his wail.

'I'd better go,' Kerrell said reluctantly.

'Wipe your face before you do,' she told him, handing him a kerchief.

He retreated, dabbing at his face. At the door, he hesitated.

'I have not been much help, my lady,' he said quietly. 'I apologize.'

'You've been more help than you'll ever know,' Ifryn replied earnestly. 'Send Doneta in, please.'

Kerrell nodded gratefully and went out. Doneta's expression when she entered was carefully neutral.

CHAPTER SIXTEEN

When gods play, men suffer. It took mankind centuries to arrive at this philosophy, and only decades to forget.

I watch him, *know the portents. What happens when men dare to play in the realm of gods?*

'I hope you have a good reason for bringing me to this ridiculous place.' Clavia glanced scornfully round the ruins of the old temple.

'Bear with me, my dear,' Verkho replied, smiling. 'I trust the climb was not too taxing.'

Clavia had just stepped from an enclosed hand-carriage, which had been borne on poles by four muscular servants. Thus she travelled privately and without effort. She gave her half-brother a cool, dismissive look, ignoring his sarcasm.

'Well?' she demanded. 'Why are we here?'

'Come with me.' Verkho led the way towards the abandoned altar at the centre of the ruins.

'Returning to the haunts of old triumphs?' Clavia suggested pointedly. 'I do hope you're not planning to conjure up more of your pretty images. They don't impress me. And if I've heard the story of your first appearance here once, I've heard it a thousand times.'

'It was quite a show for a novice,' Verkho said, laughing. 'But I have learnt so much more since then.'

He looked about appreciatively, while Clavia yawned, deliberately flaunting her boredom.

'You know, sister, the old pantheon can teach us much,' he remarked. 'Their legends could be our truths.'

'Stop talking gibberish,' she said disgustedly.

'Meyu, Elcar, Zidon . . . they knew how to roll the dice,' Verkho went on, undeterred. 'Whole worlds would change hands, spring into being or be annihilated on the chance of one throw. Our games must seem pale and uninteresting to them. No wonder they've lost interest in us.'

'And us in them,' Clavia added sourly.

'Never say so!' he exclaimed. 'They were magnificent. Such recklessness, such intrigue, such knowledge! Who better to model oneself upon? Even Gar, who lost everything, is an example of their spirit, their eternal guile.'

'"If you gamble with gods . . ."' she quoted.

'"You lose,"' Verkho completed for her. 'Or do you? Shall we put it to the test?'

'What madness are you planning?' Clavia demanded. She was worried now; Verkho was in a strange mood, his eyes glittering even more than usual.

'I can see that I should get to the point,' he said, laughing. 'I have brought you here to witness a little experiment, a demonstration, if you like.' He paused, laying a hand on the pitted surface of the altar. 'Those images you mentioned earlier, they are just that – memories embedded in the fabric of this place, in the stone itself. They are trivial things, easily drawn forth, but serving no purpose. They have no substance of their own. True ghosts, on the other hand, are spirits of people who were once in this world. They are as real as you or I. Therefore they can be put to work.'

Clavia snorted derisively.

'You have finally gone mad,' she stated. 'Ghosts can't affect anything, nor can you predict when they'll appear. How can you put them to work?'

'What if I said to you that I could not only predict but summon?' he asked.

'I'd say you were lying.' Clavia hesitated, uncertain now. She had underestimated her half-brother before.

'All it takes is a little knowledge,' the Chancellor went on, 'and a source of power.'

'A source?'

'It's simple enough,' he replied, obviously pleased by her confusion. 'Something that was connected to a particular person while they were in this world. Something imbued with the patterns of their life, their emotions, their memories. A hook to draw them back.'

'Such as?' she asked, no longer so dismissive.

'A ring, perhaps,' he suggested.

Verkho held out his hand. In his palm was a man's ring, a large flat emerald set in a thick gold band. Clavia took it carefully and weighed it in her hand, studying the craftsmanship.

'It's very beautiful,' she said covetously.

'Beautiful, old and valuable,' he agreed. 'But more than that. Look at the inscription inside the band.'

'Io RK. Aiamm, Lias, Eccoi. IA,' Clavia read, squinting at the tiny lettering.

'To RK. Love, Life, Forever. IA,' Verkho translated.

'I know that much of the old language, brother!' she snapped irritably.

'It was a gift from one Ileana Areta to her husband-to-be, Rowan Kihan,' the Chancellor went on placidly. 'He wore it all his married life. It should have gone to his grave with him, but no doubt one of his heirs became greedy.'

Clavia felt his gaze upon her, expecting some comment, but wisely said nothing and Verkho let it pass. She gave the ring back to him.

'What's all this leading to?'

'Rowan Kihan is buried here,' he replied. 'Right below your feet in fact.'

Clavia stepped aside quickly and looked down at the worn flagstone on which she had been standing. The tomb's inscription was mostly illegible, but it was just possible to make out the name once she knew what she was looking for.

'Shall we see if he is still in residence?' Verkho asked.

For a moment, she thought he meant to open the grave but then realized what he intended and felt a sudden chill. She stepped back, distancing herself from the 'experiment'.

Verkho fixed his gaze upon the ring, his eyes flashing as he focused his thoughts. He muttered under his breath, but Clavia could hear none of the words. Momentary images flashed and fluttered about him, but they were discarded instantly and none was seen clearly. The air began to sparkle and shift as if in a sudden heat haze – but Clavia felt her skin grow cold.

A spectral hand appeared above the stone, writhing and grasping at nothing. Then slowly a man emerged, struggling against the invisible forces which seemed, quite literally, to be dragging him up from the grave. His face was contorted with pain and anger.

At last the ghost stood in the open. He quietened, giving up his fight against the unnatural powers of his enemy, and met Verkho's stare with a gaze of implacable hatred. The Chancellor remained unmoved and even smiled, holding up the ring as if to taunt his victim. Rowan's face contorted with anguish and he snatched at his long-lost treasure. Verkho laughed as the spectral hand passed impotently through his own. The ghost was speaking now, silent curses spat into the void. Otherwise he stood still, held rigid by unseen bonds.

In spite of herself, Clavia was impressed – but she had no intention of admitting it.

'So you've proved your point, brother,' she said. 'What does this gain us? He's here but he can't do anything.'

'Shall I make him dance?' Verkho asked unexpectedly. He twisted the ring in his fingers, muttering again. Rowan's shade performed a grotesque parody of courtly dance steps, his limbs moving jerkily, like a poorly operated puppet.

'Or smile?' Verkho was enjoying this.

The spectre's face twisted into a painful rictus, resembling the grin of a madman.

'Or do handstands perhaps?'

'Enough!' Clavia cried, feeling almost sorry for the dead man. 'You've proved your point!'

'My dear, I never knew you were prey to finer feelings,' Verkho purred in mock surprise. 'You have concealed your weakness well.'

'Such tricks are still useless,' she retorted angrily. 'He dances in another world.'

'But what if he were to speak in this one?' he asked.

'You know that's . . .' Clavia began, but got no further.

Rowan's lips moved and a deep voice boomed out, reverberating among the ancient stones.

'Repent, ye sinners, and worship me!'

For a moment, Clavia was stunned into silence, but then she realized what had happened.

'*You* did that!' she accused.

'Of course,' Verkho admitted, then bowed to the ghost with sarcastic courtesy. 'You may go now.'

The phantasm sank back into the ground and Clavia felt the warmth of the sun on her skin once more. She noticed that her half-brother was perspiring slightly, but she could not tell whether this was from excitement or exertion. She struggled to hide her own relief at the end of the experiment.

'So what does this ventriloquism achieve?' she asked caustically.

'Here, nothing,' Verkho replied. 'But think of the re-action if, say, Southan's father returned with advice for his son. Or the late, lamented King Fyles visited his daughter with instructions about the upbringing of his grandson. Would they achieve nothing? Would they be ignored?'

'Wouldn't people see through such deceptions?'

'People believe what they want to believe,' he told her, almost childishly gleeful at the thought of the possibilities.

159

'And items pertinent to such people would be easy enough to come by,' Clavia said cautiously, finally catching up with her brother's thinking.

'Of course, my technique will improve with practice,' Verkho went on enthusiastically. 'I will make their movements more natural.'

'More life-like, you mean,' she commented, smiling.

'Aptly put,' he agreed, laughing. 'And once I am proficient, I can go on to greater things.'

'Such as?'

'I used this ring to wake Rowan Kihan from his sleep in the world of the dead,' the Chancellor replied, his eyes glittering. 'What if I were to tell you that I had located a ring, metaphorically speaking of course, that once belonged to a god?'

CHAPTER SEVENTEEN

*The mind is a dark labyrinth, full of monstrous creatures
and burning sprites. Their moves are restricted by the
rules of the game, but each uses its own weapons – talon
and beak, horn and flame, tooth and claw. Brute power
and speed. All thought is thus. It can achieve nothing but
carnage for friend and foe alike. Unless . . .*

Unless some higher order directs the game.

*I have glimpsed the light at the heart of the dark maze,
but I will never reach it now.*

The day after his successful experiment at the old
temple was the eve of the anniversary celebrations, and
Verkho hosted a banquet for a select few in his
sumptuous personal chambers. The eleven male guests
were either senior officials in the Ministry of Information
or high-ranking officers in the military liaison division –
all except one, a relatively junior officer named Claros,
who was both amazed and nervous about his inclusion in
such exalted company. The twelve women were there,
in the Chancellor's own words, 'for decorative purposes', and would be available to provide anything
their temporary partners might require. They were all
beautiful, but Verkho had also chosen them for their
mental abilities; he liked a genuinely appreciative
audience for his conversation. Several of the women had
worked for him before in a variety of capacities;
intelligence work was far from being an exclusively male
preserve. Moreover, although indiscretion was unlikely
at his own table, the women provided Verkho with a

fascinating means of monitoring his subordinates.

The room in which they dined was one of a warren of halls and chambers given over to all manner of pleasures. Among these were several bedchambers, furnished to suit all tastes, a small theatre for musical and dramatic presentations, and several gaming rooms. The dining hall was furnished in typically luxurious style. An exquisite mahogany table stood upon the polished wooden floor, the walls were decorated with tapestries, paintings and valuable rugs, and the vaulted ceiling was hung with banners and adorned with delicate carvings. A group of musicians played sweetly from a balcony at one end of the room while servants brought in the various courses of the meal and the wines which accompanied them. The food served in Verkho's quarters was known to be unsurpassed in all the Empire, delicacies from many countries supplemented by rare fresh vegetables and fruit, combined by expert chefs and served with delicious and imaginative sauces. For those who appreciated such things, the wines were even more remarkable; they had been hand picked from the best vintages housed in the extensive imperial cellars, and added the final luxurious touch to the meal.

The talk flowed as they ate, with Verkho, quite naturally, dominating proceedings from his position at the head of the long table. He held court with consummate ease, relating amusing anecdotes and giving his guests the benefit of his opinion on all manner of topics. At the same time, like a perfect host, he ensured that everyone there had the chance to participate where appropriate, and listened to their words attentively. To have been invited to this table was a sign of the Chancellor's approval and of a successful career, and everyone contributed eagerly – although they were all careful not to offend their master. They needed no confirmation of where ultimate knowledge – and therefore ultimate power – lay, a point reinforced by an incident during the meal.

As one of the many courses was brought in, one of the guests realized that he had been served something quite different from all the rest. At first he thought it must be a mistake, but was too embarrassed to question the silent waiters. Then he began to worry that some subtle point was being made at his expense. It was not unknown for Verkho's underlings to be publicly chastised and punished at such events – and the Chancellor's knowledge of poisons reputedly encompassed those venoms which do far worse than merely kill. The official desperately searched his memory for any recent act which might have given offence. However, after observing his troubled guest with restrained amusement for a few moments, Verkho relented.

'My apologies, Deion,' he began. 'It was only when you arrived this evening that I realized that the dish the rest of us are eating would not agree with you. The mushrooms would have produced an allergic reaction in your blood – and would have made you quite lose interest in the rest of the meal,' he added jovially. 'I trust our hurriedly prepared replacement is satisfactory.'

'Most certainly, Chancellor,' Deion replied, almost comical in his relief.

As the meal neared its end, Verkho became even more expansive. Alcohol did not affect him – unless he chose to allow it to do so – but he seemed especially merry this night. When the conversation turned to politics and the impossibility of democracy as a viable system of government, Verkho decided not to join the one-sided debate but to provide a rare glimpse into his own past.

'The Triphenians came closest to making democracy work,' he declared, and smiled at the polite expressions of disbelief around the table. 'Yes, it's true,' he insisted. 'I saw their government at work when I was young. It was very educational.' He sipped his wine, remembering. 'Their elders would elect a representative from each town and village, and these emissaries would gather together in the capital whenever an important decision had to be taken. They would debate the matter back and forth, then take a vote. But that was not the end of it. Later in the day, they all got roaring drunk – then held a second debate and took a second vote. If the result was the same, the decision stood. But if it was reversed, they waited until the next morning, when they were all sober again, and started anew. The whole process continued until two votes in a row – one sober, one drunken – were in agreement. The process could sometimes take several days.'

'If their wine was as good as this,' one of the officers declared, holding up his goblet, 'then I'm not surprised.'

'What a ridiculous system!' Deion said, amid the subsequent laughter.

'It has its merits,' Verkho responded. 'Different aspects of the human mind are dominant when one is sober or drunk. Balancing both has its advantages.'

'But so cumbersome!' Deion persisted. 'How did anything ever get done?'

'The Triphenians were perhaps not the fastest thinkers in the world,' his host admitted, 'but they were persistent. One of their generals once spent six days trying to destroy the gates of an enemy city with massive battering rams. His men suffered terrible losses as the defenders rained arrows, burning oil and rocks on to their heads, and they succeeded only in breaking off a few splinters from the gates. Finally, the commander of the besieged town took pity on them and opened the gates – revealing the solid rock behind them. The gates were false. The soldiers had been trying to smash through six paces of solid stone with a tree trunk.'

'But why did the commander reveal the trick?' another officer asked. 'They would have gone on trying for ever.'

'Quite correct,' Verkho agreed, 'but the town's supplies were already running low. They could not afford to wait for ever and the castellan calculated, correctly, that the general's shame at having been caught by such a trick would drive him to despair. The besieging army withdrew that night, slinking away like a beaten dog in the darkness. They never came back.'

'Would that all *our* enemies were that stupid,' one of the soldiers commented gravely, provoking nods of agreement.

'Come, gentlemen, this is a time for celebration,' the Chancellor remonstrated gently. 'Tonight the perils of the Empire are far away. I do not diminish them. In fact, if it were not for us,' he continued, indicating the whole gathering, 'it would be in a sorry state. But we are strong, if all our borders are not. Without information, even the many skills of our redoubtable General Kerrell and his staff would not save the Empire from crumbling. But that is where we have the advantage over all the barbarians beyond the rim of civilization. They may be cunning, but they will never see the wider view. Their realms are limited; ours is the whole world.'

'Long may it remain so!' Claros exclaimed, feeling that he must make his voice heard.

Verkho eyed the younger man thoughtfully, with a hint of amusement beneath his gaze that made his guest nervous.

'We may drink to such a toast,' the Chancellor said, raising his goblet, 'but we need have no fear on that score. Through my efforts – *our* efforts – the Empire is harnessing many sources of power far beyond the scope of our enemy's minds. Here in Xantium we already have the greatest concentration of talents that has ever been seen in this world, and more arrive each day. The Far-speakers are only the most obvious. You all know from our own work of various developments in these fields. Together, there is nothing we cannot achieve.'

A ministry official spoke up eagerly as his master finished, wanting to display his own special knowledge.

'We are even beginning to understand communication with the world of ghosts,' he said. 'Have you news of the boy from Zalys?'

'Ah, yes. Bowen Folegandros,' Verkho replied. 'I look forward to his arrival. Even a bungler like Farrag couldn't help but notice him. With luck the boy will be on the mainland within a day or two.'

'There were a lot of ghosts at the old temple late yesterday,' the woman at the far end of the table said. She was one of Verkho's favourites, and felt secure in her place of honour. 'People were talking. I was sure you had something to do with it,' she added with an ingratiating smile.

'Perhaps, my dear.' The Chancellor's smug expression hid the fact that he did not know why the ghosts had congregated after his departure. 'But there is still much to learn before we understand all.'

'Can such beings help us fight the barbarians?' one of the most senior officers asked.

'Who knows?' Verkho answered. 'Our foes are superstitious, so perhaps . . . In any case, knowledge is power. We will know how to use it when the time is right.'

'Some of our enemies are closer to home,' another soldier remarked.

Unexpectedly, Verkho's face lit up.

'But that is the essence of the game!' he asserted. 'Without opponents such as the Swordsman to sharpen our wits, how could we ever expect to deal with greater challenges? It would almost be a disappointment if we were to catch him now – not that I expect you to stop trying!'

He laughed and the others joined in, grateful for the Chancellor's good mood. Most of them knew Verkho well enough to realize that his evident relish for his work was due to the success of recent plans – or to those schemes he was about to put into operation. The game, as he called it, was everything to Verkho.

'We must always be vigilant,' he continued. 'Watching for the chance to learn and then to act. The festivities tomorrow will present many such opportunities.' His gaze fixed suddenly on Claros and he stared at him with piercing certainty, although his smile never faded.

'How do *you* intend to spend the day, Captain?'

Claros' face had turned chalk white with sudden terror. *Here it comes*, he thought helplessly. *Oh gods, preserve me!*

'I . . . I had not decided, my lord,' he stammered, aware that everyone at the table was looking at him.

'You must have wondered why you were asked here tonight,' Verkho remarked. Although his tone remained pleasant, his eyes held the look of a feral cat contemplating a cornered mouse.

Claros managed to nod, his throat having closed up. He was suddenly acutely aware that he had drunk too much for his own good.

'It has come to my attention, Captain,' the Chancellor went on, 'that you are in considerable debt – in breach of the long held traditions of your calling.'

The room grew very still and silent. Claros swallowed painfully and waited to hear his doom. The other guests looked away from him now, distancing themselves from the condemned man. Even the woman at his side had drawn away.

'However, I have decided to allow you to make amends,' his tormentor said, and Claros looked up in sudden wild hope, his heart hammering. 'You will perform a special task for me tomorrow,' Verkho explained. 'One perfectly suited to your talents.'

'Anything,' the young man croaked.

'I will give you the details before we retire,' the Chancellor concluded, then looked around at the apprehensive faces of his guests. 'Come, ladies and gentlemen,' he cried, reverting to his earlier genial tone, 'we have more wine to finish. Corton will never forgive me if I return any of his chosen bottles. He would only let me have a few of the older vintages as it was!'

There were hesitant smiles round the table as goblets were raised and refilled. Corton Magna, the master of the imperial wine cellars, could never have refused Verkho anything of course – the very idea was absurd – but his miserly and high-handed attitude was legendary within court circles.

Corton stared at the labyrinth board, his long-fingered hand poised delicately above one of the major pieces, as though he were about to make a move. His thin lips moved silently, as if he were whispering to himself, but otherwise he was quite still. He had held this position for some time now, much to the disgust of his opponent, who had wandered off and was now shuffling around at the far end of the room, muttering to himself. Grongar, who had but the one name, was a self-proclaimed barbarian and found waiting difficult. He came back to the table now and grimaced.

'You'd better move soon or we'll miss the stuffin' anniversary celebrations altogether!' he growled.

'They are not until tomorrow,' Corton told him shortly.

'Exactly!' Grongar stomped off again, but Corton's concentration did not waver. He would take the rest of the night to make his move if he wanted to.

The two men were so unalike that they were practically opposites, and the fact that they spent so much time together baffled all who knew them. The wine-master was delicately built, ascetically thin both in body and limb, with close-cropped grey hair, and was always neatly dressed in sober attire. His approach to life was fastidious. He had lived in Xantium all his life and was unmarried. As far as anyone knew, he had never kept the company of any woman, although he was nearly forty years old. Love – indeed, any untidy emotion – seemed alien to him. When it came to his job, however, he was without peer. He had taken over the post as wine-master from his father – who had been similarly obsessed, to the point where people wondered how he had found the time to sire a child – and he took it very seriously. What Corton did not know about wine was not only not worth knowing, it was probably wrong. Little else mattered to him, although he did appreciate music, poetry and good food – to enhance the wine. He was the ultimate aesthete.

Grongar, on the other hand, could not remotely be called such. He was built, as he himself had been heard to remark, like an upright pig. His torso was almost as wide as it was tall and his limbs were short and thick. His face and head – and presumably the other parts of his body, which were hidden by his stained and threadbare tunic – were almost entirely covered by a long, matted thatch of light brown hair, from which protruded an oversized, flat, red nose. His mouth and ears were invisible except when he tried to remove some debris from them, and his feet were almost as filthy as the battered leather sandals which encased them. His origins were obscure, his age indeterminate, and he was evasive on the subject of marriage. If all his stories were to be believed, however, he had known a great many women intimately – and would, given the slightest encouragement, describe his adventures in such graphic and foul-mouthed detail that all but the strongest-stomached would blanch or blush.

He earned his living as court master of hounds. These beasts, most of whom would terrify any sane human being, loved him as one of their own – and he made sure that anyone who dared meddle with them unwisely would think twice before doing so again. Hunting was obviously impossible on the Deadlands, and the dogs were kept for ceremonial and guard duties, as well as for the occasional wagering fight in the Stadium, but Grongar still referred to them as hunting hounds. One of his favourite pastimes was getting hopelessly drunk – on ale, even though he believed that Xantium's brews were like piss-water compared to the beer of his remote homeland – and singing incomprehensible old hunting songs in a loud, off-key voice, accompanied by the howling hounds. Grongar considered wine too fancy for his taste, and never touched the stuff. This was probably just as well – his habit of 'acquiring' things would not have sat well with Corton had it been applied to the imperial cellars.

About the only thing the two had in common was a passion for the game of labyrinth. This was a complicated battle game, played with pieces of varying strengths and abilities on a chequered board of a hundred alternately black and white squares. Yet even in this their approaches were quite different. Corton's strategy was to consider each possible move, analyse any possible developments beyond that, and only then to make his choice. Grongar played by instinct, reacting almost instantly and analysing nothing. It was a constant source of irritation to Corton that the barbarian won as many games as he did.

And yet, against all the odds, their friendship remained strong, a bond neither understood but neither questioned.

They played their games in series. The first to win ten games outright treated the other to a keg of ale or a special bottle of wine, and then they would start again. However, the oft-repeated wager was only secondary to their enjoyment. The battle was what mattered. And the game currently in progress mattered more than most because the tally was now nine apiece, and the winner would not only claim the prize but also bragging rights for the next few days. Of course, Corton's bragging took the form of discreet satisfaction and a few well chosen quips, but Grongar was not so reticent – and with the prospect of plentiful free beer on the morrow, the idea of his friend's drunken boasting was painful to Corton's noble sensibilities.

At last, he completed his calculations and moved his eagle two squares forward, then sat back triumphantly. Grongar stomped up immediately and took one look at the board.

'All that time, just for *that*?' he exclaimed derisively. 'Stuff me!'

He picked up his own bull and moved diagonally one space, banging it down so hard that the board shook and one of Corton's sprites fell over. He quickly righted it, wondering why he had not foreseen his opponent's move – which seemed so obvious now – while Grongar ambled away again.

'Come on,' he muttered. 'I'm stuffin' thirsty.'

Corton did not hear him; he was too busy working out all the new combinations. Surely Grongar's move had been a mistake. That was why he hadn't considered it. There must be an opening somewhere! He remained still, crouched over the board, and did not even notice that his friend was no longer in the lamplit room.

Grongar returned some time later. He had found a tankard of ale somewhere, foam dribbling unnoticed over the rim, and he drank noisily as he reached the table by way of announcing his arrival.

'Not moved yet then?' he remarked carelessly. 'I've known noble ladies that'd lift their skirts faster than you play.'

Corton ignored him.

'Someone was asking for you in the kitchens,' the barbarian went on. 'He's probably following me here.' He took another swig of beer and belched volcanically. The meaning of his words finally filtered through to Corton.

'What?' he asked, looking up.

'Nervous looking young chap,' Grongar replied, affecting a wholly incongruous, refined accent. 'Name of Claros.'

CHAPTER EIGHTEEN

Why do men revere dragons so? They are just one more race which has become extinct, like the long-tusked river-horse or the flightless jarlock bird. I have no doubt that the storytellers have embellished their tales; a little fire here, a few steel-hard scales there, heroes vanquished and virgins devoured by the score. But dragons remain dead, for all their mythic fame.

Who will turn our deeds into legend once we are gone? Once mankind is extinct?

It was well past midnight when Claros finally located the out-of-the-way storeroom where the two friends played their endless games. The captain knocked, and entered without waiting for an invitation. He strode up to Corton, who was still seated at the table – although he had not been able to concentrate properly once he knew that someone was looking for him. Claros did not notice Grongar, who had been standing behind the door when he came in.

'Master Corton,' Claros began, speaking far louder than was necessary. 'I have need of your services.'

'At this hour?' The wine-master looked incredulous. 'The cellars are locked. And I have a full day of duties tomorrow.'

'This cannot wait,' Claros said, his face wet with perspiration.

'I'm afraid it will have to, Captain,' Corton told him icily.

'I need a bottle of Embarragio,' the younger man

172

insisted, his voice rising to a shout. 'And now!'

Corton's face could not have registered any greater shock if he had been asked to supply bottled sunlight or pickled pieces of the moon.

'Ridiculous!' he spluttered, colour rising in his pale cheeks. 'How dare you ask for such a thing. There are only three bottles of Embarragio left in the entire world, and there will never be any more.'

The vineyard in question had been near the centre of what was now the Deadlands, and its last vintage had been produced over sixty years ago.

'I know,' Claros snapped. 'I have need of only the best.'

'You think I am going to hand over something so rare, so expensive, merely at your request?' Corton's disdain was unmistakable. 'Please leave now, Captain, before you make an even bigger fool of yourself.'

'You leave me no alternative then,' Claros threatened, and drew forth a dagger. Corton stood quickly, knocking the table and tipping his chair over. He stared at the blade in disbelief.

'Take me to the cellars and get me that bottle,' Claros ordered.

During this exchange, Grongar had remained silent and still. As it grew heated he moved closer, treading remarkably quietly, and when the soldier drew his knife, the barbarian responded in kind. In the blink of an eye, he transferred his beer mug to his left hand and held a thin steel blade in his right. Unlike everything else in his possession, the metal was shiny and well kept, and it rested easily in his gnarled fist. The needle sharp point jabbed delicately near the base of Claros' spine.

'Don't move,' Grongar told him succinctly.

The captain went rigid. He was already close to breaking point.

'Give me one good reason,' Grongar said conversationally, 'why I should let you keep your dinner *inside* your stomach.'

173

'I . . . It's for . . . for someone very important,' Claros stammered.

'Who?' Corton asked.

'I . . . I can't tell you.'

'Then I fear I shall have to introduce you to your liver,' Grongar remarked happily. 'How would you like it? Sliced or minced?'

'No! Please listen,' Claros said desperately.

'I dislike listening to someone who threatens me with a knife,' Corton pointed out.

'I'm sorry.' The soldier let the blade fall from his shaking hand. 'Let me explain.'

'This had better be good,' Grongar commented gravely. 'You've spoilt our game. I've gutted men for less.'

Corton glanced down at the board. Sure enough, the pieces were spread in chaos, sent spinning by his own abrupt movement.

'I was winning too, you ignorant stuffer!' Grongar complained bitterly.

That night, Ifryn dreamt that she was alone in a forest clearing. It was beautiful in the sunlight but she was afraid, knowing that she was lost, and unable to decide which way to go. All the trees seemed to hide dark and perilous pathways.

Help me.

A horseman appeared out of nowhere. One moment there was nothing, the next she could hear the creaking of the tack, smell the sweat of the tall brown horse and see its white breath clouding in the cool morning air. She looked up at the rider and saw Kerrell. He was naked to the waist, the muscles of his chest and shoulders shiny with a dew of perspiration. His hair was tied back in his usual style, and he was smiling down at her.

Time stood still. How could he be real?

Is it really you?

Ifryn stepped forward, stretched out and touched the

coarse material of his leggings. It felt rough and strong, the flesh beneath warm and very real.

He reached out a hand to help her up. She took it in her own . . .

. . . and woke up, hot, and with her heart fluttering like a frightened bird.

Southan Azari, heir to the throne of the Xantic Empire, made his first public appearance the next morning, aged five days. He lay in his mother's arms as she and Southan sat on a balcony atop the court walls, acknowledging the processions in The Domain below. They heard all manner of music, saw entertainments of all kinds – fire-eaters, jugglers, acrobats and clowns; guild representatives decked out in their finery trooped by, followed by units of the Imperial Army in ceremonial uniforms, their horses groomed to perfection. It was a colourful, noisy scene, full of planned pageantry and spontaneous gaiety, but Ifryn could not enjoy it. Beneath her graciously smiling exterior, her emotions were in turmoil. Already saddened by her father's death and worried about the possible threats to her baby son, she was further confused and a little frightened by the passions raised by her dream. She was still tired from childbirth and lack of sleep, and viewed the celebrations only as an ordeal to be survived. Hence she retired as soon as protocol permitted and took no further part in the day's events – until the grand banquet that evening, from which there was no escape.

However, the rest of the city was determined to make the most of the occasion. Such a perfect excuse for a riot of pleasure was not to be missed. The streets were thronged with people in bright costumes; there was dancing everywhere, music, food and drink. Entertainers plied their craft – and so did the pickpockets. Stalls selling every kind of merchandise – from cheap souvenirs to supposedly aphrodisiac elixirs – had sprung up on every corner, and there were fairs in every open space with games of skill, strength and luck. And, of course, for those who wanted to chance their hand for more serious stakes, the Great Dice Hall hosted tournaments in every imaginable form of gambling. Fortunes were won and lost on the roll of dice, the turn of a card or a spin of one of the giant carousels. There were also smaller tables, some of them in private rooms, for more intimate contests of labyrinth, gammon and emperors, on which both the participants and spectators wagered enthusiastically.

There were other contests elsewhere, most notably in the Stadium, and these too provided ample opportunity for betting on the outcome, and attracted vast and vociferous audiences. First came the athletic events – foot races, weightlifting and a variety of gymnastics – between the champions of four teams. Most of the inhabitants of Xantium supported one team or the other out of family tradition, habit or guild loyalty. The rivalry between the spectators often spilled over into violence, fuelled by drink and the passions engendered by winning and losing, but this was all considered part of the event.

Most of the athletes were slaves, owned and trained by powerful families for the precise purpose of winning their chosen events and thus bringing honour – and money – to the household and their team. The best of them lived circumscribed but pampered lives, basking in the brief glory of triumph and the adulation of the mob.

Next came the military contests, between equally competitive army units. Those who won the team events – archery, spear-throwing, wrestling and so on – would carry champions' pennants together with their unit's colours until the next competition. Although not arousing such fervour in the crowds, these skills were contested just as fiercely and watched by a knowledgeable and appreciative audience – not least by their fellow soldiers and officers.

But the climax of a day of spectacle in the Stadium was undoubtedly provided by the slaughtermen. These were a group of seemingly fearless men who, armed with only a single weapon of their choice, would individually face wild and ferocious beasts in a battle to the death. Enraged bulls, starving wolves, specially bred fighting dogs, wild boar – which were underestimated only by the most ignorant spectators – and even giant, poisonous snakes were butchered with routine flamboyance and crowd-pleasing savagery until the sand-covered floor of the slaughter-pit was splotched and discoloured with drying blood. A spitting, snarling and infuriated bear had provided the best entertainment of the day so far by killing two slaughtermen with crushing blows from its mighty paws, before it too met its bloody end. But this penultimate bout was soon forgotten when the last was announced. The crowd had been promised something special, something unique – and they were not to be disappointed.

The criers who announced the beast to the crowd called it a genuine sea-dragon, and informed them that because its teeth carried a fatal venom, any bite from its mighty jaws would be deadly. The creature had been discovered swimming off a remote island in the southern archipelago and brought back in a steel cage by a naval captain – but only after it had killed and eaten three of his crew.

A clamour of anticipation grew until the beast was released. When it waddled into the pit there were gasps of amazement. Some cynics had been expecting a large crocodile – something exotic but hardly unique – but this truly was a monster. It most resembled a lizard grown to an outrageous size – its tail alone was longer than the height of a tall man. Its four legs were massively thick, ending in heavy black claws, and its snout ended in square jaws housing a multitude of dirty, vicious fangs. Although clearly a creature of the land rather than the sea, it had no wings like the mythical dragons of old. It did not breathe fire and it was not covered in scales, but its skin looked tougher than leather and was the mottled colour of toads. Small red eyes looked around lazily, unconcerned by the uproar. No one had seen anything like *this* before.

Slaughtermen were a pragmatic breed, answering only to themselves, and many chose their bouts wisely, prolonging a lucrative career beyond the bounds of youthful vigour. However, their reputations were important, and new challenges were few and far between. In any case, the prize money being offered for slaying the dragon was so vast that there was no shortage of volunteers.

The first was a young champion whose handsome face, blond locks and bulging, tattooed muscles made him a favourite with the crowd. It was not until he jumped down into the pit that anyone realized just how fast the dragon could move. It charged immediately, fangs gaping, moving at an incredible speed for something of such bulk. The champion evaded two attacks narrowly, and even got in two glancing blows with his heavy spear, but it was soon clear that he was running for his life. Eventually he was cornered and, with a single snap of its terrible jaws and an almost casual toss of its neck, the dragon tore away one of his legs and flipped the mutilated body halfway across the pit. Within moments the man was dead and half devoured.

By now the crowd was in a frenzy, calling for their own favourites to take on the monster. The odds in the wagering had already changed dramatically.

Four more of the best slaughtermen were soon dead, while the dragon was hardly scratched. The place was in an uproar, but the pit-master knew that the situation was desperately serious. They could not afford to lose more good men – and those that were left were no longer willing to face the beast. But it was unthinkable that the creature should survive; the crowd would run riot. So they called up archers to fire on the dragon, and although at first the mob whistled and shouted their disapproval, this novel sort of archery soon became a sport in its own right. Most arrows glanced off the thick hide but a few struck home, enraging the dragon and drawing cheers from the spectators. Before long the wagering was back in full swing, with individual bowmen being encouraged by their backers.

Finally, with perhaps a dozen shafts protruding from its body, each wound seeping thick, dark blood, the dragon appeared to slow down. And then a lucky shot pierced one mad, red eye. The creature screamed, thrashing about in enraged agony. The next slaughterman saw his opportunity and jumped down, his two-handed sword ready, to face the crippled beast. Even so it was a good long contest, as the man had to avoid even a scratch from the bloody, poisonous teeth. But at last the heavy blade crashed down, splitting the monster's skull in two. It collapsed, twitched massively for a moment, then died, as the swordsman accepted the crowd's roar of approval.

CHAPTER NINETEEN

Every person tells a story. Some are no more than a brief paragraph, while others are as long as an epic, but each is complete, with a beginning, a middle and an end. There are those told as adventures or romances, while others range from tragedy to farce, but most are a mixture of all these things and more. We all write our own stories, even the epilogues.

I have no need of books.

Corton and Grongar did not meet again until late afternoon. They had both been fully occupied with official duties but now they had a spare hour, and retreated to their usual chamber. Grongar had found the time to get drunk while Corton was cold sober, but they were both having second thoughts about Claros.

'Were we right to believe him, do you think?' Corton murmured.

'Dunno,' his friend replied. 'S'only bottle'f wine.'

Corton was used to Grongar's appalling lack of sensibilities, and made no comment.

'That's not the point,' he said. 'He seemed so desperate.'

'F'you'd wagered somethin' you couldn't get, you'd be desp'rate too,' the barbarian argued. ''Specially if you were an Information Offisher. They're not s'posed t'gamble, you know,' he added gravely.

'What possessed him to do such a thing?' the wine-master wondered aloud.

'Honour! There is nothing else!' Grongar declaimed

loudly. 'Petty stuffin' noblemen're all th'same. Idiots, ev'ry one. Who says th'Empress even likes that muck?'

'The Empress Ifryn has good taste,' Corton told him coolly. 'Unlike some. She could not fail to appreciate such a gift.'

'Hah! From her own cellars,' Grongar snorted. 'Some gift!' He had taken the precaution of bringing a small keg of his own favourite beverage with him and now went to refill his tankard.

'And if he hadn't done as he'd vowed when he lost the bet,' Corton went on, as though trying to convince himself, 'he'd have lost everything. His position, status, family . . . for a man like that it would have been complete and utter ruin. He might even have killed himself.'

'Good riddansh,' Grongar muttered through a foam-flecked moustache.

'You wouldn't want a man's life on your conscience?' his friend exclaimed.

'What conscience?' The barbarian laughed, then belched loudly.

'Even *you* would never renege on a gambling debt!' Corton declared. It was as close to a sacred law as Xantium possessed.

'No,' Grongar admitted sagely. 'But I'm not dumb 'nough to make such a bet in first place. Wha's wrong with money? He promised you plenty las' night. Whether you ever see any's 'nother matter.'

'Don't you trust his word?'

'Don't trust anyone trained by Verkho.'

'Then why did you go along with my decision last night?'

Grongar grinned mischievously, affording his companion a rare glimpse of discoloured teeth.

'I wanted t'see you suffer,' he explained slyly. 'Partin' with your preshious wine.'

'Why?' Corton demanded, feeling thoroughly aggrieved.

'I know you knocked the game over on purpose,'

Grongar accused. 'You knew I was on the verge of winning.' Suddenly he didn't seem so drunk any more.

'Rubbish!' the wine-master cried.

The two men stared angrily at each other, then burst out laughing and, by tacit agreement, began setting out the pieces for a new game. Honour would be satisfied.

The grand banquet had already lasted several hours, and Ifryn was very weary. She had eaten sparingly of the excellent food and drunk only water, but she still felt bloated. She consoled herself with the thought that there was only one more ordeal to get through before she could retire gracefully, the recent birth of her son giving her ample excuse to forego the dancing that was to follow. All she had to do now was join her husband in accepting the gifts which court officials deemed the most worthy from among the hundreds of petitioners who wanted to mark the occasion personally. Most of these offerings would be from merchants or craftsmen hopeful of future imperial patronage, but others would be tributes from all parts of the Empire and, even in her weariness, Ifryn could not help but be a little excited. It reminded her of her childhood and the name-day celebrations for a young, carefree princess – whom she hardly recognized as herself any more. She wondered if there would be anything from Idiron. It would be like a gift from her father's grave.

All the guests at the banquet sat at the outer sides of long tables set out along three sides of a large rectangle, leaving the area inside free for entertainers and later for the gift-bearers. Beyond the tables the Great Hall housed a constant bustle as servants went back and forth, replenishing the tables. The walls were brightly decorated, with some of the banners reaching all the way up to the rafters. The whole scene was illuminated by hundreds of oil lamps, which outshone the moonlight coming through the windows set just below the vaulted, wooden roof.

At last the procession began. The gifts were all brought forward for inspection and, once formal approval had been given, the chosen items were then discreetly taken away by treasury officials. The cavalcade was nearing its end when Claros entered, with an attendant, his eyes fixed upon Ifryn. When he was a few paces away from the table, he knelt abruptly, to the consternation of the officials in attendance.

'My Emperor, a humble captain begs a special boon,' Claros said quickly. 'Grant me leave to speak.'

'Proceed.' Southan was obviously curious.

'This wine came my way in a game of honour, your majesty,' the soldier began. This was a polite way of saying he had won it in a wager. 'But I accepted it on condition that it should be tasted by one whose qualities are rarer and more admired than those of the vintage.' He waved his servant forward to place a tray on the table. 'I have had the wine decanted, as is proper, your majesty.'

Southan picked up the bottle, which now contained only a few dark dregs, and studied the label.

'Embarragio!' he exclaimed. 'This is a rare gift indeed, Captain.'

Claros bowed his head in acknowledgement.

'My contentment and my honour would be complete,' he stated, 'if the Empress Ifryn would agree to taste the wine, for there is none in all the world so honoured and admired by all.'

Ifryn stared at the still kneeling man, touched by his sentiments and by his shy sincerity, even though she was made uncomfortable by such fulsome compliments. She glanced at her husband who was looking at her, his eyebrows raised.

'Well, my dear? This is nectar indeed.' He added softly, 'A little will not harm the baby – and it will do you good!'

'Thank you, Captain,' she said warmly. 'I will taste the wine.'

A fresh goblet was produced and Claros rose to pour the dark, red liquid himself, then retreated deferentially. Ifryn took the cup, sniffed the rich, heady aroma and touched the rim to her lips. When Verkho's hand caught her wrist she started, spilling a few drops of wine.

'Chancellor?' she queried, looking up in shock.

'What is this?' Southan demanded. 'How dare you?'

'Allow me, sire,' the Chancellor said calmly. He took the goblet from Ifryn and tasted the wine himself. A cold look came into his eyes as he turned to face Claros.

'It is as I feared,' he said. 'The wine is poisoned!'

At his words, many of the guests rose to their feet and a group of guards, already alert, came forward quickly.

'What treachery is this?' Southan roared, standing himself.

Claros appeared terrified, but made no effort to escape. Instead he fell to one knee again as the soldiers closed in upon him.

'I swear, I did not know it was poisoned!' he declared, his eyes wide with frightened innocence. He knew his part well and now had no choice but to play it to the full. 'I . . . I was forced to bring the wine by another. *He* is the real traitor.'

'Who?' Southan demanded.

'I do not know his real name,' Claros replied. 'He calls himself the Swordsman.'

'He's lying!' Kerrell's voice rang out above the clamour that this claim provoked.

'No. I swear it's true,' Claros went on desperately. 'I was deep in debt. For one of my rank . . .' and he glanced at Verkho, '. . . it was fatal folly. He forced me to this.'

'I warned you of such, my lord,' Verkho told Southan, then turned back to the hapless captain. 'Where do we find this Swordsman?'

'I do not know,' Claros answered. 'As the gods bear witness.'

'Your actions have earned your death,' the Emperor grated.

'Let my men take him,' Verkho spoke up quickly. 'We will learn the truth before he dies.'

'Think yourself lucky I do not slay you here and now,' Southan said, spitting fury with every word. 'Take him away.'

Ifryn had sat, stunned and silent, throughout the exchange, trapped in the eye of a storm she did not understand. She wanted to cry, but could not.

At the Chancellor's signal, four guards marched the prisoner away. At the door, Verkho himself took the squad leader aside and issued some quiet instructions. The soldier nodded, then strode after his men.

'Down to the dungeons, lads,' the leader ordered when they reached Verkho's quarters.

'No!' Claros cried. 'That's not right. You're to let me go.'

The soldiers laughed.

'Why would we do that, sonny?'

'Verkho promised . . . if I did this for him . . .' A terrible doubt crept into his voice. 'I would leave Xantium a free man, all my debts paid.'

'Oh, I don't think you need worry about your debts,' the leader replied, prompting more laughter as they continued down the stone stairway.

'Please, you must believe me,' Claros pleaded, desperate now. 'Verkho arranged all this. He believes that the Swordsman is a high-ranking member of the court – or that he had friends there – and . . . this was to help expose him. I was just play-acting. The wine wasn't poisoned!'

'A pretty story,' his guard remarked sarcastically.

'But true, I swear.'

'You don't seriously expect me to believe that?'

'Ask Verkho, he'll tell you!' Claros begged. 'Please.'

The squad leader's smile faded and his expression became grim.

'Shall I tell you what the Chancellor said to me just now? Eh?' he growled.

Wide-eyed and white-faced, Claros could only nod. Inside he was screaming. From further down the corridor, someone else was shouting, unheeded.

'He said,' the soldier went on. '"Make his death painful but not *too* slow. I already know all I need."'

Verkho returned to the top table and picked up the crystal jug. Red wine winked seductively in the lamp-light.

'This will not harm me.' He sniffed thoughtfully. 'And, if my suspicions are correct, this particular poison would have had no permanent effect upon the Empress, but the consequences for your son could have been serious.'

'Are you all right?' Southan was seated beside his wife, holding her hands – which were cold and trembling. Ifryn nodded, but her face was pale and she could not speak. Verkho fetched a clean cup and filled it with white wine.

'Drink a little,' he suggested. 'It will help to calm you.'

Ifryn obediently raised the goblet to her lips, but was again prevented from drinking as a flickering shadow swooped down from the rafters and flew straight into her face. She screamed, dropping the goblet and spilling its contents on the ground. In an instant, the bat disappeared into the darkness above, but Ifryn had had enough. She could not cope with any more. Southan escorted her back to her apartments, but then had to return to complete the day's formalities. The Empress retired thankfully to her room.

Alasia was waiting for her there, her pale eyes full of worry.

CHAPTER TWENTY

The shadows draw closer, staining the sky like wine. They paint a rainbow of a single hue, an archway the colour of blood.
   Who will march through this liquid gate?
   Must I drink from the poisoned cup of augury again?

'You were actually there?' Grongar asked enviously.

'Of course,' Corton replied. 'Occasions such as last night's banquet . . .'

'Spare me the professional pride,' the barbarian cut in. 'Just tell me what happened.'

'Claros came in with the wine, just as he said he would,' his friend began.

'The same bottle?'

'Certainly,' Corton answered. 'Quite properly, the stewards called me to the preparation room to verify it. It was decanted under my supervision.'

'Go on,' Grongar said impatiently.

'He practically begged Ifryn to drink, but then Verkho stopped her and announced that it was poisoned!'

Grongar chuckled.

'I bet that caused a pretty stir,' he remarked.

'This is no laughing matter,' Corton rebuked him. 'Then Claros swore that he'd been put up to it by the Swordsman, and that he hadn't known it was poisoned. He said he was forced into it because he was in debt.'

'A slight variation on the story he told us,' Grongar commented wryly.

187

'Then Verkho's men took him away,' the wine-master concluded.

'I'm glad I'm not in his shoes!'

'But questions are bound to be asked,' Corton added anxiously. 'I may be implicated.'

'Could he have got the wine anywhere else?'

'No. The chances of a bottle surviving and my not knowing about it are negligible.'

'But not impossible?'

Professional pride battled with common sense.

'No,' Corton admitted finally. 'Not completely impossible.'

'Then it may never lead to you,' Grongar deduced. 'And even if it does, the truth will suffice. All they can accuse you of is stupidity.'

'And of helping a traitor!'

'Unknown to you.'

'But there's more to it than that,' Corton said quietly. 'I tasted the wine before it was sent in.'

'And are you all right?' Grongar asked, genuinely concerned.

'I'm fine. No ill-effects at all,' Corton replied. 'I'd stake my reputation on the fact that the wine had not been tampered with in any way.'

'Oh.' Grongar's hirsute face grew solemn as the significance of his friend's words sank in. 'I'd keep quiet about that if I were you.'

In another part of the city, Sagar Folegandros sat on his pallet, not knowing what was happening in the world above, and wondered how to keep himself from going insane. He clung to the theory that if he was still able to formulate the question – Am I mad? – then, to some degree at least, his sanity remained intact.

He reckoned that he had been incarcerated in the dark cell for six days or more. Daylight was an all but forgotten phenomenon and his only means of counting time were the signals of his own body; the desire to sleep, hunger, thirst – none of which he now trusted. More certain than any of these, however, were his meals, which he had decided were delivered once a day. The food was unappetizing, but became more palatable as time passed. It was delivered by an ugly young man in a ragged uniform, who had about him the air of another prisoner rather than that of a gaoler.

When the young man had first appeared, Sagar desperately tried to get him to talk, to get some information out of him, some hope . . . But he had received only incoherent grunts in return. When he tried again, the man simply shoved the tray through the lower opening and then stared at him through the slit in the door. He opened his mouth wide and gaped contemptuously at Sagar, who recoiled in disgust and horror. The man's tongue had been cut out.

After that, Sagar's pleading was less enthusiastic and he got no response at all. His life became one long, unbearable wait, with nothing to do except brood – until a few hours ago. He had been on the point of falling into his usual uneasy sleep when he heard the heavy footsteps of several men, and voices – one pleading, others laughing and arguing. Sagar could not tell what they were saying, but could hear the fear in the prisoner's voice. Even so, he could not resist calling out, hoping for a response, any response. But he was ignored.

Later he heard prolonged screaming, but when that stopped, the footsteps retreated again and this time he did not call out. He felt sick. Perhaps it was better to be forgotten. Yet now, only a few, interminable hours later, he was already longing to hear a voice, a footstep, anything . . . He hovered near the door, waiting for the gaoler. Even he seemed attractive company now, a link – however tenuous – with the living, breathing world.

A light flickered in the corridor and Sagar jumped up, peering as far round as the slit in the door allowed, but there was no sign of the gaoler. Instead, he saw two ghosts, the man who had visited his cell before and a tiny woman. They stood a few paces away, talking earnestly to each other, and their presence was the source of the pale luminescence. His initial disappointment was replaced by intrigue – anything that relieved his deadly routine was welcome – and then he stiffened when he realized that he could hear them whispering. That wasn't possible! The words themselves weren't audible, but the faint susurration was unmistakable.

'Hey!' Sagar shouted.

The woman turned her pale face to look at him. *She heard me!*

'Help me, please!' he cried. 'Tell me what's going on. Why am I here?' But she raised a finger to her lips and looked away.

'Please,' Sagar entreated. 'You can hear me. Talk to me!'

For answer the man vanished into thin air and the woman drifted away like a luminous cloud, disappearing from his narrow field of vision.

'No!' Sagar yelled. 'Come back!'

He felt himself crumple with despair, and began to cry softly. Then he heard the clumping of his gaoler's boots on the stone floor and knew why the spectres had left.

Clavia was with her half-brother, discussing the events of the previous day, when the Focus came in and handed Verkho a message. Evidently it was in a special code, because she had taken the trouble to write it down. She showed no interest in the contents and left silently as Verkho scanned the lines. He beamed with satisfaction.

'Something to make up for yesterday's mixed fortunes?' Clavia enquired.

'Something to make them pale into insignificance,' he replied. 'This calls for a celebration – and I have just the thing!' He opened a cabinet and took out a crystal jug, pouring two glasses of rich red wine. Clavia eyed her glass suspiciously, but Verkho laughed. 'Drink,' he instructed. 'It's exquisite – and the worst it will do is give you a rather impressive hangover.'

'What are we celebrating?' she asked.

'The talisman was brought ashore this morning at Brighthaven,' he answered, hardly able to contain his excitement. 'In a few days it will be in my hands!'

CHAPTER TWENTY-ONE

What instinct draws stone to stone, eye to eye? Is it possible to hear so much, yet see so little? The wind is full of words – gossip and speculation – but an innocent ear catches nothing.

Sleep, little one. My friends will guard your flight.

Natali hadn't felt safe, especially after Ia went to sleep and couldn't talk to him any more. All he could hear then were the voices that weren't there – the silly ones, the laughing ones, others crying, and the one who frightened him, the one who was always asking questions.

He had gone out to look for his mother, knowing that he would be safe with her, but the voices had followed him and he hadn't known where to go. Natali did not remember how he reached the southern edge of the town but it was then that he saw the cart, waiting by the bridge. It had high sides but the back was down, forming a ramp, and the inside was full of loose hay. It looked warm and soft and inviting. Perhaps it would be safe in there.

Natali climbed up, tunnelled into the grass and lay still. The voices followed him, but he was comforted by the darkness and the dry, musty smell. He dozed – and then his world was invaded by squealing monsters, burrowing and nuzzling, bouncing erratically as their hooves scrabbled on the wooden floor, and bringing with them a pungent smell. Natali squealed too in surprise, but no one heard him amid the din and the animals did him no harm, apparently accepting him as one of their own. He felt their rough, hairy skin and wet, inquisitive snouts, and his fear turned to pleasure. He did not even notice when the back of the cart was lifted and the patient donkey coaxed into movement. Natali felt warm and happy with his new friends, but he could hear men's voices now – voices that were real – and he was afraid to show himself in case what he had done was naughty. He lay still and listened.

'Gods, what a filthy day,' the driver moaned.

'Only the sow drowned,' his companion pointed out. 'Not the family. And we saved the litter.'

'If they'd had any sense they'd've moved her up too,' the other grumbled, refusing to be comforted.

'You know Junio had a mind of her own. And at least there'll be plenty of bacon now.'

'I just hope this lot survive.'

'Why shouldn't they? They're big enough now – and they'll be better off out of town.'

The driver grunted and twitched the reins irritably. The cart rumbled on in the evening quiet; Natali's head began to fill with questions again and he shivered, wondering if these men were his friends.

'We'd have been all right if it hadn't been for those eddies,' the first man said eventually, still intent on airing his grievances. 'Damn these tides!'

'There've been a lot of strange currents recently,' the other remarked. 'All the fishermen are complaining.'

'I sometimes think Zalys is doomed,' the driver said gloomily. 'Things are getting worse all the time.'

His companion laughed.

'You always were a pessimistic sod, brother. Let's stop at Runton's tavern on the way and cheer you up.'

'It'll take more than ale. We need the help of the gods.'

'You haven't been listening to that daft talk, have you? You'll have us sacrificing virgins next.'

'You do ill to mock!' the grumbler snapped, angry

now. 'All this started when people stopped believing. I remember when . . .'

'Spare me,' the other interrupted. 'I'll rely on my own strength, not on garbled legends.'

'Will your strength save Nkosa from drowning? Rid us of Farrag and his kind? You've not done much so far.'

'Time will tell,' his companion answered, growing heated himself now. 'At least I'm trying to do something, not abdicating the responsibility to gods!'

There was a long silence. Natali had not understood much of what had been said, but he knew that both men were angry and so was even more determined to remain hidden. Eventually the driver spoke again, sounding obdurate and sullen.

'There've been calls for a gathering at the Arena, for some of the old rites. If it happens, I'm going.'

'Suit yourself,' his companion answered resignedly. 'Just don't expect miracles. There's nothing there now except a lot of old rocks.'

'We'll see.'

Some time later, the cart rolled into a small village.

'Do you want that drink or not?' A measure of good humour had returned to the man's voice.

'Might as well, now that we're here,' the driver replied grudgingly.

The donkey came to a halt, and the cart shook as the men left the seat and jumped to the ground. Natali listened to their retreating voices, then stood up gingerly and looked around. It was almost dark but he did not hesitate. Saying goodbye to his new friends, he climbed carefully out of the cart. He left the village by a side path and set off up a hill, his little legs moving determinedly. He knew now where he would be safe.

Farrag was almost beside himself with glee, although of course he could not show it in front of the Far-speaker. His experiment was producing its first positive results.

'Well, Iceman, what are you hearing now?'

The boy responded with an ear-splitting, inhuman squealing which both shocked and angered Farrag.

'Have you gone mad?' The Marshal wondered if the Far-speaker had had a complete breakdown; that sometimes happened if they were pushed too hard.

'Pigs,' Iceman replied simply, his eyes faraway.

'What?'

'He's with pigs. Lots of them.'

Farrag shook his many-eyed head. The depths to which these island peasants sank never ceased to amaze him. Pigs indeed! And this boy had seemed one of the brighter prospects.

'Movement,' Iceman reported.

The bare cell was silent for a while, then the Far-speaker began repeating fragments of a conversation, as if it was only half heard, mimicking the rough voices of two men. Farrag bit down on his frustration, knowing that he would get no more by badgering his servant.

'"Filthy day . . . none of the family . . . you know Junio had a mind of her own."'

Junio? Farrag wondered. It was the name of one of the old gods, the ludicrous pantheon which had long since vanished from the world.

'"Why shouldn't they? . . . better off out of town."'

There was a longer than usual pause, and the Marshal fretted impatiently. He tried to tell himself that this was just the first step. However inconsequential this particular eavesdropping proved to be, there would be more to come.

'"Damn these tides! . . . strange currents recently . . . worse all the time . . . pessimistic sod . . . sacrificing virgins next . . . "'

The tone of the voices changed, becoming angry.

'"Spare me . . . not on garbled myths . . . rid us of Farrag and his kind?"'

The Marshal's curiosity was abruptly rekindled. Perhaps this conversation was more interesting than it had appeared.

'"... do something, not abdicating ..."'

Another long pause tested Farrag's patience, but he resisted the temptation to force Iceman. Just when he had almost given up hope, the Far-speaker began again.

'"Arena, for some of the old rites ... suit yourself ... old rocks."'

The Arena? Old rites? That would bear investigation, Farrag thought. It amused him to think of their primitive superstitions. How little they understood.

'"... as well, now that we're here."'

'Where is he?' Farrag asked.

'Alone,' Iceman replied in his own voice. 'Moving again, but I can't locate the source.' There was silence for a while, then he added, 'Contact lost.'

'Lost?' the Marshal queried.

'Gone. No longer relaying.'

'Nothing at all?'

'Nothing,' Iceman confirmed.

Farrag wondered how it was possible to lose the crystal's resonance like that, once linked in. The Amari boy had been the first of the children to relay anything more than indecipherable fragments, but their remote presences had never just disappeared like this. Even so, it was a start.

'Discard the pair of moons, Iceman,' he said, ending the session.

Ia's confession had shocked and dismayed all her family, and had sent Antorkas into a paroxysm of rage. Etha, her own eyes fiery in response to her husband's anger, made sure that he took none of it out on their youngest daughter, who still clung to her skirts. Antorkas was left to vent his fury in a stream of unfocused invective about the stupidity of letting Natali keep his pendant.

As usual, it was Dsordas who calmed everyone down.

'He can't have gone far,' he said confidently. 'We'll find him.'

The search was quickly organized; everything else had

gone from their minds. Only Gaye and Ia remained at home; everyone else – even Torin – would help, in spite of their tiredness. Nason was sent home to gather more aid, if possible, and the others set off in pairs. Etha and Anto left on foot while the rest went in two of the boats so that they could cover the city as quickly as possible.

Dsordas and Fen naturally went together, rowing in unison with the ease of long years of practice. Like the others, they questioned everyone they met, enlisting promises of help whenever feasible – but most people were desperately weary from the day's exertions and had problems of their own. And no one had seen hide or hair of Natali.

The night drew on and the search widened, growing more frantic by the hour. The boy had simply disappeared.

As time went by, Dsordas began to assimilate other information. Through contacts made in whispers over the dark water, he checked on many of the other pendant children – but none of them was missing, or reported to be behaving in any way out of the ordinary. Fen was not sure whether to be reassured by this or not.

Their growing fear was that Natali had drowned. Although he could swim well enough and was well-schooled in the ways of water, the unusual tides and currents might have taken him unaware and swept him away. The water was behaving strangely still, a fact emphasized by one eerie moment during their search.

They had just returned to their boat, after searching another alleyway, when Fen pointed into the canal.

'Look! What's that?'

Below the inky surface, a peculiar luminescence wavered, like a living creature of silver light. As they watched, it rose towards the surface, sending shadows dancing and making the black liquid glitter. Then it simply vanished, breaking up into small globules before fading into nothing. The water swirled as if reacting to its departure, and there was a sinister gurgling noise.

'What was it?' Fen whispered.

'I've no idea.' Dsordas dismissed the mystery briskly, but his voice betrayed his anxiety.

'What if Natali was caught by one of those?'

'It's only a trick of the light,' he told her, though he did not sound convinced. 'It's not real. We'll find him.'

But they didn't find him, and nor did any of the others.

At some time after midnight, they began arriving back at the house in varying states of exhaustion. Antorkas, whose body ached intolerably, and Torin, who was practically asleep on his feet, were forced to admit defeat and go to bed. Gaye and Ia had been waiting up, desperate for news, but were now sent to their beds. The other four ate quickly, trying to restore their flagging energy and spirits before resuming the search. As they ate, they studied an old map of the town, wanting to ensure that they did not waste time by duplicating their efforts, and planning their next moves. They were doing everything possible, they knew, but they were running out of ideas.

Gaye was flying again, one among thousands, each waiting their turn to leave the vast, gloomy caves which were filled with the shapes of sound. Her time came, and she swooped into the starlit night, leaving her mountain home and flitting across the rock and tree-lined slopes, her myriad companions surrounding her like a liquid, singing cloud.

Amid the clamour, she heard an alien voice.

The Stone Eye must be reawoken.

And she thought, *It's blind. Like me.*

The Arena hung below her, an empty bowl under the light of the silent red moon. And there was the Stone Eye, staring blindly at the sky. *And there*, within the pupil of the eye . . .

Gaye woke with a start and called out excitedly,

hoping someone would hear her. Moments later, Fen and Etha hurried into the bedroom.

'What is it?' her mother asked breathlessly.

'I've seen Natali!' Gaye declared. 'I know where he is!'

CHAPTER TWENTY-TWO

*An eye blinks and, in the momentary darkness, sees
everything. A wave curls and within the mirror of its fall
there are reflections of the fire. The fire that burns under
water.*

*Does a beacon's light achieve anything if there is no one
to see it burn, no one to pass the message on?*

At first, Gaye found it hard to convince the others, but
she insisted that she had *seen* Natali, that it had not been
just a dream.

'But how could he possibly have got to the Arena?'
Dsordas asked.

'I don't know,' she retorted, 'but he *did*!'

She finally managed to persuade them to take her
seriously – after all, what did they have to lose?

'I'll go,' Dsordas volunteered. 'I know the path better
than you,' he added as Anto started to object.

'I'm coming too,' Fen put in quickly.

'It doesn't matter *who* goes,' Gaye exclaimed impatiently. 'Just go!'

'You sound more like your mother every day,'
Dsordas remarked with a sideways grin.

Fen and Gaye smiled in spite of their worries, and
even Etha reacted in the way he'd hoped, giving him a
half-hearted punch. Only Anto remained vexed, and
Dsordas placated him by giving him another area to
cover in case Gaye's premonition proved to be wrong.
By this time Ia was awake and wanted everything

explaining to her, but Etha took charge of that and waved the others off.

Fen and Dsordas took a boat to the southern edge of the town, leaving it moored near the main bridge, and set off at a brisk pace, new hope and urgency giving fresh life to tired legs. Once they were away from the lights of the town, their eyes soon adjusted to the dark, and they made good progress along the well-remembered track. They had little spare breath for talking but, once up in the hills, they did stop briefly to look out to sea. Several luminous patches were glowing ominously in the darkness of the water, less bright but far bigger than the one they had seen earlier. From this distance they could not tell whether the lights were moving, but at least one winked out of existence as they watched.

'What's happening out there?' Fen whispered. 'What's going on?'

'I wish I knew,' Dsordas replied firmly, 'But we've no time for that now. Come on.'

At last, breathless, aching and sweaty from their exertions, they came in sight of the stone. From the angle of their approach it was impossible to tell whether anyone was inside, but as soon as they reached the rock, Dsordas climbed to the upper entrance while Fen circled round to the lower, peering in anxiously. It was very dark, and at first she could see nothing, but then she made out a shape in the middle, blocking most of the tunnel.

'He's here!' she cried. 'Natali! Come out.'

There was no reaction. The shape remained absolutely still.

'Natali?' Dsordas called from above.

Fen's joy turned to panic. Her baby brother was curled up exactly where Gaye had predicted, but was he asleep – or dead? The hole was too narrow for her to crawl inside and reach him.

'He's not moving,' Fen called, a note of hysteria in her voice. 'Natali!'

'Keep watching him,' Dsordas instructed her calmly. 'I'll get a stick long enough to reach him and wake him up.'

As Dsordas moved away, a little more moonlight shone into the tunnel, illuminating Natali's fair hair and glinting on the amberine pendant. Fen was suddenly convinced that her brother was not alive, and she screamed wordlessly, begging him to move, to wake up, to be all right. But the reaction came, not from the tunnel, but from below and behind her.

From hundreds of unseen perches in the valley of the Arena, a vast horde of bats fluttered up into the sky; the air was suddenly full of squeaks just on the edge of hearing, and of the frantic beating of a thousand wings. Fen spun around, frightened nearly out of her wits by this unexpected invasion, and almost lost her footing. Natali stirred gingerly, as if in response to the sudden noise all around him.

'Mama?' he said in a small, lost voice.

'I'm here, Natali,' she answered, almost overwhelmed with relief. 'It's me, Fen. Come to me.' In the distance she heard Dsordas' voice, the sound of running foot-steps.

'My friends are here,' Natali said, sounding happier and more confident.

He began to crawl down, and Fen encouraged him softly, reaching her hands into the tunnel to greet him. At last, she caught hold, pulled him out and hugged him fiercely. She scarcely knew whether to laugh or cry, but Natali appeared quite unperturbed, looking up at the whirling shadows with wondrous contentment.

'My friends are here,' he repeated.

'My friends too,' Fen replied, not knowing exactly what he meant but not really caring.

A momentary surge of warmth, noise and brightness – of life itself – swept through Fen, filling her with sudden awe and joy. She turned around, with Natali in her arms, and looked down into the Arena. The valley was full of ghosts, hundreds of them, sparkling like human fireflies, their faces all turned towards her.

We are still here. Call on us.

The words came out of nowhere, forming themselves in her head, then all was silence.

'Dsordas, come look!' she called out.

But as her words echoed from stone to stone, the ghosts disappeared and all Dsordas saw was the sad emptiness of the place.

'Come back!' Fen cried hopelessly. 'I *am* calling for you.' Nothing happened. Dsordas scrambled down to join her.

'Thank the gods,' he sighed, seeing Natali. 'Who were you talking to?'

'No one,' Fen answered sadly.

Natali was asleep in her arms. Even the bats had gone.

The following morning brought further relief; the wind was back in the west, lessening the risk of further flooding. But the morning also brought fresh cause for unease. Dsordas returned from an early investigation with the news that they were not the only ones who had been up most of the night. Farrag's minions had also been busy. Bills had been posted throughout the city describing an attack on an unnamed imperial officer – whom they took to be Panos – and demanding that the culprits be given up. If not, the proclamation went on ominously, reprisals would be necessary.

'We couldn't turn them in even if we wanted to,' Dsordas commented. 'We don't know who they are.'

'Someone must know,' Fen said reasonably. 'Even if only the men themselves.'

'If they're islanders.'

'Doesn't this prove it?' she asked.

'Knowing Farrag, no. It might just be a charade,' he suggested, 'giving him the excuse to take more action against us.'

'More?' Fen queried fearfully.

'Several families were thrown out of their homes during the night, to make room for soldiers whose quarters had been damaged by the floods,' he told her. 'Anyone who resisted was overpowered. Foran and the others are busy with the wounded, but there are some they can't help.'

'Dead?' Fen asked in dismay.

'Three men who made the mistake of trying to protect their families and homes, two old women who couldn't move fast enough for the soldiers' liking, and the entire Orocon family,' he listed grimly.

'*All* of them?' Fen was horrified. She had known the family well.

'Men, women and children,' Dsordas confirmed. 'They ran them through and dumped them in the canal.'

Etha came in then and saw Fen's distraught expression.

'You've heard?' she said, her usual businesslike manner hiding the shock she felt.

Fen nodded bleakly.

'We're going to have to squeeze up,' her mother went on. 'Effi Gallo and her three children will be here soon. Stavos is dead and their home has been invaded by human lice, so I've said they can stay with us for as long as they like.'

The new sleeping arrangements were discussed briefly.

'We're lucky the soldiers didn't come here,' Etha said. 'The way Antorkas is feeling at the moment . . .' She left the thought unfinished.

'We're too far from the main barracks for now,' Dsordas told her. 'But if things get worse . . .'

'I have work to do,' Etha said, trying to shrug off the pessimism they all felt.

'Me too,' Dsordas said.

'Gaye wants to see you two,' Etha told them.

'About the ghost's message?' he asked.

'I expect so,' she answered vaguely, on her way out.

'I've no time for that nonsense,' Dsordas said. 'You

204

talk to her, Fen.' There was a note of pleading in his voice.

'All right,' she agreed reluctantly, 'but I think you should listen.'

'Not now,' he said with finality.

Something else occurred to Fen.

'Doesn't one of Effi's children have an amberine pendant?'

Dsordas nodded.

'Yes. Pauli, the youngest. Let's hope he and Natali don't decide to wander off together.'

With that, he kissed her briefly and was gone. Fen climbed wearily up to Gaye's room. She found her sister alone, pacing carefully around the room, measuring and remeasuring the distances, remembering where things were and speaking softly to herself. The door was open and Fen went in.

'Fen?' Gaye asked, looking up.

'Yes. How did you know it was me?'

'I'm learning to recognize all your footsteps.'

Fen felt a sudden surge of affection for her sister, proud of the resilience she was showing.

'Where's Dsordas?' Gaye asked.

'Gone out. He's got business to do.'

'He doesn't want to hear about the ghost, does he?'

'No,' Fen admitted. 'He's afraid that if we start hoping for miracles, it'll take our minds off the real work.'

'What's wrong with using both?' Gaye asked. 'Farrag uses magic!'

'I've tried that argument. He's just stubborn, the same as with his healing. He won't admit anything.'

'Doesn't the fact that I found Natali mean anything to him?' Gaye demanded incredulously.

'Of course,' her sister replied. 'He was impressed – up to a point. But he doesn't see – and neither do I, come to that – how such talent can help Zalys.'

'How would I know?' Gaye exclaimed. 'But shouldn't we at least try? That ghost went to a lot of trouble to get

205

his message through to me. We can't just ignore it!'

Fen remained silent for a while, recalling her momentary glimpse of the forces of the Arena. She had told no one about it yet. The place was special – of that she had no doubt. The island's history, Natali's choice of hiding place, her own vision, the ghost's message – everything pointed to that fact, but she was equally certain that Dsordas could never be persuaded to recognize its obscure potential. Fen made up her mind.

'Gaye, I'm going to tell you everything that happened last night,' she began. 'But forget about trying to convince Dsordas. If we're going to reawaken the Stone Eye, then we're going to have to do it on our own.'

CHAPTER TWENTY-THREE

Fire burns paper. Paper wraps stone. Stone blunts knife. Knife cuts water. Water douses fire. There is symmetry within the circle of hands.

But in the darkness, who can tell one sign from another? Whose hand is stained with blood? And whose holds the burning sword?

Fournoi Square was crowded, while much of the rest of the city was preternaturally quiet. Imperial patrols had swept through the streets at mid-morning, herding all those outside towards the centre and rooting out others from their homes. Boats had been diverted from their courses and marshalled into the main canal and thence to the square. Soldiers were everywhere, heavily armed and unsmiling, intent upon their task. Among the islanders, the atmosphere of suppressed terror was almost unbearable. No one was in any doubt that the threatened reprisals were about to begin, but no one was prepared for the form they would take.

By the time Farrag made his expected appearance, his troops had plucked a dozen men from the crowd. Chosen apparently at random, these islanders were pulled away from their families and friends, and anyone who objected was dealt with with uncompromising violence. As wives or children cried, the men were marched to the centre of the square to wait under guard. Farrag approached alone, looking at the prisoners thoughtfully, once again flaunting his absolute confidence even in the midst of a hostile crowd. His tattooed eyes seemed to smile all around, and before he spoke, his purple-black tongue licked his lips as if in anticipation.

'You have chosen to ignore the imperial decree.' His voice carried easily to the four corners of the square. 'Will you hand over the guilty men now, before it is too late?'

His words were greeted with silence.

'It is your decision,' the Marshal said. 'The punishment is on your own heads.'

From the stillness of the crowd, a frail old figure stepped forward. Nias Santarsieri trembled, but faced his opponent squarely.

'There is no justice in this,' the Patriarch declared. 'These men are innocent.' The old man's voice could not match Farrag's power, but carried conviction nonetheless.

'Justice?' the Marshal roared. 'You demand justice? My officer lies broken, near to death, beaten and robbed by cowards. *He* is innocent. By your silence you prove yourselves guilty. You shall have *justice!*'

'The laws state . . .' Nias persisted bravely.

'My word is imperial law,' Farrag interrupted in a quieter, more menacing tone. 'And I say these men will be punished.'

'Commander Niering is the island's master,' the Patriarch said desperately. 'You overstep your authority.'

Farrag laughed.

'My actions have his full approval,' he replied mildly.

'Then let him come here and face me,' Nias insisted, though his faltering voice did not match his bold words.

'Face you, old man?' the Marshal said, still smiling. 'Your impertinence grows tiresome.' He turned to a group of guards. 'Give him six lashes. Teach him some manners.'

Two burly soldiers moved swiftly, tearing the robes from Nias' back and pushing him down on to his knees.

Another stepped forward, a whip in his hand, as the crowd gasped and whispered under the watchful eyes of the soldiers.

Metal studded leather lashed down, raising a fearful welt on the Patriarch's back, but the old man did not cry out, even as the onlookers winced in sympathy. Stubborn pride or the shock of such terrible pain kept him silent as the whip was wielded five more times, leaving his back and shoulders cross-hatched with ugly wounds and streaked with blood. At the last stroke Nias fell forward and lay still, then began to crawl painfully away, his humiliation complete. Several islanders, their faces white with anger and dismay, moved forward to help him, but Farrag's voice halted them in their tracks.

'Any man who goes to his aid, dies.'

The islanders hesitated as Nias edged forward, but one figure still moved. Habella Merini came on.

'I am no man,' she said, facing the Marshal. 'Will you kill me?'

Farrag did not answer, but at a slight signal from his pudgy hand, another sentry stepped forward and struck Habella a deliberate blow in the face with the heavy stave of his spear. She fell backwards, clutching at her mouth, blood running through her fingers. Several women went to her side and pulled her away from further harm, while the watching men burned with shame and impotent hatred. Nias still lay on the ground, unmoving now.

'Anyone else?' Farrag asked, sounding amused. 'No? Then we will continue with our business.' He turned to face the sweating prisoners, and the crowd grew quiet again. 'But to show that I am merciful, only four of these guilty men will be punished.'

The twelve men could not bear to look at each other, their dread now lifted by a grain of hope. None of them wished to suffer as the Patriarch had, and it seemed now that most of them would escape. But Farrag had another surprise in store. He snapped thick fingers and a guard approached, ushering a small girl. An amberine pendant hung around her neck. She looked apprehensive, but appeared to be reassured by Farrag's welcoming smile.

'Who better to choose the guilty than one so innocent?' the Marshal explained, then leant down to whisper in the girl's ear. She nodded, then walked towards the line of men, stopping a few paces away. None of the prisoners dared look at her, save one. He stared helplessly at his own daughter, his face a mask of pure horror.

The girl looked along the line briefly and had no hesitation in pointing to four of the men in turn. The last of these was her father. Soldiers pushed the reprieved prisoners away and the girl was led from the scene, while Farrag gloated over his chosen victims.

'Your guilt is confirmed by imperial law,' he announced. 'You are condemned to death.'

'One, two, three.'

Kato Gallo and Ia both lowered their right fists in time to the count, and on the third beat made a sign. Ia held her hand flat, palm vertical. Kato pointed with only the first two fingers outstretched.

'Knife cuts paper,' Kato said in triumph and claimed one of Ia's white pebbles.

The two girls were sitting cross-legged on the floor in Gaye's room, together with their younger brothers, Pauli and Natali. They played, not fully aware of the tragedy that had engulfed the Gallo family, while elsewhere Etha tried to comfort the distraught mother and her eldest boy, Yermasi.

'Let me play,' Pauli asked.

'Only two can play,' Kato told him, and the girls resumed their count. It was an old game, which had been played by the island's children for decades, but the pebbles used to keep score were an innovation learnt from the soldiers of Xantium.

'One, two, three.'

Kato kept her fist clenched while Ia made the same sign as before.

'Paper wraps stone.' Ia reclaimed one of her opponent's pebbles.

'Let me play!' Pauli begged again, but the girls ignored him. Natali merely watched, his small fingers moving experimentally.

Another contest saw Ia's fire – fingers apart, pointing upwards to represent flames – lose to Kato's water – a flat hand held horizontally, and then Pauli renewed his request in a grating, nasal whine.

'Let him have a go,' Gaye intervened. She was feeling very odd, desperately sorry for her visitors but irritated by their enforced intrusion, her thoughts in a jumble.

'Oh, all right,' Kato said with bad grace. 'You play with him, Ia.' She pushed over her pile of pebbles.

As the game continued, with stones going back and forth, Gaye began to feel that she was predicting the results before they were announced. It was as if there were voices in her head. She tried to concentrate, and was soon convinced that she was right – but only with one player.

'Pauli,' Gaye asked, 'could I play with you?'

'You can't see,' Kato objected.

'You and Ia can tell me Pauli's sign and keep score.'

'All right,' Pauli said happily.

The children moved over to Gaye's chair and arranged themselves around it.

'Ready?' Gaye began. 'One, two, three.'

Both she and Pauli made the fire sign.

'A draw,' Kato said in disgust.

'One, two, three.'

Two closed fists for stone.

'Again!' Kato exclaimed.

They played several more times – and on each occasion the contest was drawn.

'This is boring!' Kato exclaimed, but Ia was intrigued.

'Let's try again,' Gaye said.

She then lost six times in a row so that Pauli triumphantly collected all her stones.

'You've lost,' Ia said, sounding puzzled.

'Never mind. You play again now,' Gaye told her. She sat back in her chair, completely bewildered, wondering how she had been able to read the boy's mind.

Dsordas returned to the house shortly after noon, his face grim. He found Fen and her father in the kitchen.

'What's happened?' Fen asked quickly, immediately sensing his mood.

'It's started,' he replied and went on to tell them of Farrag's reprisals and the scene in Fournoi Square.

'A child?' Fen said, aghast.

'One of those with a pendant,' Dsordas confirmed.

'That does it!' Antorkas exclaimed. 'Natali's stone goes!' He was white faced with fury and tiredness. 'Now!' He got to his feet, but Fen put out a restraining hand.

'Wait, Father,' she said. 'Let's hear the rest.'

'She chose four men, including her own father,' Dsordas went on. 'And Farrag sentenced them to death.'

'To *death*?'

'Gods!' Antorkas breathed.

'How did they die?' Fen asked.

'You don't want to know.'

'Tell me,' she insisted, determined not to hide from the dreadful facts.

'They beheaded them, there and then, in front of everybody,' he told them quietly. 'Their heads are on poles by the main canal now.'

His words rendered them speechless, but Dsordas had not finished.

'There's worse,' he added. 'Farrag vowed to repeat the process tomorrow unless the culprits are given up – and no one's likely to volunteer to submit to that sort of "justice". Anyway, we still don't know who they were –

only that they're definitely not members of the underground.'

Fen glanced at Antorkas, and Dsordas saw her
uncertainty.

'Your father knows where I stand,' he told her, 'and
soon we won't have need of secrecy any more. We're
going to have to act now or we'll never get another
chance. Farrag's *games* are getting more deadly.'

'What do you mean?' Fen asked.

'Coincidence or not,' he answered, 'the four men who
died all belonged to the Children.'

CHAPTER TWENTY-FOUR

The stone, like curved glass, entraps the sun, concentrates its light and heat. A tulip of flame blossoms at its heart, a bright new sun, leaving marks upon the lids long after the eyes are closed.

Dark fire burns quickly, especially in tender kindling. It can only be doused with bitter tears.

Dsordas and Fen followed Antorkas up the stairs, a sense of foreboding in their hearts. Neither of them felt they could argue with him over Natali's pendant – too much had happened now – but they were still dreading what was to come. The children were playing when the head of the family clumped into Gaye's room, but they stopped immediately when the adults came in, sensing that something was wrong.

'Natali, come here.'

Obediently, the boy trotted over to his father.

'Give me the pendant.' A large hand was held out.

'No!' Natali clutched the amberine defiantly.

'I *will* have it, Natali,' Antorkas told his son angrily. 'Now!'

Out of sight, Pauli tucked his own pendant into his shirt.

'No,' Natali whispered, cowering.

His father reached for him, but Natali dodged his grasp with unexpected agility, and ran from the room. With a cry of rage, Antorkas pounded after him, and Dsordas followed. Fen would have gone too but Gaye called her back. They listened, with the other children, to the screams and tears as Natali was caught and the chain forcibly removed. The little boy's anguish, now shot through with fury, was uncontrollable – even when Etha came to try and calm her son. Antorkas, however, went back downstairs, a look of grim satisfaction on his face, with the stone in his pocket. In another room, Natali continued to scream.

Fen shut the door of the bedroom.

'Go on with your game,' she told the children, then turned to her sister.

'I can't monitor them all,' Iceman complained. 'I need more.'

Farrag gave the Far-speaker a measured glance.

'Any of the others would be happy to volunteer for these duties, you know,' he said.

Iceman's expression became sullen, and he would not meet the other's gaze.

'I can't monitor them all,' he repeated hoarsely.

'I know,' the Marshal replied. 'Concentrate on those who relay best.'

'I am,' the Far-speaker muttered. 'But I'm getting weak.'

Farrag was well aware that talented addicts could become expert dissemblers, but in this case he felt justified in taking a chance.

'Very well,' he said. 'But I expect results!'

He took out the phial, prepared a draught and handed it to Iceman, who drank it in one long gulp. Farrag waited patiently for the shuddering to subside.

'Well?' he asked expectantly.

'Playing games. Food. Sleep,' Iceman reported. 'Nothing significant.'

'There had better be soon,' Farrag threatened coldly.

'One of them has gone,' the Far-speaker added. 'I can't find his voice anywhere.'

'Must have taken the pendant off,' the Marshal grumbled resignedly. 'It had to happen sooner or later. Which one is it?'

'The Amari child.'

Farrag swore. He had had high hopes for the boy, even though he was one of the youngest chosen, and the early results had been promising. But this was the second time now that his voice had disappeared. Even so, the very fact that the pendant had been removed might be significant . . .

'Keep monitoring,' he ordered. 'I'll be back for a full report in an hour.'

Farrag left the cell. He had other matters to attend to now. His patient work was producing results, building up layer upon layer of knowledge. So far the children were merely turning existing suspicions into certainties, but they were far from his only line of attack. The Marshal's plans were all coming to fruition. Their culmination would be when he crushed the island's underground, once and for ever. Farrag smiled to himself. He planned to do that very soon. Then he would be able to leave Zalys in less capable hands and seek his own fortune somewhere more worthwhile.

Not long now, he told himself, hardly able to contain his elation.

That afternoon, five men met in a dark, damp cellar. They had never before been together as a group, and it was a measure of the crisis facing them that Dsordas had decided to risk such a gathering. The four who sat with him around the table were his chief lieutenants in the Children of Zalys, and each was fully aware of the dreadful happenings earlier that day. They were determined that Farrag could not be allowed to continue.

In low voices, they discussed the number of men they could count on, the distribution of weapons – they had been stock-piling them in secret for years – and the division of responsibilities. They were all aware that if they were to strike, it would have to be an all-out assault. Anything half-hearted would leave the entire population exposed to a terrible and swift revenge. It would be an all or nothing gamble, and with the timing having been forced upon them, no one liked the odds. However, there were other reasons – apart from the threat of more executions – why they could not afford to wait too long. The Children were itching for action. They would never be more willing to fight and die than they were now, and Farrag was obviously intent on a showdown. His provocations would become ever more violent and evil, but there were other factors working in the under-ground's favour – or so they hoped.

'We have to take a risk on Panos then,' Dsordas said. 'Agreed?'

The others nodded.

'He's the only chance we've got of getting inside the Far-speakers' complex,' Phylo Zevgari said. 'We've got to get rid of them one way or another, or any victory will be short-lived.'

They all knew that a revolt on Zalys would eventually be opposed by the might of the Xantic Empire. Unless they prevented the Far-speakers from sending the news to the mainland, they would not have the vital time needed to organize the island's defences after the chaos which the uprising would inevitably cause. Farrag had ensured that the complex which housed the Far-speakers was secure and only accessible to a few specially chosen Information Officers. None of the islanders had ever so much as seen inside. And a message to the Empire would be on its way within moments of news of a revolt reaching the complex. So the Children needed to attack there first of all. Panos was their best hope of learning how this could be done.

'Shall I handle it?' Yeori Alektora asked. He was a small man, but extremely strong, whose expertise in unarmed combat made him, and the men he had trained, ideal for the task.

'Yes,' Dsordas answered. 'But I want to interrogate him myself. At the Well,' he added, naming one of their secret hideouts.

Yeori nodded.

'I'll have him there at dusk,' he said confidently.

'Good. Next, the floodgates,' Dsordas continued. 'How's it going, Mouse?'

'All set.' The answer came from Yani Paphos, known to everyone as Mouse. 'All we need is one good blow from the east over the next few days.'

For some time, under Yani's supervision, the Children had been preparing a surprise for the imperial garrison. Most of the headquarters and barracks were on relatively high ground, but, by cunning design and elaborate constructions made under the cover of flood control measures, Mouse and his team had contrived a means of producing a vast, powerful surge of water which would hit at the heart of the soldiers' domain. Channelling an especially high tide, assuming they timed it correctly, might produce spectacular results.

'We may not be able to wait that long,' Dsordas told him.

'We'll do what we can whenever you say the word,' Yani replied. 'At the very least, we'll destroy some of their stores and mess up one of the armouries – and cause a fair bit of confusion. If we're lucky with the weather, we might even collapse the whole block of barracks with most of the bastards inside.'

'That'd be nice,' Yeori commented.

'Don't count on it, though,' Mouse went on. 'The westerlies seem pretty set.'

'Let's hope it changes,' Dsordas said. They were all aware of the irony of his words. In the past they would have wished for the exact opposite, to save Nkosa from flooding. Now they were threatened by something even worse. 'That's it for now, I think. You all know what you've got to do?'

'What about Farrag himself?' Skoulli Visakia, the final member of the group, asked.

'He's a man, like us,' Dsordas answered, immediately on his guard.

218

'Not quite. The man has powers. You've seen what he can do.'

'And think of those pendants,' Phylo added. 'The gods know what he's up to there.'

'People are saying we need magic of our own to be able to fight him,' Yeori put in.

'When we start relying on superstition, we're lost!' Dsordas said angrily.

'Right,' Mouse agreed. 'We don't need that old nonsense.'

'Suit yourselves,' Skoulli said. 'I'd as soon have all the help we can get – whatever the source.'

'Forget it,' Dsordas told him. 'We've enough to think about. Don't waste your time. We'll take care of Farrag.'

The men were about to rise when they heard a slight sound from the doorway. They immediately sprang into action, knives at the ready, but when Dsordas flung open the door he found only a small boy, his eyes wide in the gloom. He signalled for the others to relax.

'What are you doing down here, Natali?' he scolded, picking the child up. The others left, walking along a passageway which led to an underground mooring. Phylo was the last to go, and Dsordas called him back for a moment.

'One more thing,' he said. 'We're going to need to redistribute the oil – with the tides running this high, some of our fire points will be too dangerous. We could burn down half the town. We should move those at Dheftera Bridge further down the canal. Do it as soon as it gets dark. All right?'

Phylo nodded and went on his way. Dsordas, with Natali still in his arms, climbed the stairs cautiously.

'You've cheered up,' he remarked, looking at the boy's smiling face.

'Happy now,' Natali agreed.

That's one small blessing, Dsordas thought, but he did not notice Natali's small hand slip inside his shirt to touch something within.

CHAPTER TWENTY-FIVE

One of the stones here has the skeleton of a fish embedded within it. The masons preserved it carefully as a sign of good luck. How many ages have passed since it swam in that ancient sea? How long did it take to turn to stone, so that its memory echoed down the endless tunnels? It is unimaginably old.

And yet it is possible that something even older lies beneath our own seas. Something that may not have turned to stone could be sleeping still, not dead. Who would have the strength to prophesy its awakening?

Panos was shoved into the room, a black cloth bag over his head and his hands tied behind his back. He almost stumbled as Yeori pushed him again, but recovered and stood quite still.

'Don't kill me,' he whined. 'I can pay you. Honestly.'

Dsordas and his lieutenant exchanged glances but said nothing.

'What do you want?' Panos implored. He sounded truly frightened, but then so would anyone in his shoes, even if he *was* planning to double-cross his captors. They let him stew a little longer, then Yeori guided him roughly to the stool in the centre of the bare room and pushed him down on to it.

'Do I leave this on?' he asked, indicating the hood.

'No,' Dsordas answered. 'I need to see his lying face. Dim the lamp.'

Yeori obeyed and then stood back in a dark recess behind their prisoner. Dsordas donned a grotesque children's mask before pulling off the bag. Panos stared, his battered face showing new terrors.

'You're not . . .' he began, but stopped himself in time.

'No,' Dsordas agreed. 'I'm not the one you owe money to. You owe me more than that.'

'What do you mean?'

'You owe me your life. We could have killed you when we took your money.'

Panos' face registered complete surprise – genuine, it seemed to Dsordas – but then came a rapid flicker of calculation.

'That was you?' he said. 'I thought that bastard Farrag had arranged it to give him an excuse to stir up trouble.'

'What made you think that?' Dsordas asked, keeping his voice carefully neutral.

'It's just the sort of thing he'd do,' Panos replied sourly, then his expression changed again. 'What do you want of me now? The gods know, I've no more money.'

'But you need some?'

'You seem to know that already,' the soldier said warily.

'Then perhaps you can earn some,' Dsordas told him. 'We may have a job for you.'

Panos sat silently for a while.

'How much?' he asked eventually.

Dsordas wondered why he had asked that before finding out what the job might be.

'How much do you need?'

Again, the flicker of calculation. Dsordas realized that his prisoner was adding something on top of his debts, a margin to bargain with.

'Eighty imperials.'

'You *are* in trouble!'

'Don't mock me!' Panos cried angrily, though this might have been intended to hide his terror. 'If I don't get it, you might as well have killed me.'

He's consistent at least, Dsordas thought.

'I'll do anything,' the captured man swore.

'Anything?'

'Yes.'

'Tell me about your duties as an Information Officer,' Dsordas ordered.

If this request surprised Panos he did not show it.

'It varies,' he replied. 'I keep records, monitor reports from the island and other parts of the Empire . . .' He hesitated, then added, 'and I keep a watch on the gossip among the soldiers.'

'Do you deal with informers?'

'No. That's not my field. Farrag has specialists for that.'

I'll bet he does, Dsordas thought. *But are you one of them?* Aloud, he said, 'How do you monitor reports from overseas?'

Panos looked puzzled.

'The stuff from the Far-speakers, you mean?' he replied. 'We read, file, cross-reference . . .'

'You're familiar with the Far-speaker complex?'

'Yes.' Again Panos' expression was wary.

'How many of them are there?'

'Eight,' the soldier answered promptly.

Dsordas was surprised. Their previous estimates had put the number at six, and if Panos was lying it was more likely that he would deliberately underestimate their strength. How many more might there be?

'And they stay in the same building all the time, whether they're working or not?' he went on.

'Yes. What . . . what are you getting at?'

'Tell me,' Dsordas ventured. 'How much would Farrag be prepared to pay to get back one of his Far-speakers?'

'You couldn't kidnap them,' Panos stated. 'They're too well guarded.'

'Just suppose,' his inquisitor suggested.

'One on his own, nothing,' the Information Officer said, shrugging. 'The others would take up the slack.'

'And if the others were all dead or captured?' Dsordas

persisted. After a long pause realization finally dawned in Panos' eyes. 'You're serious, aren't you?' he breathed in disbelief. 'You must be mad!'

'Just answer the question.'

'He'd pay almost anything,' Panos said eventually. 'But you'd never live to collect it. He'd kill everyone on the island rather than give in to blackmail.'

'Let us worry about that,' Dsordas told him. 'Are you going to help us or not?'

The prisoner was silent for a while, apparently undecided.

'Eighty imperials?' he asked finally.

'Yes. Ten now, the rest when the job's done.'

'But you'll never be able to do it. And I need the money now!'

'That's the choice. Take it or leave it.'

There was another long pause.

'What do you want to know?' Panos said at last.

For the next hour, he answered dozens of questions on the lay-out of the complex, its entrances and surroundings, the guard strengths and duty rosters, the way supplies went in. Dsordas asked several questions to which the answers were already known and on each occasion Panos gave the correct reply. If he was lying, he was doing it very cleverly.

'You'll still never get in,' he concluded. 'You need someone on the inside.'

'Are you volunteering?'

'Do I have any choice?' Panos asked bitterly. 'If Farrag finds out what I've told you, I'm as good as dead. Besides . . .'

'What?'

'If you really go ahead with this, you'll be doing me a few favours,' the soldier replied. 'When is it going to be?'

'We'll let you know.'

'Make it soon,' Panos said fervently. 'Or I may not be around to help.'

'That's your problem,' Dsordas told him. 'This should buy you a little time.' He slipped ten coins into Panos' pocket then nodded to Yeori, who whistled softly. Another man was soon heard approaching down the tunnel. Dsordas put the bag back over Panos' head, and Yeori shepherded him to the tunnel entrance and passed him over to the newcomer.

'You know the drill?' Yeori asked.

The man nodded.

'Guard him carefully,' Yeori added with a grin. 'We don't want him being robbed again.'

After a few moments, Dsordas and Yeori were joined by Skoulli, who had watched the entire proceedings through a spy-hole.

'Well?' Dsordas asked, once the prisoner was well out of earshot.

'Either he's an incredible actor or he's perfectly genuine,' Skoulli replied. 'And those scabs are ugly.'

'Do you think he swallowed the story about kidnapping the Far-speakers for ransom?' Yeori asked.

'I don't know.' Dsordas shrugged. 'He's a slimy little toad, but perhaps it *is* all from self-interest. In any case, we couldn't risk telling him the real story.' He did not add that by pretending to be the robbers, he also hoped to avoid implicating Fen.

'I don't think he knows who attacked him,' Skoulli said, 'so he could have believed it was you. He certainly seemed to.'

'Yes, but that still doesn't prove that it wasn't arranged by Farrag,' Dsordas argued. 'He could have approached Panos afterwards, taking advantage of an existing situation – and so Panos might still be an imperial spy.'

'But *he* was the one who suggested Farrag might have set it up,' Yeori objected. 'Surely he wouldn't have done that if the two of them were in league?'

'But you know how devious they are,' Dsordas said. 'And he might have been surprised because he knew we *weren't* his attackers.'

'This is getting too complicated for me,' Yeori admitted, shaking his head.

'He seemed very interested in money,' Skoulli said thoughtfully. 'I don't think his greed was faked – and if he *were* in league with Farrag, then he wouldn't need our gold.'

'He obviously has some old scores of his own that he'd like the chance to settle,' Yeori added.

'I couldn't catch him out in a lie,' Dsordas admitted. 'We haven't much choice but to trust him, have we?'

'Which leads us back to what he's told us,' Skoulli went on. 'Even with his help, it'll be tricky. From the sound of it, the Far-speakers might as well be in a fortress.'

'That just confirms how important they are to Farrag,' Dsordas said. 'Everything we do depends on getting rid of them one way or another.'

On his way back home from the Well, Dsordas was intercepted by Malo. His colleague was dripping wet from head to foot and his expression was grim.

'We were ambushed moving the oil barrels,' he said without preamble. 'They were waiting for us, as if they knew exactly what we were going to do. It was a mess.'

'Phylo?' Dsordas asked, hoping his lieutenant had had the sense not to take part in person.

'Dead,' Malo replied gravely. 'He wasn't going to be taken alive.'

Although the news came as a shock, it was also, in one way, something of a relief. Dsordas hoped that he would be able to show the same courage if necessary.

'But I think they've got two of the others,' Malo went on. 'I was lucky to get away.'

'Did Phylo tell you anything . . . ?'

'Only about the job in hand, as always,' Malo replied, understanding Dsordas' concern. 'They won't be able to tell them much.'

The young boatman was evidently satisfied that the damage to the Children was minimal, but he and Dsordas were both aware that the captured men might reveal Malo's name. He lived alone, having no close relatives, and in a sense that was lucky; he could go into hiding without fearing reprisals against his family. Phylo, however, had had a wife and children – and Dsordas knew that they would have to be warned.

'I've been to Phylo's house,' Malo added, as if reading his leader's thoughts. 'They're already on their way out of town.'

'Good. Do you have somewhere safe to lie low?'

Malo nodded.

'I have time yet,' he said. 'Don't worry about me.'

'And the oil?' Dsordas asked. It had been intended to create flame-barriers, to prevent imperial soldiers moving by boat on certain routes.

'Lost. We can get more easily enough but we'll need to hide it somewhere else. They'll be watching by the bridge now.'

'Any idea how they knew?'

'Someone must have tipped them off,' Malo replied. 'The set up was too well organized to be coincidence.'

As if things weren't bad enough! Dsordas thought with angry frustration. He did not believe that there was a traitor within the leaders. Could there by one in Phylo's group? He even wondered for a moment about Malo's loyalty, but dismissed the suspicion instantly, feeling ashamed. It had just been bad luck, a chance word overheard, a fortuitous deduction . . .

'Keep your eyes and ears open,' Dsordas advised. 'And go carefully.'

'I thought you'd better know,' Malo said.

'Thanks. I appreciate it, but you'd better get away now, before it's too late.'

Malo melted into the darkness and Dsordas went home – where more bad news awaited him.

The first thing he heard when he went in was the

sound of a small child crying inconsolably. He thought that perhaps Natali was still miserable over the loss of his pendant, but then realized that it was Pauli – which was hardly surprising. The Gallo family had suffered a great loss. The kitchen was empty but Anto came in as Dsordas was about to go upstairs.

'Have you heard?' he asked, his young face strained with worry.

'What?'

'The fishermen are all going crazy. They say there are peculiar noises underwater affecting the fish.'

'What sort of noises?'

'Great booming sounds, like huge gongs,' Anto replied. 'And it's not just the fish. There've been sudden whirlpools out at sea, and odd patches of light – like liquid opal, one of them said. The water goes suddenly cold for no reason, and no one can read the currents any more.'

'These tides are the highest yet,' Dsordas said, without much conviction. 'Couldn't they be the cause?'

'Not according to the fishermen. And why would that produce the noises?'

'Underground caves?'

Anto was sceptical.

'Or make fish jump out of the water?' he went on. 'There are several dolphins beached down the coast, and the sea-bats are leaping. It's as if they're trying to get away from something.'

'That's crazy.' Dsordas had had enough of such talk. 'They'll be seeing giant squid the size of a ship next.'

'It *is* crazy,' Anto agreed. 'That's the problem. No one's got an explanation.'

'We can't afford to start treating the sea like an enemy,' Dsordas said. 'We have enough problems on land. How's the wind?'

'Still in the west, thank goodness,' the boy answered. 'It looks set, too. There shouldn't be much flooding tomorrow even though it's the highest of the tides.'

227

'It'll be running high for two days after that,' Dsordas reminded him. 'The danger isn't over yet.' *Nor is our chance of using the tide as a weapon,* he thought. *But it won't last for long.* For once he found himself hoping for floods.

Anto went to the pantry in search of food, and Dsordas went to look for Fen. He had never needed her company more than he did now. He joined the sisters in Gaye's room, and Fen came to embrace him.

'Thank the gods you're back!' she said. 'We need to talk.'

'If it's about ghosts or monsters under the sea,' Dsordas responded wearily, 'I don't want to know.'

'No,' Gaye said. 'It's about me – and Pauli.'

Dsordas sat down, puzzled but prepared to listen, and Gaye told him how she had been able to read the boy's mind.

'It wasn't until afterwards,' Fen said, 'when she talked to me, that Gaye realized that Pauli is one of the children wearing Farrag's amberine pendants. And we know that Far-speakers use crystals.'

'Are you saying that Gaye's become a Far-speaker?' Dsordas asked.

'Not a real one,' Gaye answered, 'because I can't control it, but since I've been blind, I have felt and heard some strange things that I just can't explain.' She spoke evenly, with no trace of self-pity. 'And I don't know why I heard Pauli's moves in the game but nothing else.'

'She knew where to find Natali,' Fen continued. 'Perhaps he told her telepathically where he was, without even knowing what he was doing.'

'Have you been near Natali since you heard Pauli's thoughts?' Dsordas asked sharply.

'Yes. I talked to him,' Gaye answered, 'though I didn't sense anything. But perhaps that's because Father's taken his stone away.'

'Where's Natali now?'

'Asleep,' Fen said.

'Wake him up and bring him here, would you?'

'But . . .'

'Just do it!' he snapped with uncharacteristic impatience. Looking upset, Fen left the room without another word.

'What is it?' Gaye cried in distress. 'What's the matter?'

'I don't know,' Dsordas told her in a gentler tone. 'Nothing, probably. Tell me if you sense anything when Natali comes in.'

'All right.'

Fen returned with her small brother in her arms and Gaye stiffened, blind eyes wide.

'He's angry and sleepy,' she whispered.

'So would I be,' Dsordas said. 'Anything else?'

'Guilt. He's hiding something,' Gaye replied slowly, looking confused. 'He feels quite different from before . . . I can't explain . . . Oh!' Her pale face registered shock and revulsion. 'It's horrible!' she cried. 'I can't bear it. No!' She put her hands over her ears, but to no avail. Whatever was tormenting her was still there.

'Take him to our room,' Dsordas ordered urgently. 'Quick!'

Fen hurried out, frightened herself now, and Gaye relaxed visibly.

'What was it?' Dsordas asked gently. 'What did you hear?'

'Something evil, poisonous,' she whispered. 'It's using him, eating away at him inside. It would have infected me too if I hadn't drawn back. It was revolting.' She shuddered.

'It's gone now. Will you be all right?'

Gaye nodded slowly.

'I'll be back soon,' Dsordas promised, and hurried to his own room. Natali was asleep on their bed with Fen watching over him. She looked up tearfully as her lover came in.

'What is it?'

Dsordas looked at the peacefully sleeping child, and tried to convince himself that all was well, but the dread would not go away.

'What if Gaye is not the only one who can hear Natali's thoughts?' he asked quietly. 'What if Farrag's Far-speakers can do it too?'

Shocked, Fen stared at him. 'Could they really do that?' she asked, her voice filled with horror.

'I don't know,' Dsordas replied, 'but it would explain Farrag's handing out those stones so freely.'

'But Natali doesn't have his any more.'

'I'm not so sure,' he replied.

'Father locked it away,' Fen objected. 'Natali can't possibly . . .'

But Dsordas was not listening. He leant over the boy and gently reached inside his night shirt.

'Then what's this?' he breathed, pulling out the pendant. Fen stared.

'It's different!' she exclaimed. 'It's Pauli's!'

No wonder he's crying, Dsordas thought dismally. He started to slip the chain over Natali's head, but the boy woke up and grabbed for his treasure. They struggled, and Dsordas was astonished by Natali's furious strength. Eventually, he got the pendant away and handed it to Fen.

'Lock it away.' He was having to restrain Natali, and had to shout to be heard over the child's continued screaming. By the time Fen returned, Etha was there too, and Dsordas explained what had happened. Natali had quietened a little and now lay sobbing on the bed. Fen's heart went out to her baby brother, but he hit out at her when she tried to comfort him.

'I hate you,' he hissed.

Etha picked up her weeping son and took him to sleep in her own room.

'Using children as spies,' Fen said, full of contempt for their enemy's methods. 'Do you think they can do us any harm?'

'I'm afraid they already have,' Dsordas replied. *Someone must have tipped them off.*

He told her of Natali's unexpected appearance at the underground meeting, his being present only for the last moment instructions to Phylo, and of the subsequent ambush in which his lieutenant had been killed. It all seemed to fit into a very unpleasant pattern.

'Gods,' Fen breathed. 'How much more might they have overheard?'

'Don't forget the other children,' Dsordas added, remembering the little girl who had unwittingly condemned her father to death. 'And the worst of it is, we can't just take all the pendants off. That in itself would give Farrag too much information, and he'd take action against all the families. We've already taken a risk here.'

'But that means we'll have to treat them all like traitors,' Fen objected. 'Shut them off from their families. We can't do that!'

'Oh yes we can,' he told her. 'We've no choice.'

CHAPTER TWENTY-SIX

I see it now, its bulk but not its shape, approaching. Grey, like a shroud upon the world, a winding sheet for the gravestones in the sky.

What use are beacons in the face of such overwhelming power? Are we all to fall before we learn to fly?

Sagar had no warning of her approach. When her pale face appeared in the door slit, he jumped up eagerly.

'You're back! Can you really hear me?' It had been two days since he had first seen the ghostly figure of the tiny woman, and he had begun to think that she had been a figment of his imagination, renewing fears about his sanity. Yet here she was, even closer than before. In the half-light, he could see her face clearly.

'I have ears,' Alasia replied audibly.

'But you're a ghost! How . . . ?' Sagar paused, seeing the slight smile on her face, smelling a trace of perfume in the stale air.

'The white owl has not flown for me,' she told him.

Sagar did not know what she meant, but realized that if a ghost wanted to speak to him, it would appear inside his cell. His visitor was real.

'Who *are* you?' he asked, his heart racing. 'Do you know why I'm here?'

'Your brother is coming,' Alasia told him, ignoring his questions.

'My brother?' Sagar was bewildered. 'Which one?'

'The beacon.'

'What?'

'He carries two burdens,' she went on.

'Help me!' Sagar pleaded, now hopelessly confused. 'I have to get out of here.'

'Wait for the Swordsman,' she told him.

'The Swordsman? He's the reason I was thrown in here in the first place,' Sagar exclaimed. He heard the gaoler approaching, and instinctively assumed that his strange visitor would flee, as she had done before. 'Don't go,' he whispered desperately. 'You must explain. I . . .'

But Alasia showed no signs of leaving. She looked round, smiling, and Sagar peered along the corridor just in time to see the man drop the tray of food and make a sign with his hands, meant to ward off evil or sorcery. Then he fled, and Sagar glanced back at the woman.

She's mad! he thought. *Completely mad.* All his hopes collapsed. *The first person I've been able to talk to in days and . . .* A black depression enfolded him. *I'll be like that soon.*

'You are free,' she said.

Sagar almost laughed, but found that he could not. Her words were the ultimate crushing irony. When she turned and walked silently away, he made no attempt to stop her. Instead he sank slowly to the floor, put his head in his hands and wept.

Even Clavia, who knew the reason for her half-brother's preoccupation, was getting worried. Important affairs were being neglected, and she had heard the mutterings among the Chancellor's staff. She watched Verkho carefully, and saw that time seemed almost to have stood still for him. Until his precious talisman arrived, nothing else mattered. He had even lost interest – temporarily, Clavia hoped – in his plot against Azari. Her own ambitions were being thwarted while Verkho frittered away his days. And now he had shut himself away from everyone. Something had to be done.

It took several attempts and all her considerable

powers of persuasion to enable her to get to see her half-brother. His servants had been told to keep everyone out, but at last submitted to her increasingly vehement demands with obvious nervousness. Yet when she strode into the room, in belligerent mood, Verkho looked up from the massive tome that he was studying and greeted her mildly.

'This has gone on long enough!' she scolded him.

'What?' he asked innocently, seeming genuinely surprised.

'You know very well!' Clavia retorted. 'You've been closeted in here for two days now, while for all you know, the Empire could be falling apart around your ears.'

'I've been busy,' he protested, then added eagerly, 'I've made a breakthrough. Ghosts are not limited by place. Watch.' He brandished the emerald ring that Clavia remembered from the old temple, and the anguished, translucent figure of Rowan Kihan appeared beside the desk.

'Send him away,' Clavia snapped angrily. 'Has something addled your wits?'

Looking surprised again, Verkho waved a hand and the spectre vanished.

'How long have I been in here?' He sounded puzzled.

'Two days,' she answered impatiently.

'It didn't seem so long,' he said thoughtfully and then, returning to something like his normal manner, he added, 'There must be work to be done.'

At last. Clavia breathed a mental sigh of relief.

The transformation was extraordinary. Within moments, Verkho had become businesslike, the faraway look in his grey eyes replaced by their usual rapacious glitter.

'What do you want?' he asked, as though seeing his half-sister for the first time.

Clavia came straight to the point.

'Have you given up your attempts to get rid of Azari?'

'Oh, that's not important now,' Verkho replied dismissively. 'He's of no real consequence.'

'Not even after being rescued by a bat?' she prompted, and saw that she had hit a nerve.

Verkho had been bothered by one aspect of his earlier failure to poison Azari, and that was the manner in which it had been thwarted. The white wine he had given the Empress had, of course, contained the poison which he claimed was in the Embarragio. That was why he had let Ifryn raise the red wine to her lips before snatching it away. Had his attempt succeeded, he would have been able to blame the unknown Swordsman and Claros, who was now conveniently dead. But someone had foreseen his purpose and had prompted the unnatural actions of the winged creature. It was sorcery of some sort, of that there could be no doubt and, because of this, his suspicions had fallen on some of his own men, those involved in various esoteric researches. However, Verkho's initial investigation had revealed nothing – and the news of the talisman's approach had driven all else from his mind.

'Whatever powers my enemies have,' he said eventually, 'will soon be swept aside. Let Azari thrive. It won't be for long.'

'Aren't you putting too much faith in one avenue of progress?' she asked pointedly.

'Perhaps I have, temporarily,' he admitted. 'But it is such a beguiling prospect.'

'And dangerous.'

'Without danger, the rewards are usually small,' he replied philosophically. 'But I have other strings to my bow. Thank you for reminding me of my duties.'

Clavia could not tell whether he was being sarcastic or not.

'You've already given me some new ideas,' the Chancellor went on. He smiled, his eyes reflecting all his usual deviousness.

'Can I help?' she asked.

'Indeed you can.' Verkho went on to tell her how.

For several hours after Clavia's departure, the Chancellor called in various members of his staff to give him the latest news from the city and further afield, and issued them with new instructions. His employees were relieved by his emergence, and pleased to see his renewed enthusiasm and energy. However hard he drove them, they all knew that Verkho worked even harder.

One of the first people to report was the Focus, and it was from her that the Chancellor learnt of recent communications with Zalys. One of the ministry officials in control of the Far-speakers had noted that several of his charges became unusually tired after linking with the island. He monitored subsequent exchanges and grew convinced that something was wrong. The Focus reported that when the official had come to tell Verkho what was happening, he had been unable to gain admittance, and so had used his own authority to pursue the matter.

At this point, the Chancellor sent for the official himself, and got the whole story, including transcripts of both the enquiry and Farrag's response. It made interesting reading. Verkho had long suspected Farrag of being over-ambitious.

'Perhaps I underestimated him,' the Chancellor said thoughtfully.

The ministry official did not respond.

'His reply seems reasonable enough,' Verkho went on, 'but it smells of evasion, wouldn't you say?'

'Shall I follow it up?' the other man asked.

'No. Leave this with me for a while. I need to think about the best approach,' his master replied. 'You've done well.'

The official left, feeling pleased with himself, while Verkho pondered this new development. It had long been considered theoretically possible to syphon off the telepathic energies of Far-speakers for other uses, but no one – as yet – had been able to put this into practice. If Farrag had really accomplished this, then Verkho had indeed underestimated him. It was not a pleasant thought. The Chancellor decided that he would have to devise a way to find out just what was going on on Zalys – and soon – and to turn it to his own advantage. But for now he pushed the matter to one side and went on with other business.

One of the most interesting of the subsequent reports came from another ministry official, one of those who had been at the Chancellor's dinner party only a few days ago. Harios Kedhara had no special talents beyond a keen intelligence and fierce ambition, but he was a good administrator and an excellent keeper of records. His prime responsibility was the section of the ministry dealing with the investigation of ghosts and communications with them – and Harios was a worried man.

The first reason for his concern was a vast and unexplained increase in the number of ghosts appearing in Xantium, especially at the old temple.

'It's given our people plenty of opportunities, of course,' Harios said, 'but there are so many it's tending to confuse things. Half the time it's impossible to locate the source of perceived responses, and trying to measure results is hopeless. We've done nothing which might have prompted such activity . . .' Here he glanced at his master in case Verkho had any explanation, but the Chancellor offered nothing. '. . . and it's making some of the talents nervous.' After giving some examples, he added, 'I'm afraid it might overload them, destroy their minds completely. They're highly strung at the best of times.'

'Can you test this theory?' Verkho asked.

'Only by risking a complete breakdown.'

'Do it,' the Chancellor ordered. 'Keep me informed.' He decided to visit the temple himself. Over the last few months he had found himself becoming increasingly intrigued by the ancient pantheon, drawn to them not by faith, but by curiosity and the promise of power. Verkho wondered briefly what drew the ghosts to the temple. Were their motives the same as his?

'What else?' he asked, returning his attention to Harios.

'There's another problem with the talents,' the official replied. 'It's impossible to say whether it's connected to the first.' He hesitated, hating to report in vague terms, but knowing that he had no choice.

'Go on,' Verkho prompted.

'You're aware that we watch them day and night, even when they're asleep.'

'You have always been very thorough.'

'Thank you,' Harios said gratefully. 'During the last two nights, many of them have been experiencing nightmares. I have a list of the names and times here.'

Verkho waved the proffered paper away.

'Have you questioned them?'

'Of course. Their answers are all in my report here.' Harios produced another sheaf of paper and placed it on the desk.

'Summarize for me,' the Chancellor instructed. 'I'll read it later.'

'I have no firm conclusions as yet,' Harios admitted reluctantly, 'but the frequency and duration of these nightmares cannot be coincidence – and, if anything, they seem to be getting worse. Something, some outside influence, is affecting them, I'm sure of it. But the only common factor in all the dreams – which are incredibly varied, even when they make sense, and the talents don't always remember them clearly . . .'

'The common factor?' Verkho prompted coolly.

'Something . . . big and grey . . . getting closer,' Harios answered, shamefaced.

Verkho nodded thoughtfully.

'They're all afraid of it, sometimes violently so,' the official added. 'That's all I can tell you now, but I hope . . .'

'You've done well,' Verkho interrupted and Harios relaxed visibly. 'Most wouldn't have noticed or recorded their findings so soon.' He tapped the sheaf of paper. 'Tell the other section heads to watch for similar phenomena with their own talents, and take charge of collating the responses – on my authority. If there's a pattern to all this, I want to know.'

'Of course, Chancellor.' Harios left, buoyed up by Verkho's confidence in him and already anticipating his new task – and the opportunities that went with it. In his excitement he forgot to ask Verkho for any news of the long-anticipated arrival of Bowen Folegandros.

Captain Ofiah was pleased with their progress. In two days' hard riding from Brighthaven, they had covered more ground than he could have hoped for. With luck, and if the weather held, they would be in Xantium in another eight days.

Against all expectations, their prisoner had proved to be a good horseman. That, combined with Chancellor Verkho's mandate, which allowed them to travel light, renewing provisions and changing mounts frequently at each imperial way-station, meant that they travelled fast. Of course, crossing the Deadlands would be a different matter, but by then they would be almost home and the six men under his command would need no encouragement to make the best possible time. It would be different for the prisoner, however. Why should he be anxious to come to journey's end?

Bowen Folegandros was required in Xantium as soon as possible, together with the contents of a small casket, which the captain had strapped to his own saddle. Ofiah had no idea why either was so important to Verkho, and although he was certainly not about to question the Chancellor's orders, he couldn't help wondering. Although Ofiah carried a key, the casket had been sealed so that he could not open it without his interference being discovered. The captain was no fool, and had no intention of inviting Verkho's wrath by disobeying his instructions. And so his speculation centred on the prisoner.

As far as he could tell, Bowen was insane. His expression was normally blank, as if his brain had been turned off while his body rode his horse, but his eyes sometimes came alive, staring wildly, filled with some unfathomable torment. At these times, Bowen also broke his habitual silence – though he said nothing that made much sense. He often called out a woman's name, Gaye – his wife, Ofiah assumed – and then had to be steadied in his saddle. The anguish her memory caused was plain to see, but the captain was a hardened, professional soldier, and felt little compassion. Even so, he took no part in his men's lurid speculation about the attributes of the unknown woman.

The prisoner's other utterances were far more peculiar. He talked wildly of grey sheets, beacons of fire and gravestones in the sky, and endlessly repeated the word 'falling'. The soldiers could make no sense of this gibberish, and had made fun of Bowen's words with nonsense of their own. However, the prisoner was in a world of his own, and did not react to their mockery. Eventually, the soldiers became unnerved by his outbursts, and the mood had turned ugly, with Ofiah having to enforce strict discipline for the prisoner's protection.

As he led Bowen into the way-station to arrange for the night's accommodation, Ofiah vowed to get to Xantium as fast as humanly possible. *After that, young man,* he thought, *you're on your own.*

'Falling,' Bowen said unexpectedly. 'Falling, falling, falling, falling . . . We must learn to fly.'

'I wish we could,' Ofiah commented. 'It'd be quicker than riding.'

CHAPTER TWENTY-SEVEN

A strange bird has built its nest here. How will it fly away amid all the smoke?

Corton had lived in constant fear since the fateful banquet – but nothing had happened. No one had questioned him about the wine, about whether Claros had acquired it from him, or about the possibility of poison. After three days the wine-master had just begun to relax, believing that the whole incident might soon be forgotten, when a rumour reached him that brought his fears flooding back. He was so distressed that he found it impossible to concentrate on that evening's game with Grongar and, as a result, he made two moves faster than he had ever done before, much to the barbarian's amazement.

'Careful,' he commented after the first. 'Move any faster and you'll sprain your wrist.' Grongar played in his usual manner, and was astounded when his opponent responded almost immediately. 'You've been at those mushrooms again, haven't you,' he remarked. 'The ones you cultivate down in the cellars. You know they always make you impetuous and irrational.'

'What?' Corton asked distractedly.

Grongar's grin faded as he looked again at his friend's latest move.

'Are you sure you want to do that?' he asked. The barbarian was in a generous mood. He had won the final game of their last series and held a comfortable four to one lead in the current competition. He always played to win, but disliked being handed any game on a plate. Corton's last move had been suicidal.

The wine-master stared at the board, saw his error and sighed.

'It's done now,' he said resignedly.

Grongar shrugged and took Corton's bull with one of his sprites, effectively ending the game as a contest. They played on for a few more moves before Grongar's victory was confirmed.

'What's up?' he asked.

Corton looked up from the board, worry written all over his lean face.

'There's a rumour circulating that the wine Claros gave the Empress wasn't poisoned after all, that Verkho arranged the whole thing for his own devious ends – and that he was the one who put Claros up to it, not the Swordsman,' he said. 'One of my cellar-lads was full of it this afternoon. Impertinent young pup! I had to reprimand him severely for repeating such nonsense.'

'It may not be nonsense,' Grongar said quietly.

'That's what worries me,' his companion agreed. 'I can understand speculation over the Chancellor and the Swordsman – but what I *can't* see is where the idea came from that the wine wasn't poisoned. Verkho's not likely to admit such a thing, and I was the only other person who knew . . .'

Grongar suddenly seemed to find the floor between his feet extraordinarily fascinating.

'Oh no!' Corton exclaimed. 'You didn't?'

'I might've,' the barbarian mumbled into his beard.

'I should have known,' the wine-master said. 'Don't tell me. Let me guess. You were drunk, no doubt, and probably trying to impress some poor kitchen maid?' His voice was thick with contempt, and Grongar was stung into looking up.

'Can you blame me for wanting a little friendly company?' he snarled. 'There's so little juice in you, I could use you as kindling!'

242

'Whereas you dribble from every pore,' Corton retorted with unaccustomed vulgarity. 'I thought I could trust you.'

'You can,' Grongar claimed angrily. 'There were already so many rumours flying before I put my nose in the trough that it won't be noticed. There's people in higher places than you who should be worried.'

'Such as?'

'Kerrell for a start. The gossip says he's in league with the Swordsman.'

'Impossible!' Corton exclaimed.

'I think so too, but what do I know?' Grongar responded sourly. 'There's even been some talk about Azari being dead. No one's seen Ifryn or the baby since the banquet – and some people think the poison might have worked. Except, of course, there wasn't any.'

Corton was left speechless, and his friend's defensive anger had run its course.

'I'm sorry. I . . .' Grongar began.

'It's all right,' Corton told him.

'We live in troubled times,' the barbarian said.

His companion nodded absently. Grongar was right. With such things afoot, no one was going to worry about a mere wine-master. Or so he hoped.

'Good morning, my love,' Southan said as he entered, his face serious. 'I'm afraid I have strange news. Kerrell has disappeared.'

'What do you mean?'

'Just that. He's vanished.' The Emperor spread his hands in a gesture of helplessness. 'No one can find him anywhere.'

'But that's absurd,' Ifryn replied, her heart racing. 'He can't just vanish.'

'That's what I said,' her husband replied soothingly. 'But half the army and most of Verkho's people have been looking for him for a day and a night now – and found no trace. It's most disturbing.'

It can't be true! the Empress thought wildly. *I don't believe this is happening.*

'When was he last seen?' she asked, amazed to find her voice perfectly steady.

'Noon yesterday, in the practice yards,' Southan answered. 'He left to go to his quarters to change, and hasn't been seen since. He had several appointments in the afternoon and a meeting with me last night but he came to none of them, and sent no apology.'

'Why didn't you tell me sooner?'

'I didn't want to worry you prematurely,' her husband replied, his eyes full of concern. 'The last few days have been difficult enough as it is, I know, and he might have been out of sight for good reason. But he's been gone too long now, with no explanation.'

'Who could have done this?' Ifryn felt as if she were shrivelling up inside. She wanted to shout, scream, throw things – but outwardly at least, she remained calm.

'Done what?' Southan asked.

'Kidnapped him, or . . . or . . .' She could not bring herself to say 'killed him', but the words were there in her thoughts.

'That's what we're trying to find out,' the Emperor said, 'but there's nothing much to go on.' He paused, then added gently, 'And there's always the possibility that it's of his own doing.'

'Don't be ridiculous!' Ifryn cried. 'Why would he just disappear?' *He would have told me where he was going.*

'There are all sorts of rumours circulating,' Southan told her reluctantly. 'Verkho tells me that some suspect Kerrell of being in league with the Swordsman. It's utter rubbish of course, but people get carried away.'

Verkho tells me? Verkho? How can you accept what that snake says? Ifryn wanted to make her demand out loud but knew that she couldn't. She merely listened as her husband went on, sounding sad but determined.

'There's even been some cruel gossip that Azari is

unwell. No one's seen either of you since the banquet.'
That had been four days ago. Seeing the pain on his
wife's face, Southan asked quickly, 'He *is* well, isn't
he?'

'Yes. Come and look.' Ifryn moved like a sleepwalker
to the cradle, and stooped to pick up the baby. Azari
smiled and gurgled happily, his blue eyes dancing
between his parents. Ifryn wanted to shake her son, to
make him see how horrible the world was – but he was
only nine days old and such pointless cruelty was beyond
her.

'Even so,' Southan said, sounding pleased, 'it would
be a good idea if the two of you appeared in public again
soon. Today if possible, to offset the gossip. I'd like to be
at your side.'

'Of course,' Ifryn responded. 'Why ever not?'

'There's an even uglier rumour,' the Emperor said,
sounding distinctly uncomfortable. 'Some filthy idiots
are saying that Kerrell has disappeared because of some
impropriety between the two of you.' Southan hurried
on while Ifryn tried to remain composed. 'Needless to
say, anyone with a grain of sense would only have the
utmost contempt for such vile lies, but it will do no harm
for us to be seen together. You understand?'

The Empress nodded dumbly.

That evening, her public duty done, Ifryn retired to her
chambers, feeling utterly weary and wretched. She laid
Azari in his cot, then straightened up as she heard
someone enter the room. She turned, expecting Doneta,
but saw Alasia curtseying. For some reason, the sight of
her friend brought all Ifryn's pent-up emotions to the
surface. She ran to Alasia and embraced her, crying like
a child.

The next thing she knew she was in bed, feeling warm
and comfortable. She had no recollection of undressing
or of sliding between the sheets, but that didn't matter
now. Sleep beckoned, welcome oblivion, but then she

noticed a figure in the shadows at her bedside and the real world returned.

'Alasia, do you know where Kerrell is?'

'No.' For once her friend gave an unequivocal answer, but it was not the one Ifryn wanted to hear.

'Will you find him for me? Find out if he is still alive?'

'My friends are here,' Alasia replied. 'We have many eyes and ears.'

'Then they are my friends too,' Ifryn said sleepily. 'Thank you.' She did not really understand the conversation, but was comforted by it nonetheless.

'We are always here for you to call on us,' Alasia said. 'I must go now.'

'No! Please don't leave me.'

'You need sleep.' Alasia touched her fingers to the Empress' forehead, and Ifryn felt a drowsy warmth spread through her. Perhaps she would sleep now. It seemed like a good idea . . .

She awoke in the middle of the night, pale moonlight glimmering in the open window. The warmth had gone, fled into the darkness, and Ifryn was suddenly very afraid. She leant over to check on her son, who was sleeping peacefully, but that did not erase her terrors. Her world was falling apart.

I'm so afraid. What is happening to me?

Ever since the first mention of a possible threat to Azari, she had been prey to waking nightmares. Sometimes she was afraid even to feed the baby, mistrusting her own body. Then there was the sorrow and grief of her father's death and her worries about her old homeland. And now, as if that wasn't enough, there were these horrible rumours, and Kerrell – of all people – had deserted her. Her main ally in the daunting games of state was gone and she felt lost, the world tilting under her feet.

Ever since she had dreamt of Kerrell on horseback, naked to the waist, her thoughts had been in a mad jumble. She kept recalling the roughness of his garment, the warm strength of his hand, his smile . . . And now, with him gone, she could finally admit – in the privacy of her own thoughts – what she had known in her heart for so long.

I love him.

Ifryn caught herself up, long years of self-denial reasserting themselves. It would have to be her secret for ever. For ever? She knew that they could never be together, but didn't think that she could bear the pain of never being able to speak her love aloud, of never holding him in her arms . . . She could feel his embrace now, enfolding her, making her blood tingle, her head spin . . .

What would his reaction be? Did he love her in the same way? And the most unthinkable question of all; could their feelings for each other have been why he had disappeared?

'Gods!' Ifryn breathed aloud. 'It's all a dream. A hopeless dream.' She began crying softly, realizing that Kerrell was gone, that he might even be dead. She might never see him again. *My friendship is something you can count on for as long as I draw breath.*

A long time later, Ifryn's misery turned to exhaustion and she slept again.

Let me dream of him, she pleaded silently as the night enclosed her.

There was no sign of the general the next day, but in the late evening, as the darkness drew over the city, the citizens of Xantium were treated to a spectacle which gave rise to a fresh wave of rumours.

At the summit of one of the stone peaks of The Spires, a light sprang up. At first it was only a dull flicker, but it grew steadily in brightness as the flames took hold and the fire took shape. By now, most of the city had come out to watch and to whisper. All eyes looked towards the top of the hill – the one place visible from almost everywhere within the city walls.

Verkho saw it, and knew it for what it was – a challenge of the most public and bold nature. There could be no refusing this gauntlet. He stared, coldly furious, and barked out orders which sent soldiers scurrying up to The Spires. Then the Chancellor turned away at an urgent summons from the Focus. He followed her inside, while far above the huge fiery torch, fashioned in the unmistakable shape of a burning sword, shone brightly against the night sky.

CHAPTER TWENTY-EIGHT

Magic is all around us. Men see what they want to see, believing they know what is commonplace and what extraordinary. Is it a fault in me that I see it backwards, hear the words in reverse?

Some grasp at this elusive magic, glimpsing it only by the light of their dark fire, not realizing that they are doomed to fail by the very act of reaching out. All they have to do is look into the palm of their own hand. It is there already.

Nkosa was haunted by more than ghosts. The public executions had given shape and meaning to the vague forms of nightmare, and some people tried to outwit fate by leaving the town, hoping for safety in the remote villages of mountain or coast. A few escaped before their imperial masters realized what was happening, but by midnight there were guards on the bridges and overlooking the river and harbour. Anyone who persisted, however much they protested about the legitimate nature of their business, was turned back by the grinning soldiers – but most retreated of their own accord when they saw the way blocked, not wanting to be recognized.

A quiet dread slipped over the town, and those who could sleep at all slept uneasily. As dawn came, few people ventured out, afraid of being cornered by squads sent to round up the new day's victims, but some had no choice. This day's tides would be the highest of the season, and even though the wind held strongly in the west, lessening the risk, they needed to be watchful. To be less than vigilant meant that they could lose their homes – or even drown.

While the sea lacked Farrag's malice, it could be an even more implacable enemy and, despite the weariness of days of toil and the wordless terror of other dangers, it had to be faced. It was soon apparent however that in spite of the strategically placed guards, there were actually fewer soldiers about than normal, and as the morning passed and nothing untoward happened, a tiny streak of optimism returned to tinge the all-pervading fear with hope. Farrag did not usually deal in idle threats – but life had to go on.

Some, even those who were desperately weary, faced the new day without the benefit of a full night's sleep. Fen woke in the middle of the night from a formless dream to instant, tangible horror. She was exhausted, and her body ached, but her thoughts were terrifyingly clear. She shook Dsordas awake and he almost catapulted out of bed, ready to defend her against any foe. But there was no enemy to be seen. Fen spoke urgently.

'We have to put Natali's pendant back on!' she exclaimed. 'We were so tired last night that we weren't thinking straight, but if we're right about the ambush, then Farrag knows Natali has been around members of the underground – and the logical place to start looking for them is with his family. Us!'

'But . . .' Dsordas began, still disoriented after his sudden awakening. 'What would putting it back on prove?'

'That we don't suspect what's going on,' Fen told him. 'If Farrag thinks we've found him out, then he'll cut his losses and we're doomed. But if he thinks he might get more information, he'll leave us alone, for a while anyway.'

Dsordas took her head in his hands and kissed her.

'And he *will* get more information,' he told her, fully awake now. 'But this time it'll be what we *want* him to hear!' He smiled fondly. 'What would I do without you?'

'Worry less?' she suggested, grinning weakly, then grew serious once more. 'Let's do it now,' she urged. 'I can't get over the feeling that he's waiting, trying to listen. His patience may be running out.'

'All right. Go and fetch the pendant from Father's cabinet,' he said, businesslike now. 'Then we'll think about what we say in front of Natali. We're going to have to be very careful.'

Dsordas had already passed word to the other families to guard what they said in front of their children, but that was mere concealment. What they had to do now was far more delicate. Whatever false information they fed to Natali – and thence to Farrag – it must be close enough to the truth to be believed, otherwise, as Fen had put it, the Marshall would cut his losses. On the other hand it must not be so close as to genuinely harm the underground. They would be treading a fine line between triumph and disaster. In this game the stakes were getting higher by the hour.

Farrag had also spent a busy night. Ever since his disruption of Gaye's wedding, he had taken an especial interest in the Amari family, and Natali's performance had only increased that fascination. Now, of course, his experiment was producing its first solid results. Theory had become practice. Three more members of the Zalys underground movement were dead, another captured, and their plans for the oil revealed. A search for more barrels was already under way, but the prisoner was the main prize. Farrag had left him alone in his cell for a few hours, giving him time to brood on his fate, and now went to interrogate the man himself.

He had waited until well after midnight, knowing that tiredness would make the prisoner more vulnerable, and the terror in the man's eyes brought a satisfied smile to the Marshal's face. Farrag was unarmed and alone – the guards had been left outside – but the prisoner did

251

not even consider trying to attack him. The Marshal's reputation and confidence were weapons enough. Even so, his initial impression of the prisoner led him to believe that he might be a worthwhile opponent. For hypnotism to work effectively the subject must be either willing or very suggestible. This man was obviously neither, so Farrag decided to forego the pleasure of toying with him in favour of a quicker and effortless alternative.

Long ago, he had found that toad venom, diluted with water and mixed with a chemical solution of his own devising, produced a truth serum which had the added benefit of making his hypnotic hold both instantaneous and unbreakable. Its only drawback was that after two or three hours of perfect cooperation, the subject lapsed into a coma and died within a day or so. By then, of course, Farrag would have learnt all he needed to know.

The Marshal produced a small, earthenware bottle from inside his robe and unstoppered it, staring into the prisoner's eyes the whole time.

'You could make it easier on yourself,' he began.

'No!'

'Very well.' Farrag shrugged. He had expected no less. 'You force me to use unpleasant methods. Guards!'

Two burly soldiers entered immediately.

'Make the prisoner drink this.'

After a brief, unequal struggle, one guard held the prisoner's head, pulled back by his hair, while the other pinched his nose and poured the liquid into his helpless, open mouth. The man spluttered and swallowed, and then was dumped back on to the floor, gagging as the dark fire spread through his body.

'Leave us now.' The soldiers went out. 'Look at me!' Farrag ordered. The man glanced up involuntarily, and found himself held fast by mesmeric eyes. 'What is your name?'

'Marath Kellaki,' the prisoner answered in a monotone.

'Where do you live?'

252

Marath told him, then at Farrag's request, gave him the names and addresses of his companions in the group. As he started on the fourth, the Marshal made a mental note to chastise the squad leader who had either not noted the man escape, or had felt it safer not to report his failure to catch the entire group. The list would have to be checked against the corpses before the fifth man could be identified and found, but Farrag saw no reason to hurry unduly. However, after that promising beginning, the interrogation became frustratingly unrevealing. Marath admitted readily enough that his section had been commanded by Phylo Zevgari – one of the dead men – but stated that he knew no other high-ranking members of the Children or, for that matter, anyone other than those in his own small group. When pressed he said – apparently believing it – that every islander was a Child of Zalys. All this was delivered in a flat, unemotional tone while tears ran unnoticed down his cheeks.

In disgust, Farrag changed tack, and asked him about the underground's operations, their plans, the locations of stores and meeting places, but Marath was equally unforthcoming. He was able to describe some past events, which were no longer of any real significance, but he had no idea of future plans – apart from the ultimate goal. Even the purpose of the oil was unknown to him. He knew of no storehouses, and all the meetings he had ever attended had been in public places, at a different location each time.

This all added minutely to Farrag's knowledge, and though it gave him small scope for future surveillance, it was nowhere near as interesting as he had hoped. In fact, the greatest significance of the interview was the Marshal's increased respect for the organization of the Children. Someone knew what they were doing.

Farrag went over old ground a few times to make sure he had missed nothing, but Marath had begun to shake now, a sure sign of his fatal decline, and his interrogator gave up.

'You're not as tough as you seemed,' Farrag sneered. He went out, leaving the prisoner to his lonely fate.

Released from Farrag's hypnotic gaze, Marath curled up in a corner, trembling uncontrollably, his mind now locked into a downward spiral from which there was no escape.

Returning to his own quarters, the Marshal found an anxious Information Officer waiting for him.

'Splinter has a message for you, sir,' he said, naming one of the Far-speakers.

'Well?'

'For your ears only, sir.'

Farrag felt a moment's unease. Such secrecy meant something important – and that usually meant Verkho. What could he want now?

However, when he reached the Far-speaker complex, Farrag found that although the message was indeed from Xantium, the codename attached was not one he had heard before. However, he knew that it must be a senior official, because the message had been relayed by the Focus, the Chancellor's personal assistant.

Despite the relief of not having to deal directly with Verkho, the message itself was alarming enough. It was couched in diplomatic language, but it was in essence a demand to know why contact with Far-speakers on Zalys consumed so much energy. It also asked Farrag to reconfirm the number of telepaths on the island, and to explain any additions to the official allocation, if there were any. As well as enquiring whether the power of the Far-speakers was being augmented with anything other than the usual amberine crystals and nectar – the standard euphemism for the toads' excretions – the communication also asked whether this power was being used for any purpose other than necessary relays between Zalys and other parts of the empire. As a postscript, it requested details of all relays to and from the island during the last three days.

At first, Farrag was stunned by the implications of

such a thorough inquisition. He had always known that his discoveries could not remain secret indefinitely, but that they should be discovered – or at least suspected – from such a distance was a shock. However, he had no intention of giving up any of his personal power without a fight, and he was soon laughing, realizing that he had the perfect excuse for the anomalies – and planning to take advantage of this unexpected turn of events. His experiment with the children and Ravel's amberine was turning out to be more useful than he could ever have imagined.

The Marshal composed a lengthy reply. He explained that it had been necessary to increase the complement of Far-speakers from six to eight because the possible failure rate on messages had become too high, due to overwork and the long distances involved. He confirmed that their augmentation was standard, and denied any use of power for anything other than approved communications. His smile as he dictated this section told its own story. Finally, he explained his use of the island's children as potential informers and put forward the theory that they were the cause of the abnormal power drain, but asked to be able to continue his experiment as it was 'close to success'. He finished his reply by saying that all details of recent messages were being collated and would be sent when ready.

'Add my code and relay at once.'

Splinter nodded obediently. A few moments later, she said, 'Message relayed and received.'

'Let me know if there's any response,' Farrag ordered and went out, finding the officer who had summoned him still in attendance. He passed on the relevant information from his interrogation of Marath, and gave instructions concerning its follow-up. Then he ordered that a record of recent transmissions be prepared, stating that he wished to inspect the list before it was relayed to Xantium.

'Right away, Marshal.'

255

'An interesting night,' Farrag observed.

'Shall I put a sweep of the town in motion, sir?' the officer asked. 'Gather a new batch for execution?'

'No. Let them cringe for a while,' the Marshal replied, smiling. 'Waiting for the blow that never comes.' He had more interesting matters on his mind now.

'Won't that be seen as a sign of weakness, sir?'

Farrag considered this and also noted the junior officer's unusual boldness in questioning an order. He might go far – but he would need to be watched.

'I don't think so,' he replied eventually. 'And it will make the real blow even more effective when it comes.'

Farrag glided away, intent on a few hours' well-earned rest and relaxation. However, he was roused at dawn by a soldier with an urgent summons from Iceman.

'He wouldn't give me any details, sir,' the guard added, 'but he says he has new information from the youngest spy.'

The Marshal sped to the complex, eager to learn the latest developments. Iceman looked up with red-rimmed eyes as his master came in.

'Well?' Farrag asked.

'Well what?' the Far-speaker said with belligerent weariness.

'You have reestablished contact with the Amari child, have you not?'

'Yes.'

'Then tell me what you heard!' Farrag demanded angrily.

'I can't remember,' Iceman whined pathetically. 'I need more nectar.'

The Marshal gave in immediately, privately deciding to replace Iceman soon. He was becoming unreliable, in spite of his considerable talent. Perhaps he should be put into a permanent trance, like the earlier two. That way he would not be wasted totally.

Iceman brightened once he had drunk, and without

further prompting began to repeat a half-heard conversation, between a man and a woman, judging by his imitation of their voices.

'"Stupid to commit list like that to paper . . . in the wrong hands . . . disastrous."'

'"Where is it now?"'

'"Pick up point . . . shelf in Garland Tunnel."'

'"Get . . . soon!"'

'"Can't risk . . . in daylight . . . after . . . being watched."'

'"This evening then?"'

'"Yes."'

Iceman's voice reverted to his own.

'That was all. One of them was the same man I heard before.' The Far-speaker looked pleased, expecting praise.

Farrag was delighted, but turned away abruptly and sought out an army captain.

'You know where Garland Tunnel is?'

'Yes, sir.' It was a stretch of one of the town's minor canals that ran beneath several buildings. It was not strictly a tunnel as it was open to the air in several places along its length, but the overall effect was the same. Inside were numerous landing stages and, no doubt, many nooks and crannies which might be used as a hiding place.

'I want it searched, Captain,' Farrag went on. 'Discreetly, mind you, but thoroughly. Get your men to do it out of uniform, and avoid any undue attention. I don't want to scare anyone away.'

'What are we looking for?'

'Anything unusual, but specifically some documents,' the Marshal replied. 'They'll probably be in a container of some sort. Clear?'

'Yes, sir.'

'Bring the papers to me, but leave everything else there,' Farrag instructed. 'Mark the spot and station guards – out of sight, you understand – to watch the place. Someone will be there this evening, and I want them taken alive at whatever cost.'

'Yes, sir.'

'You are in personal charge of this, Captain. If you have any problems, report directly to me.'

'Understood, sir.' The soldier left to begin his task. He was under no illusions about the price of failure.

CHAPTER TWENTY-NINE

War is fought on many levels. Not all weapons have sharp edges.

'What did you put in the list?' Fen asked. She and Dsordas were alone, and Natali was now securely locked away in his own room. She hated treating her own brother like a prisoner, but knew it must be done.

'A very impressive collection of arms,' Dsordas answered, grinning. 'Swords, spears, bows, arrows, cudgels. I hope they'll think it's what we've already got hidden away, or that it's what we're expecting from some outside source. Either way, it should give them something to think about. A few of the weapons I put down are a mystery even to me!'

'Such as?'

'Fire-bricks, underwater crossbows, demon masks . . .' With each item he named, Dsordas made an uncomprehending face and shrugged exaggeratedly.

'They sound good,' Fen said, smiling.

'They do, don't they?' he replied. 'I wish we really had some!'

'You didn't make it too far-fetched?' She looked worried again now.

'I hope not. Most of it was pretty mundane.'

'Is it wise using a genuine pick-up point?' she asked. Dsordas had been to the tunnel during the last hours of the night to leave the fake inventory.

'I don't see why not,' Dsordas replied. 'I'll make sure

we don't use it again. Now we have to decide who goes to make the pick-up.'

'You're not really sending anyone?' Fen exclaimed.

'I have to,' he told her earnestly. 'Otherwise Farrag will know it was just a trick.'

'But . . .' Fen struggled for words. 'They'll be walking into a trap!'

'I know,' he said coolly, 'but this is a dangerous game, and we can't play without taking risks. As far as you and I are concerned, we're already under scrutiny. One slip and they'll come for us. We have to assume we're being watched, and act accordingly. Farrag will leave us alone only as long as we're more useful to him at large, you told me that yourself.'

Fen took a deep breath and tried to steady her nerves as the full weight of their predicament bore down on her.

'Anyway,' Dsordas continued, returning to the earlier problem, 'the chances are they'll want to take the messenger alive, which might give him an extra moment or two – and there's a way out of the tunnel very few people know about. The right man could get away with it.'

'Malo?' Fen suggested quietly.

'Of course.' Dsordas nodded. 'He knows the place better than anyone, and they already know he's one of the Children. He's got nothing to lose.'

'Except his life.'

'He's accepted that. We all have.'

'But he knows who you are,' Fen objected belatedly.

'I'm already a suspect,' he reminded her. 'What they don't know is the scope of my involvement. We just have to hope that Natali's potential holds them off.' He paused. 'Even so, it'd be better if Malo thinks the mission is genuine.'

Fen found it hard to listen to Dsordas talk about such things so coldly.

'And we could arrange for him to be unable to talk if he is captured,' he went on thoughtfully.

'How?' Fen asked.

'Poison,' he replied. 'Malo's brave enough to kill himself.'

'Oh gods, no!' She was shocked beyond measure. Dsordas' deliberate tones were at odds with the obscene things he was saying.

'In some ways he'd be better off,' he told her gently.

Fen couldn't speak.

'Don't worry,' Dsordas reassured her, taking her into his arms. 'It won't come to that. He got away from them once. He can do it again.'

'Oh, Dsordas, I hate this,' she whispered. 'I wish it was over.'

'It will be soon, my love,' he told her. *One way or another.*

Although the day passed uneventfully, Nkosa was full of rumours. There was a certain amount of panic whenever soldiers were seen on the move, but no arrests were made, and no executions sullied the already stained tiles of Fournoi Square, where the heads of the four earlier victims gazed blankly. Passers-by averted their eyes from the grim reminder of what might still happen.

By midday even the guards at the town's exits had gone, and the townspeople were free to come and go as they pleased once more. However, most of them were more concerned with the latest high tides. As the highest of the season, these would have presented a serious threat but for the fact that the wind opposed them, and in the event, the morning tide passed without serious mishap. The islanders' twin enemies – Farrag and the sea – seemed, temporarily at least, to be postponing their onslaught, and the ensuing lull seemed almost unreal. In such an atmosphere it was not surprising that gossip should run wild.

Almost all the rumours began as theories about why no more 'reprisals' had been made, and were all characterized by a degree of optimism and wishful thinking which grew more preposterous by the hour. The first and apparently most logical suggestion was that the robbers had been caught, and with the guilty men either incarcerated, tortured or already killed, Farrag had no justification for further outrages. Other variations of this tale concerned the methods used to capture the criminals. Some said that their victim had recognized them and had them arrested; others claimed that they had been handed over by fellow islanders who were anxious to see no more innocent deaths. Those with more lurid imaginations suggested that Farrag had used sorcery to track them down, while a few were certain that the thieves had given themselves up, in spite of the ridicule this opinion provoked.

This was followed by an even more far-fetched wave of speculation centred on Farrag himself. The pessimists among the townspeople believed that he was merely waiting, planning something even more vile, while others concluded that the Marshal had been arrested by Niering for overstepping his authority – just as poor Nias Santarsieri had predicted – and that he was to be put on trial or even sent back to Xantium in disgrace. This in turn led to some rumour-mongers claiming that Farrag was actually dead! The reports of his demise varied considerably, but most concluded that he had been murdered, either by his own soldiers, by the Children, or by a brother of one of the executed men. One or two, however, quoted reliable sources as revealing that Farrag had died from a rare, horrible plague – brought on by his own unspeakably foul habits – while some said that his own sorcery had become too powerful for him to control.

But the most outrageous rumours of all were those that stated that Zalys would soon be free, not only of Farrag, whether alive or dead, but of the entire imperial presence. The whole garrison, so the tale went, was preparing to sail back to Xantium because the Empire was being engulfed by war. The most popular explanation of this was an invasion of barbarians from the east, a region so remote from Zalys as to be regarded as a land of myth, monsters and blood-soaked savagery. Some of the more gullible islanders even began watching the eastern horizon, hoping to see the approach of the fleet needed to transport the soldiers.

The more sober-minded citizens laughed off all such tales as utter nonsense, but as they were unable to explain Farrag's apparent reversal of policy, the rumours persisted – and were all eventually reported back both to Dsordas, via the Children, and Farrag, via his Information Officers. The reactions of the two men were remarkably alike. Both were at first angered by such stupidity, then they saw the humorous side of it all and laughed uproariously, despairing of their fellow men. However, there was another strand to the wildfire stories circulating in Nkosa that day, and when they heard of this, the two foes reacted in markedly different ways. Farrag treated the news in light-hearted fashion, simultaneously intrigued and contemptuous, and set several men to monitor developments, hoping to gain some useful intelligence – or at least a source of further amusement. Dsordas was anything but amused. He was coldly furious, and did his level best to ignore the growing weight of opinion and superstition – and to make sure that all of his followers ignored it too. If there really was to be a mass gathering at the Arena the next day, he for one wanted nothing to do with it.

Malo sculled steadily into Garland Tunnel, his expert handling of the oars making scarcely a ripple in the dark water. He was barefoot as usual, but his normal outfit of loose-fitting trousers and shirt was augmented now with a black cape thrown over his shoulders, so that it could be discarded in a moment, and a broad-brimmed hat. Dsordas' messenger had warned him that volunteering for this task would mean breaking all the rules of self-preservation which the underground's leader normally insisted upon – but making himself a little harder to recognize would do no harm at all.

Malo had had no hesitation in accepting both the job and the condition that he must not be taken alive. He knew that it must be a matter of the utmost urgency and that Dsordas would not have chosen him unless he was the best man for the task. The poison tablet was tucked into his shirt pocket, but he had no intention of getting into a situation where he had to use it. Malo had confidence in his own abilities. He had been told that the secret document – about which he knew nothing – might have been removed before he got there. If that was the case, he was just to get away as quickly as possible. If the hiding place had *not* been discovered, he was to take the papers with him into the water, destroying them as he made his escape. Either way, it was almost certain that Farrag's men would be watching the place, so his boat would have to be abandoned. Once in the water, the darkness and his undoubtedly superior knowledge of the water-filled underworld of Nkosa would work to his advantage.

Malo thought he had already spotted one observer but appeared to pay him no attention, rowing easily in the centre of the canal under the curving archway of dank stone. As he passed one of the openings between buildings, he noted the possibility of several others. Then he saw the darker space of the niche in the gloom of the tunnel ahead. It was carved into the stone, a pace or so above the high-water mark. His heart beat faster, but his rowing stroke remained unchanged until he drew level with the hiding place. Then, with a sudden swerve, he whirled the boat around and drew alongside the gently curving wall. He saw something move at the end of the section of tunnel, and heard sounds of movement elsewhere, but he ignored these distractions. First he had to find the document.

He stood and reached into the darkness. His hand fell upon the earthenware casket immediately and he pulled off the lid to delve within. It was empty. Malo swore under his breath, tossed his hat and cape aside and dived smoothly into the water. As he did so a cross-bow bolt, aimed at his legs, missed by a fraction and clattered into the stone beyond.

Shouts echoed in the tunnel, and shadows leapt as lamps were uncovered; boats appeared from their hiding places as the waiting soldiers converged, but Malo knew nothing of all this. He was swimming down strongly, trusting in the darkness to his innate sense of direction, the air in his lungs rationed by long experience. First crossing over to the far side of the tunnel, Malo worked his way along the slime covered wall until his questing fingers found the opening he was looking for, then quickly thrust himself into the submerged side tunnel. It was little wider than he was, and he knew now that he could not be captured. Either he would escape, or he would drown. There was no going back. *Not far now,* he told himself. His lungs aching, lights exploding behind his eyes, Malo swam on blindly. He had one moment of near panic when the material of his leggings snagged on an unseen piece of debris and he had to expend vital time and energy to tear it free. But then, at last, he saw a faint pool of light ahead and spurred himself on, praying that he would not find the way blocked by more rubbish. Squirming round the corner, he thrust upwards gratefully and burst into the blessed air above an entirely different canal.

Malo gasped, looking around quickly to ensure that he was unobserved, then smiled and began to swim towards the haven of his safe house.

CHAPTER THIRTY

No fire burns within the valley of ghosts, neither dark nor bright. There are only ashes, growing cold. What will it take to rake within this hollow dust, to find the fading echo of a spark? Who is there to blow it into flame?

My eyes are still blind and even the newest beacon grows dim.

'Nothing at all?' Farrag repeated.

'Not since dawn,' Iceman confirmed. 'All I've had since then are nursery rhymes, games and food.' He sounded disgusted at having to spend his time listening to such inconsequential nonsense, and as he had already explained to his master, the fleeting contacts from the other children were just as innocuous.

Farrag shrugged obese shoulders and sighed. It was the second disappointment of the day. The first had been the paper that the Amari child had led him to. The list had simply been an armoury inventory, which had included not only an impressive array of conventional weapons but also some rather more mysterious items. But it had given no mention of where these weapons were stored, or who had supplied them. If the so-called Children of Zalys really had access to such a store, then these mysteries would have to be solved, but the list on its own was useless – except in helping his soldiers be better prepared for a battle Farrag intended never having to fight. Now all he could do was wait for the prisoner in Garland Tunnel to be captured and hopefully shed some light on the document. Other than that, all the Marshal could do was brood on a rumour-filled but remarkably uneventful day.

There had been no further messages from Xantium. Farrag knew that he had not heard the end of the matter, but it would soon be of no consequence. He would have achieved his ends. He smiled, thinking of Verkho and his reaction when he discovered that Farrag had moved on – and taken his knowledge with him.

His thoughts turned then to his plans for tomorrow. Should he arrange more executions – or would it be better to allow the islanders another day of living in a fool's world? Their gossip was entertaining, and would make his eventual reemergence even more satisfying. He began to envisage various gruesome reprisals, his black tongue moistening thick lips, his eyes unfocused.

His reverie was interrupted by the return of the captain of the guard. The man was clearly uneasy, beads of sweat standing out on his brow, and Farrag assumed the worst.

'Well, Captain?' he asked sharply. 'Where is the prisoner?'

'Drowned, sir.'

'I distinctly remember ordering you to capture him alive,' Farrag said coldly.

'He was too quick for us, sir,' the soldier said. 'In the dark . . . no one expected him to dive so fast . . .' He swallowed painfully. 'But he's dead. I'd swear he never came back to the surface. We had the whole tunnel covered.'

'And his body?' Farrag's anger was building up dangerously.

'Must still be underwater, sir. We're trying to find it.'

'You *will* find the body, Captain,' the Marshal commanded. 'If you do not, you will be drowned yourself.' He turned away, dismissing the soldier. Tiny flashes of blue light surrounded Farrag's bulk as he fought to bring his rage under control.

*   *   *

That same evening found Fen, Dsordas and Gaye talking softly together in Gaye's room. The two women had known that it would be pointless even discussing the proposed meeting in the Arena with Dsordas, and had quietly made their own plans. Just now another subject was on all their minds.

'I think we should take Natali's pendant away from him,' Gaye began.

'I agree,' Fen said. 'We can't keep him locked away the whole time.'

'That's not what I meant,' her sister said. 'Whether he's shut up or not, that thing is harming him. I felt it, remember . . . it was horrible. If we leave it too long, the evil could overpower him permanently. The gods know what damage it's already done.'

Dsordas looked back and forth between the two sisters.

'We need him to keep it on a little longer,' he said apologetically. 'Taking it off now might bring Farrag's men down on all of us, and if we're right, Natali can help us a great deal.' As he spoke, he seemed distracted, glancing frequently out of the open window.

'How much longer?' Gaye asked.

'A few days at most.'

'A few days!' She was horrified.

'I'm sorry,' he said. 'We all have to make sacrifices.'

'You're playing with a little boy's mind!' Gaye exclaimed.

'I am *playing* at nothing,' he told her, with a touch of bitter anger in his voice. 'I love Natali just as much as you do. Don't you think . . .' Here he paused, having seen something out of the window. Fen followed his gaze and saw a brief flare of orange light from the roof of a building some distance away. She looked back at Dsordas and saw him relax a little.

'What's happening?' Gaye asked, sensing the change in them.

'Malo's safe,' Dsordas explained. 'That was our signal.'

Fen breathed a sigh of relief as he went to close the shutters. 'Malo?' Gaye prompted uncertainly.

Until then they had not told Gaye all the details of their plan, but now Dsordas saw no reason why she should not know. Time was growing short, and if he couldn't trust Gaye, who *could* he trust? So he explained what had happened.

'Now we *know* Natali is unwittingly feeding information to Farrag's men – and we can use that to our advantage. The alternative would mean us all going into hiding.'

Gaye still looked unhappy but accepted his argument, and Dsordas took it a stage further.

'You obviously have talent of some sort,' he told her. 'Your experience with Pauli and Natali proves that – but perhaps you could do more.'

'How?'

'What if you were to put on a pendant?'

Gaye shook her head immediately.

'No! I'd be trapped,' she said. 'Even at secondhand, that feeling I got from Natali made me feel ill, disgusting and slimy inside. I can't do it.'

'But you might be able to hear their Far-speaker messages,' he persisted. 'Turn the tables on them completely.'

'I can't!' Gaye looked both frightened and horrified.

'Leave it, Dsordas,' Fen said quietly.

He nodded, accepting their decision, and realizing that it might have been too dangerous. He smiled inwardly at the irony of the conversation. These two wanted him to use magic, but when presented with a possibility that might actually make some sense, they shied away.

'I won't ask again,' he said softly. 'I'm sorry.'

Later that evening, Dsordas met Yeori in one of the underground tunnels accessible from the cellars of the house. His lieutenant reported on Panos' behaviour during the day. Nothing unusual had been seen, and no changes in the routines of the Far-speaker complex had been noted.

'All right,' Dsordas responded. 'Keep watching. When we move, we'll need to contact him quickly.'

Yeori nodded confidently and went on his way.

So far so good, Dsordas thought as he climbed back up the stairs. *Now if only the wind would change!*

However, the following morning dawned clear, warm and settled, with the westerly wind blowing steadily. Dsordas set about his tasks for the day, intent on advancing their preparations as far as he could and unaware, until much later, of the unusual movement in the town.

People began leaving Nkosa in ones and twos; overland along the southern coastal path or through the hills; by sea in a number of small but well-crewed boats. The island's fishermen had been prime movers in arranging the gathering, feeling themselves to have borne the brunt of the untoward abnormality of nature. The travellers all moved at their own pace, but all had one destination – the Arena.

Farrag's observers noted the migration quickly and monitored it but, on the Marshal's instructions, they made no move to interfere. Farrag wanted the meeting to go ahead, but kept the whole affair under close scrutiny, both with spies among the throng and from more remote positions.

Fen and Gaye travelled most of the way in the back of a farmer's cart, unwittingly following Natali's route of three days earlier. The climb from the fishing village was laborious and awkward, but there were many willing hands available to help the blind girl and her sister. When they finally reached the vale itself, there was still an hour to go until noon, but there were already several hundred people gathered in the Arena.

For a long time the atmosphere was awkward, the air

full of the murmur of desultory talk. Gaye felt very uncomfortable. The group had no natural leader to turn to, and no one seemed to know what should happen next. Nias was still abed – and near to death, according to some – and the island's most influential and wealthy citizens were also absent, perhaps feeling that such a foolhardy display of superstition was beneath them. It was as if everyone felt that merely meeting there had been a bold enough step, and that some greater power – perhaps even the place itself – should take over now and relieve them of the responsibility. Eventually, one of the older fishermen, who was widely respected for his age and skill, climbed on to a boulder and called for silence. As the Arena gradually became quiet, Fen found herself looking not at the sailor, but at the Stone Eye. From where she sat, she could look through the tunnel which framed only a small patch of blue sky. *How do we re-awaken it?* she wondered, gazing at the distant lens. *How do we call on the magic here, the ghosts, the memories?* She was at a loss, and was further downcast by the fact that Gaye felt nothing special about the place; whatever her talent was, it was not attuned to the Arena. Their earlier vow seemed like an empty promise now. Equally disappointing was the fact that the Arena had not re-sponded in any way to the largest gathering it had witnessed for more than a decade. Where were the ghosts she had seen? Then her attention was reclaimed by the voice of the fisherman, whose name was Latchi Irini.

'You all know why we are here,' he cried in a cracked voice. 'Zalys has been abandoned by the old gods, as we have abandoned them. There are signs everywhere. Apart from the evil dangers we already face – which we've faced for long years, and will eventually throw off . . .' He must have known that he was risking his life by speaking in such a way about the imperial forces, but he had been pushed beyond endurance by recent events and did not care who overheard. 'As well as this,' he resumed, 'the forces of nature, which the gods control, have turned against us. Zalys is sinking! Even though the wind sits happily in the west now, it won't always do so, and Nkosa and other places will drown.' He paused, and for a time the only sound was the soughing of the wind. 'The sea has gone mad,' Latchi went on, looking around. 'You've all seen it. Lights and whirlpools, noises and sudden cold. The fish are no longer where they're supposed to be. They behave like mad things, leaping from the sea or beaching themselves . . .'

Now that Latchi had made a start, others interrupted, eager to take up his theme. One fisherman told how his father and brother had been killed when a giant sea-bat leapt upon their boat, shattering it to kindling. He had only escaped himself by great good fortune. Another described how his friend had been engulfed by a luminous mass while swimming, and was never seen again. Others claimed to have heard singing or drums beating beneath the waves, or to have seen impossibly brightly coloured sharks or giant crabs with claws as long as a man's forearm. And the list would have gone on but for a lone voice rising above the others.

'We've all heard these tales,' the man cried, 'but what do they mean? Why have we come here today?'

'To summon the old forces,' Latchi answered. 'The memories of the gods, our old allies. This place used to be special. We came here to ask for help.'

There were shouts and mutterings of agreement.

'But how?' Fen recognized the new speaker as a sometime acquaintance of Dsordas, a man called Skoulli. 'What exactly are we supposed to *do*?'

That silenced the crowd for a time, and then an old woman, in worn black robes, spoke up.

'All the rites of this place were stories of a kind,' she shouted hoarsely. 'Words, music, memories. We need to remember the stories.'

'What use are stories?' someone called. 'We need action.'

The argument split into a hundred fragments, a chaos of opinion and doubt.

'They're never going to get anything done,' Fen commented to Gaye.

'It's looking at us,' her sister said, sounding preoccupied.

'What?' Fen glanced up instinctively and gasped when she saw that the pupil of the Stone Eye was now black, as if the eye were blinking; she almost cried out, but then a small child tumbled out of the tunnel, leaving the unchanging patch of blue sky once more. She shivered, and the moment passed.

'I want to go,' Gaye said. 'I'm scared.' She was trembling in spite of the day's heat.

You do *feel something,* Fen thought. 'What are you frightened of?' she asked.

'I don't know.'

'How can we reawaken the Stone Eye?' Fen persisted. 'Surely that's why we're all here.' She was becoming frightened too now, without knowing why. *I'm so afraid. What is happening to us?*

Gaye shook her head, looking dejected and miserable.

'I've no idea,' she whispered. 'I want to go.'

'Oh, well,' Fen decided. 'Nothing's going to happen here.' She stood up and helped her sister to her feet, feeling the overwhelming sadness of the place once more. She had no more idea than Gaye about how to call on the dormant powers of the Arena, the faces she had seen once so fleetingly. *It's all a dream. A hopeless dream.* They set off home in a mood of deep depression, knowing that any prayers said in the Arena that day were fated to go unheard.

Day had turned to evening before they got home. Dsordas had been on the move all day, and so had not been aware of their absence; although he had learnt that the meeting in the Arena had taken place, he chose to ignore the possibility of Fen having attended.

The day had passed quietly in Nkosa; even the tides

had done little damage, and Farrag had not provoked any more violence, but even so, Dsordas was suffering from a crushing headache. For all his efforts and those of his men, which were bringing them to the brink of readiness, the fateful decision had still to be made – and Dsordas was the one who had to make it. He knew he was running out of time.

CHAPTER THIRTY-ONE

Is this how it feels?

It is not my destiny to know love in this world. I will never have a child, never watch with parental pride as she takes the first faltering steps of discovery, speaks her first real words. But my life has its joys as well as burdens. This day feels as wondrous to me as the day I learnt to fly myself.

'We go with this evening's tide,' Dsordas told them.

The decision was greeted with a mixture of relief, excitement, and misgiving. After waiting and planning for so long, it was hard to believe that the time for the uprising had actually come.

That morning had brought news which gave them all a renewed sense of urgency. Farrag's patience had evidently run out overnight, and eight more heads now decorated bloody poles in Fournoi Square. The new terror of midnight raids had been added to the sufferings of Nkosa's inhabitants.

'Everything ready, Mouse?' Dsordas asked.

'As ready as they can be,' he replied. 'Tonight's tide will be the last for a while to give us a chance, but unless the weather changes I don't think we'll be able to do much damage.'

'Just do what you can. At least it should cause some confusion.' Mouse nodded and Dsordas turned to Yeori. 'Can you get to Panos quickly enough?'

'Yes. He's easy to find.'

'You know what to tell him?'

Yeori nodded.

'Don't worry,' he said. 'We'll take care of him – and the Far-speakers.'

'I'd like to take some of them alive if we can,' Dsordas went on, 'but not at the expense of a message getting through to Xantium. Any danger of that and they have to be killed.'

'I know.' Some of the Far-speakers were reported to be little more than children, but Yeori knew that he had to be ruthless. There was too much at stake.

'So who's taking over from Phylo?' Skoulli asked.

'Malo,' Dsordas replied. 'I've already spoken to him.'

'I thought he was dead,' Mouse said.

'He's in hiding. Malo knows what to do,' their leader reassured them. 'You'll have your backup.'

Skoulli, always the most methodical of the lieutenants, wanted to make sure they had thought through all aspects of the operation.

'Are you sure this is wise so soon after the meeting at the Arena?' he asked. 'Old Latchi was saying some pretty stupid things . . .'

'I think he realizes that now,' Yeori commented grimly. 'His son was one of the men killed last night.'

Skoulli swore under his breath.

'I didn't know that,' he said. 'But won't Farrag be on his guard after . . .'

'I'm hoping he'll see it for what it was,' Dsordas cut in impatiently. 'The mumblings of an old fool and some superstitious idiots. If Farrag really thinks the people in the Arena yesterday are the enemy he faces, then he'll be less prepared for us.'

'It was asking for trouble,' Mouse added, 'but I reckon it makes what we have to do more urgent, not less.'

'Anyway, I'm hoping to mislead Farrag about the timing,' Dsordas said. His lieutenants all knew about the children and their amberine pendants, but the full story was now explained.

'So Natali was responsible for Phylo's death?' Yeori asked carefully.

'Unwittingly, yes,' Dsordas replied. 'Me too. I should have realized what was going on. We have to make their sacrifices worthwhile.' His eyes were haunted.

'So what are you going to tell Farrag?' Skoulli asked.

'I don't know yet,' Dsordas said. 'I can't make it too obvious, but whatever it is, I hope to help us catch him off guard.'

'I've an idea,' Yeori said. 'There's a ship from the north due here in about three days, but it's a bit of a mystery because no one knows what cargo it's carrying. I heard the lads on the docks talking about it. Couldn't you imply she's got weapons on board . . .'

'Fire-bricks and the like,' Mouse added with a grin.

'. . . and say that we can't make any move until they arrive,' Yeori concluded.

Dsordas nodded thoughtfully.

'Better still,' Skoulli went on. 'Say she's actually going to drop anchor off one of the northern villages to unload before coming to Nkosa. That way we might even get some of the troops out of town.'

'Yes!' Yeori agreed, looking at Dsordas.

'What's her name?'

'*The Frozen Star*,' Yeori answered. 'Romantic northern name!'

'What if Farrag knows what's on board?' Dsordas asked.

'It's not likely,' his lieutenant replied. 'She's not an imperial vessel.'

'Have you got any better ideas?' Skoulli asked as their leader still looked doubtful.

Dsordas shook his head.

'All right,' he said. 'Anything else?'

'You're going to face some opposition,' Skoulli told him. 'Some of the hostage families are still against any direct action. Costa Folegandros, for one,' he added, naming Bowen's father.

'Do they walk around with their eyes shut?' Mouse exploded. 'Aren't those heads in Fournoi Square direct enough for them?'

'They don't come from their own families,' Skoulli pointed out. 'And they're in enough trouble already.'

'If we take out the Far-speakers,' Dsordas said calmly, 'then the hostages will have at least a short period before Xantium knows what's going on. We might even be able to think of some way of warning them, but we can't let their situation stop us. We've gone too far now.'

'In the meantime,' Yeori added, 'don't tell anyone you don't trust completely *anything* about tonight.'

'Right,' Dsordas agreed. 'We must be coordinated, so spread the word. But be careful – and, above all, don't let anyone tip our hand by panicking. No one is to evacuate their homes, or send wives and children out of town. We're all in this together, and we can't afford to let individual sentiment get in the way now.'

The men nodded solemnly.

'Right. Let's go.'

The meeting split up, and Dsordas went to find Natali. His head was pounding again, but he ignored the pain. His thoughts were with his family – and especially with Fen. Did he really have the right to risk their lives as well as his own? It was a heavy burden to bear.

Since the failure to capture the man in Garland Tunnel, Farrag had made Iceman concentrate solely on the Amari child, assigning the monitoring of the rest of the children to other Far-speakers. Iceman had been jealous at losing the total responsibility for this project, and had been uncooperative for a while, especially as nothing of interest had come through. However, the change of policy seemed to be paying off now.

Farrag was with Iceman when he said that Natali had been joined by others. Then the Far-speaker's voice changed, and he repeated a conversation – presumably from the same couple as before – which came through practically complete. The woman spoke first.

'"Shouldn't we attack now, before any more people are executed?"'

'"No. We have to wait for the weapons. We can't move until then."'

'"But *The Frozen Star* isn't due for another three days. What are we supposed to do until she gets here?"'

Farrag looked puzzled. Were they talking about the right vessel?

'"Nothing,"' the man's voice said flatly.

'"Will she dock in Nkosa?"'

'"No. That'd be crazy. We'd never get . . . off secretly. She'll anchor off the north coast and ferry the stuff ashore before coming on here."'

'"I hope you know what you're doing."'

'"We've no choice. The ship would have got here earlier if she could, but . . ."'

There was a pause, then the woman spoke again.

'"Come on, little one. Time for your bath."'

'Relay ended,' Iceman said in his own voice. 'I've lost the link. They must have taken the pendant off.'

Farrag smiled.

Well now, he thought. *I wonder how they intend to fight armed with a cargo of grain, pickles, timber and goats?*

You must come with me, Gaye.

Gaye jumped. She had been alone in her room for once, a rare occurrence in the last few days, and had not heard anyone approach.

'Who is it?' she asked before she realized that no one had spoken aloud.

A friend.

'Are you a ghost?'

In this world, yes. You must come with me, he repeated.

'What do you mean? Where to?'

To the Stone Eye.

279

'I can't go there,' Gaye protested, fear welling up within her. 'I'm blind!'

I will guide you.

'How?' she demanded, on the edge of hysterical laughter. 'I can't see you and you can't touch me!'

Let me show you.

A sensation stole over Gaye then that was so unnerving, so unlike anything she had experienced before, that she had to fight against screaming. It felt as though tendrils of awareness, neither pleasure nor pain – but *alive* – were growing within her entire body, becoming a part of her and yet alien, an invasion of her self. Gaye shivered.

'What's happening to me?'

The ghost did not answer; indeed, Gaye was not sure whether he was still there. But then her visitor disappeared from her thoughts, because – suddenly – she could see! Yet what she saw was no world she had ever known.

Her room had gone, the whole house too; Nkosa no longer existed. She was adrift in an endless, weightless chasm, its warm light stretching away to infinity. Gaye floated, lost in silence, knowing that she was not seeing with her eyes, and wondered if she was going mad.

At first there were no variations in the all-encompassing glow, but then she saw – or rather felt – quick wingbeats and black shadows. She was flying with her dream-friends, listening to their measuring voices. Realization made them potent; dark shapes in an unreal sky, flying.

You must come with us, Gaye.

'How?'

A woman's face appeared, pale beyond imagining, yet smiling.

You have learnt to fly. Come.

Gaye flew.

Here. Where was here? In this nether-world, there was no sensation of movement, no whistling of wind or change of perspective. No effort, no distance, no time. And yet Gaye flew.

Then the dream collapsed into darkness, and the stillness of her own world reasserted itself. A warm breeze ruffled her white hair, bringing with it the scent of flowers, earth, trees and sun-baked rock. She was sitting, and she felt around her. Her bed had gone; beneath her now were tinder-dry blades of grass.

'Where am I?' Her words echoed softly – and she knew where she was, knew that she was being observed, and was afraid.

The Arena greeted her in watchful silence.

Etha was beside herself with worry. Her usual monumental calm had been frayed by the unexpected demands of recent days and by her expanded household, all of whom had preoccupations of their own. But Gaye's disappearance was the final straw. Her daughter had been alone in her room since breakfast, with the door closed. Both Etha and Fen had been in the house the whole time, and both were prepared to swear that Gaye had not left her bedchamber. Yet when Etha had gone to take her her midday meal, she was gone.

No one could even suggest an explanation. She couldn't possibly have climbed out of the window – her blindness made movement slow and difficult – but a search revealed nothing. Etha collapsed, weeping, her nerves giving way, while Antorkas held her, looking helpless. He had always relied on his wife to cope with life's trials, to guide him through. Now their roles were reversed, and neither could cope.

Fen was as mystified as her parents, and as frightened. She did not know what to do, and wished that Dsordas would come home. She had not seen him since they had acted out their little play for Farrag's benefit that morning. Fen knew that the fighting would start soon, and not knowing where Dsordas was left her feeling bereft and full of terrors. And now her sister had vanished. *I don't believe this is happening.*

Unable to remain still, Fen went out to search for her lover.

The noonday sun shone brightly in the mostly deserted alleyways of Nkosa, but Panos saw shadows everywhere. He walked quickly, glancing behind him frequently and inspecting each doorway and alley as he passed by. The Information Officer had every reason to be nervous. His debts were still overdue, he was a traitor whose life would be forfeit if he was discovered, and he was at the mercy of islanders who were his natural enemies. Hedged in on all sides, he lived from moment to moment, grateful for each new breath.

When he saw the prearranged signal that summoned him to a meeting with his underground contact, whose code name was Falcon, Panos' heart raced, but he went immediately to the appointed place. A door opened and he stepped inside after one last nervous glance around. The room was warm, dark and stuffy, evidently an old storehouse of some sort and, as usual, Panos could not see the face of the man who spoke to him.

'I have good news,' the Falcon said. 'We will be raiding the Far-speaker complex tonight.'

'So soon?' Panos gasped.

'I thought that was what you wanted.' Yeori, alias the Falcon, sounded amused.

'Of course.'

'I hope you're not having second thoughts.'

'No!' Panos was committed. He had a slim chance of salvation, but it was better than nothing.

'Good. Listen carefully,' Yeori told him. 'This is what we want you to do.'

A short time later, having faithfully repeated all his instructions, Panos left by a different door, leaving the Falcon to his own devices. He went straight to the Far-speaker complex, glad that his duty roster meant he would be there legitimately that afternoon and evening.

It would have been awkward if he had had to make excuses to swap shifts. Instead he simply reported to the guards on the outer doors and went inside, his brain running through everything he had to do – and hurriedly making a few plans of his own.

However, all this flew from his thoughts when the duty officer he was relieving told him to go at once to Iceman's cell. When he got there, the Far-speaker was absent. There was only one person inside, and he was smiling evilly. Panos suddenly felt very sick.

'You should be aware that I've been taking a considerable interest in your activities over the last few days,' Farrag told him evenly. 'I think it's time we had a little talk.'

CHAPTER THIRTY-TWO

I listen to the screaming. Playing with dark fire has its perils – it burns both inside and out, across the worlds. But that does not mean it has no power. Beside it, the purer flames are as bright as candles in the sun.

How can we yet prevail when our very nature stacks the odds against us? Cast the dice and defy prophecy. Who would wager on rolling The Circle in one throw?

Fen had not been able to find Dsordas, and was now on her way back home, with Gaye's disappearance still weighing heavily on her mind. She was rowing steadily, feeling weary and miserable, when a hiss made her pause. She looked around and could see no one, but the sound was repeated and she spotted Nason, peering out of a hatchway, beckoning to her urgently. Fen manoeuvred closer. The boy's face was red, either from exertion or anger, she could not tell which.

'I've come to warn you,' he whispered. 'Farrag's men are on the way to your house.'

Fen's heart sank. She was so very tired, and it was all too much to bear. She wanted to cry, but found strength from somewhere.

'How do you know?'

Nason's face went redder still.

'I overheard my father giving them directions,' he said. 'I hate him!' Shame mixed with outrage in his young face. 'You have to get away!'

So the ruse failed, a small rational part of Fen's brain concluded. *Something went wrong and he knows we were using Natali.* At the same time, a far greater portion of her mind was pleading for help. *Oh, Dsordas, where are you?*

'I was on my way there now,' Nason went on, seeing her distraction. 'Do you want me to warn them?'

'No.' Fen pushed her fears aside. 'I'll be quicker by boat. You go home.'

'You'll have to move fast,' he told her. 'Make sure you don't get caught on the way.'

Fen nodded absently.

'Thank you,' she whispered as an afterthought as she pulled strongly on the oars.

It took all her willpower not to panic, knowing that a smooth stroke would get her there faster. As she drew nearer home, plans began to form in her head. She knew the escape routes; Dsordas had explained them all to her, but she had never really expected to use them. She found herself hoping desperately that Nason's father – curse the man! – did not know of the underground passageways.

Reaching the mooring, she leapt ashore without bothering to tie the boat up properly and ran to the front door. To her great relief she had seen no sign of the approaching soldiers, but she wasted no time. She burst into the kitchen, finding her parents, Anto, and Effi Gallo sitting at the table, their expressions full of worry.

'We have to get out. Now! All of us!' Fen shouted over their startled questions. 'Soldiers are coming! Down to the cellar. Quick!'

The urgency in her voice forced them to their feet, bewildered though they were.

'Where are the children?' Fen demanded.

'They're all in Gaye's room, I think,' Etha replied. 'I'll get them.'

'No,' Fen told her quickly. 'You help Effi. Anto and I'll get them. Papa, you go down and open the panel to the boat passage.'

285

Such was her almost manic persuasive power that they all did as they were told. Anto was already on his way up the stairs, and Fen ran after him. In Gaye's room, they found only Kato and Ia.

'Where are the boys?' Anto shouted.

'Pauli's under the bed,' Kato answered. As she spoke the boy crawled out, wide-eyed. 'The others went to play in the attic.'

Fen swore under her breath.

'Down to the cellar, both of you. Move!' she yelled, then scooped up Pauli, as Anto set off up the ladder to the attic. The girls were crying as Fen shooed them down the stairs.

In the cellar, Antorkas had got the panel off, and Etha and Effi were making their way slowly down the dark passageway. The girls were pushed after them and Pauli thrust into Antorkas' arms.

'Go!' she ordered her father. 'Get the boat ready. The others are coming.'

As she spoke, there was a clatter of footsteps as Anto, Tarin and Yermasi ran down the stone stairway.

We're going to make it! Fen thought in disbelief. 'Come on!' she urged aloud.

They all edged their way towards freedom, reaching the secret boathouse to find the two distraught mothers already in the spare boat. Antorkas and the children piled in, making the boat sit very low in the water. Their perils weren't over yet. Fen prepared to cast off.

'Where's Natali?' Etha asked shrilly.

'Gods!' Fen remembered that Dsordas had locked the boy in his room after his 'bath', to prevent any possible disclosures. 'I'll fetch him,' she said quickly. 'You leave now. We can swim.'

'No!' her father roared.

'Yes, Papa, you *must*,' she insisted. 'Otherwise we could all be caught.' She threw the rope aboard and pushed the boat away from the stone steps. 'Be as quiet as you can.'

Anto was already struggling with the oars and his father joined him, while their passengers tried to comfort each other. Fen turned and ran back up two flights of stairs. She reached the door, thankful that the key was still in the lock. As she turned it, the house rattled as someone crashed through the front door and she heard the soldiers shouting. *Now what?* There was nowhere to hide. Where could she go?

Fen opened the door and saw Natali sitting on his bed. She stepped forward, then stopped dead. A ghost stood beside her brother, watching him intently and, as she stared, both spectre and Natali slowly faded out of existence, vanishing into thin air.

'No!' she screamed and, too late, threw herself towards the bed. But she was alone in the room.

Fen was still stunned and sobbing when the soldiers found her and dragged her away.

Gaye felt the weight of their presences all around her, their eyes upon her. But she was blind again, and dared not even move from where she sat. There were many places in the Arena where a misplaced step could lead to a possibly fatal fall.

'What do you want?'

You know. It was a man's voice, one she had not heard before.

'I don't know how to wake it!' she told them. 'I'd do it if I could.'

All knowledge is available to you. Call on us. This time it was a woman who spoke.

'Who *are* you?'

Our names mean nothing. We are your friends.

'Then let me go home,' Gaye pleaded.

We cannot do that. You have work to do.

Each time it was a fresh voice, and Gaye remembered Fen telling her of the sparkling multitude.

'No. I can't. I'm scared . . . I'm blind!'

Yet you are here.

There are other ways to see.

You have time yet.

We will leave you to reflect.

The pressure of their regard vanished, and Gaye was left quite alone, shivering despite the warmth of the afternoon sun. None of this made any sense. How could she have got here? What was she supposed to do? Questions filled her head, but she had no answers. Gaye sat there for a long time, but had resolved nothing when the ghosts returned.

It is time.

'For what?'

To awaken the Stone Eye.

'Look!' Gaye cried, anger mixing with her tears. 'I don't know who you are or what you expect of me, but you've no right! I can't do it. I don't know how. I'm here – the gods know how – but I'm in the dark, with no knowledge, alone . . .'

Not alone.

And then another voice, young and familiar, sounded not in her head but in her ears, and a small hand crept into hers.

'The man with the sword said you wanted my necklace,' Natali told her. 'But it's *mine*.'

Iceman screamed.

Farrag watched as the Far-speaker writhed, his eyes rolling up until they showed only white.

'What's happening?' the Marshal snapped unsympathetically.

'It . . . hurts . . . hurts,' Iceman gasped. 'Burning . . .'

Farrag slapped his face.

'Pull yourself together!' He wondered whether Iceman had finally been stretched beyond his limits.

The Far-speaker stared, still racked with pain, shaking.

'Burning . . . light . . . took him away . . . not there now . . .'

'What are you talking about?' Farrag demanded. 'Have they taken the pendant off again?'

'No,' Iceman replied between shuddering breaths. 'Something else . . . ahh.' He relaxed suddenly. 'Back now,' he announced with immense relief, and his voice changed to that of a little boy.

'"The man with the sword . . ."'

Then Iceman fainted, and Farrag could not revive him. Muttering darkly to himself, he glided out of the cell, meaning to set another Far-speaker to monitor the Amari child. But he was intercepted by a soldier.

'Well?' he barked.

'The raid on the Amari house will be happening about now, sir. Where do you want us to put the prisoners?'

'Bring them here and put them in separate cells, away from the Far-speakers.'

The captain saluted and went on his way. Farrag wondered why the raid should have caused such a problem with Iceman. Something else had happened, he was sure of it. He began to look forward to interrogating the family. They should have some interesting tales to tell.

The conversation he'd overheard about *The Frozen Star* had been most enlightening. Farrag knew the vessel; the commander was an old acquaintance of his who had made several deliveries for the Marshal that he had wanted keeping from his imperial masters. He also knew her present cargo, and so the pretence that she was carrying weapons for the underground told him three things. Firstly, someone – he would soon find out who – had discovered the secret of the pendants, and was using it for their own ends. That meant that the Amari child was now worse than useless as a source of information. Secondly, it confirmed the family's involvement with the underground, and lastly, they were trying to mislead him about the timing of some action. As a consequence he had ordered the arrest of the entire household, and had put the garrison on full alert. He had even sent a few squads out of town to the north, supposedly reacting to the false message. The soldiers had orders to return to Nkosa within two hours, but it would be interesting to see the islanders' reactions to such moves.

And, of course, Panos had provided him with even more fascinating intelligence. The kidnapping story was nonsense, certainly, but the Information Officer's tale had confirmed that *something* was going to happen this very night.

Panos had had to be forced into a confession, but that had been easy enough. Once another of the Marshal's special poison solutions had been administered, he'd been only too cooperative. He would live long enough to play his part in the trap Farrag was setting for the Children, but then – unless he received the promised antidote – he would die a particularly unpleasant, painful death. Such a prospect was enough to ensure the temporary loyalty of even a rat like Panos. Farrag's patient surveillance of his foolish officer was now paying off.

The Marshal allowed himself a smile of self-congratulation. Even a few minor setbacks, like Iceman's apparent breakdown, could not stop him now. His enemies were playing into his hands.

Fen's mind refused to function. She was aware of light, sound and the world around her only in abstract terms. She saw, heard and felt nothing as the soldiers marched her towards the boat and then rowed towards the centre of the town. Too much had happened, too much had gone wrong; there was a limit to how much horror she could absorb – and she was long past that point. Gaye, and now Natali, had disappeared, in her brother's case right before her eyes. She had no idea where Dsordas was, but knew he couldn't save her now. What was more, the plans of the Children seemed to be collapsing, the end of all their long-cherished hopes . . . She clung to one tiny particle of hope – that her family had escaped – but she could not even be sure about that.

The boat arrived at a small landing stage near Fournoi Square, and she was taken ashore, into a labyrinthine building which some tiny portion of her tortured mind recognized as garrison headquarters. After walking down apparently endless corridors, they came to a bare passage with locked cells on either side. *The Far-speaker complex?*

And it was there that Fen saw something which broke her last fragile hold on sanity. As she was marched along, two soldiers in immaculate uniforms came the other way, grinning at her as they passed by. Fen's throat felt as if she had just swallowed a lead weight. They were the two men who had robbed and beaten Panos. Farrag had known all along!

Darkness filled her head, matching the black void in her heart, and Fen embraced oblivion gratefully.

Dsordas heard the news that his home had been raided as he made his cautious rounds, preparing for the evening's attack. His face was a mask as he listened to the bearer of bad news, and the man hurried on, hoping to soften the blow with some hope.

'We think the family got away, though.'

'All of them?' Dsordas asked.

'We're not sure. We'll check as soon as we can.'

Dsordas found himself praying to gods he did not believe in. *Please let them be all right,* he begged. *Fen, please be safe!*

'Are we still going ahead tonight?' the man asked.

'Yes,' Dsordas replied, as firmly as he could. 'The tide's already on the way in. We can't turn back now.'

The messenger went on his way, promising to bring more news soon. Dsordas steeled himself to continue and waited, helplessly, for further information. When it came it brought little comfort. Most of the Amari and Gallo families had reached a temporary safe haven – but Gaye, Natali and Fen were missing. Gaye had apparently disappeared earlier in mysterious fashion, but it was assumed that Fen and Natali had been taken prisoner. Dsordas wanted to abandon all his plans and go to try and save his love – but knew he could not. He couldn't expect others to obey the rules he had laid down if he flouted them himself. *We can't afford to let individual sentiment get in the way now.*

His only hope was that Fen and Natali could be rescued when they stormed the Far-speaker complex and the garrison headquarters. But Dsordas was too realistic to set much store by that.

Fen, I'm sorry! he cried silently. *Oh gods, keep her safe!*

CHAPTER THIRTY-THREE

My eyes have been opened by ghosts. I wish I had time to listen to all their stories, but the ashes are too deep. I will leave it to her.

She has fire enough for us all.

'It's all right, Natali,' Gaye told him. 'I don't want your necklace.' She felt the boy relax, and he snuggled into her side.

'Where did all these people come from?' he asked.

'They're ghosts,' she answered. 'They live . . . they belong here. How did *you* get here?'

'I flew,' Natali replied, sounding not in the least concerned, as though he took such things in his stride every day. 'What do they want?'

I wish I knew, Gaye thought. 'They want my help.'

'What with?' he continued with childlike persistence. 'Is it to do with the stone with a hole in? I like it there. I went to sleep inside,' he added proudly. 'After the pigs.'

Natali's innocent questions brought Gaye up with a jolt. What did he know of the Stone Eye? Even a little boy could see that it was important. *I have to try!*

'We can try together,' Natali said.

He's reading my mind! Gaye thought in amazement.

'Don't you want to?' he asked, sounding confused.

Let him help you.

For a few moments, Gaye had forgotten about their unseen, spectral audience.

He does not read thoughts, but he is sensitive to your

feelings. Only when something is projected strongly do specific ideas get through.

Gaye realized that this made sense of her being able to predict Pauli's moves in the game. They had been the single focus of the boy's thoughts at the time.

Hold the pendant, another voice advised. *He need not take it off.*

'But . . .' Gaye started to object, but then realized that she could no longer sense the ugly power behind the crystal. She was still afraid, but willing to try, to take one step at a time. 'Natali, can I hold your necklace? You can keep it on.'

Her brother placed the polished amberine into her palm. Gaye flinched, expecting the touch of evil, but all she felt at first was the warm, smooth surface. Then, all at once, her mind filled with sounds, vibrations and echoes. Music reverberated, words spilled forth in a profligate cascade and memories flooded through in waves of sound; the crash of storm-tossed waves, wind in the olive trees, the songs of birds and the whirr of insects. It was a joyful, sad cacophony – beautiful and hideous, calm and hectic, glorious and defiled. Conflicting emotions raged within her.

And through it all, Gaye heard again the words of the old woman. *All the rites of this place were stories of a kind. Words, music, memories.*

'It's too much!' Gaye cried aloud. 'I can't control this!' Beside her, Natali was gurgling with delight.

'Sparkly!' he exclaimed happily.

Gaye had no idea what he meant.

'Help me,' she pleaded.

Choose a story.

'Choose? Which one?' There were so many. 'What will that achieve?'

You will be able to concentrate. To make it real.

'Real?'

A face appeared in Gaye's permanent darkness, the same pale woman she had seen when she was flying.

Trust your instincts, the stranger told her calmly, *however foolish it may seem. Choose as your heart dictates.*

'And then what?'

The ghosts will play their part. By the force of their retelling they will make it true, but they need you to make it real in this world.

'You're not a ghost, are you?' Gaye said. 'Who are you?'

My name is Alasia. We see each other through the Stone Eye. And you must use it to spread the story to the sky.

'To make it real?'

Yes. Choose now. The face faded from view and the noise returned. Gaye wanted Alasia to come back, to tell her *how* to do it, but the woman was gone.

'It's all sparkly, and it blinked!' Natali reported excitedly.

'What?'

'The hole in the stone.'

Choose. The ghostly command overrode all else in its urgency.

'I can't think,' Gaye protested. 'There's too much noise!'

'That one,' Natali said. 'The big waves.'

One strand within the maelstrom of sound stood out abruptly, and Gaye felt a rush of relief, of gratitude. Instinct overcame logic, and she chose. At once, all the other sounds vanished and the story began.

The storm raged for only a few hours, yet in that time great damage was done. Rain and spray lashed the island, driven on by the dark easterly gale . . .

'This can't be right,' Gaye protested feebly. 'It'll destroy Nkosa!' Yet she knew in her heart that this *was* right, that it was meant to be. And she had to make it real.

'Whee!' Natali cried, thoroughly enjoying himself. '*Crash!*'

Gaye listened intently, wondering what she was supposed to do now. The description was so vivid that she could see the storm's approach in her mind's eye. *Use it to spread the story.* The Stone Eye; she felt it above her, looking down. No! Look outwards, to the sky. *It's all sparkly, and it blinked!*

In that instant, Gaye knew what she had to do. She took her internal vision of the story, the words of the ghost-tellers and the images they conjured up, and concentrated all her emotions, sending it spinning out into the world. Like a funnel in reverse, the Stone Eye channelled the story and threw it into the blue sky beyond. The Arena spoke with the voices of the gods.

Far away, on the eastern horizon, storm clouds began to gather.

When Fen came to, she was lying alone in a bare cell. Immediately, all the appalling memories of the last few hours crashed down on her, leaving her too drained and miserable even to cry. Her own fate seemed unimportant now. Everything was going wrong, everything she loved was doomed.

She pulled herself up and was sitting propped against the wall when the door opened and Farrag glided in, a hateful smile on his round face. Fen shrank back into herself, wishing she was still unconscious, almost wishing that she was dead.

'I'm glad you're awake,' he remarked. 'I have some questions for you.'

'I've nothing to say to you.'

'One way or another, you *will* answer,' he told her. 'But your cooperation would make it *so* much easier on the rest of your family.'

Fen looked up, trying to guess whether they too were in this monster's grip, but his smile gave nothing away. She bowed her head again, not wanting to look at him.

'I don't think you realize quite who you're dealing with,' he gloated. 'You should be honoured that I am attending to you personally. I am going to become one of the most powerful men in the world.'

Fen did not react to Farrag's boasting.

'Shall I show you?' he asked, sudden venom in his tone.

He thrust out a thick forefinger and a violent force slammed Fen's head back so that it banged painfully against the wall. She stared at him perforce, her eyes wide.

'Do you think such power is commonplace?' Farrag demanded. 'Not even the great Verkho is aware of the secrets, the powers I have uncovered.' His voice rang with sarcasm.

Still Fen chose not to respond. The longer her captor gloated, the longer it would be before he returned his attention to her.

'Aren't you even curious?' he asked contemptuously.

'Tell me,' Fen responded apathetically.

Farrag laughed.

'I can see it will take rather more than a brief display to impress a woman like you,' he remarked. 'Perhaps I should teach you some manners.'

Fen waited, tensed for further punishment, but nothing happened. The Marshal had evidently thought of a better idea.

'Far-speakers are chosen because of their innate talent,' he said, as if beginning a lecture. 'Like your little brother. But to become effective they have to be trained. Nectar increases their potential enormously, of course, and the amberine focuses their thoughts so that they can speak to each other over long distances. But we never needed them all at the same time, so I devised a method of leaving them inert, so as not to waste energy. Then I found that the energy didn't go away. It was still accessible to one who knew how to harness it and – with my own use of nectar – I did!' His cruel eyes were shining now, his face animated as he basked in his self-styled glory. 'And as more of them were brought together, the network on which I could draw grew ever more powerful. Two of the Far-speakers here are in a permanent trance now, feeding all their energy to me, and I can draw on the others whenever I wish.'

'Very impressive,' Fen mumbled half-heartedly. She was too dazed to take in all he had said, but knew that something was expected of her.

'I should have known better than to expect any appreciation from a peasant,' Farrag said dismissively. 'You've lost your northern heritage – you're just the same as these moronic islanders.' His expression grew serious. 'We've wasted enough time. Now you will answer my questions.'

Using the last drop of her fading defiance, Fen told him what he could do with his questions.

'Then you leave me no choice,' he said coldly, producing a small earthenware flask from his robe. 'I have no time to spare now. A colleague of yours was most cooperative after the guards made him drink some of this. I'm sure they will enjoy administering it to you even more.'

'Can't you do it yourself?' Fen asked. 'So much for your *power*.' She was shaking inside, but she put as much contempt as she could into her voice. If she could just get him to come close enough . . .

But Farrag was not to be drawn. He regarded her with amusement.

'Guards!'

Fen did not even have the chance to struggle. She found herself choking and swallowing the foul grey liquid, before being released and slumping to the floor once more. The soldiers went out, unnoticed, as the evil fire burned through her body. Already tortured and abused, her mind teetered on the edge of the black void but she remained conscious. All willpower evaporated. Nothing mattered any more. Farrag's eyes shone like beacons.

'Who is the leader of the Children of Zalys?'

Fen heard a voice she hardly recognized say, 'Dsordas. Dsordas Nyun.'

'Ah. Good,' Farrag said. 'Now . . .'

His words were interrupted by an unexpected crash of thunder, rolling across the unseen sky. Then the whole room shook violently and shouts echoed in the corridor. Farrag glanced around in consternation, then slid from the room.

Fen did not even notice him go. There were needles in her veins, fires behind her eyes and formless music in her head; pain was everywhere, the fathomless dark looming beneath her. For a moment she thought she saw Gaye's face, a strange light in her blind eyes. *Help me!*

Fen began to fall, swirling round in a nightmare whirlpool, slipping ever closer to the darkness below.

The storm hit Nkosa with the force of a thousand battering rams.

The wind had veered round so suddenly and so completely that it defied anyone's understanding, but Mouse and his men had not questioned their good fortune and had set in motion the sequence that would maximize the surge directed at the imperial barracks. An hour later, they were worrying that it was going to be too powerful to control. The lagoon was rising at a terrifying rate, and currents swirled violently as the clouds approached from the east like a purple wall of doom.

As the sun set, the moment came, and the deluge was unleashed. The storm arrived at the same time. The man-made tidal wave smashed along its predetermined path, carrying all before it, while the rain lashed down, the wind howled and lightning blazed. The sky roared.

The leading edge of the wave boiled and shook, twice the height of a tall man and moving faster than a galloping horse. In its path, boats were smashed or hurled aside, the sides were ripped off buildings and, despite Mouse's best efforts, several people – both his own men and others – were swept away. Its unexpected size and ferocity meant that the surge overflowed its banks in many places, causing smaller waves to radiate out through the town, but the plan succeeded in its main objective – only too well.

The main barracks, the target for that first wave, were still crowded because no one had had time to organize an evacuation. An immense wall of churning water slammed into the building, which simply collapsed like a house of cards amid a vast explosion of spray and rubble. Within moments, the continuing weight of the pent-up flow had carried almost everything away – from the smallest piece of wood to the largest block of stone. The men inside stood no chance.

But the wave was not finished there. It rolled on, its progress no longer so devastating, but still bad enough to inundate other parts of the town and throw them into utter chaos.

Mouse surveyed his handiwork in stupefied awe, knowing it was quite beyond his control now. Even away from the deliberate destruction, the storm had turned the floods into a terrible force, getting worse by the moment. One way or another, Nkosa would never be the same again after this night. Even if the Children won a great victory, there might be little left of the newly liberated town.

His thoughts turned to Dsordas and Yeori, who were to lead the attack on the Far-speaker complex.

They'll be going in about now, he thought and wished them luck.

Farrag grabbed a passing soldier.

'What was that?'

'There's a storm broken, sir. Flooding everywhere. The barracks have been hit badly.'

'And the complex?'

'We should be fine here, sir. There's no reason to change our plans. Panos is in position and so are all the men.'

300

'Good,' Farrag said, forgetting about Fen for the moment. 'I'll come with you. I want to see this for myself.'

As they approached the outer sections of the complex, they noted the troops waiting, their weapons at the ready. A door was slammed and barred as Panos emerged, and in the distance another boom rang out.

'Like rats in a trap.' Farrag smiled.

Panos approached, out of breath and sweating, his eyes pleading.

'They're all inside,' he gasped. 'No way out. I've done what you asked. Please, let me have the antidote now.'

The Marshal's grin became malicious.

'There is no antidote, you pathetic fool,' he said. 'And even if there was, I wouldn't give it to scum like you.'

Panos' face contorted and he rushed at Farrag, who raised a contemptuous finger. A pulse of blue fire knocked Panos flat.

'Throw him in a cell,' the Marshal ordered. 'Now let's go and see what we've caught in our trap.'

As he spoke, the first crashing sounds came from the far side of the inner door.

CHAPTER THIRTY-FOUR

I float amid the hand-wrought stone, on an altogether different island. An island of clouds. I long to be elsewhere, in the middle of the storm, but I dare not disturb their dreaming.

The dark fire sleeps.

Gaye listened to the storm raging all around her. She and Natali were safe, cocooned in serene warmth, dry and still. Something protected them. The ghosts? But they could not accomplish anything in the real world. The Arena? That made no sense. Nothing made any sense.

She heard a crash of thunder roll round the hills, and imagined the tumultuous waves, the howling wind. She pictured Nkosa under siege, devastated. *What have I done?* Yet the feeling that she had done the right thing persisted. Gaye held Natali in her arms, and waited. The voices were silent now; the story was telling itself.

Help me!

Fen's voice came out of the fire, bringing with it a dark, revolting ugliness that made Gaye recoil instinctively, but she forced herself to confront her fears. Fen could not possibly be the source of such evil; something had been done to her, she was in trouble and needed help. But how?

Choose a story. Make it real.

Without prompting, Gaye called upon her friends.

'Tell me another story,' Natali said sleepily.

'I'll tell you a new story,' Gaye replied, a sudden confidence growing within her. *And I'll make it real!*

* * *

In a distant way-station, Bowen stood on his bed, looking out at the night sky through the bars in his cell window. But his eyes saw more than stars.

The storm played out in his mind; he saw its terrifying onslaught and rejoiced as he felt the rain sting his face, heard the wind screaming in his ears. He loved the storm. And he knew who had brought it into being.

'Gaye,' he whispered jubilantly, and began to fly.

The winged creatures were all around him, their purpose certain. Leaving the mountains behind, they swooped down in their thousands, their world defined by the shapes of sound. It was exhilarating, this flight of freedom. But best of all because *she* flew alongside him. No longer falling.

For a few precious moments they were reunited, allowing Bowen to be happy and whole. He revelled in it, basking in the glow of her love; he felt her respond, felt her joy. Time vanished for Bowen – but when it returned he was doubly bereft. Blood ran down his wrists from where he had gripped the rough metal so tightly, his throat was hoarse from the shouts he had not heard, and his face was wet with tears.

Captain Ofiah, who had been summoned by the irate goaler to quiet his unruly, lunatic prisoner, watched as Bowen collapsed on to his pallet, his earlier yells now reduced to whispers.

'Gaye. Gaye,' Ofiah heard him say. 'We learnt to fly, but we're still not together.' The anguish in his voice was hard to bear, even though his words made little sense. Later he became even less coherent, repeating one word over and over again.

'Flying, flying, flying . . .'

The storm had caught everyone by surprise, but the Children lost no time in taking advantage of it. Together with twenty or so hand-picked men, Dsordas and Yeori made their way towards the outer buildings of the garrison headquarters, on the far side from the doomed barracks. Many of the alleys were already awash with rain and floodwater, and most of the sentries had retreated inside. Those who had not were disposed of with ruthless efficiency.

Even from their remote position, the noise from the impact of Mouse's tidal wave was colossal, rising above the pounding of the thunder, the hiss of the rain and the roaring wind.

'Now,' Dsordas said, and the signal was passed.

Simultaneously, two doors and two shuttered windows were attacked with axes. The sound of splintering wood was lost in the tumult of the storm and the men surged in, taking several soldiers by surprise. Dsordas led one group, his sword at the ready, and himself accounted for two guards before they could even draw their weapons. Elsewhere the fighting was fierce but brief, for this part of the garrison was relatively unimportant and not heavily guarded.

Once inside, the attackers' essential asset was speed. The men regrouped and Dsordas led them along a corridor, following Panos' instructions, heading directly for the Far-speaker complex at the heart of the imperial enclave.

Although they were occasionally intercepted by defenders, their advance was relentless. At last they came to a solid, iron-studded door which was the entrance to the complex. Here, as expected, they met fierce resistance. In the confined space, the battle was brutal and ruthless. Men sweated and grunted, smashing and parrying, manoeuvring for space, wet boots slipping on a floor made treacherous by a sheen of blood. Their ears were filled with oaths and cries of agony, their nostrils filled with a metallic stench.

Dsordas fought like a man possessed, releasing all his demons in an onslaught of fury. His blade ran red with blood, some of it his own from an unheeded wound in his forearm. He would have suffered far worse but for

Yeori's axe, which split an opponent's skull as he moved in for the kill.

It only took a short time to overcome the guards, though it seemed to last an agony of hours, and soon Dsordas was able to go to the door and hammer out the signal with the hilt of his sword. *Panos,* he thought, *don't let us down now.* To his great relief, he heard the sound of bolts being drawn back, and the door opened a crack as their accomplice peered out. Dsordas thrust the door wide open and his surviving men surged through after him. Inside it was just as Panos had described; a long corridor with cells on either side, but the officer – looking understandably nervous – grabbed his arm.

'Farrag moved them!' he yelled. 'This afternoon.'

Dsordas swore. 'Where to?'

'I'll show you. Come on.' Panos ran off down the corridor at a surprising pace, with the others trailing in his wake. Rounding a corner into another corridor, he sprinted ahead as the rest struggled to keep up. Ahead of them another solid wooden door stood open, and before anyone could prevent it, Panos threw himself through and the door was slammed shut with a resounding clang. As they heard securing bars coming down into place, the sound of another door closing came from behind, its boom echoing hollowly through the dark corridors and empty cells.

They were trapped.

Dsordas cursed silently, desperately, but then realized that some of his men were close to panic. He could not allow that. He had to keep them busy.

'Check all the corridors and rooms,' he ordered brusquely. 'See if there's a way out of here.'

The men spread out obediently, breaking down inner doors, running through the silent complex. They reported back soon, and they were all in agreement. Yeori put it most succinctly.

'All the cells are bare. There's not even any furniture. The only windows are high up and out of reach, and barred. The only way in or out are those two locked doors.'

'Well, there's no point going out the way we came in,' Dsordas said, trying to sound confident. 'Let's get to work on the other.'

Soon, half a dozen axes were thudding into the hardened, reinforced wood. Although at first they raised little more than a few splinters, eventually slow progress was made. But it was tiring work, and they all knew that when the breakthrough came, they would be facing an enemy who had had plenty of time to prepare for them. And all the time they had to be on the alert for an ambush from the rear.

At last the door seemed on the point of giving way, and Dsordas called a halt to organize their sortie. It was unnervingly quiet now that the axes had stopped. Nothing moved behind the battered door, and each man silently wondered about the nightmare they were to face. No one knew what lay beyond, no one knew the layout of the prospective battle ground, which was soon to become a dying place. It would only take a few bowmen, strategically placed, and the first men through the door would be dead before they had gone more than a few paces. But there was no alternative. To stay where they were only delayed the inevitable and gave the enemy even more time to prepare for them.

'Right. Everyone know what to do?' Dsordas asked.

In the gloom, each man nodded grimly, expecting to die within the next few moments.

'To your places then.'

The axemen who were to complete the job stood ready. Dsordas and Yeori were immediately to either side, ready to lead the assault, when the look-out at the junction of the two corridors cried out in alarm. Within moments they all heard it – an unearthly squealing, almost beyond hearing, together with an ever-growing beat of flapping wings. Dark shapes flitted within the shadows above.

'Bats?' Yeori said incredulously. 'Where did they come from?'

Other sounds came from beyond the door; screams, shouts of anger and confusion.

'Now!' Dsordas yelled urgently to the men with the axes. 'Go! Go!'

The heavy blades crashed down in unison and the door burst asunder. The two leaders leapt through to be faced with a macabre, lamplit scene. Before them was a large open space, with several corridors leading away like spokes from the hub of a wheel. There were soldiers everywhere, but they were all preoccupied with the dark, flapping creatures that clustered round their heads. Their fox-like muzzles and huge ears gave the bats a sharp, demonic appearance. No one had ever seen them act like this before. They seemed intent on attacking the imperial troops, several of them to each man. Sharp fangs glared and clawed forearms raked the air as the membrane wings beat frantically. Beating one away only meant that two more would take its place from the hundreds swarming above. And all the time more were streaming in through the high windows, joining the dark, milling mass.

Some of Dsordas' men glanced up anxiously as they surged through after their leaders, but they were not targets, and so they joined their colleagues in the battle which the bats had changed beyond recognition. There was no time to wonder at the strange turn of events.

The fight became a slaughter. The archers' weapons were useless when they could not see to take aim, and the other soldiers were so preoccupied with the flying furies that they became easy victims for the islanders' blades. Soon the conflict was spreading out along several passages, with the garrison in retreat everywhere despite their numerical superiority.

Dsordas spotted Farrag at the end of one corridor, and led the charge that way. The Marshal was shouting and screaming – there were bats around him too – but the forces between him and the islanders were retreating, ignoring his orders. Farrag turned a corner and disappeared before Dsordas and his colleagues could reach him.

Yeori caught his leader's arm.

'Look!' he gasped, pointing to the cells on either side of them. 'Far-speakers!'

As the other men rampaged after the stricken imperial forces, Yeori and Dsordas made a quick check of the cells. The Far-speakers, identified by their grimy, loose-fitting robes and amberine headbands lay in various helpless poses.

Dsordas ran into each of the four cells on one side of the corridor. One of the Far-speakers was dead, blood still oozing from wounds in his chest and throat. The other three were alive but seemed to be deeply unconscious. Dsordas began to hope for success as he headed back into the passage.

'Four this side,' Yeori reported. 'Two dead, the other two in some sort of a coma. I can't wake them.'

'All eight!' Dsordas exclaimed with a grin. 'We've done it!'

The two men embraced briefly, filled with relief at their good fortune.

'The signal?' Yeori asked.

'Yes!' Dsordas replied. 'It's now or never.'

'I'll do it myself,' his lieutenant declared and ran up the passageway. Soon, Dsordas knew, beacons would be burning on several rooftops, a sign to all the remaining Children that the first, vital stage of their efforts had been completed and that they were to join the long-awaited revolt. There was a lot of fighting still to do, but at least it had begun!

Only now, as the enormity of what was happening sank in and the fight moved on, did Dsordas have time to wonder about their unlikely saviours. Without the bats, it would all have been for nothing.

On impulse, Dsordas went to examine the Far-speakers more closely, starting with the ones Yeori had counted. *How young they are,* he thought, grieving at the misuse of such talent. One of the dead bodies was covered in blood, having obviously died in the fighting, but the other was curled up in a corner, with no outward signs of harm. His robes were thrown over him, and only the back of his head was immediately visible. *No headband,* Dsordas realized, assailed by sudden doubts. Hastily, he pulled back the robe, revealing islander's clothes beneath, and saw the man's face.

Dsordas swore viciously. *Oh, Yeori, you idiot!*

In his haste, Yeori had merely checked that the man was dead, assuming him to be one of the Far-speakers. The mistake was understandable, but hard to forgive.

The body was that of Marath Kellaki, one of Phylo's men. One of the Far-speakers was missing.

CHAPTER THIRTY-FIVE

He is angry. I can feel it, amid all the shouting. That pleases me, but it should not. His anger will cause suffering that I am powerless to prevent.

He sings more songs than I.

Farrag was in a mountainous fury, blue flames flickering around his corpulent form. He now knew of the destruction of the barracks and was reconciled to the temporary loss of all but one of the Far-speakers. That sorcery was part of his enemy's weaponry was now almost certain, and he knew that the whole town would soon be convulsed in battle. The Marshal was in no immediate personal danger, but he had to prepare for the possibility that the garrison might be completely destroyed. And that, much as he hated the idea, meant only one thing.

'Message for Chancellor Verkho,' he snapped. 'For his ears only.'

He and Iceman had retreated to Farrag's secure quarters, with the Far-speaker stumbling blindly under hypnotic compulsion. Now installed in the Marshal's private study, Iceman nodded obediently.

'The Zalys garrison is under serious attack from a full-scale uprising of island traitors. It is possible that control of the island may be lost. Recommend you send punitive force to recapture with the utmost urgency. It is imperative that I be protected, as recent discoveries . . .' Here Farrag paused, wondering how best to put this. 'Recent discoveries in the manipulation of excess Far-speaker power will be of great value to the Empire. Add my code and relay immediately.'

'Message relayed and received,' Iceman said a moment later.

'Good,' Farrag said. 'Discard the pair of moons, Iceman.' As the Far-speaker collapsed gently, the Marshal's thoughts turned to his own survival, and how he could best use his powers to help what was left of the garrison.

At the urgent summons from the Focus, Verkho tore his eyes away from the burning sword that was casting its spell over Xantium and went inside.

'There is a message from Farrag on Zalys, Chancellor,' his assistant reported, handing him a transcript.

As Verkho scanned the words, his anger increased. Such incompetence was beyond belief! And such arrogance! 'Imperative that I be protected' indeed! Then the Chancellor remembered recent reports. Just what *had* Farrag discovered?

'Send a message to Admiral Barvick in Brighthaven. Top priority,' he ordered. 'Instruct him to send two full squadrons from the southern fleet and enough army divisions to retake Zalys.' He went on to describe the situation, and gave detailed instructions. 'The population of Zalys is to be punished severely,' he concluded. 'All leaders and all those active in the revolt are to be executed. Marshal Farrag is to be arrested for dereliction of duty and transported back to Xantium under guard. That's all.'

The Focus relayed the message and reported its arrival in the port. Verkho was still fuming, and his thoughts turned to the hostages from the island. They, like their compatriots, would pay dearly for this insurrection!

On the rain-swept streets and canals of Nkosa, the revolution was truly under way. As the first of the oil-soaked signal flares burst into flame, others passed on

311

the fiery message and the Children sprang into action. Every willing man old enough to hold a sword or string a bow was directed to collect a weapon from the long-secret hoards. Among them were Antorkas and his eldest son Anto. They, along with many others, were intent on making their way to Fournoi Square and thence to the garrison headquarters, where the fiercest fighting was. The scene about them was apocalyptic. The canals churned with fierce currents and sudden waves, buildings were on fire, and all around them the cries of war and the clash of weapons rose above the clamour of the elements. Nkosa was at war, and all was chaos.

But Antorkas and his son knew their destination. If Fen and Natali were anywhere in Nkosa, they were in the imperial stronghold – and the two men would allow nothing to stop their search for their missing family.

Dsordas hesitated only for a moment before realizing what he had to do. He tried to recall which way Farrag had gone – for that would surely be where the missing Far-speaker was. Yet perhaps it was too late – perhaps the message was already on its way to Xantium, sealing their eventual fate. Even so, he had to try.

He ran down the now empty corridor, and glanced in either direction at the turning. Corpses lay still in the lamplight which glittered on the blood-stained stone floor, but there was no sign of Farrag. Dsordas walked slowly down the passage to his left, glancing into each room as he passed by. In one he saw Panos, curled into a ball on the floor. Dsordas kicked the door down, and shook the double traitor roughly.

'Where's the last Far-speaker?' he yelled. 'Where's Farrag taken him?'

Panos did not respond. His eyes rolled, his mouth gaped, revealing a blackened tongue, and he shook uncontrollably. It was obvious that Dsordas would get no sense from him. He threw him down and went on his way.

A voice hailed him from the far end of the corridor.

'Dsordas, come quickly! Farrag is holed up in his own quarters.' It was Yeori, back from lighting the signal flare. He sounded desperately worried. 'Some of the men think they saw a Far-speaker go in there with him,' he added. '*Quick*, man!'

'You go!' Dsordas yelled back, not moving.

'But . . .' Yeori stared, not understanding.

'*You go!*' Dsordas roared. He had no intention of following Yeori yet. Farrag, the Far-speakers, the Children, the whole of Zalys could go to hell for all he cared. He had just seen Fen.

She lay unmoving on the floor of a cell, curled up in a pose reminiscent of Marath's.

No. Please let her not be dead. Please.

Dsordas' calm and calculating mind had lost its moorings; he was adrift in an unknown sea. For all his selfless words – *we can't afford individual sentiment* – when faced with the sight of her like this, he was helpless. She mattered more to him than anything. Anything! And now it might be too late.

He flung himself down beside her, cradled her in his arms. He felt for a pulse in her neck, and his heart leapt when he found one – albeit shallow and erratic.

'Fen, my love, wake up. It's me.'

From deep within the black well, Fen heard a voice far above, muffled and faint. It did not seem worth the effort of finding out who it was, but something made her force her eyelids open. Seeing Dsordas' distraught face so close to her own brought her back to life for a moment, and she smiled through the intolerable pain. Was he worth coming back for? She had been sinking into darkness, the pain receding slowly, but now . . . he wanted her to return to the agony. Struggling to make sense of her muddled thoughts, she tried to speak.

'Dsordaaa . . .'

He saw her black-tainted tongue, and knew the worst.

'I'm here, my love,' he said. 'I'll help you.'

313

There were tears in his eyes, and Fen wondered why. She relaxed in his arms, feeling the comfort of his embrace, his desire to help, but knowing it was hopeless.

'Poison,' she whispered. 'Dying.'

'Don't say that!' he cried. 'You're going to be all right.'

'No. Just hold me. Feels nice.' Fen closed her eyes again.

The lump in Dsordas' throat made it impossible for him to speak. His denial of her plight was instinctive, but his rational brain knew the truth. Even though his embrace seemed to ease her, he could see that she was fading, could feel her slipping away from him.

'No!' He raged against fate, wordlessly howling his anguish to the heavens.

Fen opened her eyes again.

'Don't be angry,' she said softly, as if she were more worried about him than herself.

Then, through the pounding ache in his head, through the tortured regrets and self-recrimination, Dsordas heard Etha say, 'Your mother was a healer, and so are you!' 'Much good it did my mother!' he had replied. 'She died.' Now he would gladly die to save Fen.

Help me! Dsordas pleaded silently.

He felt another presence in the room. He raised his tear-stained face and saw his long-dead mother standing before him, arms folded, her eyes full of long-suffering love.

It took you long enough, the ghost commented.

Dsordas stared.

'I can hear you!' he exclaimed.

That's because you're listening at last.

'Heal her, please,' Dsordas begged. Surely that was why she had come.

I cannot. You can.

'How?'

Lay your hands upon her. Then let the healing flow. It's not hard, she told him, with a touch of impatience.

Dsordas' world was crumbling around him. Nothing made sense any more. There was so much he wanted to say, but there were no words, and there was no time. He shifted Fen and slid his hands next to her soft skin, one supporting the back of her neck, the other on a shoulder inside her shirt. He felt the clammy coolness with rising dread.

Close your eyes. Shut out everything but Fen. Let it happen naturally.

Dsordas tried to do as his mother said, but it seemed impossible. He didn't know what he was doing, and his thoughts went round and round in hateful circles.

Stop this absurd self-pity, his mother scolded him. *Do as you're told!*

Perhaps to her I'm still a little boy, he thought, and the idea made him relax a little. At the same time, he became aware that his hands had grown tremendously hot. He concentrated on them, trying to feel, to sense, as much as he could.

The cell, his mother's ghost, the entire complex disappeared. All that was left was his awareness, and Fen. At first he didn't realize what was happening, just felt sick and filled with a stabbing pain. Then he saw that it was not his pain, but hers. Tendrils of awareness grew from his fingertips until he could sense her whole body, her whole being. The ravages of the poison appalled him. How could anyone endure this? It was no wonder that she was dying.

No! He would not let that happen.

His sense of justice fuelled his determination, love gave it shape, and he released the long pent-up energies bottled up within him. It happened in a rush, a tidal wave – too fast, too violent. He felt Fen shake, jerking in his arms, and he calmed the flow deliberately, let it happen naturally.

In the end it was as easy as breathing. He did not need to think about it. Lines snaked out, feeding, warming, healing. He saw the poison retreat, felt the needles of agony dissolve in her veins, warmth and colour return to her pallid cheeks.

Dsordas opened his eyes to find Fen looking up at him with wonder in her clear green eyes. The ghost had gone.

'What happened?' she asked hoarsely. 'Why are you crying?'

Dsordas couldn't speak. He hugged her to him, weeping, great silent sobs shaking his entire frame, while Fen held him tight, not understanding.

'What's going on?' she asked at last.

'Are you really all right?' he said, drawing back to look at her.

'I feel like I've had toothache in my entire body,' she replied, 'but it's gone now. I'm fine.'

'Thank you,' Dsordas breathed, glancing around the empty room. He realized that his own headache had gone completely, for the first time in days.

'What?' Fen looked more puzzled still.

'Never mind now,' he told her. 'We have work to do!' He hugged her again, unable to believe his good fortune, his second chance. 'I love you,' he whispered.

'I know,' Fen replied. 'I love you too.' Then she remembered suddenly that she had terrible news to report. 'Panos double-crossed us!' she exclaimed.

'I know, but it doesn't matter now,' Dsordas said calmly. 'We've taken all but one of the Far-speakers. The battle's begun. All we need now is to get Farrag.'

Another memory stirred in Fen's reviving brain.

'Are the other Far-speakers dead or alive?'

'Two dead. Five in some sort of a coma,' he replied. 'One escaped, so he's the only one we need to worry about.'

'Not necessarily.'

'What do you mean?'

Fen explained that Farrag was drawing power from the unconscious Far-speakers.

'That's where he gets his magic!'

'You mean we'll have to kill them all?' Dsordas would

316

do it if necessary, but was repulsed by the idea of such cold-blooded murder.

'Perhaps not. What if we just remove the amberine?' Fen suggested. 'Without that, he may not be able to draw power.'

'It's worth a try,' he decided. 'Can you stand?' Dsordas got up, feeling unutterably weary, and pulled her to her feet.

'Who were you talking to just now?' Fen asked.

'No one,' he replied. 'Come on.'

CHAPTER THIRTY-SIX

The dark fire wakes.
  Can I hold my hand within the flame without flinching?

The battle for Nkosa centred on Fournoi Square. Most of the garrison outposts and patrols had been attacked and overrun in the first wave of the rebellion, in operations carefully orchestrated by Skoulli. The unexpected ferocity of the weather and the tide played havoc with both sides, but by far the greater advantage fell to the islanders, especially as so many imperial soldiers drowned without ever leaving the ruined barracks. Even so, any movement – let alone any fighting – was a hazardous business that night, and casualties among the townspeople ran high. As many were swept away and drowned as were cut down by their enemies. Even the most experienced boatsmen were having difficulty controlling their craft in the swirling waters.

At first it was only the Children who fought, using weapons from the secret hoards, but before long most of the population of the town were out in the open – either forced from their homes by the fear of flooding or of the buildings collapsing, or drawn by the lure of revenge upon the hated imperial forces. Women, old men and even children were caught up in the fever of rebellion, fighting with anything they could lay their hands on; knives, oars and pitchforks. The imperial garrison, in spite of their horrendous initial losses, still outnumbered the well-armed and well-prepared Children, but they were soon facing an enraged mob of islanders as well.

The long years of indignity, suffering and unjust oppression had left an indelible mark on the people of Zalys – and now they were intent on washing it away in a sea of blood.

Skoulli and the other commanders of the Children did their best to keep the most vulnerable away from any real fighting, but in the chaos of battle this was impossible.

For his part, Commander Niering did the only thing he could. He was a personally brave but ineffectual leader, quite unsuited to his post, but once the battle began in earnest he reorganized his shattered troops as best he could. But they were always pressed back, and the area of combat grew smaller and more concentrated. Niering died with an arrow in his neck, and the retreat continued. The imperial forces seemed doomed – until Farrag appeared in Fournoi Square.

Antorkas and Anto were already there in the thick of the action, trying to force a way through and thinking only of Fen and Natali. Although Antorkas was carrying a nasty wound in his side, it only made him all the more determined, while Anto was on the point of exhaustion but unwilling to leave his father's side. They were among the first to see Farrag emerge and they, like everybody else, fell back in awe.

The Marshal was travelling at speed, a blue aura of power shining all around him like a shield. His eyes glowed as he charged towards the nearest islanders and thrust out a pointing hand. Cold fire blazed forth, sending four men crashing backwards. They landed in crumpled heaps, unmoving. Reflections of the sorcerous light bounced around the wet stone of the square, like visible echoes of death.

'Thus all traitors are despatched!' Farrag roared, and his troops cheered with renewed hope as another blast smashed into three more rebels and scattered many others.

'Xantium is already aware of your folly!' the Marshal

bellowed. 'You will all pay dearly for this treachery. Forward, men!'

The soldiers were rallied by this spectacular reinforcement, and they surged forward, renewing their last ditch defence and turning to attack. The milling, undisciplined throng could not match the newly heartened guards, and the resulting carnage was terrible. At the same time Farrag continued his advance, seeming to glide effortlessly over the water-covered stones and the bodies of the fallen, his blue fire concentrated on the few men putting up sterner resistance.

Antorkas and Anto were driven back with the rest until they were on the northern rim of the square, with only the raging waters of the canal behind them. Although there were plenty of boats milling around on the far side of the barrier wall, there was little hope of any escape. This was a fight to the death.

They struggled on, the insane scene lit by lamps, fires and occasional bursts of lightning as well as by Farrag's flashes of power. Both men were now terribly weary and afraid. Between them, they managed to kill their latest opponent but when they looked round, breathing hard, they were faced with the Marshal, safe within his pulsing shield. Farrag raised a finger to point at them and smiled.

'You take that side. I'll do this,' Dsordas instructed. 'Hurry!'

Fen dived into the first cell and wrenched the headband from the comatose Far-speaker, then darted back out into the corridor and on to the next. Dsordas was doing the same.

'He's dead!' he called as he ran on. 'Go on to the next one.'

Fen obeyed and returned to the passageway as Dsordas emerged from the last of the cells on his side.

'Done!' he declared.

'Take them off the dead ones too,' Fen said. 'Just to be sure.'

That done, Dsordas shoved all the stones into a pocket.

'I have to find Farrag now,' he said. 'To see if he's still powerful. You stay here. It'll be safer.'

'Are you quite mad?' she exclaimed. 'I'm not letting you out of my sight now.'

Dsordas hesitated. He wanted to keep Fen by his side, but did not want her embroiled in the violence. Fen stooped to pick up a short sword from one of the dead soldiers.

'Come on,' she said firmly. 'Let's go. You can't keep me out of this fight. I have a score to settle.'

'Just be careful,' Dsordas said, his eyes full of worry. 'I couldn't stand it if . . .'

'I'm always careful,' she told him briskly. 'Let's go!'

Antorkas knew that he was about to die. He had been hit by a blast of Farrag's power before, but that was nothing compared to the fury being unleashed now. He could not move.

But Anto had still not given up. He dived at his father, sending them both tumbling to the ground, hoping to avoid the thunderbolt.

But it never came. Just as he prepared to kill them, Farrag's aura flickered and grew marginally less bright. Moments later it happened again. The Marshal hesitated, frowning – and was suddenly afraid, his intended victims forgotten.

Antorkas and his son looked up, watching the process in amazement. The shield flickered three more times and, at the last, the blue aura was only just visible. The Marshal tried to retreat to the safety of his own troops but he could not move, and the jubilant islanders converged quickly, weapons ready for slaughter. The first sword slashed down but bounced off the vestigial shield in a shower of blue sparks. Farrag pointed at his attacker, who cowered away – but no blast came. More attempted blows were parried by the Marshal's waning power, to the islanders' growing frustration.

Then someone yelled, 'Into the canal with him!' and the cry was taken up.

A mass of people gathered round, heaving their helpless victim over the flood wall and into the swirling water. Farrag sank like a stone, bubbles of fear and fury rushing from his gaping mouth. The last of his aura was evidently no protection against drowning.

A huge cheer went up from the islanders as the news sped round the square. The tide of battle turned once more, with the garrison in disarray, retreating to their last strongholds.

It was at this point that Fen and Dsordas found their way out of the complex and entered the rain-soaked fray. Working their way towards Fournoi Square, they arrived just in time to see the final charge which pushed the soldiers back against the southern walls. Antorkas, feeling invincible now after his last-moment reprieve, was in the forefront of the battle, his sword flailing savagely. Anto had long since been left behind in the mêlée. Fen saw her father and tried to call to him, but was unable to make herself heard over the tumult. She and Dsordas fought their way round, intent on reaching his side, but before they were within thirty paces, Fen saw her father slip, half fall and lose his blade. An imperial guard saw his chance and slammed his spear through Antorkas' chest. Fen screamed as her father, eyes wide in disbelief, slumped to the wet ground. He was dead before the soldier pulled out his spear.

Fen was rooted to the spot, stunned and convulsed with grief as Dsordas glanced around helplessly, ready to defend her. But then a commotion on the far side of the square drew their attention. Farrag erupted from the canal in a volcano of spray and blue fire, shooting up into the air and hovering ten paces above the heads of the astonished, terrified onlookers.

'Prepare to die!' the apparition roared in a voice like the thunder of doom.

Bolts of blue flame sped left and right, spreading panic and devastation among the horrified crowd.

'It didn't work,' Fen breathed, aghast.

'Yes it did!' Dsordas replied. He had been listening to the amazed comments of the people around them, and realized what had happened before they reached the square. 'He's getting power from somewhere else.'

When Gaye had reacted instinctively to Fen's remote plea, she had not expected to find herself flying alongside Bowen. She had no idea how it had happened – or even *what* had happened – but she felt his joy, and shared her own with him. *We have learnt to fly.*

And now, even though he was gone, a remnant of that happiness remained; the ashes of what had been a glorious fire warmed her still. Bowen was alive; they might fly again some day. It was not enough, but it was enough for now.

She and Natali had not moved from their extraordinary haven in the Arena, but the bats were flying still. She heard with their ears, sensed their satisfaction, and knew that she had done all she could for Fen. Now she had to wait – and hope.

Natali was asleep in her arms, and Gaye was also very weary. *Talking to ghosts is tiring,* she thought and smiled to herself, content now just to rest. But then Alasia's troubled voice sounded in her head.

Farrag threatens them still.

'What do you mean?'

He should be dead. He drew strength from the dark fire of the Far-speakers on Zalys, but they are denied to him now. So he grows more daring. He is taking power from another source. Alasia paused momentarily. *He oversteps his abilities and will pay for that eventually, but before he does, he can do great harm.*

'What other source?' Gaye asked.

323

The children.

When Gaye realized what Alasia meant, she was aghast. She shook Natali but could not rouse him. He was limp in her arms.

'What is he doing to them?' she asked, close to panic.

They are unformed talents, but the latent power is there, Alasia replied sorrowfully. *It will not last long – Farrag knows that – but he still hopes to regain the Far-speakers, and in the process he will destroy the little ones' minds. We must stop him.*

'We?'

Do you still doubt your talent, my pretty beacon? Look about you.

'I'm bl . . .' Gaye began, but got no further.

The world had become a network of glowing lines, infinite and strange – and she was part of it. She saw at once that in the midst of the glory was sickness and a corrupting fire, spreading from a single point.

'Farrag.'

Yes. We cannot attack him – that is beyond our strength. We can only cut him off, deny him the childrens' power.

'How?' Gaye responded eagerly. 'Like this?' In her thoughts she pulled, twisted and tried to break one of the strands.

No! Alasia said quickly. *You will harm the little ones. Like this.*

A subtle flare of light cleansed a tiny section of the polluted network and allowed the connected strand to heal itself. However, as Gaye watched, the illness seeped back along the line, spreading out once more.

We have to heal each line at the same time, Alasia explained. *While he has one child, he has them all.*

Together they divided the work.

Ready?

'Yes.'

Now.

All the lines radiating from the heart of the evil flamed

brightly for an instant, turning from vile wrongness to natural perfection. The dark fire at the centre vanished – and then so did the whole network and Alasia's voice. Gaye was alone again within her own dark world.

Natali stirred uneasily in her arms.

Farrag soared above the petrified crowd, unleashing blue lightning that killed and maimed. He reached the centre of the square, blazing like a miniature sun.

'Bow down before your god, fools!' he roared, his voice reverberating even above the noise of the storm. 'Or prepare to die!'

Then suddenly he lurched to one side and was forced to right himself quickly. Moments later the blue fire vanished completely and Farrag fell.

There seemed to be an eternity between the beginning of the fall and the moment when he struck the unforgiving stone. Standing motionless and mesmerized, everyone in the square watched his downward path.

As Farrag hit the ground, his 'carriage' splintered under his weight and was revealed as a mere chair, while the Marshal sprawled upon the paving, broken and pathetic. Gradually the people drew nearer, forming a circle, watching silently as Farrag squirmed. His bloated body was helpless, his flabby, atrophied legs shattered and bloody.

No one wanted to go any closer. Although the crowd still retained a little of the fear he had inspired earlier, most people were revolted by what they saw now. Farrag was reduced to something truly pitiful, something no longer even vaguely human, disgusting and evil but no longer a threat.

Dsordas pulled Fen towards the silent, watching ring. She had wanted to go to her father, even though he was clearly beyond help, but she knew that Dsordas had work to finish – and he would not let her go from his side. For him, she had to see it through. But when they came to the edge of the circle to look on their fallen enemy, they too could go no closer.

'Well, what are you waiting for?' Farrag rasped. 'No one got the guts to finish me off?' He laughed painfully, blood spilling from his lips.

Still no one moved. No one could bring themselves to approach this creature.

No one, that is, until a little girl moved forward slowly, rubbing her eyes as if she had just awoken from a deep sleep. A pendant hung round her delicate neck. It was the same child that Farrag had forced to condemn her own father.

Her step never faltered, as every eye – including the Marshal's – followed her progress. She stood before him for a moment, then looked directly at Dsordas.

'He's hurting,' she said quietly. 'You should stop him hurting.'

Dsordas looked into her innocent eyes, then nodded solemnly. As he strode forward, the girl went back to find her mother.

Dsordas stared at Farrag one last time, shocked to see the malice which still shone in the Marshal's helpless eyes. Then steadily, almost gently, he slid his blood-stained blade between the man's ribs and into his tainted heart. It was the last act of the old era. Farrag gasped, and then with a final shudder, he lay still.

In the silence that followed, few people even realized that the rain had stopped. The storm was abating. Overhead, a huge swarm of bats circled unseen, then turned and headed back towards the mountains.

In the distance, one of the rebellion's signal flares still burned atop the tallest warehouse near the docks, and Fen found her eyes drawn to it.

It's shaped just like a burning sword, she thought numbly. Then she turned, and with Dsordas at her side once more, went back to find her father.

CHAPTER THIRTY-SEVEN

Stone blunts knife. Water quenches fire. Greater powers will soon be in the game, but at least we have made a start.

Small victories are sometimes the most important.

Somehow, time still passed.

The night ran its course, the sea retreated and the winds blew gently from the west once more. Morning came and with it the beginning of new and, in some ways, even more arduous tasks for the islanders. The last few pockets of imperial resistance had long since crumbled and the remaining soldiers taken prisoner. Now began the long aftermath of war; tending to the wounded, clearing up the mass of debris, the endless repairs, rehousing the homeless. And, of course, the burial of the countless dead.

Yet a new spirit had come to Nkosa, arriving with the new era, and even though the people were sombre, recognizing the weight of all their problems, they set about their tasks with determination and energy. Freedom, possibly only short-lived freedom, had been bought at a terrible cost. Almost every family was in mourning for one or more of its members, but that put all the survivors on an equal footing, uniting them in sorrow as well as in hope for a very different future.

Most people looked to Dsordas for leadership; he vowed publicly to do whatever Zalys required of him, and promised to organize their defences against the expected arrival of the imperial fleet. But for now the needs of his family came first, and he left the direction of the salvage operations to his deputies.

The Amari family returned to their home, finding it relatively unscathed. The front door needed replacing, several of the rooms showed signs of the guards' search and the cellars had been flooded, although the water had receded now; otherwise the house was sound. But it was full of tears.

Antorkas lay in his bedroom, his body cleansed and prepared for burial. Etha was heartbroken, unable at first to accept her husband's death. She sat beside him, talking quietly and pausing as if expecting him to reply. Anto was plagued with guilt, blaming himself for not being able to keep up in the battle, his failure made all the more acute by his own – in his eyes, shameful – survival. Fen tried to comfort them both, but her own heart was heavy, and she raged against the fate which had killed her father when victory was in sight. She missed him already, his handsome smile gone for ever now.

With the burden of looking after the solemn, withdrawn Tarin and the tearful Ia, Fen was weighed down by her responsibilities, and was very glad that Dsordas was with her constantly, helping wherever he could. He looked after the mundane necessities of life, and also tried his best to talk to Anto, to persuade him that what had happened was not his fault. But most of all he was just there, proving to Fen that life was still worth living, that love was possible in a cruel world.

On top of this, Gaye and Natali were still missing. The rest of the family had listened to Fen's tale of Natali's disappearance, but although they seemed to accept her word, Fen was not sure that they really believed her. They had tried to organize a search, but this had proved almost impossible in the shambles, and they were not surprised when it revealed nothing. Could a blind girl and a little boy have survived the night's events? All they could do was wait and hope.

Noon brought Fen and Dsordas a rare moment alone together. They were in the kitchen, a place so filled with happy memories that the recent horrors seemed hardly credible. All their words had been used up on others, and now they merely stood, wrapped in each other's arms, crying softly.

They were interrupted by the sound of slow footsteps on the stairs. Etha appeared in the doorway, her face pale and drawn but dry-eyed.

'Mama?' Fen said, wiping her tears away.

'Oh, Fen. He's really gone,' Etha cried, as if she had only just realized.

Fen glanced quickly at Dsordas, who smiled encouragingly and went to talk to Anto again. Fen held her arms out to her mother, and soon Etha was weeping for the first time, helpless sobs that racked her whole body. Fen held her tightly, knowing that this had to happen. Eventually Etha drew back and looked into her daughter's tear-filled eyes.

'The stupid man,' she said. 'Why did he do it?'

'Because he had to,' Fen replied gently.

Etha nodded.

'He never did know his own limitations,' she said with a wan half-smile.

'If he had,' Fen told her, 'he'd never have been able to bring you back here from the north.'

Upstairs, Dsordas knocked firmly on Anto's door. There was no answer but he went in anyway, and found the young man lying on his bed, staring at the ceiling.

'Soldiers die in battle, Anto,' Dsordas began. 'That's the first thing everyone learns.'

At first there was no reaction.

'He wouldn't have been killed if I'd kept up with him,' Anto said eventually.

'So you're invincible, are you?'

Anto sat up, his angry face a younger version of his father's.

329

'He had no right to die!' He even sounded like Antorkas.

'He had the right of every man,' Dsordas replied with equal passion. 'He died fighting for what he believed in, for what he loved. And he succeeded!'

'He's dead!' Anto said in disbelief.

'But Fen, Etha and all of you are alive – and Zalys is free.'

'For how long?' Anto wondered bitterly.

'That doesn't matter,' Dsordas told him. 'Yes, there'll be more fighting before this is over. You'll have the chance to prove your worth to yourself. But in the meantime, you do your father's memory no honour by shouldering blame that is not yours to take.' His voice had been harsh, but grew more gentle as he added, 'Forgive him. And forgive yourself.'

Anto was on the point of responding angrily, but then he let his head fall.

'Where is he?' he asked quietly.

'In his room.'

Anto stood, and walked slowly towards his parents' bedroom. Dsordas followed but kept a few paces behind and waited outside, letting the boy say his own farewells. Downstairs he could hear the murmur of female voices.

A sudden scream sent Dsordas pounding down the stairs, followed soon after by Tarin and Ia who came scrambling down from the attic, and then by Anto.

As Dsordas flew into the kitchen, he saw the cause of the commotion. Gaye stood on the threshold of the shattered door, with Natali in her arms, and was engulfed by Etha and Fen amid shouts of joy and disbelief. Behind her stood a pleased but nervous looking fisherman. Dsordas went to greet him, leaving the women to their reunion.

'Come in, friend. You have brought great joy to this household.'

'Thank you, sir, but I must get back,' the man replied

gravely. 'The storm did much damage to our village last night.'

'Village?'

'Moulia, near the Arena.'

'How . . . ?' Dsordas began.

'These two came down from the hills this morning,' the fisherman said, shaking his head. 'The boy was guiding her, I think. They'd been out in the storm all night, but they were dry and warm somehow. Come to no harm at all! They told me they were from Nkosa, so I brought them back in my boat.' He was clearly mystified by the whole affair.

'Thank you,' Dsordas said. 'Are you sure you won't come in?'

'No. I'd best be going.' He went back to his boat.

As Dsordas turned to see the reunited family all in a huddle, the excited conversation stopped and everyone fell silent, suddenly aware that one painful piece of news had to be passed on.

'Gaye,' Etha began. 'Your father . . .'

'He's dead. I know,' the blind girl said quietly.

'What? How did you know?' her mother asked.

'His ghost spoke to me in the Arena.'

'What did he say?' Etha asked in a voice choked with emotion.

'Just goodbye,' Gaye replied. 'His story is part of the place now.'

That night, Fen and Dsordas lay in each other's arms.

'Will it ever be the same again?' Fen whispered.

'No. We can't go back,' he answered. 'But we *can* be happy again.'

'Gaye won't ever be happy unless Bowen comes back.'

'Maybe,' Dsordas conceded. 'But she's learning a lot about herself.'

'Yes,' Fen said. 'And *you* can't deny magic now. Even if you don't believe her about the storm, you can't

331

explain the bats. Not to mention the way she and Natali got to the Arena.'

'There's a lot I don't understand.' It was the closest he would get to an admission of defeat.

'Including your healing?' she asked, smiling.

'You're here,' he said seriously. 'That's all that matters.'

'But you can't deny your own talent now, can you?' she persisted.

'No,' he confessed, grinning. 'I never could argue with my mother.'

EPILOGUE

It screamed as it broke the surface.

The huge triangular wings beat slowly in massive undulations as the giant manta ray erupted from the sea and took to the air in an explosion of spray. But this time the great creature did not fall back to the water with the usual earsplitting thunderclap. Instead it flew on blindly, ever higher. Free at last from the constricting ocean, it screamed its malevolent triumph to the skies, then turned and flew ponderously towards the island.

Deep in their mountain caves, the sentinel bats measured the sound of its screaming and reacted nervously to the approach of their new foe.

THE END

SHADOW-MAZE
by Jonathan Wylie

The attack began at dawn. By the time the sun rose, the only people left in the village were dead. They were the lucky ones . . .

On what should have been a day of celebration – the day marking their transition from boys to men – Varo and Brostek's lives were changed for ever. Their village was destroyed by the Knifemen of Bari, leaving them home-less, orphaned and alone in a world in which the men of power cared little for their sufferings.

And so they have dedicated their lives to the seemingly hopeless task of protecting others, and to their own relentless, obsessive search for revenge.

Only in the extraordinary crater-city of Trevine, in the company of their friend Magara, are the two warriors able to find a little peace. Yet it is Magara's investigation of the past which reveals the first clues to the unimaginable secrets which lie behind the Knifemen. And her attempts to solve the deadly puzzle only lead her deeper and deeper into the shadow-maze.

Jonathan Wylie, author of DREAM-WEAVER and the SERVANTS OF ARK and THE UNBALANCED EARTH trilogies, has created a mysterious world in which humour, violence and magic co-exist within a tale of great emotional power and unrelenting pace.

0 552 13929 7

OTHER JONATHAN WYLIE TITLES
AVAILABLE FROM CORGI BOOKS

THE PRICES SHOWN BELOW WERE CORRECT AT THE TIME OF GOING TO PRESS.
HOWEVER TRANSWORLD PUBLISHERS RESERVE THE RIGHT TO SHOW NEW
RETAIL PRICES ON COVERS WHICH MAY DIFFER FROM THOSE PREVIOUSLY
ADVERTISED IN THE TEXT OR ELSEWHERE.

☐ 13929 7	**SHADOW-MAZE**		£3.99
☐ 13757 X	**DREAM WEAVER**		£4.99
☐ 13101 6	**SERVANTS OF ARK I: THE FIRST NAMED**		£3.99
☐ 13134 2	**SERVANTS OF ARK II: THE CENTRE OF THE CIRCLE**		£2.50
☐ 13161 X	**SERVANTS OF ARK III: THE MAGE-BORN CHILD**		£3.99
☐ 13416 3	**THE UNBALANCED EARTH 1: DREAMS OF STONE**		£3.99
☐ 13417 1	**THE UNBALANCED EARTH 2: THE LIGHTLESS KINGDOM**		
			£2.99
☐ 13418 X	**THE UNBALANCED EARTH 3: THE AGE OF CHAOS**		£4.99

All Corgi/Bantam Books are available at your bookshop or newsagent, or can be ordered from the following address:

Corgi/Bantam Books,
Cash Sales Department,
P.O. Box 11, Falmouth, Cornwall TR10 9EN

UK and B.F.P.O. customers please send a cheque or postal order (no currency) and allow £1.00
for postage and packing for the first book plus 50p for the second book and 30p for each additional
book to a maximum charge of £3.00 (7 books plus).

Overseas customers, including Eire, please allow £2.00 for postage and packing for the first book
plus £1.00 for the second book and 50p for each subsequent title ordered.

NAME (Block Letters) ....

ADDRESS ....

....